CRATE FULL OF CHAOS

28 FIENDISH TALES

IAIN ROB WRIGHT

ULCERATED PRESS

For Sue Crouch & Family
Thanks for you support.

Words are sexier than flesh.

— **<u>Clive Barker</u>**

A short story must have a single mood and every sentence must build towards it.

— **<u>Edgar Allan Poe</u>**

And didn't they say that, although curiosity killed the cat, satisfaction brought the beast back?

—**<u>Stephen King, Four Past Midnight</u>**

PREFACE

Short stories are a craft all of themselves. A novel affords space and time to tell a story. A short story, though... a short story is like a one-night stand. It can be forgotten instantly in a blackout-blur, or... or it can stay in the memory forever—a mysterious stranger that comes into your life for a fleeting moment only to put its mark upon you.

On the pages to follow are 28 of my best attempts to make an impression on you, to linger in the corners of your mind forever with just the merest of touches. 28 brief kisses of horror await.

I hope you are prepared.

Iain x

SPAGHETTI NECK

Aaron grinned in the coppery glow of the fire. The warmth on his cheeks was like a lover's caress—at least he imagined so.

He loved this. Being outdoors at night, sitting on the frigid ground, surrounded by trees—each one a different, silent sentinel watching over him. Most human beings feared the moonlit woods. But he loved the thrill.

Aaron's friends were in equally chipper moods, but mainly because of the supermarket brand vodka in their tummies. Shelly swigged from the bottle even now, her plump lips pressed around its slender neck. Callum and Leon watched her, mesmerised no doubt by the phallic connotations.

"So," Aaron said, cross-legged, with his hands on his knees. "Are you guys ready to listen, or what?"

Shelly took the bottle away from her lips and passed it over. Callum and Leon both snatched at it, but Callum, being closer, and the bigger of the two, claimed victory.

Shelly pulled a face at Aaron. "We already said we were ready, so go on."

"Yeah, get on with it, mate," Leon grumbled. "Do your worst."

The bet was simple. Aaron would tell them a horror story, and if it scared them, they had to let him drink as much as he wanted. If he failed, then he wouldn't drink at all.

Callum took a swig of vodka and winced. With a croaky voice, he showed his disdain. "I laughed all the way through Sinister, so there's nowt you can say to freak me out, man."

Aaron narrowed his eyes. "You've never experienced anything like this before, I promise."

Shelly clapped her hands suddenly, hard enough to fan the campfire, which was small and rather pathetic. But Callum and Leon had given it their best shot. The problem was airflow, but Aaron wasn't going to give them a lesson about that right now.

"Okay," he said. "I'll start at the start." He looked around, pretending to check that the coast was clear. "The local kids around this town, back when our parents were our age and our grandparents their age, used to say that Spaghetti Neck was once just a normal kid—born totally healthy. Good at sports, clever in class. Someone that was just average and okay. His parents were both scientists in a lab, working on viruses and stuff, so perhaps that's what led to what eventually happened, but at first Spaghetti Neck was no different to any of us."

"So what happened?" Shelly asked, rolling her eyes.

Aaron frowned disapprovingly. "So impatient. Let me get there, will you?"

Leon swigged from the vodka and chuckled. "Best hurry up, then, or there'll be nothing left for you to drink."

Aaron grinned, confident he would get what he wanted in the end. "David French. That was Spaghetti Neck's real name. He lived in West Park back when the houses there were first built."

"Posh." Shelly smirked. "I fucked a kid from there once. He could barely get it up."

Aaron rolled his eyes, suspecting Shelly was still a virgin. They all were, if they were honest, himself included. "Yes, he was a rich kid, but not stuck up or selfish. In fact, all agree that David French was kind and easy to like. His favourite thing in the entire world was to perform. Dancing, magic, singing, he loved the spotlight. Loved to put a smile on people's faces."

Leon picked up a twig and snapped it, tossing both ends into the fire. "What a loser. Bet he got bullied to shit, man."

"Perhaps," Aaron admitted. "But it's hard to bully a pure spirit–there has to be something for a bully to latch onto, some hint of defiance, but David would always take everything with a smile."

"Sounds like a nice dude," Shelly said.

"Anyway, as you might imagine," Aaron went on. "David's dream was to be on stage one day, to play Oliver or the Cowardly Lion, et cetera et cetera. He had a good shot of succeeding too–decent looking, well-spoken, and genuinely talented. Rich parents didn't hurt either."

"So when does he turn into a freak?" Callum asked, the vainest of the group with his shoulder-length blonde hair that made him look like an Italian footballer.

"It depends how you define freak?"

"When does he get all the weird shit on him? When does he turn into Spaghetti Neck?"

"At thirteen years old," Aaron answered. "An unlucky number, some would say." He chuckled, in what he hoped was a sinister manner, wanting to add to the atmosphere. "Most who know the story say David's mum brought home some nasty virus on the bottom of her shoe. Others swear he was cursed by a jealous theatre kid rival from a Romanian family. Truthfully, nobody knows. The only thing anyone can agree on is that the change began slowly."

"The neck veins," Shelly said, smirking. She had the vodka bottle and absentmindedly offered it to him. Aaron declined, not wanting to interrupt his flow or cheat on his wager.

"The first changes were subtle. Just a red patch on the side of David's neck. He scratched at it, and assumed it was eczema, but after several weeks, it still hadn't gone away. In fact, it was getting worse, and a throbbing blue vein had popped up right in the middle. That's when the other kids started avoiding David."

Callum shuddered. "Not surprised. Bet that shit was gross to look at."

Aaron nodded. "You're right. It wasn't through spite that people shunned him; just simple, unintended revulsion."

"Poor kid," Shelly said.

"Yes. Poor David. The kid who loved the spotlight, now suddenly couldn't get a single person to look at him."

"That actually kinda sucks," Leon admitted, his eyes red and bleary from the alcohol. It was he who had brought it here, stolen from his dad's wardrobe stash. "I feel bad now."

Callum tutted. "Mate, you wouldn't have gone near that kid either. You proper made Stephanie Gibson's life hell when she got that cold sore."

"It made her look like a fucking corpse. It was all over her mouth."

"It gets worse." Aaron said, trying to silence them. He narrowed his eyes and looked around at the shadowy trees and spiky bushes. "More bulging veins appeared on David's neck. His parents paid to have him seen by the best private specialists, but none could work out what was happening. In fact, they panicked."

"Why?" Callum ran a hand through his golden hair, made brighter by the fire's warming glow. "Why panic?"

"Because the bulging veins had broken free and started to grow on the outside of David's neck. Look closely enough and you could see them coursing with blood, pulsing in time to his heartbeat."

Shelly covered her mouth and groaned. "If that was me, I would kill myself. No one would ever shag a veiny freak."

Aaron declined to mention that her chronic bad breath wasn't exactly a turn on. "Sex was the least of David's concerns. All he wanted was for things to be the way they used to be. He missed his friends, missed entertaining people with his singing and dancing. But over the weeks, his existence grew lonelier and lonelier. He spent his school lunch breaks stroking the stray cat that used to hang around the playground—the only living thing that didn't care about his condition. Of course, the other kids wouldn't even let him have that in the end. They threw rocks at the cat until it stopped visiting. The nickname Spaghetti Neck started not long after."

Leon pouted, his arms folded. "Kids can be so nasty. Even I wouldn't go that far."

Shelly pulled a face at him. "You started the nickname 'Lewis Hamilton' for Chrissy Monroe when she broke both legs and had to use a wheelchair for six months."

Callum sniggered. "Yeah, you're the biggest bully out of us all."

"I still have a heart, though, man. Not my fault some people can't take a joke."

"You even bullied Aaron for a while," Shelly said, nodding at Aaron. "When he first joined our school."

"We all did, not just me. Anyway, that was before we realised he was sound."

Aaron didn't respond to their bickering. He just wanted to finish the story. "Eventually, David's parents had no choice but to take him out of school. They would have homeschooled him, but both were working full time, so David just ended up even more isolated. All the while, the veins on his neck kept on growing, more and more of them running all the way down from his ear to his shoulder. The large ones pulled away further, looping and tangling like a bunch of telephone wires. Occasionally, he would carelessly snag them on things and hurt himself. Fortunately, they had become so thick it would take a hacksaw to puncture them."

"And the doctors still couldn't figure the shit out?" Callum asked, shaking his head.

Aaron glanced towards the trees, alerted by what he thought was movement. Had he seen something? Was it merely the shadows?

"The doctors didn't have a clue. They wanted to run more tests and document David's condition, but his parents wouldn't agree. They tried to make their son happy by buying him everything he wanted–video games, toys, and books–but nothing could improve his mood. All David wanted was to be normal and have friends. By now, the pressure from his veins distorted his vocal cords so he couldn't even sing to himself. The weight of them messed with his balance, and he could no longer dance. He spent his days watching old musicals, knowing he would never get to tread the boards himself."

Shelly frowned. "What does that mean?"

"It's a theatre expression," Aaron said, peering towards the trees again. The night was growing cold, the fire now a dying flicker. They were a twenty-minute walk from the nearest paved surface.

"David's first kill was shortly before his own death," Aaron explained. "They say it was the act that damned his soul, the thing that transformed him from victim to monster."

"Who did he kill?" Callum asked, leaning forwards eagerly. All three of his friends were enjoying the grisly tale, just as he'd known they would.

"He killed a bully," Aaron said. "Although, ironically, not one of his own."

"What do you mean?" Leon asked.

"I forgot to mention a key detail. Forgive me. David had one friend left in the world. His little brother."

"He had a brother?" Leon tutted. "You kind of left that out, mate."

Aaron shrugged apologetically. "David had a younger brother named Samuel. Samuel was eight years old, and he loved his big brother dearly. He even thought his veins were cool; used to call them his brother's 'pipes.' Cute, I suppose."

"Yeah, lovely," Shelly said, pretending to gag.

"David used to sit in his bedroom after school and look out at the street, watching the other kids ride their bikes up and down the pavement. When Samuel got older, he began hanging out with them. The problem was that Samuel was a shy boy—a shy boy with a freak for a brother. Eventually, the local kids turned on him too, especially when he refused to make fun of David. I guess they considered him a freak sympathiser."

Leon chuckled. Along with Shelly and Callum, they had now drunk the large bottle of vodka down to halfway. It had put them all in a bleary-eyed state. Relaxed. Stupid.

"David saw his brother rolling on the ground one day," Aaron said, rubbing his hands against his thighs to keep them warm. "He'd been pushed into the road by a bigger kid named Ryan. Ryan was twelve. David, by this time, was fifteen. When he saw his brother being attacked, he saw red. He bolted from his bedroom and sprinted into the street."

Callum nodded. "Fair play. Gotta stand up for fam, fam."

"Ryan never even saw David coming, which is why Ryan fell so awkwardly when David shoved him. The side of his skull cracked against the kerb and his brains oozed out onto the road. It was a freak accident, committed by a freak."

"Jesus." Callum wrinkled his nose. "That's grim, mate.

"What happened to David?" Leon asked, sitting up and eagerly awaiting more.

"Well, his little brother Samuel was horrified and immediately began to wail. The local kids had been bullying him, sure, but he had weathered it with a smile, tougher than his brother gave him credit for. He didn't want this. He didn't want violence and death. David, however, didn't seem to care one bit. He simply turned and went back inside the house. When the police arrested him half an hour later, he was eating cereal at the kitchen table as if nothing had happened. His veins hung like dreadlocks around his shoulders."

"Let me guess," Shelly said, her eyes shifting slightly to the side as a twig snapped somewhere nearby. "He ended up in a mental hospital?"

"Nope." Aaron shook his head. "The whole thing was put down to an unfortunate accident. While David admitted to shoving the boy, it was determined to be a terrible tragedy born of self defence. Witnesses admitted to Samuel being pushed, and some even blamed poor Ryan for what happened. A bully facing the consequences of his own actions, they said. Ryan's parents didn't think so, of course. Most think it was them who started the fire."

"The Witch House," Callum said.

They all knew about the ruined house behind the mesh fencing on Randall Church Street. The entire block had been flattened in the nineties to build shops, but one single plot had been left as rubble, its foundation charred and uneven. Of course, there was no way it was David French's house. The kid had died forty years ago. A ruin would not be left to fester that long in a residential area, but all the local kids swore it was the resting place of Spaghetti Neck. Go there at night, and he might just appear and strangle you with his bulging veins.

"The fire started deep in the night," Aaron said. "David woke up first and raced to get his parents, who then hurried to rescue Samuel, knowing he was the most vulnerable. By this time, the smoke was a thick blanket, making it impossible to see. At the same time, the roof timbers were rapidly weakening and threatening to collapse." Aaron took a deep breath and let it out slowly. The campfire tilted away from him, lighting up his friends. They were all equally enraptured, awaiting the final part of the story. The woods seemed to close in on them, the trees creeping closer.

"David's parents assumed he had got out of the house, old enough to take care of himself, but the truth was that he was still in his room, trying to gather some of his belongings—just ordinary kid's stuff: books, craft projects, and treasured photographs. By the time David was ready to leave, his family had already fled outside. The roof caved in."

Another sound of snapping twigs. Shelly flinched, her fingers digging into the hard soil as if she were ready to push herself upwards and run. Leon smirked and told her to chill out. "Probably just a fox or something. We are in the woods, you know?"

"If I see a fox, I'm out of here. They carry disease."

"It's not a rat," Aaron said. "Listen to the end of the story."

Shelly nodded. "The fire."

"Yes, the fire was blazing, and a big piece of timber collapsed through the upstairs ceiling. It was right above the landing where David was currently heading for the stairs. It missed his head by inches, but it struck his left shoulder. The shoulder where his tangled, distended, disembodied veins grew."

Callum expression twisted into a grimace. "Ouch!"

Aaron narrowed his eyes and lowered his voice. "The burning timber tore the veins from David's neck, severing them in two. The agony and shock didn't stop him, but he began to bleed heavily. He made it down the stairs and staggered out into the street, smouldering and blackened from the flames. He collapsed into his mother's arms but it was too late. He died right there on the front lawn. Witnesses said his torn open veins were like pressurised hoses, whipping back and forth, spraying blood everywhere."

Callum hooted and then slapped his hands against his knees. "Christ almighty. That is proper messed up, mate."

Shelly glanced at the trees uneasily, her arms wrapped around herself as the fire struggled to stay alive. "S-so when did David come back from the dead?"

"I think you mean when did Spaghetti Neck start preying on young, unsuspecting teenagers?" Aaron corrected.

"Yeah," Leon said. "When did he become a monster?"

"The very next night, when his body disappeared from the morgue. Nobody ever located it, although there were many sightings of a strange, blood-covered kid wandering the streets at night. Some said David was still alive and had wandered out of the morgue in a trauma-tised daze, but the coroner remained adamant that the young man had been stone cold dead, with barely a drop of blood left in him. Despite the rumours, the locals eventually moved on to other things and forgot about poor David French. Until, exactly one year after the fire, when three local children were found strangled to death in their beds. Each had been part of the group who had bullied young Samuel back when David had still been alive—all nasty kids with a history of being mean. Authorities eventually let slip that the children were strangled with some kind of rubbery, hose-like material."

"Veins!" Callum shouted, making Shelly flinch. "Gross!"

"And that's when the legends started, right?" Shelly giggled nervously. "If you're a bully, Spaghetti Neck will come and strangle you in your sleep with his thick, throbbing veins?"

"Yes, that was when the stories started," Aaron said with a grin. "And they only intensified when three more children died three years later, and three years after that, and every three years since. Over three dozen in total so far."

"Including Tessa, Drayton, and Millie from our school," Leon added, swallowing a lump in his throat. "Three years ago."

"Three years ago today," Aaron added. "David French died forty years ago to this day. One year of rest, followed by thirty-nine years of killing. All bullies should beware tonight, for Spaghetti Neck will be out looking for three new victims."

Callum sneered and raised a fist. "I swear to God, that freak wouldn't last two seconds with me. I'd yank those neck veins and swing on 'em like Tarzan."

"Shut up, will you?" Shelly warned, seeming to shiver. The fire had almost died completely. Its meagre light was disappearing fast. "That's proper disturbed me."

Leon took a long swig of vodka and then handed the bottle to Aaron. "Alright, mate. You win. You got us all freaked out."

Aaron refused the bottle with a wave of his hand. He didn't drink alcohol. It was a fool's vice.

"I thought this whole thing was a bet so you could get the vodka."

"Keep it. I got what I wanted."

Shelly hugged herself tightly. "Can we get out of these woods now. I feel like we're being watched."

"Maybe it's Spaghetti Neck," Callum said, pulling a face at her and wiggling his fingers over against his throat as if they were disembodied veins.

"Stop!"

"Don't worry," Aaron said. "You three aren't bullies, right? I mean, Shelly, you don't ever say mean things to the other girls at school, right? You've never shoved anyone in Baxter's pond for a laugh. Oh, right, yeah, you did that to Sally Moon because she wears scruffy shoes and has a backpack from Temu." He turned to Callum. "And you? You've never forced anyone's head into a dirty toilet? Oh, right, you did that to me when I first started at the school."

Callum blushed. "We're mates now, though. It was just, like, you know, an initiation or whatever. New kid rite of passage. Anyway, that was months ago."

"Three months ago," Aaron said. "But you're right, we're mates now. After all, you came out here to the woods to listen to my story."

Callum smiled uncertainly. "Yeah."

"But you," Aaron pointed at Leon. "You're the worst—your bullying is all online. You gather the troops and attack people on Social Media like it's some kind of sport. Then you text your victim's phones at all hours of the day to never allow them a single second of peace. You let them know that you can always get at them, that even in the safety of their own bedrooms you can still hurt them. There are plenty of ways to bully, Leon, but your methods are truly vile."

Leon shuffled himself and straightened up. "Hey, fuck you, man. What's your problem?"

"I'm not the one with a problem. I've never bullied anyone. My self esteem is perfectly intact without having to pick on the weak."

Leon glared. "You want a slap, mate? Because you're going the right way about it."

"Yeah," Callum said. "I thought you were cool, man."

Shelly shook her head as though she were disappointed. "You're kinda pushing it, Aaron."

"Just let me finish my story," he said.

"You've finished it, mate," Callum scowled. "I reckon we're done here."

Aaron shook his head slowly. "No. Not quite. You see, I never mentioned what happened to David's family after his death. Sadly, his traumatised parents became alcoholics and soon divorced, but little Samuel wouldn't let tragedy hold him back. He became a fireman, determined to save innocent victims like his brother. A strong, moral, and courageous young man. A hero."

"Good for him," Shelly said with a roll of her eyes. "Why don't you find him and suck his dick?"

Aaron went on, undeterred. "Young Samuel eventually got married and had a son. The bloodline continued. *Still* continues."

Leon sneered. "Is this a joke? Why are you acting like a weirdo? We don't want to hear any more."

"It's no joke." Aaron fanned the fire with his flat hand, giving the flames a smidgeon more oxygen. Slowly, he lifted up his t-shirt to show his belly—the final part of the story. Emanating from his navel and rising right up to his left armpit was a thick snarl of throbbing, purple veins. "My real name is David. David Aaron French. My dad named me after my uncle."

"What the fuck!" Callum scrambled to his feet, stumbling backward as Shelly and Leon staggered alongside him, eyes wide and mouths open in horror. In the midst of their shock, they managed only a single step back towards the tree line behind them.

"Y-you're a freak," Shelly muttered at him across the dying fire.

Callum nodded, unblinking. "Yeah, a-a right fucking freak."

"That's what they used to call *me*," came a voice in the darkness behind them. "The bullies."

The three teenagers spun around to face the tree line. At first, there was only darkness, but then something pale and twisted took shape amidst the shadows.

Uncle David was deeply scarred from an awful house fire, and the thick veins on his neck were hardened and thick where once they had been rubbery and pliant. The fire had severed them, but he had held them together for eight hours at the morgue, until the gooey flesh started to re-knit itself. He wasn't truly alive, not in the normal sense, but he was here tonight. And he was hungry.

Every one-thousand-and-ninety-five days, Uncle David woke from the soil of the woods for twenty-four hours, thirsty for vengeance. As a loving nephew, Aaron was only too happy to assist.

"It started with my dad," Aaron said as his 'friends' screamed in terror as Spaghetti Neck grabbed them and wrapped his thick neck veins around their throats. "David visited him a year after the house fire and asked for help. Of course, my dad was glad to help his big brother. Then, when I was old enough, he passed that duty on to me. I found you bullies easily, and now I've brought you here to meet my uncle. I dare you to call him a freak." He knelt, picked up the vodka bottle, and upended the foul liquid onto the fire, killing it for good.

The bet wasn't about drinking vodka. It was his uncle who was thirsty.

Uncle David's neck veins were so thick and powerful that they snapped the delicate bones in his victim's necks as if they were twigs.

Shelly's eyes bulged as her head threatened to pop clean off her shoulders. Callum's tongue stuck out, his wonderful blonde hair yanked back so fiercely that his face began to stretch and split open. Leon went bright purple as he gasped for breath. None of them could scream any more, their necks constricted by throbbing purple veins.

And then those veins drank. Lined with a thousand tiny, sucking mouths, they drained the teenagers dry. The colour drained from their faces and their bodies went limp.

"Bullies beware, Spaghetti Neck will be there." Aaron walked away, but before he exited the woods, he yelled out, "See you in three years, Uncle."

THE YOFFEL

"Eddie's Storage Warehouse. Uh huh? No, sorry, I think you have the wrong number. No problem. Goodbye." Eddie Johnson dropped the cordless handset back onto its receiver and sighed. It was the only call he'd taken all afternoon, which would be okay if not for the fact half of his storage units were sitting empty. There was a time when that might have been enough to keep the lights on, but with the way things were ...

I'm going to have to put up prices to cover my costs. No point turning up every day when I can barely afford to pay myself.

Eddie stood up from behind his IKEA desk and decided to stretch his legs. The grey skies drizzled outside the warehouse, but that didn't bother him. With the hours he was putting in, chasing business, he needed to get some fresh air. He was starting to look like a vampire.

As soon as he stepped out front, he saw a familiar car bouncing up the trading estate's potholed access road. A groan escaped his lips. "Are you kidding me?"

His ex-wife, Anna, glared at him smugly over the steering wheel of her new husband's Mercedes. It was a six-year-old C Class, but you would have thought she was driving a brand new Maserati from the way she posed.

Probably for effect, Anna slammed on the brakes and skidded on a patch of wet gravel, spitting up tiny, biting stones. Rather than turn off the engine and get out, she merely lowered the window and leaned out at Eddie as he stood there in the rain. "Do I need to tell you why I'm here?" she asked, as if she were speaking to a naughty child.

Eddie cleared his scratchy throat and let out a breath. "I already told you, Anna. I'll get you your money by the end of the month. Why are you here?"

"Every two weeks, Eddie. Ella needs new shoes."

"If you let me spend more time with her, I could get her the things she needs myself."

"No way Jose. You would get it wrong. She's almost a teenager now, Eddie. You have to get the right brands—the expensive stuff."

"Hey, maybe I could, just, um, ask her what she wants and then buy that. What do you think?"

"Don't be sarcastic with me, Eddie. You're behind on what you owe me."

He hadn't even lit his cigarette yet, and his lips were moist at the thought of taking a drag. No way would he do so in front of Anna, though. She would just love to take a dig at his dirty habit and delight in the fact he had started back up since their divorce. "I don't owe you anything, Anna. We never went to court. Maybe we should."

Anna sneered at the suggestion, tapping her hands on the steering wheel. "That's the last thing you want, believe me. I'll hire a solicitor so good, you'll be lucky to keep your underwear."

"I don't want to argue, Anna. I give everything I can spare to Ella. If I don't have it, I don't have it. You can't get blood from a stone."

"I can get blood from you!"

He sighed. If he just agreed with her bullshit, she would go away sooner. "End of the month, okay? I'll get back up to date. In the meantime, why don't you ask Sean to give you an allowance?"

Damn, I almost managed it. I just can't be nice to her.

"Sean doesn't give me an allowance, Eddie. I make my own money."

"Uh, huh. Well, that's what I'm trying to do here, so can you please leave me to get on with it?"

She looked past him, at the ramshackle Victorian-era warehouse that was miraculously still standing. Its windows were so old they rattled in the breeze. But the rent was cheap–compared to other places–and access to the main roads was decent. It wasn't exactly upmarket, but neither was Eddie.

"This place was the worst idea you ever had," she told him. "You should just shut it down and get a proper job. Maybe if you'd stuck to being a plumber, you and I would still be together."

I highly doubt it.

"I just want more for myself. More for Ella. Is that so wrong?"

Anna rolled her eyes, but then she softened a little. "Well, hang in there, I guess."

Eddie actually recoiled in surprise. "Um, thanks."

"Because if you end up broke and unemployed, I'll make sure you have nothing to do with Ella."

Eddie sneered back at her, two snakes hissing. "Always thinking of our daughter's happiness, eh? Just get out of my face, Anna. I'll get your money, okay?"

She chuckled at him, and it sent shivers of rage through his veins. He wasn't a violent man, but sometimes the thought of just letting go and...

Don't let her get to you. Ella is what matters.

Anna wound up her window and sped off. The gravelly access road looped around the other side of the warehouse and then back out onto the main road. It was too narrow to turn around in place, penned in by old buildings on both sides.

Eddie felt a pressure remove itself from his chest. His throat was still killing him, but he pulled out a cigarette and placed it to his lips anyway. His hand shook as he did so.

Calm down. A heart attack is the last thing I need.

As soon as the cigarette was lit, things became bearable. He took a deep drag and felt himself relax. There was a time when he'd been a heavy drinker, as well as being a chain smoker, but he had decided to settle on just the one way to slowly kill himself.

"She's got you by the short and curlies, mate," said a voice that caused Eddie to wince. There would be no peace for him today, it seemed.

Eddie turned to see Christie leaning against his black Audi TT. The younger man shared the old warehouse with Eddie, which was divided in two by a partitioned wall. While Eddie had a series of twelve storage containers spaced evenly on his side, Christie ran a weight lifting gym on his. Eddie spent most of his day listening to muscle heads grunting and groaning on the other side of the wall, waxing lyrical about their particular brand of protein powder.

"Ex-wives," Eddie said with a shrug. "Every man should have one."

Christie chuckled, but he couldn't help but flex his shoulders and arms like a posturing gorilla. A thick, gold chain rested on his upper pecs, glistening in the rain. "Nah, mate. Once I get a woman, she never wants to leave."

"How wonderful for you. Maybe wait another fifteen years and see where you're at then."

Christie crossed his thick arms, not seeming to notice the chill or the drizzle in his skin-tight black vest. "I'll have taken over your half of the warehouse by then, and probably opened another six locations. Treadmill never stops for a guy like me." He grabbed his gold neck chain and rattled it. "Twenty-four-carat living, bro."

"Life's that easy, huh? All those steroids must give you a plenty of self-confidence. Small balls as well, from what I hear."

Christie stomped over to him, trainers sploshing in the puddles. "Just move out, Eddie. I'm going to get your half of the warehouse eventually. I already spoke to Georgio about it, and he said one more late rent payment and you're out. Why not leave now on your own terms? Stop getting in the way of people who actually know how to succeed."

Eddie took a drag from his cigarette and blew the smoke in Christie's face. They'd had this conversation before, and every time Eddie got a little closer to giving in. Was the stress worth it? He was his own boss, sure, but he got less respect than ever. "Maybe I'll just burn this fucking place to the ground with you in it, huh?"

For a moment, Christie clearly didn't know what to say to that. Eventually, he settled on a derisory sneer. "You got issues, mate. No wonder your old lady left you."

"Actually, I left her." *For fucking the pub landlord at our local boozer.*

Rather than wait for Christie's reply, Eddie went back inside. When he reentered his office, the telephone was ringing.

"Hello, Eddie's Storage Warehouse."

For once, it wasn't an incorrect number. But it wasn't good news either.

"Oh, dear," said Eddie. "I'm very sorry to hear that. Yes, of course. I can get that to you along with a final bill tomorrow. Right-o. Thanks for calling."

Eddie put down the phone and let his head drop. Already he needed another cigarette. A long-term customer had just died.

The call had come from the executor of Mrs Katchatori's estate. Apparently, the old lady had died alone at home from a heart attack. Detailed instructions told what to do in the event of her death, and that included details of her container lease at Eddie's warehouse.

It was business he couldn't afford to lose, but he could barely blame the old lady for dying.

Shit! This day just keeps getting worse.

Shaking his head with mild despair, Eddie went and unlocked the safe in the corner of his office, then pulled out a steel lockbox full of keys. Mrs Katchatori's container was number 9, so that was the key he grabbed. He had so few customers he knew them all by heart.

The old lady had been an odd one, with a glass eye and a spooky accent. He recalled she might once have claimed to be from Romania. *The old country,* she called it.

The partition at the far end of his space wobbled as some brute on the other side slammed weights down on the floor without regard. A door on the left side of the partition allowed Christie to swan in here from time to time, which was always an unwelcome surprise, but it was against fire and safety to lock it, so Eddie was powerless to keep the arsehole at bay.

Twelve containers in total, purchased from a defunct shipping company. Some storage places had nice plaster-walled units with temperature control. Eddie's setup was much simpler. Shove your stuff inside and he would store and protect it from theft. A basic, honest service.

Which no one wants.

If not for the larger storage company in the town centre, Eddie suspected his business might be doing better, but he had no way to compete with their location or number of units. Advertising only ever cost him money.

The containers were aligned in two rows of six. Eddie went over to the last-but-one on the left. The executor had requested an inventory, which Eddie didn't have. Privacy was one of his business's key promises. He held little interest in the lives of strangers.

I'd take a rotten corpse so long as they paid me.

He cleared his sore throat.

Mrs Katchatori visited once a week for the last two years, always empty-handed and always leaving the same way. Eddie's assumptions ranged from her coming to look over old family photographs and heirlooms, to her withdrawing cash from an illicit stash and tucking it into her bloomers. It actually filled him with a small amount of excitement, knowing he was about to find out what the woman's secret was. He valued his client's privacy, but she was dead now.

He stepped up to the container and grabbed the heavy duty padlock that kept the vertical locking bar in place. After a moment's pause—to remind himself that he was about to disturb the possessions of a dead woman—he unlocked the container and yanked down on the handle.

A musty smell wafted out and filled him with a momentary panic.

Shit! It's a corpse. I knew it!

But then he calmed down and realised the smell wasn't that bad. It was more of a farmy odour than something rotting—like the smell in one of those homes where the owners had more pets than space.

But there were no animals inside this container. In fact, there seemed to be barely anything inside it at all. A battery-operated sensor light came on overhead, but all it revealed was a single wooden crate about the size of a dishwasher. Atop the crate was a piece of cream-coloured material, like an oversized doily. A dark object sat directly upon its centre.

Eddie frowned. He considered exiting and just listing 'box' on the inventory form. No one had permitted him to inspect any further than that, so it was probably best not to interfere.

But it was so odd. People usually hired storage containers to hold their furniture in between moves, or to hold on to a bunch of stuff inherited from a deceased relative. Why had an old lady paid full rental on a container for years, only to fill it with a single wooden crate? Something that could easily have fitted inside a garage or shed.

And what is that sitting on top of the cloth?

Eddie couldn't help himself. He stepped forwards and inspected the small, dark object. When it provided no answers, he picked it up and examined it further.

A stone.

A nice stone. But just a stone.

It might be a rare mineral, but he knew nothing about that kind of thing, so to him, it was merely a perfectly smooth black stone about the size of a ping-pong ball. It was flattened on the bottom, which had allowed it to sit securely on top of the crate.

"Weird. I'm gonna put this down to the old dear being 'foreign.'" Despite not being particularly religious, Eddie did the sign of the cross. "Rest in piece Mrs Katchetori."

He leaned forwards to put back the stone, but as he did so, the crate rattled. Something thumped on the inside.

Eddie hopped back. "What the...?"

The crate rattled again, the cloth on top billowing slightly as stale air slid beneath it. Whatever was inside the crate possessed a decent amount of force.

A person? No... no way.

So an animal, then? That would explain the smell. But it's not possible.

Eddie's thoughts got stuck in the u-bend of his brain, questions stacking up on top of each other. No way could the old lady have kept a pet in here without him knowing about it. Plus, she'd visited only once per week. If that had been to leave food for a dog or a cat stuck inside the box, then the woman was nuts. Or evil.

You can't lock an animal inside a box and leave it.

But the crate moved again. Something was definitely inside. Something alive.

"God damn it." Eddie was now compelled to open the crate. It was against the terms of his business to store anything living, but he also had a moral duty to let whatever it was out.

No, I have a duty to call the authorities and let them deal with it. I don't need to open the crate myself.

But he couldn't shake the image of a miserable little dog cowering in the dark. Every second the poor thing stayed locked inside now was because of Eddie's delay.

Dogs didn't scare him, so he was willing to get nipped if it meant getting the poor bugger out of there.

Now angry, Eddie grabbed the cloth from the top of the box and tossed it aside onto the dusty floor. The crate was topped with a featureless wooden panel, with no key holes or handles. He grabbed at its edges and yanked, but found the wooden board nailed in place. The movement inside grew more frantic.

"Okay, boy! I'm going to get you out of here. Just... hold on."

Eddie stormed out of the container and headed to his office. Conveniently, he actually owned a crowbar. He had bought it to pull up some old laminate flooring in the office when he had wanted carpet. It leaned up against the side of the filing cabinet. He took it back to storage container number 9 and realised that he still held the smooth, black stone in his other hand. He put it in his pocket for now.

It was a satisfying feeling when the crowbar's sharp flat edge slid perfectly beneath the wooden lid and immediately loosened it by a few millimetres.

"Hold on, just wait a minute." Eddie stopped, both hands placed on the crowbar as he prepared to throw his weight on it. "Am I getting carried away? Is this the right thing to do?"

The crate bumped again.

"I guess that's a yes."

Eddie shoved down on the crowbar and popped the lid. The nails were short and came out easily, so it only took a single pry to slip his hands underneath the wood and pull it aside.

The mild, farmy odour inside the container now became a full on stink.

The battery light flickered overhead.

Eddie peered inside the crate.

"What the...?"

The light inside the container wasn't great, so his first thought was that he was failing to see what was in front of him. It was an animal, just as he had feared, except...

What the hell kind of animal is that?

What breed of dog am I looking at?

As Eddie looked down into the crate, its occupant peered back up at him. It wagged its tail, perked up its ears. Friendly.

A friendly little... thing.

The closest breed Eddie could ascribe to the creature was that of a pug. Except, it had a long, coiling tail that was more feathered than furry, and its ears were mere flaps of skin, like that of a cat. Its flat white face did not seem squashed, as with a pug, but instead, again, more like a cat's. If not for the way it wagged its tail excitedly, he might have described it as feline, but its body language was definitely more canine.

This is probably a bad idea.

"Okay, buddy. Let's get you out of here."

Eddie reached down cautiously into the crate. The sides were low enough that he could bend at the waist and place both hands around the creature, but he didn't know if it was dangerous or not.

A shudder spiralled through his spine in anticipation of being bitten, but nothing bad happened.

Feathers?

Like its tail, the creature's short body was covered with a feathery coat. Eddie felt his fingers slide into the plumage as he lifted the animal up and studied it. His hands were shaking.

"Don't bite me, okay?"

The creature did nothing to attack or even to escape his grasp. It just peered at him through gentle green eyes set in a round, almost owl-like face.

What the hell are you?

The creature's tiny mouth opened and made a *clup-clup* sound. Its body shimmered with various pleasant shades of green, made up from short, soft feathers. Its tail was twice the length of its body, hanging almost to the floor. Its ears perked up as it stared at Eddie.

"Whatever you are, you're a cute one, huh? What were you doing inside that box? Why would someone do that to you?" He truly couldn't believe the cruelty. He also couldn't believe that this animal wasn't a feral mess of fear and aggression.

It was wearing a collar.

Eddie was only getting more confused. The creature wasn't heavy, but it was substantial enough that he needed both hands to lift it. In order to study the collar, he had to raise his arms and lean forwards.

No name. No address. Just a mobile telephone number below the word CALL IF FOUND.

"Huh? Did the old woman worry about you getting lost?" Eddie pulled his arms inwards and placed the creature against his chest. It made more *clup-clup* sounds as it settled against his shoulder. Warmth radiated from its body. Its scent was very dog-like.

Wet dog.

"What am I going to do with you, buddy? Suppose I should call someone, huh?"

Eddie flinched as something sounded behind him, but it was only a meathead on the gym-side of the partition wall roaring on a final rep.

What would he say if Christie suddenly swaggered in?

Who cares? This is nothing to do with him.

Even so, Eddie couldn't help but tiptoe as he went back inside his office. It felt like he was doing something naughty, and he couldn't deny feeling a little afraid. Life had taken an odd turn, and he didn't feel fully in control of what was happening. His increasingly sore throat didn't help matters.

Creeping over to his desk, Eddie paused a moment. Was it safe to put the creature down? Nothing about its body language suggested it was eager to run away or cause mayhem.

"Okay, buddy. I'm just going to just place you down here." He lowered the creature to the desk, waiting for it to place down its back feet and then its front. It had claws sharp enough to dig into the wooden grain of the desk.

Geez! Wouldn't want to get on the wrong side of those.

The creature stayed put, as he'd hoped, tilting its owllike face curiously as he moved to grab the telephone. "Okay, let me just call... um, the RSPCA, right? They take animals of all sorts, I think."

He just needed to look up the number. He could use his mobile phone in his pocket or the laptop on his desk, but once he called them, he wasn't quite sure what to say.

"Oh, hey," he said to his empty office. "I just need you to come get a bird-cat-dog-thingy from me. Oh, where did I find it? In a wooden crate inside my warehouse. Yes, it's been there for abut two years."

Eddie cleared his throat and thought for a moment. There was another option. The number on the collar. Most likely it belonged to Mrs Katchatori, but he might get through to someone who knew what they were dealing with. They could explain what exactly this strange creature was, and why it had been locked up inside his warehouse.

"Okay, let's follow the breadcrumbs, shall we?" Eddie reached out carefully and tugged at the animal's collar. Placing the telephone handset down on the desk with the keypad facing up, he tapped in the number and then lifted it to his ear. It rang twice, clicked, and then delivered a message in a robotic voice:

If you have come into possession of the yoffel, it is now your responsibility to keep it contained until a new guardian arrives. Please state your location after the beep and—

Eddie ended the call and put the phone facedown on the desk. He wasn't willing to leave his address without thinking things through a little longer. Something about this whole situation was starting to feel off.

"And what the hell is a yoffel?"

The creature—apparently a yoffel—gave a happy *clup-clup* and then moved towards Eddie's arm. He reacted too slowly to get out of the way, but he ended up chuckling when the feathery little animal started to lick the back of his hand. At the same time, it whipped its tail back and forth across the table, knocking several papers onto the floor.

"All right, all right. I like you, too, buddy." Eddie patted the yoffel on its head and it made a purring sound. "That's nice, huh? Tell you the truth, I like it too. Nice to have someone around here that appreciates me. Maybe you can get rid of that lunkhead next door so we can have a little peace and quiet."

Clup-clup.

"You agree then? He needs to go!" Eddie shook his head and tittered. "I wish."

Clup-clup.

Eddie's leg vibrated. For a moment, it confused him, but it was merely a text on his mobile coming through. He reached into his pocket and felt something hard and cold–the strange black stone–and then managed to locate his phone. He pulled it out and groaned when he saw the text was from Anna.

The message read: *Spoke to Sean, and he said if u don't pay what u owe by Friday, he'll be coming to c u himself.*

Eddie gritted his teeth. He had little fear of Sean, but the arrogance of Anna made him furious. The pissant pub landlord had nothing to do with how much Eddie paid for his daughter's upkeep.

And I barely even get to see her. I miss every Christmas, every birthday...

Maybe I should bite the bullet and go to court. Even if I lose everything, I won't be any worse off than I am now. Ella is all I care about.

Eddie started to text back, but a sudden tiredness washed over him and he decided it wasn't worth it. An argument would only ruin his evening, and he was feeling increasingly under the weather. He just wanted to go home and sleep this day off.

But he had something to take care of first.

He looked at the yoffel–he really struggled to use the word–and still had no idea what to do with it. What he did know was that if he called the RSPCA now, they would probably take an hour or more to arrive. In the meantime, he would be stuck here, tired and ill.

He looked at his watch. It was almost five.

I don't want to be here all night.

"Do you think we can deal with you tomorrow, little fella?"

The yoffel tilted its head at him. A tiny feather came loose from its neck and floated down onto the desk. *Clup-clup.*

The creature had been trapped inside a wooden crate for god knows how long. One night in an office shouldn't hurt it.

"I'm going to leave you here, just for tonight, okay? You can have the run of the place. I won't even blame you for shitting. I just... I can't deal with the aggravation right now. Whatever you are, I'm guessing you're going to cause a fuss when people see you." He patted the yoffel on its head once again. It pushed against his hand, purring away. Maybe, once he found out what the hell it was, he could consider keeping it as a pet. He was no animal expert, though, so it was unlikely he would be allowed to adopt an animal so exotic.

"Okay." He nodded, took a moment, then nodded again. "Right. I'm going to close up and deal with you in the morning. That's the plan. Good."

Clup-clup.

The yoffel gave no sign that it minded when Eddie turned off the lights and closed the door. Nor did it cry out when he locked up the warehouse and went home. He resisted the urge to key Christie's Audi as he walked past.

———

WHEN EDDIE AWOKE in his bed, the first thing on his mind was a cigarette. The second thing was the yoffel. He laughed at the word. "What the hell is a bloody yoffel?"

He got dressed slowly, huffing and puffing as he struggled to breathe through a blocked nose. He put on the same jeans as yesterday and found the smooth black stone still in the pocket. It caused him to wonder why it had been left on top of the crate. It was as bizarre as the recorded message he had listened to. The yoffel was an enigma.

And this morning I'm going to have to deal with it.

Eddie got in his car and drove the fifteen minutes to work. It was a grey and dreary morning, and he shivered as he walked over to the entrance on his side of the warehouse.

Christie's Audi TT was already parked outside, which was strange as the guy rarely turned up until noon. He had a cleaning lady who opened up at 6AM for the morning workout psychos, but Christie was a late riser.

I can't imagine anything worse than exercising at dawn. Ergh!

Eddie switched on the lights from a panel on the wall and blinked as the fluorescents flickered and then came on. The doors to container number 9 were still open, and he shuddered as he imagined the old woman's zombie shambling out of it to eat him.

Then he shook his head and chuckled. It was unlike him to be so morbid. Cynical, sure, but not morbid. He lacked the imagination for it.

He stopped outside his office and listened for a moment. As a kid, he'd had a poodle that would howl like mad when left alone, but the yoffel was silent. Totally calm.

Maybe I imagined the entire thing. Could've been a fever from my cold. Or perhaps, I've finally snapped.

When he saw the office door ajar, he panicked. Had the creature got loose? The warehouse all seemed to be in order, but...

What if Christie walked in last night and found it? Is that why he's here this early? He's taken the yoffel for himself?

Eddie barged into his office, now fuming, but he stopped in his tracks when he saw his feathery friend sat on top of his desk. The light was off, so he could not see the greens and whites of its coat, but he could see its long, swishing tail whipping back and forth. Could see the shine of its eyes and hear its *clup-clups.*

Eddie switched on the light and said hello. "Thought you'd escaped for a moment there, bud. How did you..."

Something was different.

"Did you *change?*"

The yoffel was larger, its head wider and less like an owl now. Its ears were folded over and longer. The shimmering green feathers were darker and covered a larger trunk.

Eddie took a step backwards, moving into the doorway.

Clup-clup. The yoffel wagged its tail and tilted its head, clearly pleased to see him.

"How did you grow? How did you get bigger?"

It made no sense. The creature before him was more alien than ever, but it was also purring away and chirping happily. It meant him no harm. Somehow, he was confident of that.

Something glinted on Eddie's desk and caught his eye. "What do you have there, buddy?"

The yoffel had something beneath its front paw, a thin length of something shiny and metallic. Eddie thought he recognised it, and as he stepped closer, he was certain he did.

"Is that Christie's neck chain?" Eddie grabbed the length of gold and gave it a gentle tug until the yoffel removed its paw from atop it. It was heavy—made for a thick neck of a meat head gym owner's. And it was definitely Christie's.

But what's it doing on my office desk?

"Was he here last night? Did he come into my of—" Eddie gasped as he realised the gold chain had stained his palm with blood. It glistened all over the rounded, metal links.

Clup-clup.

Eddie gawped at the yoffel and saw that there were flecks of blood all over its plumage, spattered amongst the shimmering layers of green. Also, there was a...

He reached out a hand and plucked a piece of something pale from between two large feathers. It took only a second to realise it was an ear lobe. "Jesus."

Eddie hurried around his desk and grabbed the wastepaper basket. He filled it with vomit, then groaned when he realised it was made from metal wire, so the puke spat out and left his shoes soaked with last night's microwave curry.

He turned to the yoffel, wiping his mouth and unsteady on his feet. "Did you... Did you eat Christie? That's bad. That's a bad yoffel."

The yoffel opened its mouth and let out a belch.

Eddy reached into his pocket to grab his phone, but his hand came out with the black stone instead. It irritated him to keep finding it in his pocket, so he placed it down on the desk.

Immediately, the yoffel began to hop about and grumble. It clearly did not like the stone, and it caused the animal to glare at Eddie. He quickly picked it back. "Okay, okay, I'm sorry."

The yoffel wagged its tail and purred at him.

Eddy ran his thumbs over the stone's smooth black surface. "This is linked to you, huh? Is that why it was on top of your crate? To keep you inside?"

Eddie had taken the stone with him last night, allowing the yoffel to eat Christie from the looks of things. Or it had at least taken an ear.

"This can't be real." He brought up the address book on his mobile phone and called the gym next door. A man answered, but not Christie.

"Viking Iron Gym."

"Um, hi. Is Christie there, please?"

"Nah, mate. No one knows where he is today. I've tried calling him, but there's no answer. Who's this?"

"Oh, just an old friend. I was thinking of joining the gym."

"Yeah, you should come along and join up. Best gym in town, bruv. You want to leave a message?"

"No. I'll call again tomorrow."

"Suit yourself." The line went dead.

It had probably been one of the long-term gym users who had answered the phone. Christie had a little group of buddies who basically lived at the gym with him.

But they didn't know where Christie was.

Because he's been eaten.

His car's still parked outside.

Eddie stared at the yoffel. "You can't eat people."

Clup-clup.

Eddie huffed and leaned against his desk. "Or, I dunno, maybe you can. Not like I made you do it." He examined the smooth black stone in his hand. "Did I?"

Still ain't murder. I didn't know this animal was capable of eating people. Or maybe he just attacked Christie of his own volition. Wouldn't surprise me if he was snooping around my office late last night. That stupid door in the middle of our warehouse.

He nodded at the yoffel. "You were just guarding my property, right? Whatever happened, Christie had it coming?"

The yoffle wagged its tail as if to agree. It padded back and forth on the desk and turned in a circle. Then it took a dump the size of Eddie's arm.

Eddie wafted a hand in front of his face. "What the hell, buddy? Let me at least get something to put down first."

Eddie grabbed two entire rolls of blue roll from the toilets, along with the mop and bucket. When he returned to the office, the yoffel was on the ground, sniffing around the carpet. The massive turd took up most of the desk. Thankfully, it was firm and easy to pick up. Eddie dropped it in the mop bucket to dispose of later.

He had to decide what to do with the yoffel.

But first he needed a cigarette.

Eddie was about to leave his office when Anna appeared and caused him to dodge back inside. "Whoa! What the hell are you doing here?" He glanced around the office in a panic, but the yoffel was crouched underneath his desk, crammed into the footwell. Was it hiding?

"You're not welcome in here, Anna."

Anna opened her mouth to speak but then gagged and held her nose. "What the fuck, Eddie? Did you fart?"

"What? I... Yeah, sorry. I didn't know you were about to come in, did I? Why are you here again? I said I'd get your money."

She let go of her nose and grimaced. "I know you did. I was..."

He shook his head. "You were what?"

"You never replied to my text last night."

Eddie shrugged. "Why would I? You were just making stupid threats."

She grunted, but to his surprise, she also nodded. "I'd had a glass of wine. I was trying to cause an argument."

"Why doesn't that surprise me?"

"Don't start, Eddie. I came here to check on you. I thought maybe..."

He sighed. "That I'd hurt myself? I did that once because of you, but never again. You can fuck who you like. I don't care."

She stepped back towards the door, probably surprised by his venom. During their marriage, he'd put up with a lot, and rarely complained. But when it had all become too much, he had taken an overdose of sleeping pills. He always picked a non-confrontational way of dealing with things. He just didn't care for conflict. Didn't care much for anything anymore.

Except for Ella. I care about her.

"I want to see more of Ella," he said. Demanded it, in fact.

"After what you just said to me? Forget it. Pay me what you owe me and I might let you see her once a week—if you're lucky."

Stop! You're losing your temper. Don't do it.

"I want her at Christmas, Anna. I mean it. It's not fair on her or me."

She scoffed. "I make the rules."

"I'm warning you, Anna. You need to let me see my daughter."

"Are you threatening me?"

"Yes, I am."

I really am. No more being bullied by you. No more!

"Oh, that is it." She shook her head in disbelief. "Just wait until Sean hears about this. You're dead."

"No," Eddie said, his voice even and firm. Confident. He raised the smooth black stone above his head. "You're dead, Anna! Yoffel, kill!"

Anna frowned, but her confusion turned to horror when the yoffel leapt up onto the desk and snarled at her, extending its feathers like an angry peacock. She screamed for only a single second before the creature leapt on top of her and started ripping her throat to shreds. As it did so, it slurped hungrily, and all the blood went into its mouth. It swallowed her flesh in great, greedy mouthfuls. Devoured her noisily.

Eddie threw up again, this time all over the floor.

"What... what the hell did I just do?" He had no idea where the anger had come from, but once it came it was like venom jetting out of a wound. He hadn't been able to stop it.

He had just ordered the yoffel to kill for him. He was a monster.

I need some air.

Eddie staggered out onto the warehouse floor. He bumped right into Ella, who was standing there like a statue, all the colour drained from her cheeks as she watched the yoffel eating the last of her mother.

Oh, god, no.

Eddie choked, his sore, swollen throat full of phlegm. "E-Ella? What are you doing here?"

"M-Mum said I could come in and say hello. Sh-she told me to w-wait here." She couldn't take her eyes off the yoffel. Her voice was like a distant whisper.

Eddie grabbed her by the shoulders and looked her in the eyes. "It's okay, sweetheart. Let's get you out of here."

"M-Mum?" She pushed Eddie aside and started screaming. "Oh my God, Mum!"

Eddie tried to grab her again, but she dodged past him and ran into the office, perhaps to try to help her mother. But it was too late for that. Anna was beyond dead. She was leftovers.

Eddie put his hands to his cheeks in silent despair.

The yoffel glanced up at Ella and growled. Its jagged feathers fanned out in a threatening display.

"No!" Eddie held up the black stone and roared frantically. "Get away from her! Get back."

The yoffel looked at Eddie and wagged its tail, suddenly calm and happy.

"That's it... just, stay. Stay, boy."

The yoffel wagged his tail even more enthusiastically.

Then it leapt at Ella and tore her face off.

Eddie and his daughter screamed in unison.

———

EDDIE SAT cross-legged on the floor of the warehouse, rocking back and forth slightly. His daughter's remains sat in a glistening pile beside his ex-wife's. No longer recognisable as human, just chunky red puddles. Soup.

The yoffel was the size of a cow. Its feathers fanned in and out constantly, flicking blood and guts into the air and staining the concrete floor. Its ropey tail was like a hosepipe, whipping back and forth with heavy *thwumps*. It was a creature of evil–some kind of ancient demon. Mrs Katchatori had been its guardian, keeping it contained inside a crate inside a locked container. Now the old woman was dead and the demon was loose.

Because of me. I let it out.

The yoffel's collar snapped free when it had grown again. Eddie now held it in his hand, rubbing away a slick layer of blood with his thumb. He dialled the number on the tag.

If you have come into possession of the yoffel, it is now your responsibility to keep it contained until a new guardian can be selected. Please state your location after the beep and help will arrive shortly.

Eddie left his address and warned of the yoffel having fed. Then he tossed his phone across the warehouse and watched it smash on the ground. He didn't need it anymore. The only thing left in his possession was the smooth black stone. He had assumed it had given him control over the yoffel, but it hadn't. It only protected him. Him alone. The creature didn't obey orders.

Christie must have entered the warehouse last night after Eddie had left. The yoffel had fed.

Then it ate Anna and Ella.

Anna... she brought my daughter to see me. All this time, I've been fighting with her. Maybe she was right to keep Ella away. I am a loser. Always have been.

The yoffel stomped around the warehouse, sniffing at the ground and licking its bloody lips. Eddie had no idea who was on the way, but he hoped they could contain it, or even kill it. It wasn't an animal. It was a vile monster. A devourer of children.

Before today, Eddie had possessed little reason to live. Now he had none at all.

"Hey?" He put two fingers in his mouth and whistled. "Hey, you son-of-a-bitch. You see this?"

The yoffel turned in his direction and wagged its tail. Its feathers retracted back against its trunk and it lowered its head.

Eddie held the black stone out in front of him.

Then he flung it against the side of Mrs Katchatori's container. It bounced off the steel panel and hurtled out of sight.

The yoffel tilted its head like a curious puppy.

Then its feathers sprang back out like razor blades and it let out a demonic screech.

The beast rushed towards Eddie, its beak opening wide.

Eddie closed his eyes.

And waited to be eaten.

CALL ME BOB

Dennis took a bath. He was usually more of a shower guy—the superior way to get clean–but he was feeling weary and wanted to relax. Sometimes there was nothing quite like a long, hot soak.

He lay back in the steaming water and tried to find a comfortable position for the back of his head. His student flat wasn't up to much, but the bath and shower had been new when he'd moved in, so he made the most of it whenever he wasn't at a lecture or down the pub. Or lying in bed, riddled with anxiety.

Philosophy was turning out to be more difficult than Dennis had envisioned, and studying at York when all of his family were down in Peterborough left him feeling unsettled and alone. To make matters even worse, he was struggling to make friends. Whenever he went on a night out, he tagged along with his fellow students, but usually ended up sitting quietly in a corner. As much as he tried, he just couldn't make an impact. He felt invisible.

Nothing was the way he had hoped it would be when applying to universities last year. This was supposed to be the time of his life. It just wasn't.

"You need to find like-minded people," came a softly spoken voice.

"That's the key. For instance, there's a polite young chap named Kyle Patterson studying first year History. The two of you would get on very well."

Dennis jolted, struck with the sudden panic that reasonably arrived at finding a stranger in your bathroom. He tried to leap out of the tub, but his feet slipped on the bottom and he ended up beneath the water.

I'm going to be murdered. I never should have left home. My mum will be heartbroken.

Dennis came up spluttering and found himself staring at an old man sitting on the closed lid of the toilet. The stranger, with long white hair and a flowing grey cloak, offered out a wizened hand. "Settle down, son. I mean you no harm."

"Who... Who... Who in the hell are you?"

The old man winced. "Who in the heavens would be more accurate."

Dennis sat up and wiped water from his eyes. "I... I don't understand." He realised he was completely exposed. He tried to cover himself with his hands.

"Don't be bashful," said the old man. "Hold still."

Dennis froze, confused, and then he felt something. The water began to fizz, tickling him and making him want to itch. Then it frothed up with thick, cloudy bubbles. Within a few seconds, a lather rose up from the tub that covered Dennis's nakedness.

"H-How did you...?"

"Strawberry scented," said the old man. "My favourite."

"You added bubble bath? You didn't even move."

"It's nothing. I am God, after all."

Dennis was expressionless for a moment. Then he spluttered out a laugh. "What is this? A practical joke? Who set this up?"

"It's not a joke, son. I need some advice."

Dennis laughed again, then blinked several times, wondering if he was dreaming. He felt entirely lucid, however. The bath water was warm against his skin. The bubbles hissed as they burst. This was no dream.

"Y-You need some advice?"

"Yes, son."

"And you believe you're God?"

"You can call me Bob. No need to be formal."

"You're a lunatic. Where have you escaped from?"

"I wish I knew. Look, Bob is a perfectly fine name for anyone. It's short, impactful, and it reads the same back to front, which is just lovely, don't you think?"

Dennis shook his head, realising how absurd this was. He needed to call the police, or the men in white coats at the very least. This old man had escaped from a home, suffering with dementia.

He put his hands on the side of the bath and started to push himself upwards.

"The world is going to end." The old man waved a frail hand through the air and suddenly Dennis's shoulders felt as if they were made of solid iron. He could no longer lift himself and plunged back into the water.

"Wha... Stop it!"

"I truly apologise, son. It's unlike me to be so hands on, but I really do need your help. Stay where you are, I insist."

Dennis felt his shoulders return to normal, but he didn't risk getting up again. "How can I help you? I'm a student."

"You're a philosopher."

"I'm nine months into a foundation year; I wouldn't exactly name me Socrates."

"But you have a philosopher's mind, and you're young, which means you haven't been jaded by life or influenced by the teachings of others. You have that spark of pure human spirit I'm looking for."

"You think you're God?"

"Must I keep repeating myself? Yes, I am God, but you can call me Bob."

"You're God, but you've come to sit on my toilet while I take a bath?"

"The lid is down, so it makes a good seat. As for you being in the bath? Well, that's just where you happened to be when I sought you out."

"You're not God," said Dennis, waving an arm and displacing some bubbles. "You're insane, is what you are."

"What is insanity, son? A departure from the norm? Well, in that case, I suppose I can accept that label."

Dennis shook his head, staring at the bubbles on his hands. "Maybe *I'm* insane."

The old man sighed, so gently that he barely moved. He lifted a leg, revealing leather sandals, and placed a foot across his knee. "Look, neither of us is insane, son. You want to meet insane people, then go visit Stockton-on-Tees." He shook his head. "It's quite a place, I can tell you. But, for the purposes of this conversation, I am very much in touch with reality, okay? My presence here is not on a whim. There's a quandary with which I need your help."

Dennis rubbed at his face, checking for signs of a stroke. With his eyes closed, he said, "What quandary?"

"The world is going to end."

Dennis opened his eyes and looked at the old man. He seemed so old and frail, yet there was not the merest sense of poor health about him. His robe was spotlessly clean and his hair shone with purity. Even his toenails were pleasantly shaped—and Dennis hated feet.

"What do you mean the world is going to end?"

"I mean it's a ticking watch about to run out of battery."

Dennis huffed. "Well, if you're God, can't you do something about that?"

"There are several things I can do, but I'm not sure which one is right."

"Aren't you *all knowing?*"

"I know all, yes, but that doesn't help me make decisions. If anything, it's the exact opposite. Sometimes, having too much knowledge and too many options is a curse. I can't see the future, you see, so I don't know what will happen from one minute to the next. That's what I want to talk to you about, Dennis. Help me choose what to do."

"About the world ending? Why would you choose me for something so important?"

"I already told you. You're a young philosopher. You can help me see the virtue of my decisions. The humanity, I suppose."

"There must be someone better than me." Dennis shook his head and tutted. "Am I really having this conversation?"

"You're as qualified as anyone else."

"You really expect me to believe you're God? Prove it."

"Really? I'm not really one for parlour tricks. It's a lot of effort in lieu of simple words."

"Effort? Didn't you create the heavens and the earth?"

The old man looked away sheepishly. "I didn't, as it happens. One day, long ago, I just... came into being. My conscience formed and I found myself floating in an endless void. I sensed I was not alone, so I reached out and touched the earth. It was dark, so the first thing I did was put some lights on. That was my first mistake."

"Your first mistake?"

The old man nodded and stared at the floor tiles wistfully. "Yes, as soon as I added light, things began to grow. Ice melted and formed water, and that water filled with tiny little life forms. Eventually, those life forms changed and grew and made it onto dry land. Before I knew it, there were great big lizards stomping about everywhere."

"Wait? Are you saying life formed on Earth by accident?"

"More as a reaction to my actions. Everything was already in place, all the... matter and whatnot. When I ignited the sun, it really kicked things off, though. The dinosaurs were just settling in well when I knocked one of Saturn's moons with my elbow and sent a chunk of it flying into the earth. Killed nearly everything on the planet, it did. A bad day."

Dennis put his face in his hands. "I want to get out of this bath. Will you let me leave?"

"Once you've helped me make a decision, yes. Shall I continue?"

"I suppose so."

"Anyway, after I wiped out most of life on earth I, of course, felt bad. It's hard to describe, but I sensed this well of power at my disposal. Not much, but enough to get a few things going again. I reached into that pool and used the essence inside to create new life."

"Humans?"

"No, the duck-billed platypus. I admit, it didn't exactly go to plan. I mean, it was my first try at making something. To be honest, I have no idea how those bloody things survived. Have you seen them?"

"So, you didn't create the dinosaurs, but you created..." Dennis frowned and rubbed at his temples. "Not sure I'm following you very well."

"I never made the lizards or the insects, son. They evolved all on their own from the muck of the earth. No, I only created the mammals and the birds. The cute, fluffy things–they're all me. Why would I want to make a snake or one of those stupid beetles that push balls of poop around? Nope, they had nothing to do with me."

"Okay, fine." Dennis thought about trying to make a run for it, but he felt that heavy feeling in his shoulders again, almost as if the old man could sense his intentions. Was Bob really God? Impossible. Ridiculous. And yet... there was something wrong about the man. "So you created all the animals? Great. Well done."

"Thank you. I learned a lot in those early stages and every iteration of creature was better than the last. Eventually, I became skilled enough to create my greatest of all life forms."

Dennis nodded, needing to pretend this was a normal conversation. "Humans?"

"No, the slow loris. Have you seen how cute they are? I really nailed it. It was my final creation because I had nowhere to go after that."

"Wait? What? So when did you make people?"

"Oh, I made humans quite near the end. I admit, I got you mostly right. Went too big with the brains, though. Caused all sorts of problems. I had been working too hard, needed a rest, and I forgot I'd left you growing. By the time I got back, I had this chubby giant headed baby looking at me. Killing it would have been cruel, so I signed it off and let humans evolve. Now you've reached a point where you're going to destroy everything. I really don't have the energy to start again."

Dennis groaned. "I don't believe you're God. Please, just tell me what this is and let me go."

The old man closed his eyes for a moment. "You humans do make things hard, don't you? If I showed myself to a llama, it wouldn't doubt what I was. Only people question what they see before them."

"All I see in an old man."

"Fine. What would you like to see? How about someone famous? You like Cliff Richard, don't you?"

"What? No, I don't. Why would I like a guy that old?"

"Because he was your grandma's favourite and you used to listen to his songs together when you were a little boy. Here, watch!"

The old man began to vibrate and shimmer. Suddenly, Cliff Richard was sitting on the toilet smiling at him. Still wearing the same grey robe, though.

Dennis choked on his own tongue.

"I can't do the voices," said Cliff Richard—or Bob the God. "I'm terrible at doing voices."

"Turn back," Dennis said, choking. "I don't like it."

"No problem." Cliff Richard shimmered back into an old man. "Believe me now?"

Dennis shivered, unable to talk.

"Water getting cold?" Bob nodded, and the water in the bathtub heated up a few degrees.

"Y-you're really God?"

"Yes. Can we move past that, please?"

Dennis nodded. "Okay. I believe you. You want my help to stop the world ending?"

"Not necessarily. I'm weighing up my options about what to do. Last time I got involved directly, things didn't go quite to plan. Couple thousand years ago, when mankind was last getting out of hand, I tried to change the way of things. I sent Jesus and Ed to help mankind change its ways."

"Jesus was real?"

"Of course."

Dennis smiled, comforted by that. "Hold on a minute, did you just say Jesus and *Ed*?"

"Yes. Jesus was a carpenter and Ed was a stonemason. I sent them to earth to erect great structures and improve the infrastructure of the Middle East. They were to build mighty monuments in my name and spread the word of... well, the word of *me*. People were being so greedy and unkind, you see, so Jesus and Ed were going to build homes for the homeless and bring water to the desert."

Dennis licked his lips and blinked slowly. "Um, right. So, what happened next?"

"Well, there was a snag, you see? Ed got drunk one night and ran off to start a band. He was quite handy with a harp, and it tended to attract the females a lot more than his hammer and chisel. Anyway, I never heard from Ed ever again, and Jesus ended up a bit short-handed. He did what he could, but you maniacs nailed him to a cross. I mean, why do that? If you didn't like a chap, just kill him. To make pageantry of it is just perverse."

Dennis started laughing. It felt like he was losing his mind slowly out of his ears. "What do you want from me? Please, I can't take any more of this. It's crazy."

Bob leaned forward, bony elbows on his knees. "Right, let's get to the point, shall we? Mankind is on the brink of destroying itself. Mass greed and corruption has led to wars, poverty, and climate crisis. Right now, there are multiple unhinged individuals working on nuclear weapons and devastating viruses. I give you all..." He shrugged. "Three or four hundred years, max."

"Four hundred years?" Dennis scoffed. "I thought you were going to say the world is ending next week."

"Well, it is as far as *I'm* concerned. I've been around for millions of years, son. Four hundred years is a clap of a fart to me."

"I suppose it would be. Okay, so how do we stop it from happening?"

Bob sat up straight. His robe slipped a little and almost exposed his naked body beneath. He didn't seem bashful about it, but he did refasten it. "Not sure that we even do want to stop it. Way I see it, you people have run your course. The problem is, you'll likely take all other life with you when you go. Goodbye platypus, goodbye slow loris, goodbye Keanu Reeves."

"You care more about the animals than us?"

"I care about you all, but it's impossible to help you humans. My powers are finite, and I don't want to waste what essence I have left in the pool on a lost cause. That's why my decision is so important. I might only have one shot at this before I become impotent."

Dennis raised an eyebrow. "Impotent?"

"Yes, impotent. Powerless."

"Oh, right. So, what can you do?"

"Not sure, really. I could wipe you all out prematurely, of course. I could, um, pump Katy Perry full of a doomsday plague and have her explode all over the audience at her next show. Might be a little grim, but it would get the job done."

Dennis grimaced.

"No, no, you're right," Bob said, scratching at his beard. "There wouldn't be enough people in the audience. Maybe we do Lady Gaga instead. Ooh, Olivia Rodrigo, I like her!"

Dennis swallowed a lump in his throat. "Um, what else you got, beside a pop star plague bomb?"

"I could try and find Ed? Give him one last chance to spread love and warmth throughout humanity."

"I don't think that would work. Besides, if you have to prove the existence of God to get people to behave, then they are only really doing it through fear or want of reward."

Bob chewed at his lip for a moment. "You see my predicament? I don't want to see mankind extinguished, but if I'm not careful, I could lose everything–all life on earth. You really have got too big for your boots."

"Some of us understand that, Bob. The biggest evils are committed by a select few. Most ordinary people are decent, at least if given the chance."

"Really? Dennis, do you honestly believe that the average person, if presented with the chance to take something for themselves at the expense of someone else, wouldn't do so?"

Dennis opened his mouth but found it hard to speak. He had to force out his answer. "Yes. Yes, I believe that most people are good."

"So tell me what to do, son."

"What? You want me to choose the fate of mankind?" His eyes almost bugged out of his head, and the bath water seemed to turn cold, but it was likely just the sudden surge of adrenaline. "Why don't *you* choose?"

"I don't want the guilt of it. I'm going to leave mankind's fate to a man. Can't say fairer than that, can I? You tell me what to do and I'll do it. Do I wipe out all of humanity right here and now in order to secure the future of all other life on Earth? Do I make you all blind and dumb? Do I level your empire with a second great flood? Should I make donkeys smarter so that you have competition for dominance? Come on, let's get some ideas out."

Dennis shook his head, mind awhirl with a thousand different possibilities. What the hell should he do? All he had wanted was to take a bath. This shouldn't be his problem, his decision.

"Come on," said Bob. "What adjustment—big or small—would make the world a better place?"

"I... You could..."

"Spit it out, son."

Dennis's eyes went wide as the right decision suddenly hit him like a wet fish across the face. A perfect way to instantly make the world a better place. It could fix everything.

"I know the answer," he said.

"What is it?"

"Kill all the billionaires."

Bob smiled.

And Mankind thrived.

For a little while, anyway.

THE FADING OF THE BLOOMS

"I'm thinking this might have been a bad idea." Stef put her hands on her hips and surveyed the house standing before her—a mixture of dream home and financial nightmare surrounded by two acres of land. The ramshackle two-story farmhouse was like something off the cover of *Country Magazine*. Having grown up on a council estate, Stef always dreamed of living somewhere rural like this. Somewhere without loud neighbours and car-clogged kerbs.

Michael entwined his fingers with hers as he stood beside her. "We always knew it was going to take a bit of work, but it'll be worth it in the end. We'll make this place ours." Just as he said it, a squirrel darted across the overgrown lawn and scooted up the thick trunk of what looked to be an elderly yew tree.

Stef took a breath of fresh air and smiled. *It might have been growing here since before the house was even built. What a memory it must have.*

"The Bloom House," Stef said, staring at the wildflowers growing around the building's foundations. Dandelions, buttercups, and crowfoot.

Michael looked at her. "What?"

"That's what we should rename the house once it's all done. Bloom House."

"Seriously? I had to convince you to take my surname when we got married. Now you're ready to name a house after me?"

"After *us*, and I was only funny about giving up my name because it felt like part of my identity."

He nodded awkwardly, having already heard her thoughts about the matter. "I know, honey."

She turned and put her hands on his chest, looked into his eyes. "Eventually, I realised I wanted a fresh start. With you."

They kissed, then Michael chuckled. "So you don't want to keep the existing name for the house?"

"Unknown Cottage? It's the worst name I've ever heard. Seriously, who names a house that?"

"Right?" Michael shook his head with a grin. "There must be some history to that. We'll have to find out."

"*History-shmistery*. Who cares about the past? We bought this place for the future."

"*History-shmistery?*"

She smirked. "You heard me."

It was true that they had bought the house for what it could be not for what it was. Michael had finally qualified as an architect, while Stef had conquered her ambition of having a first romance novel published. Life had clicked in all the right places, so after tying the knot nine months ago, they had both agreed on finding the perfect house to be a family. A home that was unique and cosy and all theirs. *Bloom House.*

"This is gonna be great," Michael said, still smiling.

"It's gonna suck," she said, referring to the work that lay ahead of them. "But you're right. The end will be worth it."

———

THEY HAD VIEWED the house several times before putting in an offer, so its disrepair wasn't a shock to them, but now that it was finally theirs, the responsibility suddenly became overwhelming. A professional survey had found the bones of the house sturdy and well-built, but the wooden floors were chipped and damaged, the tiles in the large, country-style kitchen were badly cracked. The walls needed re-plastering and the light fixtures needed replacing. The bannister on the stairs had completely collapsed.

But the bones. The bones are good.

Stef and Michael sat silently on the white leather sofa that had travelled with them from their former two-bed terrace. It was badly out of place in the cottage and would have to go, but for now the two of them relaxed into its soft cushions and took a moment to reflect.

Stef's thigh vibrated, and then followed an irritating *ping!* Reaching into her jeans pocket, she pulled out her phone and looked at it. "Oh, it's mom. I texted her earlier when we got the keys and..." She frowned.

Michael sat forwards and perched his forearms on his knees. "What is it?"

She turned her phone so that he could see it. The text message was indeed from her mother, but it read simply: **Who is this?**

"Huh? Has she lost your number or something?"

Stef frowned. "Even if she had lost it, it should be obvious from my message that it was me. How many other people would text her about getting the keys to a house today? I'm going to call her."

And she did.

Her mother answered immediately. "Hello? Who's this?"

"Mom? It's me. Are you serious?"

"What? Oh, it's you, Stephanie. How are you?"

As she held the phone to her ear, she scrunched up her face in confusion. "I texted you. We got the keys to the house. Did you not get the message?"

"A message? Let me... Oh, yes, here it is. You got the keys? Great."

"Yeah. About two hours ago. Me and Michael are just sitting in the lounge wondering what the hell we've done."

"Getting married?"

"What? No, mom, I'm talking about the house. There's so much work to do. Are you all right? You sound confused. Have you..."

Been drinking all day?

"...have you been busy today?"

"Busy? No, not really. I went to Brenda's for a cuppa and then to the shops, but other than that I've been at home watching television. You know me. Life of excitement."

Stef laughed, relieved to hear her mother slip back into a normal tone. For a moment, she'd sounded like a stranger.

"Well, anyway, Mom, I just wanted to check in with you and let you know we're in. It's a bit empty at the moment, but we'll have you around for tea soon, okay?"

"That'll be nice, dear. I can't wait to see it all done up. Lovely, being out in the countryside. Nice and private and so far away."

Stef rolled her eyes at the last comment. "We'll see you soon, Mom, I promise."

"Right-o. Well, speak to you soon then, Sarah."

"Huh? Sarah?"

"Oh, I meant to say Stephanie. How silly."

"Yeah... goodbye, Mom."

She ended the call and turned to Michael, who had been watching her the whole time. "Everything okay?" he asked.

"Not sure. She sounded weird."

"Drunk?"

"No. No, I don't think she was. She was talking clearly, but she was... confused."

Michael slapped his thighs and stood up. "Hungover, then. Come on, let's go find the box with the kettle in. I need a cup of tea before we do anything else."

———

THE FOLLOWING DAY, Stef and Michael headed out to discover the nearby village of Daveton. They'd only moved twelve-miles from their previous home in Milton Keynes, but they knew little of the precise area in which they now lived. They parked their car next to a circular green with a blossom tree in its centre and a small paved area with a war memorial. A quaint and lovely place to have nearby, that was for sure. Most of the tiny shops surrounding the green were independent, with only a bank and a newsagent bearing the name of a corporation.

"Ooh," Stef purred. "There's a little tea room over there. Let's go in and get a sandwich."

Michael gently squeezed her hand. "Wow, are we country folk now? Sandwiches and tea for lunch?"

"We're more the living in a derelict house in the middle of nowhere kind of folks, but we can aspire."

A bell chimed above the door when they opened it, and a plump, smiling old lady welcomed them from behind a rustic brick counter. Lace table clothes covered the small round tables and an elderly-looking spaniel lay in one corner, snoring softly.

"Good morning, my lovelies. How are you today?"

Stef couldn't help but grin. "We're good, thank you. We just moved into the area, the old farmhouse. Unknown Cottage?"

"Oh, I know it," she said with a chuckle. "Everyone knows Unknown Cottage. Ha!"

"Ironic," Michael said. "Is it okay if we sit?"

The woman put her hands on her bulging hips and shook her head at him. "No. We don't like strangers around these parts." Then she laughed and waved a hand dismissively. "Of course you can sit down, deary. I'm Sandra, but everyone calls me Gertie."

Michael frowned. "Why do they call you that?"

"Long story. Now, what can I get for you both?"

Stef sat down near the spaniel and stroked its head. It woke up briefly to look at her, but then went back to sleeping. She then picked up a small laminated menu from the table and gave it a peruse. "Um, can I please get the... brie and cranberry panini?"

"Of course, deary. And for you, young man?"

Michael sat down and took a quick look. "I'll have the roast beef baguette, please."

"Any tea or coffee?"

"Two teas, please," Stef said, knowing Michael hated coffee.

Gertie gave a thumbs up. "Coming right up."

While the woman toddled over to the coffee machine to fill two mismatched mugs with hot water, Stef leaned in close to Michael and whispered. "She's lovely."

He pulled a face. "Dunno. I'm getting a whole Sweeny Todd vibe. I better check the roast beef before I eat it."

She punched him on the arm and cackled. "You idiot."

Gertie came over with their teas a moment later, plonking them down and standing back from the table with her hands on her hips again. Her apron had flowery, blue embroidery around the edges. "So what made you two buy the old cottage down the road, then? Needs a lot of work, I would have thought."

Michael snorted. "You're not wrong, but we'll be doing most of it ourselves."

"The only way we could afford to live out in the countryside was to buy a fixer upper," Stef explained. "Luckily, Michael's an architect, so he has an interest in doing up old buildings."

"An architect? How impressive."

"And Stef's a writer," Michael said, directing the attention away from himself. "She just had her first book published."

Gertie gasped and looked at Stef as if she were a famous painting. "My word, you're joking? A real life writer in my tea room, eh?" She gave Stef a little tap on the shoulder. "Maybe you could type up a few chapters in here. Then, when you get super famous, I can advertise that you used to work here."

Stef blushed. "I wouldn't bank on me being the next Danielle Steele, but I would love to pop in now and then to work. Especially while the house is a mess. I don't even have an office at the moment."

Gertie motioned with an arm. "Let this be your office. What name do you write under, my love?"

"Stephanie Bloom. I plan to have a rose on every cover of every book I publish. Kind of like a branding thing, you know?"

"So it's romance, is it? I'm more into my true crime. Love a bit of murder, me."

"Same," Michael said. "Bloodier the better."

She gave him a wink of agreement. "Anyway, I'll go make your food. Won't be too long."

Mike reached out a hand. "Um, before you go. Do you happen to know how long our house has been empty for? We couldn't find out much about its history."

Stef tutted. "Michael likes to know the stories behind old buildings. It'll drive him crazy if he doesn't find out."

Gertie turned back to face them. "The previous owners? Well now, there's a question. Seems like the old place has always been empty, but no..." She wagged a finger. "There was a family who lived there, actually. They were... hmm." She frowned like she had a headache and then flapped her arms in defeat. "Nope. I'm afraid the old age is getting to me. You're best off asking someone else."

"No problem," Stef said. "Thanks, Gertie."

"My pleasure, Susan." The woman toddled off into the kitchen.

Stef turned to Michael who was laughing underneath his hand. "That's the second time that's happened," she said. "Mom called me Sarah on the phone yesterday. Now, I'm bloody Susan."

Michael was in hysterics, and he had to hold his breath to keep from cackling. "Susan's a nice name. Let's stick with it. Susan Bloom."

"It'll be back to Stef *Pilkington* if you keep on." She tapped him on the side of his thigh under the table. "Seriously, though? Is my name so forgettable?"

"Must be. But I wouldn't worry about it too much, Steve."

She whacked him playfully again, a little harder."

Gertie came back out of the kitchen and went behind the counter. She didn't seem to notice them for a moment, but then she flinched, waved, and gave them a welcoming smile. "Good morning, my lovelies, how are you today?"

Stef and Michael glanced at each other, both of them bemused.

What?

Michael cleared his throat and shifted in his chair. "Um, good, thanks. Didn't you already ask us that?"

Gertie frowned. "Did I? Age must be getting to me. Oh well, what can I get for you both?"

Stef chuckled, not sure if this was a joke. "A brie and cranberry panini and a roast beef baguette." She lifted her mug of tea. "You already gave us our drinks."

Gertie stood frozen, like a robot whose operating system had crashed. For a moment, it looked like she might have been suffering from a stroke, but then she shook her head and tittered. "Of course, of course. I remember now. What on earth is wrong with my brain today? I'll go make your food."

Stef smiled until the woman disappeared back into the kitchen, but then she turned back to Michael and said, "What the actual fuck?"

He shrugged, sipped his tea, and then shrugged again. "Magic mushrooms. Has to be. Either that or the old bird is whacked up to the eyeballs on black tar heroin."

Stef rolled her eyes and smirked. "Did I really agree to marry a clown like you?"

"Yes, and it's binding. So shut up and drink your tea, Simone."

———

BACK AT THE house that evening, Stef helped Michael organise the kitchen cupboards. After spending a few hours in Daveton, they had gone to see a movie at the cinema in Milton Keynes and grabbed a McDonalds on the drive home afterwards.

Placing the toaster beside the kettle on the counter, Michael shook his head and chuckled to himself.

Stef growled. "You're thinking about Gertie again, aren't you?"

"I'm sorry. It was so surreal. Like, she went into the kitchen and completely forgot who we were."

"It's not funny, babe. She might have dementia or something. Or what if she was having some kind of fit? We should have checked to make sure she was okay."

"She was fine. My roast beef sandwich didn't even have any finger-nails in it. Was pretty nice actually. I would go back again."

"I might go back tomorrow."

"What? Why? Was the panini *that* good?"

"I feel guilty, Michael. She was so lovely, but we slunk out of there in a hurry as soon as we finished our food."

He nodded. "Yeah, so fast we forgot to pay."

"What? You're joking? I thought *you* paid."

"I didn't even think about it until we were in the car but, yeah, we didn't pay the bill. Gertie just waved as we left."

Stef put her hands to her face and moaned. "Oh my God. I can't believe we did that. Now I'm definitely going back tomorrow. Hopefully she'll laugh it off."

"Shit happens. I'm sure she'll be fine about it."

They continued unpacking for the next hour, getting most of the kitchen done. In a few months, they would likely rip out all the counters and cabinets and replace them with something new, but for now all they needed was for it to be functional. Michael wanted to start by putting up a new stair rail and changing the electrics before moving on to anything else.

Stef unsealed another cardboard box and reached inside. "Ooh, our wedding album. What's this doing in a kitchen box?"

"I think it was on the counter when we were packing. I just shoved it in with the baking trays."

"Charming. Thankfully, it's not caked in grease."

She placed the album down on the counter and opened the cover. The first picture was of the two of them standing together at the altar with the vicar between them. She had needed to drop a stone-and-a-half to squeeze into her sleeveless wedding dress, and she had already put half of it back on.

I'll never look as good as I did right at that moment; slim and gorgeous and young. But I'm excited to grow old with Michael. This is the happiest I've ever been.

Michael moved to put his arm around her and looked at the album as she flipped through the pages, taking in each glossy print one by one. Pictures of them getting ready in the morning, the wedding itself, and the party afterwards. To finish would be the pictures of their morning breakfast with the two dozen guests who stayed over at the hotel, as well as her favourite photograph of all: a candid shot of her and Michael kissing in the corner of the hotel's lobby, stealing a moment for themselves and unaware they were being photographed.

Where is that picture? On one of the last few pages, right?

She started flipping back and forth.

"What's wrong, hon?"

"The picture," she said. "The one of us kissing. I can't find it. Where is it?"

"Last page, I think."

"Uh huh." She flipped all the way to the end, then back again. But she could not find the photo. In fact, there seemed to be a quite a few missing. The one of them standing in the hotel's gravel courtyard. Another of them sitting in the back of the Mercedes's wedding car. "Michael, some of the photographs are gone."

"How? It's a *printed* book. Maybe the pages are stuck together."

Stef rubbed at the pages with her thumbs, trying to pry them apart, but there were none stuck together. She examined the inside of the spine and saw no ragged edges suggesting ripped out pages either. "I don't understand. It's like they were never here."

Michael put a finger to his temple and grimaced. "Let's think about this, because it's not making any sense. How could the last few pages of our wedding album suddenly be missing?"

Stef peeked back inside the cardboard packing box, checking for loose pages, thinking that perhaps the binding glue had come loose. But there was nothing except a few baking trays and a cheese grater. "What did you do, Michael? You must have done something. Did the pages fall out?"

He folded his arms and frowned at her. "What? I didn't do anything, I swear."

She went back over the album and flipped through the pages again. The pictures were still missing. Their wedding. Their memories.

"W-we have them all backed up on a USB stick," Michael said, keeping his distance by the counter. "We can print another one."

For a second, she wanted to yell at him—to tell him this was the original album, and a reprint would somehow be less special—but he was right. She was overreacting. "I... I just don't get it. And it's not just the album. The last couple days have just felt... *off*. You know?"

"It's been an upheaval for sure. Even though we wanted this, it's a bit spooky being out here on our own. It'll take a little getting used to."

Stef let out a long sigh. Was that the problem? Staring out the kitchen window at the vast, unbroken darkness of the countryside evening, she wondered if she was simply feeling unsettled by the move. It was so quiet here. Silent.

But it was more than that, though. Something in her gut was shifting constantly, like her very DNA itself was yelling out a warning.

"Maybe I just need to get some sleep," she said, pinching the bridge of her nose and closing her eyes. "In fact, I think I'm going to call it a night."

She kissed Michael on the cheek and left him standing in the kitchen. It was the first time since getting married they'd gone to bed separately.

————

THE NEXT MORNING, Stef found herself unsettled still, although this time she could attribute it to a tangible cause. The shame of not having paid for her lunch yesterday gnawed at her, and she needed to go back into the village to pay off her debt to Gertie.

"You want me to come?" Michael asked her, although he did so in a tone suggesting he would rather stay home and continue unpacking.

"No, it's fine," she said. "I'll just pop in and pay for our lunch, then I'll come back home to help."

Michael smiled at her and wrinkled his nose.

Stef frowned. "What?"

"You said *home*. It was nice."

She kissed him on the cheek. "I'm sorry about last night, for storming off to bed."

"It's fine. You were stressed. If things are too much, just leave everything to me, okay? I don't mind."

She went over and kissed him. "No way could I leave it all to you, but thank you. I love you."

"Love you too. See you in a bit."

Stef left the house and took the car back into Daveton. She parked in the exact same space beside the village green. As she got out and approached Gertie's tea room, a breeze came across the grass that seemed to surround her. It left her shuddering as she pushed open the door and jangled the bell.

"Hello, deary. How are you?"

Stef smiled sheepishly. "I'm good, thanks. You probably know why I'm here."

Gertie put her hands on her hips. "A nice cup of tea, I'd imagine, what with this being a tea room. Ha!"

"I need to pay my bill from yesterday."

Gertie frowned. "Sorry, must be my old age. What bill are you talking about?"

"We forgot to pay yesterday. I'm so sorry. It was a total accident. Michael thought that—"

"I think you've got the wrong place, my deary. You were never in here yesterday. I never forget a face and yours I definitely haven't seen, pretty as it is."

A spluttering gasp exploded from Stef's mouth. Was the woman trying to save her from embarrassment?

No, she's being weird. Just like yesterday.

"Gertie? I was here yesterday with my husband. We had a baguette and a panini."

The woman looked utterly lost. Either a fine actress, or she was being truthful. "I really think you have the wrong place, my deary. I'm so sorry."

Stef put a hand over her mouth and was at a loss for words for a moment. The woman had to be having some kind of memory issues. "Gertie, are you okay? Your memory... is it?"

"Nothing wrong with my memory, miss. I've run this place for twenty years, and I can still name every customer who comes through my door. You and I have never met, I promise you."

"J-just let me pay for the food we had yesterday."

"You didn't have any food. Not here." She shook her head, growing irritable. "Look, I'm not sure what to make of this. If you want to sit and have a cuppa, you're more than welcome, but if not then you'll have to leave." She took a step forwards, hands on her hips. "You're getting me all het up."

"Um, sorry. I'll leave. I didn't mean to bother you, I just..." She stared hard at the woman, hoping for some spark of recognition, but there was nothing. "Sorry, Gertie. I'll leave you to it."

The woman squinted and tilted her head.

She's wondering how I know her name. She really doesn't have any recollection of me at all. How is that possible?

Stef left the tea room and went into the shop next door. She didn't check what it was before going in, but it turned out to be a nail salon. A heavily tanned woman with thick blue eye make-up smiled at her from behind the counter. A massive grey cat with tufty ears lay asleep on top of it. "Hello. You okay?"

"Yeah, I'm good," Steph replied. "I just... um... is the old lady next door okay?"

The woman frowned slightly, her facial muscles barely moving. "Gertie?"

"Yeah. She seems a bit confused. Does she have a problem with her memory? Alzheimers or something?"

"Gertie? She's as sharp as a nail. I grabbed a coffee from this morning and she was fine. Do I need to go check on her?"

"No, no. Sorry. It's just I was in yesterday and she has completely forgotten me. I must have a forgettable face. Ha!"

The woman grinned, but her forehead and cheeks didn't move a millimetre. "Nothing a bit of brow shaping and facial waxing can't fix. I'm free now if you want to book in?"

"What? Oh, no, not right now. I'll come in soon, though, I'm sure."

"Okay." The woman turned away, disinterested. Both of her beautician's chairs were vacant, and the place was spotless.

Stef exited the shop and got back in her car. She sat for a moment behind the wheel, unsettled by the conversation with Gertie. How could the woman have no memory of her? It was bizarre.

A minute later, the woman from the salon exited onto the street and went next door into the tea room. Another minute after that, Gertie stepped out onto the pavement and scanned the car park. When she saw Stef, she started heading in her direction. The woman from the salon was right behind her.

"Oh, fuck this," Stef said, and she took off out of the car park and sped onto the main road. "Try to be a nice person and where does it get me?"

She gripped the steering wheel tightly as she hit the first bend, her jaws clamped together. "If the old bag can't be bothered to remember who I am, then she deserves to not get paid. Sod her."

It took Stef half the journey home to calm down, her heart finally settling to normal speed only as she neared home. "Jesus, what is wrong with me? She's just a confused old lady. Let it go, Stef."

When she pulled into their weed-covered driveway, Michael came out to meet her. He appeared frantic.

———

"WHOA, WHOA, WHOA," Stef said, putting out both hands to keep Michael from crowding her. "Calm down. What's wrong?"

"Just come inside. Um, yeah, inside. That's best."

Stef followed him into the house, wondering what on earth had happened in the last hour that had got him so out of sorts. He led her directly into the kitchen and sat her down at the small wooden breakfast table. A large, dusty book sat right in the middle of it.

"I found this in the shed outside," he said. "I was putting the jet washer and the strimmer away when I noticed it on a rotting wooden shelf."

She leaned forwards and studied the book. Its cover was a faded red leather. No text or title information. "What is it?"

"A scrapbook, or a photo album." He shrugged. "A whole mess of things."

"Okay. So why has it got you so excited?"

"I'm not excited. I'm freaked out."

"Why?"

He opened the book to the first page. There was a black-and-white photograph of a five person family. Dungarees, jeans, and overalls suggested they were farmers. Underneath the picture were the names of the people along with a date.

March 1914. Mr and Mrs.... and their children...

Stef grunted.

"Read the names," Michael told her.

"I am."

March 1914. Mr and Mrs... and their children...

"What are their names, Stef?"

"It says right here. Mr and Mrs..."

Michael nodded, his eyes wide and manic. "You can't say them, can you? Neither can I."

She looked away from the album, fearing she was going mad. "It's like I can see the names, but as soon as I read them they slip from my mind. I can't grasp them long enough to keep them in my head."

Michael nodded, his brow creased, his expression earnest. "Now look at their faces."

Stef glanced back at the photograph and studied the collected faces. She saw noses, eyes, and other features, but she could put none of them together. It was as though her brain were blocking her from seeing a complete image.

Michael reached out and turned the pages, revealing more old photographs. She could make out none of the faces, none of the names. They were all... *vague*, like trying to remember a dream. Interspersed with the blurry photographs were erratic scrawlings and scraps of text. One message in particular caught Stef's eye and worried her. In a jagged script, made with a bright red pen, it read simply: **We're gone.**

Michael turned to the final page, to a single remaining photograph—glossy, bright, and modern, and the only one she could make out fully. She recognised the two smiling faces immediately as she read out the names printed beneath. "April 2024. Mr and Mrs Bloom."

"We're in the album," Michael said. "The album I found buried in the shed that's probably been here for years."

Stef slammed the album closed and glared at him. "What the fuck is this, Michael? Are you pranking me?"

"No, of course not. I don't know what this is, but it doesn't stop here. I tried to log in to my work account earlier to check my emails, but no matter what I tried, I couldn't get access. Then I checked the company's website where it lists all the personnel."

Stef nodded. She knew the page he was talking about. Michael had been so proud when his picture and bio had appeared on Thomas Webb Structural Design Solutions' official website.

But he showed her the page now and his profile was missing. No mention of him at all. No picture of him in his dark blue suit, smiling.

"I called into work to ask why my details were gone," he said. "They told me they'd never heard of me. Joan at reception, who I bloody well saw last week, acted like I was a crazy person. She put the phone down on me."

Stef's vision began to tilt back and forth. She feared she might fall off her chair, so she grabbed ahold of the table. Her gorge rose as she spoke. "When I went back to pay Gertie for our lunch yesterday. She had no idea who I was."

Michael tapped a finger against the album's leather jacket. "Something is very wrong, babe. I think it has something to do with this house. Unknown Cottage."

Stef leapt up from her seat and whimpered. Her breath came in shallow gusts. "I-I need to call my mom. I need to..." She reached into her jeans and pulled out her phone. She brought up her recent calls and pressed on the word **MOM**. The call went through immediately.

"Hello? Who's this?"

"Mom! Mom, it's Stef. I really need to see y—"

"Who?"

"Stephanie. Your fucking daughter!"

Her mother huffed irritably. "I don't have a daughter, so whoever this is, you have the wrong number. Go swear at someone else."

"Mom!"

The line went dead.

Stef dropped her phone and it bounced on the old kitchen tiles. Slowly, she turned to look at Michael. "She... she doesn't know who I am. She genuinely didn't have a clue. My own mother."

"We need to get the hell out of here," Michael said, and he got up to join her.

The two of them raced out of the kitchen and through the hall. Michael yanked open the front door.

Both of them froze, staring outside in horror.

The world was gone. Unknown Cottage floated in a sea of inky darkness, all other existence fading to nothingness a mere twenty feet down the driveway.

"It's all gone," Stef muttered, fearing she might pass out as she slowly realised the truth.

"No," Michael said. "It's us. We've vanished. We no longer exist. We're gone."

"Unknown," Stef said. "Forgotten."

Michael turned to her and frowned. For a moment he said nothing, but then he turned angry and demanded, "Who are you? What the hell are you doing here?"

Stef let out a scream, in a voice she no longer recognised.

CAPTAIN TRIPPS

Malcolm got up off the sofa when he heard the familiar hiss of the autoclave activating. Two minutes later, Dr Reid emerged from the small sliding access door at the end of the short corridor, steam rising from his space suit and making him look more like a spirit than a scientist. From inside his Perspex bubble helmet, he offered his usual friendly smile. "Malcolm, how are you doing this morning?"

Malcolm twisted at the hips and motioned to his living space. Forty square metres, with a single bedroom and one bathroom. "My morning has been much like every other morning, Doctor. How about yours?"

"I've been working on a cure, same as always. We're close, Malcolm, I promise you. Last night, we had a breakthrough."

Malcolm rolled his eyes. "I remember you saying that when I was eight. And when I was twelve. Also last year around this time."

"Sometimes it takes several breakthroughs." Reid pulled up a chair on the other side of the inch-thick glass that surrounded Malcolm's habitat. It was always awkward for him to sit down in his bulky white biohazard suit—even more so when he came inside the habitat and had to hook himself up to an air hose to pressurise his suit. It would inflate to twice the size, forcing him to plod inside like a walrus. Afterwards, he would always have to go take a chemical shower.

All because of me.

Reid settled in the chair, placing one turquoise gloved hand on top of the other. When he looked at Malcolm, he seemed troubled–perhaps even sad. "It's your birthday in a few months," he said, shaking his head inside his bubble, which remained fixed in place. "Sixteen-years-old. I can't believe you're suddenly a man."

Malcolm pulled up a chair of his own, a light wooden one with spokes on the back. He thought of it as his visitor's chair, because he always used it to chat with Reid and other members of staff at the Thorny Brook Institute for Deadly Materials.

The TBIDM was a massive facility built on the western coast of Portugal, but Malcolm had never seen any of it besides what was inside his habitat. He supposed the fact he'd grown up there made him Portuguese, but Reid was English–and the closest thing he had to family.

"You think I'm a man?" Malcolm smirked. "Does that mean it's time for me to go out and get a job? Hey, I was thinking, for my birth-day, maybe we can go visit *Chuckie Cheese*? I hear the pizza's really good."

Reid pulled a face. The last year or so had aged him, his short brown hair now suddenly flecked with grey. It was as if his body had been encoded with a start date for getting old– and he had passed it. "They only have those in America, Malcolm. Maybe try *Pizza Hut* if you're ever after a slice."

Malcolm felt a twinge of embarrassment. He always did whenever he got things wrong. "Well, I wouldn't know where they have *Chuckie Cheese* because I've never been outside this room, have I? I'd settle for McDonalds. They have those everywhere, right?"

"They really do," said Reid with a smile. "Largest real estate company in the world."

"I thought they made fast food."

"A mere side gig." He let out a sigh which crackled through his suit's intercom. "I know it's frustrating, Malcolm, being stuck in quarantine–"

"Prison."

"You're not a prisoner, Malcolm. You're a patient with a very dangerous virus living inside your bone marrow. No one wants to see you live a normal life more than I do, but–"

"I know, I know." He grunted. "I'm human asbestos."

Reid chuckled, and then he broke into full on laughter. A moment later, Malcolm started to laugh as well. That was how things usually went with the two of them. Reid might have been forty-years older than Malcolm, but sometimes he acted like a big kid.

Guy's a goofball.

Reid visited almost daily, usually just to chitchat, but occasionally he would go full spaceman and come inside Malcolm's habitat to take blood or urine. Mostly, though, they just hung out. The science team already had more than enough of his blood and tissue to work on a cure, so there was little need to prod him anymore. It happened perhaps once per year at most.

Reid got control of himself and cleared his throat. "We really are getting close to a cure, Malcolm. Thirty world-class scientists are working around the clock to find it."

"Wish I could take your word for it."

"What do you mean? Malcolm?"

He shifted in his seat and averted his eyes. Reid was his best friend–the only person he ever spoke to about the things on his mind–so it was unusual to be grumpy with him. But lately the walls of his habitat seemed to be closing in. Every year that passed filled him with an increasing certainty that he would never get out of there. Never get to stare up at a blue sky or walk on green grass. At least not in the flesh. He saw those things often on television, which only depressed him further. "I looked online to see if anyone knows about me being here," he admitted. "There's absolutely nothing. I don't exist as far as anyone else in the world is concerned."

"You don't." Reid nodded as if it were no secret. "You were raised here and have never left."

"But you said you're the good guys, and that the entire world is working on trying to find a cure for me."

Reid nodded again, his suit rustling. "The scientific community,

Malcolm. This lab is funded by multiple nations, but everything we do is protected by the highest levels of secrecy. You're not the only Jack-in-the-box we have here. If people knew the dangers we—"

"Super ebola, right? I read about it."

"Trust me, that's one of the nicer things we have here." He let out a sigh, causing more crackles through his intercom. "We've been through this. I thought you understood. We *are* the good guys, Malcolm. A lot of people dedicate their lives here to undoing the sins of others. Every time some madman engineers a virus, it's up to us to engineer a way to kill or contain it. Every time there's a malfunction in nature, we fix it."

"Is that what I am? A malfunction?"

Reid's expression fell to misery, an emotion he rarely displayed. In fact, the only time Malcolm had ever seen the doctor cry was when his wife, Samantha, had died three years ago from some kind of cancer. "What you are is a desperately unfortunate young man who did nothing to deserve the fate he's been given. I promise you, Malcolm, I will see you leave this place one day. I will see you live a normal life."

"You can't promise that. What if there *is* no cure?"

Reid's expression lifted. "Polio, Small Pox, HIV—mankind has prevailed against them all. Every living thing is built a certain way, with a certain set of instructions. The key is simply figuring those instructions out. Then it's just a matter of time and money—and both we have in abundance."

They sat in silence for a while. Usually they chitchatted and joked until it was time for Reid to leave, but Malcolm didn't feel like it today. He felt low. Searching himself up on the internet, and finding out he didn't exist, had affected him in ways he'd not expected.

Reid broke the silence. "What would you like for dinner tonight? Any special requests?"

Malcolm shrugged. "I fancy pasta. Can you get the kitchen to make up that king prawn *Arriabata* I like?"

"I'll see to it personally." He stood up, nylon fibres swishing between his thighs. "I'm afraid I have to get back to work. Longer I spend lollygagging with you, the longer it will take to cure you." He turned to leave, to head back inside the autoclave that would spray him with chemicals and make sure none of Malcolm got out of the level 5 lab with him, but halfway down the corridor he turned back. "Oh, before I go, what are we watching tonight?"

"Huh? Oh, yeah, I wanted to watch *IT: Chapter Two*. You game?"

"Pennywise the Dancing Clown? Sign me up. We can discuss it in the morning."

Malcolm smiled. "If you manage to make it through the whole thing."

"I'll do my best. Have a good night, Malcolm."

Yeah, I'll have myself a little party, here on my own.

Malcolm got off his chair and headed into the middle of his living space. He had a seventy-five-inch television with every games console you could name, as well as an expensive laptop he could use to surf the internet—although he had no email address or social media accounts. In fact, there was a member of staff employed purely to monitor what he was doing online, and to make sure he didn't communicate with the outside world. A security risk, he was told.

Last year, they'd given him an Italian leather sofa, which cruelly featured three seats he would never fill. He had everything—and yet he had nothing.

He turned on some music via his laptop and sent it to the speakers in the ceiling. He didn't know what counted as cool or current, so most of what he listened to was random. He did have a fondness for a band named *Disturbed* though, especially when he was feeling down.

Get down with the sickness, you fucker.

He went into his bathroom and stripped down. Unlike Reid, and most of the staff, his skin was dark. He was black, which was probably supposed to mean something to him, but the only thing it made him feel was different. A few of the doctors and nurses shared his skin colour, but he didn't see them often. When he once asked Reid, as a young boy, why they looked different, the doctor had simply explained that it was because a hundred-thousand years ago, some black people had gone to live in colder parts of the world where a lower amount of sun had altered their skin. That was all, a simple adaptation, which had no bearing on anything else. From what Malcolm saw on TV and online, it seemed more complicated than that. White people kind of sucked.

But not Reid. He's the nicest person I know.

Malcolm switched on the electric shower and stepped beneath the stream. He liked the water hot, and within seconds he was moaning with pleasure. Later, he would be eating his favourite meal and watching a kickass horror film. Life could be worse, and from what he saw online, for most people it was. He was safe, fed, and entertained.

But I'm still a prisoner.

And I want to get out of here.

———

ONE OF THE nurses came by at ten-thirty with a cardboard box full of books. Her name was *Ivanka*, and she was from a country called *Slovakia*. She was one of Malcolm's favourites, and while he could only see her face with her biohazard suit on, her light green eyes were beautiful and hard not to stare at.

"Good evening, Malcolm," she said with an accent. "We had a new shipment of books come in. Dr Reid wanted me to hand them to you tonight. He knows you like to read to get to sleep."

It was true. Getting to sleep at night was tough. While he tried to exercise in his cell, he was usually still full of energy by the time bedtime rolled around. Besides mealtimes, his life lacked any kind of schedule.

"Thanks, Ivanka. Anything good?"

"Lots of scary books, as usual." She winked at him through her bubble. "You have a very morbid imagination."

"I'm a human plague, what do you expect?"

She stepped up to the glass and looked at him. "It must be so difficult for you, Malcolm. You must dream of getting out of here."

"Well, yeah, of course I do." He was surprised because the staff usually avoided talking to him about leaving his habitat. It wasn't up for discussion. Only Reid spoke to him about things like one day being free. "I want to get out of here," he said, "so I can take you out to dinner."

Shit, did I just say that?

Whoa!

Ivanka's wonderful eyes widened, and she gave him the most amazing smile. "You're too young for me, Malcolm. Perhaps in a few years. Deal?"

"Deal?"

"Stand back and I'll give you these." She readjusted her grip on the cardboard box. It was obviously heavy, so she probably wanted to put it down.

Malcolm stood back from the glass while she moved over to an airlock in the corner of the glass habitat. She put down the box, slid open a large metal drawer, and then lifted the box back up to place it inside. As soon as she closed the drawer, there was a violent hiss as a vacuum sucked every molecule of air out of the container. A minute later, a green light illuminated on Malcolm's side, letting him know it was safe to open the drawer. The main reason for the protocol was to protect him from bugs and bacteria. His cell was a closed environment, and while he was often given supplements and healthy gut bacteria to help maintain his immune system, the truth was he was vulnerable to even the mildest of viruses.

"Enjoy your night," Ivanka said with a wink. "Don't stay up too late."

"I won't." He watched her swish away in her white nylon suit and imagined what her body might look like inside. Sweaty, smooth, hot to the touch.

He groaned in frustration as she entered the autoclave and disappeared. To keep himself from getting further het up, he went over and retrieved his box of books. Book day was the best day. Inside, he found a couple of massive Stephen King novels, along with lots of other smaller paperbacks from various writers. Some he knew—like Jack Ketchum—others he was yet to discover. By the end of the month, he would've read them all. He could manage a book a day when Netflix was light on new releases.

He removed the leftover pasta from the coffee table and stacking the books, one by one. He flipped the covers as he placed them, giving the pages a deep sniff—one of his favourite smells. All of the books were new. Everything they ever gave him was new. Reid must've been right when he'd spoken about an unlimited budget. He often referred to the institute as mankind's most vital investment.

An investment in what, though?

He put aside the Stephen King novels. He'd just read *Revival* and was looking for a change, so his attention turned next to a book by an author named Matt Shaw. When he went to flip the cover open, he found it didn't match the dust jacket. The book contained within was actually by an author named *Cpt. Donna Tripps*. The book was titled: *The Racial Exchange*. It didn't seem like fiction—let alone horror—and when he read the summary on the back, it was some kind of academic text about changing population levels. Unlike the other books, this one seemed old—*used*.

"Boring!" He tossed the book onto the rug where it landed with its cover open. The first page—meant to be blank—seemed to have something pencilled on it.

Malcolm frowned. For a moment he sat there on his knees next to the coffee table and wondered why he'd been sent a book he had no interest in reading. Reid sometimes picked books out for him, but the truth was he didn't know who did the ordering most of the time. Probably just some low-level admin worker.

He shuffled on his knees and picked the book back up, examining what was written inside. It was etched in dark graphite, smudged in several places. It read:

> *Don't believe their lies.*
> *You're not sick.*
> *Captain Tripps would be proud. Your only friend.*

Malcolm dropped the book, his mind full of sparks.

———

MORNING ARRIVED AFTER A SLEEPLESS NIGHT, but it didn't matter. It wasn't like he had anywhere to be or anything to do. When your days consisted of playing video games, reading, and surfng the web, there was very little problem with being exhausted.

But the constant yawning was annoying.

Reid arrived early, along with breakfast. It was something he did once or twice a week. Most of the scientists lived at the institute so they could turn up at all hours.

"Morning, Malcolm. I must say, *IT: Chapter Two* wasn't a patch on the first, but I did enjoy that opening scene. And that madness at the Chinese Restaurant. Ha, such fun!"

"Oh." Malcolm shook his head in shock. "I can't believe I forgot. I never watched it."

Reid frowned. "Really? I don't think you've ever missed one of our movie nights before. Oh well, I shall seal my lips. No spoilers here. Is everything okay? You look tired."

"Didn't sleep well." He considered telling Reid about the message in the book. It made no sense to him, and when things didn't make sense, it was usually Reid he turned to.

But it said not to believe their lies. Does that include Reid? Is he lying to me?

"Well, maybe you should take a nap after breakfast." He placed a plastic tray into the air-lock drawer and sent it through. Malcolm pulled out the tray and said *thank you*. A plate of scrambled eggs, beans, and sausages—something he liked very much, but his appetite this morning was strangely absent. He placed the food down on the table and went over to his chair in front of the glass wall.

"What would happen if this glass wasn't between us, Doctor? And if you weren't wearing that suit?"

"You know what would happen, Malcolm." He sat down the chair on the other side, one turquoise gloved hands one on top of the other as usual.

"I know I would make you sick, but what exactly would happen. I don't think you've ever told me. It's something I give off, right?"

Reid sighed, fogging up his bubble. Whenever he spoke, it was picked up by a small mic inside his helmet and emitted from a tiny speaker on his suit's chest plate—which was then picked up by a ceiling-mounted microphone outside the habitat and piped through the speakers inside. Even sound couldn't make direct contact with Malcolm. "Why do you want to talk about this?"

He shrugged. "I'm becoming a man, aren't I? Isn't it important for me to understand who I am?"

"This virus isn't who you are."

"Are you serious? This virus is the *biggest* part of who I am. My entire life is shaped by it. I want to know what would happen if I ever got out of here."

Reid leant forwards as much as his cumbersome suit would allow. "Are you planning to escape, Malcolm?"

He shook his head. But the thought had occurred to him. "No. I just want to know what would happen. I want to know the reason I've never been hugged. Never been kissed. Never been touched by another human being."

"Because it would be a death sentence for whomever did so."

"Why?"

"Because you emit a pheromone that acts as a necrotoxin." The doctor paused, as if his statement was supposed to shock Malcolm. When he saw that it did not, he continued. "Within the first fews seconds of exposure, anyone near you would experience a runny nose, itchy eyes, and other allergy-like symptoms. Then, within a minute or so, the thin membranes inside their sinuses would start to break down, leading to severe nose bleeds and eventually coughing up blood. The last stage happens two or three minutes later."

Malcolm took a deep breath, wondering if he really wanted to know. "What is the last stage?"

"The breakdown of lung tissue. It happens rapidly. The victim would grow short of breath, and then be completely without. Blood would fill their throat, and they would either suffocate, or choke to death on their own decaying tissues. A painful and terrifying death."

"How do...?" He felt a little woozy, and had to take a moment. "How do you know this? I've never been out of this room."

"Yes, you have, Malcolm. The doctors and nurses who delivered you were exposed to the toxin, as was your mother. They all died in the delivery room as soon as you were born, with you still attached to your umbilical cord. Several others responded, but they quickly died too.

Eventually, the hospital was sealed off and a hazmat team took you into custody. You've been here ever since."

Malcolm gasped, and rocked back in his chair so hard that he almost toppled over. There were many questions he'd never dared to ask—and Reid usually avoided discussion of how Malcolm had come into the world—but today was different. Today, he wanted the truth. "I killed my own mother?"

Reid sighed, the sound crackling through his speaker. "As we discussed yesterday, you're a man now. Also, I have seen your frustration growing lately, and I understand it. Perhaps the truth will remind you that no one is keeping you here to be cruel. There's simply no other choice."

"You could just kill me? Why keep me around if I'm so dangerous?"

"You're an innocent boy, Malcolm. At first, you were kept safe because various entities wanted to study your makeup—and no doubt try to formulate a bioweapon—but thankfully sanity prevailed and the UN put forth a resolution that all efforts must be put towards finding a cure, and that no one could seek to weaponise whatever is inside of you."

"Does anybody else have what I have?"

"No. You are unique. As are we all in our own ways."

Malcolm huffed. "Not as unique as me."

"Indeed. I'm sorry. You'll never know how much."

Don't believe their lies.

Captain Tripps would be proud.

"What was my mother like? Did you know her well?"

Reid smiled inside his bubble, but the expression didn't reach his eyes. "You already know we worked together for several years. She was brilliant. A visionary."

"You said she was scientist, like you?"

"She was. The two of us worked together at Porton Down in the UK. I was a virologist. She was... a genius. There were so many letters after her name it would take ten minutes to name them all."

"So she was smart?"

"As smart as a human being can be. It was an honour to work with her."

Malcolm smiled. He'd seen pictures of his mother, even had a few in his bedside cabinet, but he asked about her rarely. It hurt. Whenever he thought about being in this place for his entire life, it took on a kind of normalcy, but when he considered that he had once had a mother—even if only for a minute—then it felt like he'd been ripped away from an ordinary life—that he hadn't always been destined for this room. "There's something else, isn't there? I can see it in your eyes."

Reid nodded. "Your mother was as troubled as she was gifted. She had a tendency to obsess. Some days, if she watched the news, she would spend the rest of the day ruminating on the world's problems. She wanted to fix everything. But she had a gap in her mind."

"What do you mean, a gap?"

"Your mother would go to any lengths in pursuit of her work. No sacrifice was too great if humanity improved and moved forwards as a species." He let out another crackling sigh. "If it had been up to your mother, we would have performed all our experiments on human beings instead of rats. She used to pester the UN for more funds, even at the expense of other humanitarian projects like famine relief. As much as I respected he, and even cared for her, she was an egotist of the highest order. Worse even."

Malcolm laced his fingers together and felt a chill. "Worse?"

Reid shrugged, his suit rustling. "It's possible she was sociopathic—a narcissist, at the very least. Brilliance often comes with trade-offs. In most cases, they were worth it with your mother because of how brilliant she was. Do I ever tell you she engineered a strain of wheat that grows twice as quickly as what we had before, and is ten times hardier? You see, that's how your mother's mind worked. She took money away from famine relief, so that she could work towards finding a permanent solution. Today, Africa is well fed, and many would put that down to her, despite the fact that some people starved to death while she worked on a solution. Her cruelty always had a purpose. She only ever saw solutions. People to her were just data."

"It doesn't sound like you actually did like her, Doctor."

"I did, son. I liked her a great deal. But she scared me, too, I won't lie. Some people aren't like the rest of us. They exist on a level we can't understand. I believe they are the people who move humanity forward, but change never comes without casualties. Anyway, let us talk about things more cheerful."

"You don't like me knowing the truth?"

Reid frowned, clearly confused. "I would never lie to you, Malcolm, but that doesn't mean I enjoy being the bearer of the bleak and moribund. It brings me no joy to see you hurt." He lowered his gaze inside his bubble. "I see her in you sometimes. It even feels like..."

Malcolm shook his head. "Like what?"

"Like I'm your father. At least as close to one as you've ever had. You and I have had fifteen years together."

Malcolm looked away. He felt that, too, but the two of them had never spoken in such terms. He'd known Dr Reid since birth and had received nothing but friendship and kindness. Maybe even love.

But he's still my jailor. Is being nice simply part of his job? An act?

Don't believe their lies.

You're not sick.

"I'm tired, Doctor. I think I'm going to eat my breakfast and go back to bed for a bit. Is that okay?"

"Of course it is. You're free to do as you like."

Malcolm raised an eyebrow as he stood up. "Not that free, but thank you."

Reid stood up as well, but with a frown. "Thank you, for what?"

"For caring about me. I care about you too. You're the only person that matters to me."

Reid smiled, but as Malcolm turned his back, he couldn't do the same.

I need to get out of here. I can't last another sixteen years waiting for a cure that might never come.

That I might not even need.

Malcolm spent the day reading *The Racial Exchange* by Cpt. Tripps, the mysterious author who would apparently be proud of him.

Why? Who am I to them?

The book was a difficult read, full of statistics and forecasts about the future of humanity. The author wrote about an eventual tipping point, where racial tensions would escalate into a war of supremacy. Billions would die and worldwide infrastructure would be in ruins.

Whites would no longer rule the world or control its resources. Their numbers were already dwindling, while those in Africa and the Middle East were exploding. A new world order would emerge—on the back of a mass genocide. But it was all contingent upon mankind refusing to resort to nuclear exchange.

Malcolm tossed the book down at about the halfway point. He couldn't understand why people would fight each other because of the colour of their skin. He understood there were lots of countries, and that they all wanted to be the best, but didn't they also work together? The United States, the EU, and NATO—countries cooperate with each other to make the world better for all. Why would they go to war? Why would white people fight black people and vice versa?

People like me fighting people like Reid?

It didn't make a lot of sense to Malcolm, nor did it interest him that much. What did interest him was the author. Who was Cpt. Tripps?

One way to find out.

He brought up the *Eversearch* browser on his laptop and started typing. Then he hit enter.

A photograph of his mother came up. He knew her only as Donna, a woman who existed in a few pictures on his side table and a smattering of Reid's stories. But now he learned that she was actually British Army Major Donna Tripps MRes, MSc, PhD and MBE—although she must only have only been a captain when she had written the Racial Exchange. She had died fifteen years ago in childbirth when she had been the current Head of Research at the UK's Porton Down Science Park.

Everything Reid told me is true.

Except where it said that her only child had been stillborn. It didn't say anything about Malcolm, or a deadly necrotoxin.

But why would it? I've been kept secret my whole life.

He kept reading, bringing up further articles. One was about his mother's final projects before she'd died. It appeared she was trying to eradicate malaria in Africa. After her death, the project was taken over by Deputy Head of Research, Dr Harlan Reid, who eventually shut the project down—some say at the behest of several of the larger pharmaceutical companies. Malaria remained rife in Africa.

Reid took over my mother's role. He benefited from her death.

And then he shut her project down. She was trying to help people. Black people.

Did she put the cure inside me? Is that why I'm here? So that I can't spread an end to malaria and affect the rich white man's profits?

Malcolm sat in silence for a long while. The habitat lights mimicked sunset. By the time he got off the sofa, it was likely early evening.

His mind had been swirling around and around, like a spider trapped in a drain. His theory about him possibly having a cure to malaria inside of him was based on very little, and he was also very resistant to thinking Reid might be an immoral opportunist.

But someone wrote that message in the book. They wanted to warn me.

Your only friend.

"I have to find out the truth," he said in a whisper, under no illusion that people were listening in and watching him in his habitat. Even now, they were probably figuring out what to do about his recent search history. If not for the book he'd been given, he never would have known what to look for. Never would have learned who his mother truly was. A hero.

His name was Malcolm Tripps, and his mother had been a great woman.

For the first time in his life, he decided to break out of his cell. The plan was already in his mind, formulated over many years of boredom.

He walked into the middle of the room and fell straight through the coffee table.

———

THE RESPONSE CAME WITHIN MINUTES.

Malcolm lay face down amongst shards of wood, the coffee table in pieces underneath him. He had his eyes closed and was trying to be as still as possible, but a bead of blood running ran down the side of his head and made him desperate to wipe it away and stop the tickle.

Just got to keep still a few minutes more.

His living space could be accessed through an air lock at the front of the room, in the same section as the vacuum drawer. It was a circular portal that connected to a pressurised, nylon tunnel. He could hear them unfolding the tunnel now and hooking it up to machinery outside on the wall. Once connected, air would blow into the living space, ensuring nothing came out. Fully-suited individuals could then come inside.

He waited.

Minutes went by.

Voices called out to him, trying to get him to respond.

"Are you okay? Malcolm, can you hear me?"

I hear you all right. I hear your lies.

He heard the hissing of the pressured tunnel, too, and a moment later he heard the *swish-swish* of someone stepping inside. He had expected Reid to come, but none of the voices belonged to him. Probably better that way. If his friend were here, it would be harder to do what he had planned.

"Malcolm? It's Doctor Chowdry. We've only met a few times, but I'm here to help you. Can you hear me? Are you awake?"

He let out a pretend moan and half-opened an eye. "H-help me. I need help."

Chowdry waddled over in her air-filled suit. It looked like you could tie a string to her leg and fly her like a balloon, but the image wasn't as funny as it might have been. "What happened, Malcolm?"

"Can't see. All black."

"Okay, Malcolm. I'm going to roll you over."

As soon as the glove touched him, he leapt up with a shard of the coffee table's wooden leg in his hand. He lunged at Dr Chowdry, causing her to scream inside her bubble helmet and retreat backwards. "Malcolm, what are you doing?"

"Freeze!" He positioned himself between her and the portal. Every time she tried to move, he swiped the shard of wood at her. "I said stop. One nick in your suit and you're dead, right? Or is that just a lie?"

"A lie? What are you talking about? Malcolm, are you okay? This is very serious."

"You're damn right it is." He turned his head and saw two members of the science team working to unfasten the portal tunnel. If they managed to reseal the habitat, he would be trapped inside. There was a window of opportunity, but he had to take it.

Dr Chowdry yelled at him to stop, but he turned and sprinted for the hole in the glass. He leaped through the giant metal O ring and landed inside the pressurised tunnel. It was hard to breathe as the wind rushed at his face, but the tunnel was short. He quickly made it out the other end.

Two men in unpressurised biohazard suits waited outside. One tried to grab Malcolm, but he slashed at one of the man's gloved hand with the shard and caused him to curse into his mic. The other man snatched at him as well, but missed.

Malcolm sprinted right by them, much faster due to not being encumbered by a heavy nylon suit. He raced right for the autoclave, his heart beating out of his chest, his chest filled with exhilaration.

I'm out. I'm outside of my habitat.

I'm not an animal.

He reached the autoclave, having no idea how to work it but hoping it wouldn't be too complicated. There was a big green button on the wall that Malcolm had seen people punch, so that's what he did too. Then he grabbed the silver handle on the small sliding door and cried out with joy when it moved aside easily.

But when he tried to open the next door, it was stuck.

I have to close the previous one first.

He turned back and saw the two suited men behind where he'd left them. Both were still standing. Neither were clutching their throats and dying.

Lies.

He slid the first door shut, and there was an electronic chirp. Immediately, the ceiling began to hiss as jets of hot steam sprayed down on him. The pain was immense, forcing him to cover up and wail. Thankfully, it was over in just a few seconds. His skin sore to the touch, but he didn't think there was any serious damage.

He grabbed the handle of the next door and yanked it open.

The entire world opened up.

It was pathetic, really, but it was new and mind blowing.

Malcolm found himself in a room not much bigger than his habitat, yet it felt vast and alien. It was filled with shelves of chemicals and supplies, and there was an open shower in the corner. Along the longest wall was a row of biohazard suits. Caution signs covered the wall along with safety instructions and protocols.

All because of me.

Am I really dangerous? Would they go to all this trouble to fake it?

Don't believe their lies.

There was a door at the far end of the room. He threw down his wooden shard and raced over to it. There was a keypad on the wall, which caused him to deflate, but when he tried the door, it opened. When Malcolm had collapsed, the panic must have made Dr Chowdry forget to rearm the lock.

This is meant to happen. I'm supposed to leave here.

My mother would be proud.

He shoved open the door and stepped out into a white-tiled hallway.

Doctor Reid skidded to a halt in front of him. "M-Malcolm? What are you...? I heard you had fallen ill?"

Malcolm took a step forwards, and when Reid didn't flinch, he became even more sure that he was right about not being sick. This man was not wearing a suit. In fact, it was the first time Malcolm had seen him in normal clothes. Shirt, trousers, and lab coat.

"It's all lies, isn't it? I'm not sick. I'm here because my mother was trying to make the world a better place. You took her job and cancelled her work. I saw it all online. Captain Tripps was my mother."

Reid gasped. "How did you find out? No one ever told you your mother's last name."

"I have a friend apparently. I know who my mother was. She was a hero."

"Oh, Malcolm. I wish that were true."

Malcolm felt his fists clench. He'd never known his mother, and he felt completely felt robbed of it now. "She was trying to cure malaria."

"No, she wasn't. Malcolm, that's what she was supposed to be working on, but when I took over her work, I found out what she was really doing–what she did to *you*. That's how I came to be in charge of your care. I have your mother's research. I understand it better than anyone."

"I don't want to hear any more lies."

"Donna engineered a virus, Malcolm–something she knew she could never sneak out of a maximum security lab. Not unless she was able to hide it."

Malcolm's stomach sloshed uneasily, empty from missing breakfast and lunch. "She put a cure for malaria inside me, so that I would spread it to the world for free. She didn't want the medicine companies to take it and force people to pay."

"She put a doomsday device inside of you, son. A virus designed to kill every Caucasian on earth."

"Caucasian? You mean white people?"

Reid nodded. He rubbed at his eyes, a tear spilling down his cheek. "She was probably the smartest, most accomplished woman of colour there's ever been, but her intelligence made her paranoid–or maybe not, I don't know. Maybe what she predicted is destined to be true."

"The genocide? White people and black people going to war?"

"It's a little more nuanced than that, Malcolm, but in a nutshell, *yes*. Your mother was convinced a global race war was inevitable and that the world would end in nuclear annihilation. She wanted to stop it. She wanted to get it over with quickly and painlessly by creating something that would wipe out every last white person on earth, and thus avoid the need for any war. As smart as she was, your mother was terribly naive. Mankind will always be at war. Race is just one excuses of many. It's the core of us that is diseased, not the surface."

Malcolm took several steps forwards. Still Reid did not flinch. He showed no signs of fear at all.

If I'm so deadly, why isn't he afraid?

"Are you..." Malcolm shook his head. "Are you my father?"

Reid stepped forwards and wrapped his arms around Malcolm in a tight, all-embracing hug. "I'm not your father, but I would be proud to be. You are strong, intelligent, and kind, which is why you need to go back inside your habitat."

"Why? I'm sick. It's all lies."

Reid eased him away, causing Malcolm to gasp. His nose was gushing with blood. His eyes were streaming with tears. "I love you, son," he said in a wheezing voice. "I've never told you a single lie since the day you came here. Your mother was an amazing scientist, but a very flawed human being. You weren't her child—you were a delivery mechanism for a virus designed to wipe out billions of lives. But I love you, Malcolm, and many people here care about you too. Trust them, okay? Let them find a cure for you. One day they'll succeed. I promise. I know it."

Reid fell, causing Malcolm to lunge and catch him. The doctor's body was rattling, and his neck was starting to bulge. Blood seeped from his lips, and a terrible whistling emanated in his chest.

"No! No, Dr Reid, what have I done?"

"Y-you made a mistake. It's okay. You can fix it. Go home."

Malcolm nodded, tears streaming from his own eyes. Reid was turning blue in the spaces where blood didn't cover his face. He was suffocating. Dying.

Because of me.

Malcolm lowered Reid to the ground and waited for him to die.

Alarms sounded. Lights flashed red.

"What have I done?"

He turned and ran, not for freedom, but for captivity. He raced back inside the staging area and hurried through the autoclave, crying out in anguish when steam burnt his skin all over again—but really his cries were cries of grief. He'd just killed the closest person he'd ever had to a friend—to a father.

He was all I had.

In the corridor leading up to his habitat, Malcolm encountered Dr Chowdry and one of the two men who had tried to stop him. The other man was lying on the ground, completely still.

I cut his glove. He breathed in my toxin.

I'm a murderer.

Chowdry and the other man backed away from Malcolm, clearly terrified. As they should be. He was a weapon of mass destruction.

Without word, Malcolm stepped through the nylon tunnel and hopped back into his habitat. Then he went into his bedroom and lay down on his bed, sobbing his heart out. A few minutes later, he heard them reseal the portal. He would never try to leave again. This was where we would stay. Forever.

————

THREE MONTHS LATER...

Malcolm smiled at the people assembled beyond the glass of his habitat. They couldn't eat birthday cake inside their suits, but they had gone to the effort of bringing colourful little flags to wave at him.

"Happy birthday, Malcolm," said Dr Chowdry.

Since Reid's death, Chowdry had taken over as lead scientist working on a cure for Malcolm. They weren't friends, but she had listened to his woes and helped him through his grief during the last few months. She was a nice lady, and no one had punished him for what had happened. Everyone was just sad about it.

It turned out that the nurse Ivanka had delivered the book for a colleague named Dr Max Panesar. Panesar had worked as a junior researcher for Captain Donna Tripps at Porton Down. Dr Reid had hired him out of familiarity, not realising the man had been a secret advocate of Donna's true mission. He too wanted to see people of colour inherit the earth.

The nurse Ivanka was guilty of nothing other than trusting a colleague, but she had quit out of shame, even after being cleared and found innocent. Malcolm missed her kind eyes.

Dr Chowdry had made a few changes since taking charge of the lab. Malcolm now received many more visitors, often for little more than socialisation. While wary at first, nurses and doctors now popped by frequently for a chat. A television screen had been erected outside the habitat and connected via bluetooth to speakers inside. Movie nights were twice a week. Lots of people attended.

Malcolm no longer felt as alone as he once had, but he missed his friend dearly. Perhaps Reid hadn't made all the right decisions regarding his care, but the man had not flinched at Malcolm's presence in that hallway. Instead, he had chosen to hug Malcom in his final moments. If Malcolm never left his habitat ever again, he would die knowing what it felt like to be embraced by someone who loved him. His life would forever be a little less empty.

As people chatted outside his habitat and celebrated his sixteenth birthday, Dr Chowdry moved up to the glass and caught Malcolm's attention. "I just wanted to tell you," she said. "We're getting really close to a cure."

Malcolm smiled. "That's great news, Doctor. I'm sure I'll be out of here in no time."

"Maybe in time for your next birthday."

"Sure." He turned away, his smile fading, and went to sit down on his three-seat sofa to eat birthday cake alone.

BREATHE

Sophie's head banged like a metal cup on prison bars. Her tongue was a dead slug between cracked lips.

"Oi, I really hate last night me." She held her head and groaned before exiting her warm bed and heading out into the hallway of her flat. She must have killed an entire bottle of wine last night, and that was after two double vodkas. A celebration, but now all her positivity was gone, and she felt utterly depressed. A pustule of dread throbbed in her brain, threatening to burst, and the urge to check her social media was overwhelming. She needed to take a whizz first and swig a heckload of water. "Someone please just kill me."

After sitting on the toilet and taking a mammoth wee, she stood over the sink and gulped from the cold tap. Gradually, she felt a little better. Besides the dizziness and a little nausea, things slowly became bearable. Her sense of dread ebbed away, replaced by a numb realisation that she would just have to get through today.

Turning off the cold water tap, Sophie lifted her head and appraised herself in the oval mirror above the sink.

"Jeez Louise. I look like hell."

Her eyes were bloodshot, and her blonde hair was a seagull's nest.

Thank God she hadn't brought a man home from the club last night, because she would be mortified to face one looking like this.

She let out a breath and winced at the smell of stale alcohol. The mirror fogged up, and then began to clear. But it then misted up again as she let out a second breath.

Except she hadn't let out a second breath. The condensation seemed to form out of nothing—a ghostly mist upon the mirror that faded more slowly than her breath had.

She stared hard at herself, blinking and testing herself for delirium. It was as if her mind were a few microseconds behind reality and couldn't quite catch up. Her reflection didn't even seem right. It was *her* blonde hair and *her* blue eyes, but it was like looking at a badly drawn image of herself, the edges scrawled in chalk.

"I'm never drinking again," she said, and then went back into her bedroom to sleep for another hour.

———

A ONE HOUR lie-in turned into a four-hour coma, and when Sophie finally roused, she felt even worse than before. Her back was drenched in sweat and she felt feverish. Her skin was sore. Was she getting ill in addition to being hung over?

The promotion she'd got at work yesterday was now a past joy, dampened by present misery. Her confidence about taking on the role of Senior Sales Executive at Prime Canning Works was pushed aside by anxiety—and a dreadful certainty that it would all be too much to cope with.

"I'm gonna puke!"

Sophie leapt out of bed and only just made it to the bathroom across the hall. Her vomit hit the bowl with a high-velocity splatter that sent splashes of dirty water up into her face. She groaned in misery as her stomach spasmed, and her feet rattled against the floorboards as her entire body shuddered. Once again, she hated her last night self; that foolish, grinning imbecile who had felt so invincible. Could she not have shared a single thought for the morning after?

"Shoot me, I'm done."

But the salvation of death was out of reach. Instead, Sophie got to her feet and staggered over to the sink. Wrapping her lips around the cold tap, she gulped for several seconds before pulling away with a gasp. Sour saliva filled her mouth, and she almost puked again, but she held it back. It took several deep exhalations to send the nausea fully packing.

Once again, she stared at herself in the mirror. Once again, her breath fogged up the glass. She wiped the condensation away with the sleeve of her pyjama top and paused.

Her reflection took a breath. The mirror fogged up once more.

Sophie stepped back from the sink and gasped. "What the fuck?"

Her reflection had visibly exhaled, but Sophie had been holding her breath. In the foggy reflection, she saw the slightest of movement.

She wiped away the condensation again and continued to scrutinise herself. After a while, she had to laugh and question her sanity.

"It's just me," she said, watching as the other Sophie in the mirror matched her lip movements exactly. "I'm just hungover and dizzy."

She went back to bed and switched on the TV. She then tried to check the messages on her phone, but when the screen lit up, it showed nothing but a plain white screen.

"Fantastic," she groaned. "There goes a week's wages buying a new mobile. God, I'm never drinking again."

―――――

BY SIX O'CLOCK, Sophie had been laying in her bed for almost the entire day, watching Judge Judy back to back and fading in and out of a half-asleep daze. Several times, her body went numb, and she panicked each time, fearing she wouldn't be able to move her limbs ever again. But it seemed her brain was simply slow in sending out commands.

Her skin still felt sore. Her head still ached. And her increasing fever was like having flies buzzing inside her head. To add to her discomfort, she was also struggling to get warm, no matter how tightly she wrapped herself up in her duvet.

She glanced at her phone again, hoping the frozen, featureless screen would suddenly come back to life, but it remained broken. Her friends had probably called and texted–hopefully just to check in with her, and not because she had done something awful or embarrassing. She kept trying to remember the events of last night, but she only recalled lots of dancing, chatting, and drinking. A good night, she became more and more sure of that. Nothing bad had happened.

Everything was okay.

After spending so long in her bedroom, the air had turned stuffy, and she needed to get some air. Going out into the living room, Sophie pulled open the double-glazed doors that led to her flat's Juliet balcony. The painted steel bars were cold against her clammy forearms as she leaned out, and the evening chill sent a shiver down her spine. But she sighed with pleasure as her body cooled down and the flies inside her head buzzed a little more quietly.

Tomorrow was Sunday, so if she still felt ill she would have to brave a trip to get some cold medicine from the garage around the corner. She was almost certain now that she was coming down with something. In fact, she had a faint image in her head of Jill having the sniffles last night. Had they sat too close or shared a glass? With a shrug, she decided it didn't matter. It had been a while since she'd last been ill, so it was overdue. Although, it would look bad if she started her new promotion by calling in sick.

Darkness arrived early outside, which wasn't unusual for late October, but it seemed darker than it should be. It took her a moment to realise that none of the lampposts were lit, and only the merest flicker of light came from the terraced houses across the street. It felt like the entire world had gone to bed.

Where was all the traffic? The odd pedestrian heading to the 24-hour garage or the Winchester Inn? Had there been a power cut?

Sophie shivered again and decided she was cool enough. Closing the doors to the balcony, she went into her flat's tiny kitchen. Her stomach was finally a little less delicate, so she went over to the fridge to get herself a snack.

The small block of cheddar was wrapped in clingfilm. Unrolling the plastic at one end, she ate the block as if it were a chocolate bar. Caveman behaviour, but there was no one there to see. And she was too depressed to cook.

A minute later, Sophie was back in the bathroom, leaned over the toilet bowl and ejecting the cheese from her body.

Seriously, just kill me. Argh!

Wiping the vomit from her mouth, she choked out a sob. "Nope. Not ready for food yet."

She wanted her mum. Twenty-five years old, and she still hated being ill by herself. If her mum were there, she would rub Sophie's back and hold her hair before rushing off to make a nice, soothing cup of tea. Instead, all Sophie had for comfort was the cold, ceramic floor tiles and the sour stench of own stomach contents.

"Just breathe, Soph," she told herself, echoing what she knew her mum would be saying right now if she were there. "Breathe and let it pass. Let your body do what it has to."

She breathed for many minutes until the sickness went away. Then, for the third time that day, she hobbled over to the sink and washed the acidic foulness from her mouth. Even after swilling thoroughly, she had to spit for several minutes before the wretched taste went away. "I bet kissing me right now would be like licking a drainpipe."

With a pitiful chuckle, she lifted her head to check out the state of her face. Her reflection was looking to the left.

This time, there was no doubt what she was seeing was impossible. She was looking at the side of her own head in the mirror, staring directly into the small dark hole of her ear canal.

Before she knew it, she was screaming.

Sophie's reflection turned to face her, and let out a voiceless howl in reply. The mirror fogged up.

Sophie sprinted out into the hallway, still screaming. Making a beeline for the front door, she grabbed the handle and yanked on it with a wail. But it didn't budge.

"Damn it, damn it." She turned and frantically searched for her keys. If she'd been paralytic last night, she would have acted on autopilot, which meant...

My bag.

She raced over to the sofa where she was sure she would find her clutch bag tossed onto the cushions. Sure enough, there it was. Pink and sparkly with sequins. "I locked the door and put the keys back inside my bag. I know I did."

She fumbled inside the purse and groaned when she found only loose change, a sanitary pad, and lipstick.

Then her fingers blessedly found the keys.

She snatched at the Mickey Mouse keyring and raced back to the front door with the keys jangling. Her hands were shaking as she struggled to insert the right one into the lock, and she realised she was still screaming. Her neighbours must have thought she was being murdered.

Calm down. Just calm down.

"My reflection isn't real," she said, comforted by the sound of her own voice, despite how taut with fear it might be. This was a dream. She was hallucinating. Freaking out over nothing.

Had somebody spiked her drink last night?

God, she wanted more than ever to speak to Jill or one of her other friends from last night. What the hell had happened to make her feel so ill and so... *mental?*

Hands still shaking, she tried to force herself to calm down. She took a deep breath and held it, growing more certain by the second that she was having some kind of manic episode–because there was absolutely no way her reflection had actually been moving of its own accord.

She slid the key in, turned it, and yanked the handle.

It still wouldn't budge.

"What the hell? What the fuck? No, come on."

She twisted at the key again, but now it wouldn't budge in either direction. She couldn't even slide it back out. Beating at the door, she yelled out for help. Didn't her neighbours hear her?

Out of answers–and unable to even think straight–she stepped back into the centre of the room and put her hands on her head. She was hyperventilating and trembling like a leaf. "It has to be drugs," she said, her voice quivering. "Someone drugged me at the club. I'm having a bad reaction. I need help."

She wanted to call an ambulance, but the only way was with her mobile, which still wasn't working. She had left it in the bedroom, but hesitated at the thought of passing the bathroom again.

The mirror.

Her reflection.

I have no choice. I need to call for help.

Like a drunken gazelle, Sophie lolloped down the hallway, picking up speed as she passed the open bathroom door. With the panicked sensation of being chased, she leapt up and landed on her bed, hastily spinning around to face the doorway. Nothing came crashing through after her, of course.

She was acting insane.

Panting, she grabbed her phone from the bedside table and thumbed at the screen frantically.

It was completely dead. It wouldn't even light up anymore.

"No, please. I need help."

She dialled 999 and pressed send, hoping that just the screen was dead, but there was no dial tone.

"The battery!"

Maybe she just needed to give her phone some juice. Thankfully, she had a charger plugged in beneath the bedside table. She wasted no time and plugged it in.

"Just need to give it a minute," she said, trying to keep herself company while she waited long enough to give the battery at least a few percent of life.

After three minutes, she could wait no longer.

She dialled 999 again.

Still no dial tone.

Sophie shuffled up her bed and lay against the headboard, her stare fixated upon the doorway, as if she expected a ghoul to rush in and attack her at any moment. A sob escaped her, but she bit it back and tensed her jaw to keep from crying further. The last thing she needed was to get even more hysterical.

She rubbed at her burning red cheeks, her entire face sweating. Maybe she was having a fever dream.

"I need to calm down." She put her fingers to the edge of her eyes and pulled her lids sidewards. It distorted her vision and reset her frazzled thinking enough to calm down a tiny amount. "Okay, okay, just stay calm and deal with this, Soph. There's no doppelgänger in the mirror. It's all in my mind. Something's wrong. I just... I just have to breathe."

She sat on her bed for several minutes, feeling unwell but undeniably lucid. Nothing told her she was seeing things or having some kind of fit. Her vision didn't blur. There were no flashes of light or strange shapes. Just her, lying in bed and feeling worse for wear.

"Just me. Just plain old boyfriendless Sophie."

Her mind oscillated back and forth between the surreal and the mundane until she actually started to get bored—or perhaps merely frustrated. Staying in her bed all night and freaking out wasn't an option. The situation needed dealing with. If this was all down to a fever or drugs in her system, she needed to do something about it. She needed to cool herself down and try to restore her lucidity.

A cold shower.

Sophie slid her feet off the bed and stood up. If she was burning up, then she needed to get in cold water, but that meant going back into the bathroom. Not an enticing prospect.

"If this were a horror movie," she said, "then this would be the bit where the audience screams at me to not be an idiot. Oh God." She shook herself. "Right, let's do this."

She exited the bedroom and went back into the bathroom. There, she had to force herself to look into the mirror. It sent bile up into her throat, and every second that passed caused her to tense up further as she waited for her reflection to do something it wasn't supposed to.

But her other self behaved, doing only as she did. She took a full five minutes to make sure, but then she chided herself with a chuckle and unclothed.

She stepped into the shower.

The cold water hitting her sensitive skin made her hiss with discomfort, but she stood her ground, enduring the frigid temperature until she was shivering with a chill. If she had a fever, it had to come down. In fact, she was already starting to feel less dazed. Her head felt clearer.

The cold shower did its job.

But, despite feeling better, Sophie was still wary as she stepped out of the glass cubicle and onto the fluffy pink bathroom mat. She glanced over at the mirror as she grabbed a towel, then glanced at it several more times as she dried herself.

Nothing else bizarre happened.

At least, not until she was about to leave the room.

"Clear."

She heard the word like a whisper in her ear. Although spoken softly, it was alarming enough to spin Sophie around, back to face the mirror. Her reflection stared back at her, backed by a glaring light behind her. A light bright enough that she had to shield her eyes.

"What the fuck?"

Sophie wanted to run, but the front door was jammed and her phone was dead. Whatever this was, she needed to face it. Despite the terror in her guts, nothing had tried to hurt her. There was no rational reason to run from her own home.

She faced her mirror-self and noticed something strange. Dead eyes— dull and lifeless. Not her own. She knew then, in that instant, she was not looking at a true reflection.

It's something else—something else in my mirror.

Sophie's reflection opened its mouth and let out another foggy breath. The glaring light cast a shimmering halo around her, slicing through the gaps in her hair.

Clear.

There was that word again. Sophie pulled back her lips and repeated it back to her image. "Clear? What does that mean? What do you want?"

Clear.

Her reflection let out another breath, fogging up the glass.

Sophie felt drawn towards the mirror, closer to its shining surface. She leaned forwards over the sink, staring into those dull, dead eyes.

Clear.

Sophie felt a thud against her chest. Grabbing her ribcage with both hands, she gasped.

Clear.

Her reflection exhaled, fogging up the glass again.

She reached out, but her reflection didn't do the same.

"What is happening? What is going–"

Clear.

The mirror shattered and a black hole appeared. Sophie tried to look away, but it pulled at her, clawed at her, drew her inward. She tried to scream, but found herself breathless.

All around her was darkness.

And then there was light.

———

DAGGERS PIERCED Sophie's eyes as she fought to open them, the light so blinding that she almost retreated back to the darkness. But something wouldn't let her. Something ordered her to wake up.

A persistent beeping slowly centred itself in her mind.

She tried to move, but found herself restricted.

The room was unrecognisable, bare and featureless. Cold.

A face appeared floating, hovering over Sophie's.

"It's okay, sweetheart. You're in the hospital."

"W-what?"

"You were in an accident. An ambulance brought you here last night, but you're okay. You're awake. Just stay calm."

She nodded, her head almost too heavy to hold up. "I had an accident in my flat? The mirror broke."

The other woman smiled gently. "No, sweetheart, you were hit by a car in town crossing the road. Your friends say you were very drunk and didn't see the car coming. It was an accident."

"No..." She had no memory of it. No memory at all. "Am I... am I okay?"

"You were in pretty bad shape," the woman told her, obviously a nurse. "But you're going to be okay. You've broken your leg, but it will heal. Just rest and let us take care of you."

She tried to move, but still found herself restricted. The bed sheets were tight around her. Stifling. "My mum. I want my mum. Please."

The nurse put a hand on her shoulder. "I'm going to go get her right now, sweetheart. She's been here the whole time, waiting for you to wake up."

Sophie fought the urge to cry, but she felt hot tears spill down the sides of her cheeks. "I'm going to be okay. I'm going to be okay."

"Yes. That's it, Sophie. Just breathe."

DEVIL'S WOODS

Dale and Blake went to Devil's Woods.

No one knew why it was called that, it just was and always had been. Dale imagined some young kid had probably said it back in the eighties or something, blagging about seeing a ghost in the trees or a witch in a hut, and the name had stuck. Anyhow, everyone called it Devil's Woods. At fourteen, though, Dale was old enough to know that ghosts and monsters weren't real. Although allegedly a kid had gone missing in the woods a few years back.

Alfie Woods, I think his name was.

Still, lack of monsters aside, the woods were creepy AF, and as the sun drifted beyond the trees, the greens of the leaves and the yellows of the sun-scorched grass turned dull. Even the air itself seemed to lose its life.

"Can't believe we're back at school tomorrow," Blake said, pulling a face that made him look a bit like a pug. "I swear those six weeks felt like two."

Dale raised an eyebrow. "Seriously? It's felt like an entire year. We've literally had nothing to do for over a month. I'm glad the holidays are over."

"Ah, you would say that, you weirdo. Most of us don't like school as much as you do. Nerd."

"Most of us don't have to live with my dad. I hate being stuck in with nothing to do."

"Um, Fortnite, mate? You should try it."

"I know, you keep saying, but it just looks dumb to me."

"You're dumb."

Dale chuckled. "Cheers."

Blake glanced slightly in Dale's direction as they strolled along the top of the grassy plateau that ran between bunches of thick trees on either side. Years of kids walking from one end of the woods to the other had seen it become an elevated path. If you looked down, you could spot batteries stuck in the dirt, or bits of coloured plastic from some old abandoned toy, as well as the commonplace crisp packets and chocolate bar wrappers caught up in the brambles. This was an area without a caretaker. The council didn't mow the grass here or cut back the trees. It was a wasteland.

No, just nature. Somewhere we haven't paved over yet.

"I guess school's all right," Blake muttered. "Be nice to see Sadie Boyd and Claire Addison again. Their legs whenever they're wearing tights..." He mimed a chef's kiss. "*Magnifique!*"

Dale smiled, nodded, and played along. His lack of interest in girls had begun to concern him more and more each day. It was all his mates seemed to talk about, but for some reason he was different. Slowly, he was coming to realise what that meant. It was terrifying.

Dad will kick me out.

Blake might not even be my friend anymore.

They walked a little longer, heading for an area right in the middle of Devil's Woods where there was a rope swing tied to a giant oak tree. Another rumour went that this tree opened up at night and demons clambered out from a hidden staircase inside—straight from Hell. If they saw you, they would drag you back down with them.

"I gotta be back by eight," Dale warned, kicking a disembodied Barbie head that dared peek out at him from a thicket. "Mum's working a night shift at Tesco and wants to see me before she leaves."

Blake started walking backwards, facing Dale as he talked. "When is she gonna get a better job, man? It must suck working through the night."

"She says she don't mind it. It's quiet, and she can just get on with her work."

"Maybe she's a vampire."

"That's dumb."

Blake chuckled. "Yeah. She's not hot enough to be a vampire. Vampires are always sexy as hell."

"Your mum ain't no looker either, mate. What was she, fifty, when she had you?"

"Forty-one, you ass hat."

They both broke out in laughter.

"Yo!" Dale stopped and pointed. "Look, a rabbit."

Blake spun around and followed Dale's finger. In the nearby bushes, a little white-tailed bunny hopped along, unaware of their presence. It didn't seem to impress his best friend very much, though.

"Yeah, amazing, bro. What do you want me to do? Catch it and put it in a cage for you?"

Dale blushed. He didn't know why he had got quite so excited. "It's just cute, that's all."

"It'll probably be in a fox's belly by tonight, mate."

Dale watched the bunny hop off into the bushes, vanishing almost instantly. "Nah, I reckon he'll be okay. The foxes around here are probably full from rummaging in everyone's bins at night."

"Tell me about it. There was one outside my house the other night that would not shut the fuck up. I swear it was trying to wind me up."

"What does the fox say?"

The two of them broke out in silly noises and then laughed. They were both being lame, but there was no one else around and they were bored, so where was the harm? Blake was the only friend Dale could be stupid around; the only person who didn't make him think too hard about what he was doing or saying.

The only person I can be myself around.

I should tell him.

"Blake?"

Blake turned back around and started walking backwards again. "Yeah?"

Dale cleared his throat. "Nothing. I was just gonna say that if you have any chance with Sadie, then you need to lose some weight. You've put on like twelve-stone this summer."

"Whoa! Screw you, dick face." He pinched his belly underneath his bright red Adidas t-shirt and wiggled some flab. He was only slightly overweight, and his big chest and shoulders helped him get away with it for the most part. "This is all muscle. Ask your mum."

"Hey, can we stop with the mum jokes?" Dale pointed a finger, although he was smiling. "I don't want to have to kill you."

"Bring it on." Blake leapt in the air and delivered a flying kick that missed when Dale stepped aside. Dale then threw his best spinning roundhouse that connected with the side of his friend's arm.

"Shit! Man, that hurt."

Dale reached out a hand to his staggering friend. "Fuck! Sorry. I didn't mean to get you. Are you okay?"

"No, man. What the hell?"

"I'm really sorry." He reached out again, trying to shake hands. "It was an accident."

Blake grabbed his arm and swung him around. "Gotcha!"

Dale went hurtling forwards, forced to follow his twisting wrist that was no longer under his control. When Blake let go, his momentum kept him going forwards.

His ankle twisted, and he staggered to the edge of the grassy plateau, where the ground suddenly sloped downwards at a steep angle. Gravity won, and his legs collapsed underneath him as he went tumbling down the hill.

"Shit!" Blake called after him. "Dale?"

Dale rolled and rolled, hurtling down the hill like a wheel of cheese. He cried out, knowing his final destination would be amongst the thorns and brambles below.

As the world spun, the sky and grass intermingled. He was vaguely aware of Blake hurrying down after him.

As expected, Dale came to a skidding halt in the bushes at the bottom of the slope, wincing as the spiky weeds bit into his skin. His button-up, short-sleeve shirt had ridden up his torso, exposing his back and belly, which were beginning to itch from the prickly limbs scratching at him. He tried to liberate himself safely from the tangle, tried to find a route through the slicing thorns and sharp needles. But by the time he made it few feet back up the hill, his arms were stinging from a dozen thin red scratches.

As his senses reordered themselves, and he recovered from the brief bout of chaos, Blake's voice gradually came into earshot. He was screaming and yelling about something, crying out for help.

Dale blinked and looked around, confused. He was the one who had fallen, so why was Blake the one screaming?

"Bro, where are you?"

"Over here. Shit. I'm gonna puke. You gotta help me."

Dale got on his hands and knees and crawled further up the hill until he could rise, cautiously, to his feet. The knees on his jeans were muddy and scuffed, as were his hands. Blood oozed from a particularly nasty scratch on the back of his hand, but he was more or less okay. No broken bones or nasty wounds. Still, Blake was getting a punch in the arm for throwing him down the hill. That psychopath.

Dale looked for his friend, but could only hear him. "Bro, chill out. Where are you?"

"I tripped and fell. I'm halfway down the hill. Please, help me."

"You tripped and fell? I was the one who got pushed down the hill."

"It was an accident. Dale, please. I need you, mate."

"Fuck. All right, I'm coming." Dale plodded along, his legs a little hollow after the physical shock of falling. He zigzagged part the way back up the hill, heading for the sound of his friend's voice.

Blake came into view amongst the branches of some nearby trees, the red of his t-shirt sticking out among the dull greens and shitty browns.

"Hurry up, man. Please. Dale, there's... there's a dead body here."

Dale's stomach turned. "What are you talking about?"

"Just come."

Sensing his friend's panic, and realising this wasn't a joke, Dale sprinted to where Blake was standing. It looked like he was stuck in place, his one leg rigid as he flailed and yanked at his ankle. Behind him, a gnarled tree trunk, three times the length of a man, lay uprooted and horizontal in the long grass.

Blake reached out to Dale as he neared him. Instinctively, he grabbed his friend and yanked on both his arms. "What's wrong?"

"I'm stuck. My foot's jammed in a hole."

Dale pulled Blake's arms even harder, but it only caused him to cry out in pain. His leg wasn't coming loose at all. From the look of things, he had stepped in a weed-filled divot, and the soft earth had closed in around his foot. "Hold on, man. Let me try to dig you out."

He was about to stoop down and pull at the weeds, but then his eye caught something else—something poking out of the thick tree trunk behind Blake. A maggot covered face. Human.

"Whoa!" Dale backpedalled down the hill.

"Don't leave me," Blake cried, reaching out like a toddler begging to be picked up. "Please, get me out of here, man."

Dale stopped where he was and nodded. His heart was pounding in his chest, but this was a moment where choices mattered. If he legged it and left Blake alone with a corpse, their friendship would be over.

And I couldn't bear that.

"Don't worry," he said. "I'm not going anywhere. Wh-who do you think it is?"

Blake glanced at the corpse stuffed inside the log but then looked away and closed his eyes. "Ain't it obvious? It's Alfie sodding Woods."

"The kid who went missing? It can't be."

"It has to be! My mum told me it happened five or six years ago. Alfie Woods had a fight with his sister and ran away from home with only a lunchbox and some snacks. After two days, when he didn't come home, the entire neighbourhood went searching for him. Eventually, they found his lunchbox in these woods." He closed his eyes and turned a sickly white. "Alfie's severed tongue was inside it."

"Bullshit!" Dale sneered, the story angering him for some reason. Was it because his friend was trying to scare him even more? "That's just a spooky story."

"My mum told me, Dale. It's true. That's Alfie Woods in there. I... I can prove it."

"How?"

Blake took a deep breath and swallowed. "Open his mouth."

Dale stared over at the ghastly, pale, grinning face—its eye sockets filled with quivering maggots and baby flies. "I ain't touching a corpse. You do it."

"I can't reach, can I? My foot is stuck. Grab a stick or something."

"No. I don't want to get any closer."

"Grab a stick and give it to me. I'll do it."

"Fine. But I ain't getting nowhere near. It probably has diseases." He glanced around at the various trees and bushes, looking for a stick or branch that would fit the bill. Eventually, he found a dead tangle of something that might once have been covered with leaves. He managed to snap off a limb and bring it over to Blake.

Blake snatched the stick from Dale and held it out like a sword. His hand was shaking, but focused on it until it became still. The corpse was about six-feet away, so he had to lean over and point the stick ahead of him. It took several attempts, but eventually he was able to jab the stick at the grinning skull.

Skin sloughed away, leaving behind a putrid red and white mess like yoghurt and strawberries.

"Shit, I can't get it between his teeth. Hold on." He inched forwards, stretching as far as he could. He gritted his teeth and went red in the face with strain. "Almost got it."

Blake suddenly screamed and fell forwards. His leg remained stuck, but something had shifted and changed angle. He came down on his front, arms sprawling out in front of him. The branch he was holding snapped with a gunshot-like *crack*!

Blake's screaming took on a new volume. His hand that had been holding the stick was now pressed right up against the sticky, rotting face. The broken end of the stick jutted out of the corpse's mouth, having entered between the teeth and pried open its jaws.

Dale screamed too, but was unable to move a muscle.

Groaning, Blake slithered away through the grass, yelling out every curse word he knew. Disgusting goo caked his hand, as if he had shoved it into a deep, creamy trifle. He clawed at his ankle frantically, but it seemed to be tangled even worse now, with wiry brown roots wrapped all around it. As much as he pulled, he couldn't get free. Eventually, he grew tired and flopped on his side, panting.

Dale had forgotten to breathe for a moment. He was transfixed by the open-mouthed, maggot-ridden skull.

Blake stopped yelling, but his voice was high-pitched, like a fridge door alarm. "Mate. Mate, get me out of here. Please. My hand. It's on my hand."

Dale pointed a trembling finger at the corpse. "Its tongue, bro. It has no tongue."

Blake turned his head, and his eyes stretched almost comically wide. "Alfie Woods."

It was unclear if the tongue had rotted away or been eaten by animals, or if it had simply recoiled into the neck like a burrowing worm, but one thing was apparent—the slimy dead jaws were empty of everything except teeth.

"Get me out of here, Dale. Please."

Repulsed, terrified, and sickened, Dale nodded and dropped to his knees. He began yanking and pulling at the roots around his friend's ankle so urgently that his fingers throbbed. But they could have been made of steel for all they refused to give. He twisted and turned them, trying to find some magic combination of movements that would loosen them up just a little. They were so tight that Blake's ankle had started to bleed through his white sock.

"I... I can't get you free," he said, looking Blake in the eye. His best friend. The coolest guy he knew. "I need to fetch someone."

"You ain't leaving me here, man. You gotta get me out." He let out a frustrated roar and pulled at his ankle again, causing the roots to bite even deeper. The pain didn't seem to bother him. In fact, he seemed prepared to cut off his own foot if it got him free.

"I don't know what to do. Blake...?"

Blake glanced at the corpse and closed his eyes. His mucky hand was stretched out away from him. "You need to find something to cut the roots."

"Like what? There's nothing sharp here. I have to go get an adult. I'll be right back, I swear."

Tears filled Blake's eyes. Dale hadn't seen him cry since they were little kids. It compelled him to throw his arms around his friend and hug him.

"I would never abandon you, Blake. You know that, right?"

Blake let out a little sob, then a chuckle. "Gay."

Dale broke away and looked at his friend. "Why would you call me that?"

"Does it matter?"

"No. I... just wondered why you called me that."

"Um... because I reckon you might actually be gay, bro."

"Shut up. I ain't gay." He moved back, wringing his sweaty, mud-caked hands together. "D-do you really think that?"

Blake was trembling, but he managed a half smile. "Am I wrong?"

"Would you care?"

Shit. What am I doing? Just deny it.

This is bad timing.

"Of course I don't care. You're my best mate. Just don't try to kiss me because I really am into Sadie. You get me?"

Dale nodded, feeling like he might be sick, but also feeling a mad rush of energy that made him want to leap up into the air. His best friend didn't care that he was gay.

Thank God.

"I'm going to go get help, okay?" Dale reached out and put a hand on Blake's shoulder. "I'll run all the way home and get my dad. If he's not already passed out, drunk, I'll get him to come with a saw or some scissors or–"

"Secateurs."

Dale frowned. "What?"

"Secateurs. They're like scissors but for cutting plants and stuff. My mum uses them in the garden."

"Well, my garden is covered in slabs and my parents haven't gardened once in my lifetime. I'll bring whatever I can find."

Blake glanced back at the corpse. Somehow, its mouth had closed, and it was once again grinning like a ghoul. Maggots wriggled in and out of its eye sockets. "Run faster than you ever have in your life, okay? And call the police too. It's a dead body. We're going to end up in the local paper. Chicks are gonna dig us."

Dale tilted his head.

"Oh, yeah, sorry. Dudes are gonna be waving their dicks at you."

"You're gonna make my life hell, aren't you? I don't even know for sure that I'm—"

"You definitely are, mate. I've seen you play football."

Dale put his hands on his hips. "You want me to leave you here and not come back?"

"Sorry. I'm just messing around because I'm scared. Go get help. Go on, before I change my mind." He looked back at the corpse and quivered. "Fuck."

"I promise I'll be quick." Dale turned and sprinted back up the hill. It felt good to let out all the pent up energy that had built up inside of him. The panic.

A dead body, for real?

"Hurry!" Blake yelled up after him.

Dale reached the top of the hill and raced for home. Overhead, the sky had lost the last of its blue.

———

"THIS WAY," Dale said, leading his dad and a police officer through a gap in the hedges. "We can cut through here."

Predictably, his dad had been drinking, but not so much that he hadn't been able to come along with his son. It had taken several minutes to convince him it wasn't a joke, and that there really was a dead body in Devil's Woods. Also that Blake was stuck right next to it.

The police officer had arrived less than ten minutes after Dale's dad had called 999, and he had listened to Dale in complete silence, only nodding grimly now and then, making it clear he would tolerate no nonsense. All that mattered was that they had agreed to following him.

The woods were silent, the birds asleep and the insects not yet awake. At least the darkness was held at bay by the torches he and his dad held in front of them, lighting up cones of woodland as they bobbed along behind Dale.

It had been over half an hour since he had left Blake alone with the corpse.

I promised him I would be quick. He's stuck waiting for me, wondering where I am.

"I'm coming, buddy," he muttered.

"What were you both doing in these woods?" the police officer asked as they jogged through the bushes. The badge on his chest read: *Jaskil.*

"Just hanging out. We were on our way to the rope swing, but we were play fighting and ended up falling down the hill. Blake got stuck at the bottom."

"And that's where the body is?"

Dale nodded. "It's all rotten and covered in maggots."

His dad grunted, huffing and puffing, as they climbed up onto the elevated pathway in the dark. "It's probably a dead fox or something. You're going to end up in a lot of trouble for wasting police time."

"Dad, it was a person. I looked at its face. And Blake is stuck. He needs rescuing."

His dad held up the small hacksaw he had grabbed from the shed. "I'll get him free. I just hope we didn't drag an officer out here for no reason."

"It's okay, sir," Jaskil said. "Better to be safe than sorry." He gave Dale a nod and a smile, almost like he understood his dad was a pain in arse and half drunk.

"We need to hurry," Dale said, picking up speed. His body burned with the anticipation of making it back to his friend. Would Blake be mad that he had taken so long?

I had to wait for the police.

"How much further?" Dale's dad asked, increasingly out of breath. Maybe if he got a job, he wouldn't be so unfit.

"Just up ahead." Dale noticed the battery buried in the mud, reflecting the torchlight. "We tumbled down the hill right here. Blake is behind those trees down there."

"Okay," Jaskil said. "Lead the way, young man."

"Blake!" Dale cupped his hands around his mouth. "Blake, I'm back. Are you okay? Blake?"

His dad plodded down the slope behind him. "I don't see anything? Where is he?"

"I... I don't know. He should be here. Blake, are you okay?" Panicking, Dale took off down the hill, risking another tumble. He couldn't think of a reason his friend wouldn't respond to his calls.

When he saw a flash of red between the trees, Dale sighed with relief. For a second, he had feared he was going mad. "Blake. Blake, answer us."

What's wrong with him?

Dale sprinted along the middle of the slope and headed through the trees. Blake was there, right in front of him, lying inside the thick log. His face peered out of one end.

When the officer and his dad arrived beside Dale a few moments later, he hadn't moved an inch. He was stuck in place, just like Blake had been when he had left. But somehow Blake had got free.

How? How did he get free?

And where is the dead body? Where is Alfie Woods?

"What the fuck?" Dale's dad spotted Blake lying inside the trunk and covered his mouth. He turned around and vomited into the bushes.

Two sharp branches had impaled Blake's eyes.. His mouth was hanging open in a silent scream, while the bloody nub of a missing tongue peeked out from the back of his throat. No sign of Alfie Woods. No sign of the rotting corpse that had been inside the log.

"I... I don't understand." Dale's legs buckled, and he fell backwards into his dad's arms.

"What on earth happened here?" Jaskil asked. His tone was harsh, and his body had turned rigid. "What the hell did you kids do?"

Dale stared at his dead best friend, his entire world spiralling. It made no sense. No sense at all. Blake was dead and inside the log. But it couldn't be true.

"It was Alfie Woods," he pleaded. "Alfie Woods killed him and took his tongue."

The police officer grabbed Dale by the arm. "I advise you to stay quiet until you get to the station. You have a lot of explaining to do, and I don't want you to say anything you'll later regret."

"Hey," Dale's dad snatched at Jaskil. "Get your hands off my boy."

Jaskil shoved him away, knocking him over on the uneven slope.

"Sir, your son might be in some very serious trouble right now. I understand your instinct is to protect him, but interfering won't help anyone. Do you understand me?"

Dale's dad turned the colour of clean bedsheets and when he looked at Blake's dead body stuffed inside the log again, a bulge erupted in his throat. He stayed on the ground, silent, staring. Shocked.

Dale halfheartedly tried to fight the officer as he cuffed his hands behind his back, but his body felt weak and he just wanted to lie down. "Blake," he muttered. "Blake, what happened? Blake!"

His dad shook his head over and over. "Son, what have you done? He was your friend. Your best friend."

"I didn't do this, Dad. It was Alfie Woods. It was Alfie Woods. Dad?"

Jaskil turned him around and looked him in the eye. "Who is Alfie Woods, son?"

"The kid who died in the woods."

"I don't know who you're talking about. What kid?"

"Alfie Woods! He was here. I swear he was. A dead body. A dead body without a tongue." He collapsed to the ground and sobbed. Nobody seemed to care. They all looked at him like he was a murderer. "He was here."

But the only dead body in the woods that night was his best friend Blake.

LUCAS

Lucas dashed for the hospital lifts, leaping forwards and keeping the doors from closing with a flamboyant karate chop. The flat metal edges hit his hand and the doors rebounded open, unable to chomp through his flesh.

"That'll teach ye, ye *eejits*," he scoffed at the doors. "Saw me coming, did ye?"

He stepped into the lift's vestibule and turned around, prodding at buttons and fiddling with the control panel. Miraculously, he hadn't spilled his coffee, which was fortunate since it was hotter than the sun. In such days of extreme health and safety, it was nice to know that negligence still existed in some places.

Looking up, he saw a desperate woman dashing towards him. "Please," she said. "Hold the doors."

Lucas reached out and held the doors at bay, not trusting the 'open' button to do it. He rarely trusted buttons.

I remember a time when the only buttons were the ones people used to keep their trousers up.

The woman hopped into the lift beside Lucas, her sensible black shoes squeaking on the metal floor. "These things have a habit of closing on me," she said with a smile as she pressed the button for the ground floor.

Attractive, brunette, and with lumps in all the proper places, Lucas imagined the woman's smile was disarming to most people. He smiled back, confident he was quite disarming himself. "Aye, lass, they have it in for me too, so they do. Perhaps it's the Lord's way of telling us to stop being lazy buggers and take the stairs." He reached into his pocket and offered her a chewing gum from a small green pack. "Something to keep the devil's mouthpiece occupied?"

She frowned at him for a moment, then let out a chuckle and took one. Popping the gum into her mouth, she nodded. "You're probably right about taking the stairs. I don't remember the last time I got my steps in."

Lucas looked her up and down, spying nary an ounce of fat. Her tight black trousers were likely chosen to show off her svelte figure, and a blue NHS uniform peeked out from beneath a trendy white leather jacket.

"Get a dog," he said, sipping his coffee again. "Great excuse for fresh air at all hours of the day or night."

"Oh no, I couldn't. I work far too many hours to take care of a pet. Even a fish would be too much."

"A nurse at this hospital, eh?"

"That's right. Are you visiting somebody here?"

"I'm always visiting someone, lass. Busy man, me."

Another chuckle, but she now gave him an intense look, as if she were attempting to figure him out. "Haven't we already met?"

He nodded. "Aye, I think we might just have, lass."

"You were on my ward." She wagged a finger at him knowingly. "I dropped a pile of blankets and you knelt down to help me gather them."

"Aye. Our eyes met, our hands touched, and then I departed, a mysterious stranger whose name ye never learned. Except, I've ended up having to hold the lift for ye. Kind of ruins the lasting image I tried to create."

It was obvious she didn't quite know his words, which was a reaction he was more than used to. She was probably used to men flirting with her, but Lucas had a way all of his own that let even the most confident of people off balance.

There was also little doubt she would take him up on any offer to go grab a coffee together, but alas he already had one. A shame.

The nurse smiled wider at Lucas, as if she had just managed to work him out. Chewing her gum on one side of her mouth, she wagged her finger again. "You're a cheeky one, you are. Must be the Irish thing."

"So they tell me."

"It's a really sexy accent."

"They tell me that too. Yer pretty well put together y'self, lass. If ye have no time to keep a wee mutt, then I take it ye got no time for a wee fella either?"

She folded her arms and leaned back against the wall of the lift. With a sensual pout, she said, "I can always find time for the right man."

Lucas tossed his empty coffee container down on the ground and grinned. Matching her posture, he folded his arms and leaned back against the opposite wall. "And what kind of fella would be the right kind, because I'll be honest, I tend to fall into the wrong side of most columns."

"Well, sometimes wrong is right." She licked her lips, leaving them glistening. "So, where are you from? I have family in County Mayo. Do you know it?"

He clicked his fingers and tapped his nose. "I'm from everywhere, lass. Man without a home, me."

"You're, what, a gypsy then?"

"More of a nomad. Hard to stay in one place when ye have a family like mine."

"Families..." she shook her head and tutted. "I hear you there. I barely see mine."

"They don't see how wonderful ye are?"

"Ha! They certainly don't. I'm the black sheep of the family. My sister's on stage in London, living the high life. My parents think she's a superstar. Me being a nurse isn't quite so fancy."

"But it's a heck of a lot more vital, what you do. People put their lives in yer hands, lass. There's no more honourable a career than giving care." He clapped gently. "Bravo."

She blushed and then fidgeted. "Um, my name's Lucy, by the way. Probably should've led with that."

"Eh, names have power. Why give it away carelessly?" He offered out his hand. "Lucas Fergus is my name, pleased to make yer acquaintance."

Like a lady of old, she slid her hand into his, in such a way that he was tempted to kiss it. He didn't kiss it though, instead he shivered and let go. "The hands of a healer," he said, a slight tremor to his voice. "I'm not worthy."

"Oh, give over." She swatted a hand coyly at him. "You make me sound like Mother Teresa."

He waved a hand back. "Ah, don't get me started on that one. Devious old crone."

"Um, okay. So what do you do, Lucas Fergus?"

"This and that," he said. "Mostly, I make improvements."

"Improvements?"

"Aye, to the world, lass. I leap about, striving to put things right, hoping that one day I can earn my way home." He shook his head and grinned. "Oh boy."

She frowned. "You've lost me. How exactly do you improve the world—other than handing out gum to strangers?"

"And holding lift doors, don't forget. But it's easy really. A little bit of kindness here, a dash of courage there. Mostly, it's about seeing who people truly are and making sure they get what they deserve."

Finally, she was unnerved, likely a rarity for a woman as confident and beautiful as her. She unfolded her arms and started fidgeting with the buttons on her side of the lift. "Why haven't the doors opened yet? We've been in here a while."

"Ye not wrong, I'm starting to take root here, eh? Let me take a wee gander." He turned to the control console and tapped at the buttons. They had no power, all of them unlit. Prodding about, he managed to yank the whole panel open on a squeaking hinge.

"Shouldn't that be secure?" Lucy said, frowning. "I don't think you're supposed to open it."

"Looks like some cheeky bugger's already been fiddling. These wires are like the insides of a mouse."

"Press the emergency button."

He raised an eyebrow at her. "Would ye call this an emergency, lass? Us standing here, chatting?"

"Yes! I have places to be. Press the button and someone will answer in the control room. The lift has obviously broken down. Go on, press it."

He did as she asked, ignoring her unpleasant tone by whistling a jaunty tune.

Somebody answered almost right away. "Hello, is everything okay?"

"Hello there, laddie, this is Lucas Fergus on the line. Thanks for taking me call."

"Um... okay. Are you having problems with the lift?"

"More like the lift is having problems with us, good sir."

Lucy hissed and shoved Lucas aside. She leaned towards the speaker panel where the microphone was located. "The lift has stopped moving and all the buttons are off. Can you help us, please?"

"Have you tried pressing door-open?"

She hissed again but humoured the request, pressing several buttons on the console. "Nothing's happening. It's completely dead."

"Okay. Stay calm, miss, and I'll contact a lift engineer right away. I'll come back to you in a moment after I've spoken with someone."

"Be quick about it," Lucy said. "I'm stuck in here with a man."

"Miss, don't worry. We'll have things sorted out quickly."

"Thank you."

Lucas folded his arms and tapped a foot, waiting for Lucy to turn around and face him. When she did, he feigned being upset. "Yer stuck in here with *a man*, eh? I've been called a lot of things in my time, but none so insulting as that."

"Sorry," she said, scrunching up her face irritably. "Are you not a man?"

"Not even close. Anyway, I thought we were getting along, but now the air in here is sourer than Egyptian wine."

"I'm uncomfortable. You might be a weirdo, for all I know, and we're trapped in here together."

He did a little jig on the spot. "Oh, ye can count on that, lass. Weird as they come, me."

"See?" She shook her head and backed off. "You keep saying strange things like that, and now you're dancing like a child."

"A child?" He gasped. "How dare you?"

She seemed to tremble, but it was merely bad acting for the camera mounted in the corner. "Y-you're scaring me."

Not wanting to cause drama, he waved a hand dismissively. "Come on, bonny lass. I'm just enjoying meself. That's what life is for, eh? I apologise if I've made you uncomfortable."

She nodded, as if to accept his apology, but her expression remained taut. "You spoke about making sure people get what they deserve. What did you mean by that?"

"I was just gibber-jabbering."

She seemed to settle down a little. Refolding her arms, she moved away from the wall and chewed her gum for a few moments. Then she looked back across at him. "Who were you visiting on the ward? I never saw you come in. You just appeared when I dropped the towels."

"I was there to visit a friend whose time is up. Old Graham."

Her eyes widened. "Oh, wow. I didn't realise Graham had anyone left to come visit him."

"Aye, he's ninety-two," said Lucas. "A good innings, for sure. As it goes, Graham does have people who care about him, but they're scattered about. I couldn't let him pass without paying my respects. Unfortunately, I couldn't stay longer because he was boring the paint off the walls."

She chuckled. "He has some stories, huh? Nice old man, though."

"Aye. I suppose ye meet a fair few, doing what ye do."

"And some not so nice ones," she added, wrinkling her nose like she smelled something bad.

"What do you do about those?"

"What do you mean?"

"I mean, how do ye get yer revenge when some old fart is groping ye during his bed bath or pleasuring himself while ye plump his pillows?"

She unfolded her arms and glanced down at her nails, which were short and neatly trimmed. "Just part of the job, isn't it? Nurses have to put up with all kinds of things."

"That they do, lass. Like I said, it's an honourable profession for those who truly hear mercy's call."

"It's a job," she said flatly. "If I could inherit a million pounds and retire, I would do. No one in the NHS works for the love of it. Maybe they used to, but not anymore. We're underpaid, overworked, and abused on a daily basis."

Lucas nodded, seeing the truth come out of her like pus from a wound. "It must boil ye piss, no?"

"Of course it does, but like I said, it's part of the job." She huffed and turned back to the console, bashing it with her fist. "Is that guy coming back to us or what? Hello?"

Lucas glanced up at the camera and waved.

Lucy pulled a face at him. "What are you doing?"

"Just saying hello."

"Just saying hello? Why?"

"Dunno, really. I see a camera, I wave. Do ye not?"

"No, I don't. God, you're so weird, Lucas. I can't figure out if I should be screaming for help or wanting to get to know you more."

He spread his arms out wide. "Ask away what you will. Lucas Fergus is nothing if not an open book."

"Okay, what do you *really* do for a living? Like, give me a job title."

"Hmm, that's a tough one. Ye could call me an odd job man, if it pleases ye."

"I thought you weren't a man."

"Aye, good point. Then, I suppose ye can call me a fixer."

She sighed. "So you're, what, a tradesman? That's..."

"Disappointing?"

"Yeah. I thought you were more interesting than that."

"Am I not roguish enough?"

"Perhaps too roguish." She ran a hand through her shiny brown hair, tucking some behind her ear. "Okay, next question. How did you and old Graham meet?"

"In a bar. Next."

"Have you ever been married?"

"Only ever to God."

She grimaced, clearly displeased by the word. "So you're religious?"

"Not in the way ye might think. God and I rarely see eye to eye."

That seemed to settle her back down. She liked to break rules and disliked authority. They had that in common.

"Are you currently dating anybody?" she asked.

"Nope. Been a while."

"Okay, well here's the biggie, then. Lucas, are you dangerous?"

He titled his head at her and smirked. "Oh aye, lass. I'm as dangerous as they come, but I'm not a pervert or a sex offender, if that's ye meaning."

"That *is* what I'm getting at. You're a handsome guy, and clearly confident, but you're also very odd. I'm thinking I might let you take me out for dinner, if you play your cards right."

"Well, colour me flattered." He did another jig on the spot, this time spinning around on one foot. When he came back around to face her, he gave her a serious stare. "Ye nay gonna poison my food, are ye, Lucy?"

She flinched. "What? Why would you say that?"

"Because a fella wants to make sure he isn't being poisoned. Common sense, wouldn't ye say?"

She shook her head, her expression souring. "Okay, you're obviously just too weird to keep it together, so let's stop the banter and just get out of this lift, yeah? I'd like to leave."

"Oh drat. Did me silly mouth let me down again?" He slapped himself on the back of the wrist. "Lucas, ye do struggle to use yer inside voice, do ye not?"

"What is your problem?"

"My problem is that I feel a wee bit nauseous being this close to ye, lass. Ye give off an eggy stench, so ye do. Infernal, one might describe it."

The face she showed him now was her true face—one full of revulsion and disgust, entitlement and ego. "Keep the fuck away from me, you weirdo. As soon as we get off this lift, you're fucked."

"Why? I haven't hurt ye." He pointed at the camera in the corner. "There's evidence I've done not a thing to ye."

"You're threatening me."

"Am I? When did I threaten ye, lass? Tell me, wouldn't ye?"

She pressed herself up against the wall and cowered, clearly for the benefit of the camera he had just reminded her of. "It's your tone, and the things you're saying to me. I'm... I'm intimidated."

He backed off against the opposite wall, eyeing her up carefully. "I'm sorry to intimidate you, Lucy. I wouldn't want to get on yer wrong side."

"What do you mean? What are you talking about?"

"Ward Nine, eh? Ye can check in, but nary can ye leave."

Some of Lucy's mock frailty dissolved, replaced by an icy disdain. "Who *are* you? Why are you saying these things to me?"

"Because someone has to. How many men and women have died on yer watch, Lucy? Frail, old people who trusted ye to keep them cosy and safe?"

"I work in an end-of-life care unit. People on my watch are *supposed* to die."

"Is that how ye live with it? Or is it the fact yer a flaming narcissist who thinks the rest of humanity exists only to help ye get what ye want?"

She lashed out, and like a striking viper, she leapt forwards and shoved Lucas in the chest with both hands. "Get the fuck away from me."

Casually, he looked up at the camera again. "I haven't touched ye, lass. In fact, it's quite the opposite."

Her eyes went wide. "Help! Someone, help me." She rushed over to the lift panel and pressed the buttons frantically. Nothing happened.

"I disconnected that while ye weren't looking," he said. "The intercom too."

"What? Why? What do you want?"

He waggled all of his fingers at her. "What am I like, eh? Silly old Lucas. Break everything I touch, me."

This time, Lucy cowered for real. She retreated into the corner of the lift and crouched. "What do you want with me?"

"To ask if ye have any regrets?"

"About what? I didn't do anything."

He waggled a finger at her and took a step forwards. "Now, now, Lucy. If I were to reach inside yer wee pocket right now, are ye saying I wouldn't find old Graham's antique pocket watch? That scratched up old thing is his most prized possession, but thanks to ye he's about to die without it."

"I don't know what you're talking about."

"Ye laced his porridge with God knows what. Just another heart attack on the old fart's ward, they'll say, but we know better, don't we?" He took another small step towards her. "Graham had another three months. Ye took them from him."

"He's in his nineties. If he's had a heart attack, it's because of old age."

"Or a bad dose of porridge, lass. I've already let yer bosses know, so I imagine they'll be looking into things as we speak. I bet there'll be plenty of evidence to be found in them leftovers."

She turned white. "You're lying. I never did anything. If there was something in that boring old sod's porridge, it's because you put it there. That's what I'll tell them."

He shook his head slowly, sadly. "No, ye won't, lass. Ye'll nay get the chance to tell anybody anything."

She put her fists up. "Touch me and I'll kick your nuts in."

"Please don't attempt it."

"You're crazy."

"Nope, just tired and newly human. It's all very upsetting."

"Newly human? You really are mad. Oh, my God."

He put his hands on his hips and glared at her. This would usually be the part where his magnificent black wings fanned out to frame him majestically. But he didn't have them anymore, thanks to his meddling brothers in the lands above. So his power pose was far less effective than he would have liked it to be. "Lucy, lass, ye've been killing old people and stealing whatever meagre possessions they have left to them. It's reprehensible."

"Who are you?" She demanded it now, unable to control her anger and entitlement even in her fear. She spat her gum in his face and growled. "Who the fuck are you, you maniac? Help! Help me. He's going to rape me."

He took another step closer, looking deep into her eyes. "Ye might be an angel of death, love, but I'm the Devil."

Lucy began laughing hysterically. "You're a nutcase, is what you are, and you're screwed once these doors open." She started screaming out for help again. Certain she could indict him through dramatics alone.

Lucas reached out and grabbed her wrist, making her yelp. "Picture this," he said, and forced a stream of consciousness into her soul, showing her exactly who he was.

She recoiled and slumped to the floor. Out of breath and bewildered, she stared at him through wide, astonished eyes. "Wh-what? No, no. It can't be. How...?"

"I know, I know, it's overwhelming, meeting a celebrity." He crouched down in front of her, elbows on his knees. "I suppose this must be what it's like for yer sister, people being star struck all the time. From what ye just showed me, she's about to get a major part in Eastenders. Ye must be right happy for her, eh?"

Her grimace suggested she was not.

Lucas tutted. "Sorry, I keep forgetting about the whole malignant narcissism thing. Yer no doubt desperately waiting to see her fail, eh? How dare she have a better life than her big sis?"

"You know nothing about me."

"I've known everything about ye since the moment our hands touched picking up those towels. Ye see, I might be newly human, but I kept a few of me old parlour tricks."

She shook her head, confused and afraid. "I don't understand."

"See, my big throbbing celestial soul wouldn't fit inside a bog standard human body. So, instead of a *Citroen C4*, they gave me a *Bugatti Veyron*. I'd say I have about three or four hundred years on this baby before it fails its MOT. Hopefully by then, me and father will have figured out our differences."

Lucy started to sob, but no tears came. The mockery of human sadness stoked a fire inside of Lucas and his fists clenched. "Have ye ever truly shed a tear, Lucy? When ye break the news, with secret glee, to the poor relatives of yer victims, do ye even feel so much as a twinge? Do ye feel anything at all? For anyone?"

Instead of answering him, she pulled out her phone—a large slab of glass and silicon inside a sparkling pink case. "I'm filming you, mother-fucker. Try anything and you're screwed."

"Oh!" He clicked his fingers at her and grinned. "We should totally take a selfie, girlfriend. Come on, let's strike a wee pose, eh?"

Ignoring her screams and restraining her attempts to struggle, he dragged her up off the floor and wrapped his arm around her waist. She squeezed her so tightly she struggled to breathe. "Go on now, get that camera loaded, lass. Let's see what we get."

With a shaking hand, she opened up her front-facing camera, but instead of saying *cheese*, she merely gasped.

"This is gunna blow your mind, Lucy, lass. One of me father's cute little decrees from on high. Listen to this." He put on a deep voice and tried to sound almighty. "*No deed nor achievement of the fallen son, Lucifer, shall be documented by man nor commemorated in mortal history.*" He shook his head and sighed. "What that means, is that I can't be recorded, catalogued, or even keep a diary. The ink dries up as soon as I try to write a single letter." He pointed up at the corner of the lift. "CCTV's no good either. You're gonna look like a right loon, lass, when you tell 'em you met the Devil."

"Fuck off!" She shoved him, and he allowed himself to be moved. Glaring at him with all the hatred she could muster, she pointed a shaking index finger right in his face. "This is some kind of set up, but it's not going to work. I haven't done anything. I don't even know what you're talking about."

"This is simple retribution, Lucy. Ye've been killing innocent souls for a long long time now—poisoning them for no other reason than ye like the feeling of power it gives ye. I'm here to see ye answer for yer crimes."

"I'll never admit to any of it. You can't prove it."

"Ye don't need to admit it, lass. I see all of ye. There's a devil standing inside this tin box and it's not me."

She leapt at him again, her short nails aiming for his eyes. He grabbed both of her wrists, easily holding her at bay. "I'll kill you."

"Time's up, Lucy. Unlike Graham, ye'll nay see yer nineties."

Her eyes rolled back and forth in their sockets. Her voice begin-ning to slur. "W-why are you doing this?"

"Oh..." He let out a long breath, still holding her by her wrists. "It goes back roughly two-thousand years, to when I met a nice fella named Jesus on the cross. Meeting him that day changed me life, and ever since..." He shook his head and tutted. "Dear oh dear, ye nae want to hear me life story, do ye?"

"I'm going to kill you," she said weakly.

He eased her back, letting go of her wrists and shoving her gently back against the wall. "Yer looking a wee bit pale there, lass. Maybe it was something ye ate."

She clutched at her stomach and frowned. Without anything approaching joy, he watched as the truth slowly dawned on her. "The gum," she said, searching the floor until her eyes settled on the green, fizzing lump she had spat in his face. "What did you give me?"

"Pretty much the same thing ye gave yer victims," he said. "I do enjoy irony. Few things are finer at my age. Ye should never accept gifts from strangers, do ye not know?"

She fell to her knees, clutching at her stomach and groaning. "Why... why report me to my bosses, if... if..."

"If I were just gunna kill ye all along?" He shrugged. "Justice for the victim's families, of course. They deserve to know the wee gobshite that killed their kin. Ye might be dead, but at least Netflix can make a decent documentary about ye now." He shook his head and muttered. "The guys that run that place are a bag of shits, but they spin a decent yarn, ye can't deny."

"H-help me." She reached out to him. "Please."

"Too late for that. We're already going down." Lucas reattached the cables inside the console and the buttons blinked back to life. He pressed the button for the ground floor and the lift descended.

"Y-you won't get away with this." Lucy clawed at his ankle, green spittle on her lips. "You'll go to prison. Please, just help me."

"I spent a millennium ruling over the king of prisons. There's nowt ye can say to me, lass. In fact, it's ye what should be afraid. Right now, yer heart is slowly stopping in yer chest. When these doors open, ye'll be gone, and all I have to do is tell them ye keeled over suddenly and that there were nowt I could do. When the ambulance arrives, I'll slip away and..." He pointed up at the camera in the corner. "When they try to track me down, they'll see nothing except a poorly lass talking to herself before dropping down dead like a louse-infested pig. Sure, the whole ordeal will confuse them, but they'll have no evidence to show I was ever here."

"M-my family..."

"Hate your guts, lass. You'll be dead, and they'll be glad. Toxic, they call you. And what about your victims? They all had families, people who loved them. Not you, though? Yer nowt, but rotting meat and fetid air. Hell is full of souls just like you."

She slumped down on her face, straining in agony as her heart froze in her chest. A last gasp escaped her lips, forming half a word. "*Plea...*"

The lift doors opened.

Lucas stepped away from Lucy's dead body and exited into the hospital's foyer. "See ye in Hell, lass. Keep a seat warm for me, eh?"

Nobody tried to stop him as he exited the building and disappeared.

Lucy made the news one week later.

Porridge Poisoner, responsible for up to fifty-four hospital deaths, died of karmic heart condition, coroner says. Mysterious witness still unidentified.

THE MONKEY

Cecily knew right away that she'd slept funny. As soon as she turned her head to check her alarm clock, she grunted in pain as lightning jolted down one side of her neck.

"Ah! Please, God, just end it. Kill me now."

It was an overreaction, for sure, but not entirely facetious.

She peeled back her duvet and pivoted her hips until her socked feet touched the beige carpet. Unable to move her neck—what a perfect start to the frikkin day.

Ready to do it all over again, Cess?

What choice do I have?

The night had been cold, so Cecily was still in her pyjamas. It was Saturday, her day off from the car supermarket, so there was no need to get dressed today. What would be the point? She had no plans besides making it through to another bedtime intact. Physically, at least, if not emotionally.

In the kitchen, she flicked on the kettle and dropped a spoonful of instant coffee into her battered Garfield mug. Caffeine—her last remaining vice. Along with cake.

Swapping one addiction for another. And around we go.

Coffee in hand, she sank into the off-white, worn leather sofa in her citrus-scented living room and closed her eyes.

To an outsider, her flat was neat and orderly, but the truth lay close beneath the surface. Stuffed drawers and bulging cupboards hid unattended clutter—a metaphor for her own life; her messiness always close to spilling out.

But I'm doing okay. Three months sober. I should be proud.

She placed her coffee mug on the side table next to the sofa and rubbed at her itchy, morning eyes. Mike's butt groove still scarred the other cushion, but he hadn't sat there for six months, at least. He'd left a few scars on her, too.

Cecily didn't know if she actually missed him, or if her mind was merely torturing her. It was too soon to trust her own feelings about the subject, because they changed so often it left her dizzy.

As she reached to pick up her coffee, again she noticed her hand was shaking. By now, the physical symptoms of alcohol withdrawal had long passed, but she still didn't feel right in herself. A constant quivering plagued her tummy, and often, whenever she got up from sitting, her head spun.

And don't even get me started on the constipation. Never thought my greatest battle each day would be with my own arsehole.

The morning news ended, and the daytime brain rot schedule was about to begin.

Only so many antique-appraising, house buying, and quiz shows you could watch without wanting to throw yourself out of a window.

Or take a drink.

Unsettled, Cecily took herself over to the living room's single window, sipping her coffee and taking in the view outside her building. To the right was Mollins Car Park, and a noisy *Tesco Express* that opened at the crack of dawn. The tarmac was more of a rockery nowadays than a flat surface, but the supermarket was always busy. She often liked to people-watch in the evenings, counting the strangers carrying crates of beer or bags full of bottled wine. Then there were those she spied with giant chocolate bars, grab bags of crisps, and tubs of ice cream. Seemed like everybody had a weakness for something.

To the left, Amberside park stretched off for half a mile, eventually meeting the edge of the next housing estate. It was just a field, really—mowed by the council twice a year and left to overgrow for the rest. Kids liked to play football on it most afternoons, and adults walked their dogs in the evenings. Sometimes, Cecily strolled around the perimeter to calm down, whenever her heart felt like it was beating a little too fast or her head was a little too disquieted.

She hadn't had a panic attack in months, but she lived in anticipation of the next one.

Maybe I should call Toni. We could go for lunch, catch up.

No, she'll have already made plans. It's too short notice.

Not so long ago, Cecily had feared she would never speak with her best friend ever again, but two weeks ago she'd sent Toni a text and had been shocked—as well as anxious—to receive a reply. It had been a wary—almost icy—response, but Toni had sounded truly happy when Cecily reported she hadn't had a drink in almost ninety-days.

But that doesn't erase me kissing Steve behind her back.

Fuck, what was I thinking? I ruined three separate relationships in one fell swoop.

The view outside her window was bleak and uninspiring today, but the sight of a blue sky lifted her mood slightly. Spring was on its way.

She took a deep breath, focusing on the smooth flow of oxygen filling her lungs. Slowly, she was finding herself able to grasp brief moments, here and there, where she could feel her soul moving back into place. *Realigning.*

Finding peace.

She decided not to text Toni. It was too soon. Her friend needed space.

Despite it being her day off, Cecily decided to fill her morning with a little work admin. It would at least make her feel productive.

She opened up her laptop and checked her emails. There was nothing much of interest—mostly sales invoices and colleagues messaging her over nothing—but then she spotted a message referenced in all CAPS.

AGAIN CECILY!

"Shit!" She opened the email from her boss, Jeff, and immediately groaned. She'd done it again; had failed to process a finance application for a customer. The end of the month had now passed, meaning the sale hadn't contributed towards their store bonus, and the customer was upset by the delay.

She'd done the same thing last month.

I'm gonna lose my job. Jeff already has me on a last warning.

Being sober was supposed to change things. No more hangovers or skiving off to catch up on sleep. But she was still screwing up. Painfully sober and no better than before.

What the hell? Why am I even putting myself through all this?

She emailed back with the most profuse apology she could muster, before sitting in silence for several minutes, feeling utterly sick to her stomach.

Eventually, she decided to take a walk. Pyjama day was cancelled; she needed distraction to keep herself from spiralling.

When she went and opened her bedroom's wardrobe, she found her clothes in disarray, piled up on the floor as if she had torn them from the hanger in some kind of rage. A strip of wallpaper at the back was torn and sagging.

What the hell happened in here?

As Cecily tried to figure things out, she looked towards the corner of the wardrobe and spotted the most unexpected of things.

"Fuck me sideways!"

———

THAT THERE WAS a monkey in her wardrobe should have sent Cecily running out of her flat and screaming for help...

And yet she merely blinked, and then blinked again. This couldn't be real.

I am not looking at a frikkin monkey right now.

But it *was* a frikkin monkey. The longer she stared at it, the surer she became. A tiny little white-faced monkey in her wardrobe, staring back at her with big expressive eyes.

A cappuccino monkey? No, that's not it.

Wait, why am I even trying to identify what species it is? What the hell is it doing in my wardrobe?

The monkey—proving it was real and not some kind of prank left behind by Mike—suddenly hopped up in the air and spun around. Something flung from its body and hit Cecily in the leg.

She looked down and let out a groan. Light brown monkey-shit caked her right shin. "Ew, you disgusting little..." She staggered backwards and stumbled bum-first onto her bed before immediately bouncing back up again.

The monkey hop-ran out of the wardrobe and leapt up onto the bedside table, knocking over a half-empty-glass of water and soaking the rug. Then it ran across her pillows, leaving shitty paw prints on the clean white fabric.

"Stop!" she yelled. "Stop making a mess!"

She hurried out of the bedroom and raced into the lounge, not knowing what else to do. The monkey remained behind, shrieking and bleating. She turned back to the door.

"Stay here. Just... stay here." She closed the bedroom door and hurried across the lounge into the hallway.

Unlocking the front door, she bolted out onto the landing and looked left and right. She shared the floor with two other flats, but she only knew Brandon, who lived opposite. She banged on his chipped green door and called his name. From the little she knew, he was an unemployed dosser who barely went outside.

The door opened almost immediately and Brandon's round, unshaven face glared out at her. "Cess? What's wrong?"

"There's a monkey in my flat."

He smirked. "The fuck?"

She put her hands on top of her head and paced back and forth. "Look, I know it sounds crazy, but I'm not even kidding. There's a little monkey in my flat wrecking the place. Come help me get it out."

"Girl, you're high. Go sleep it off."

"I'm not high! I don't even do drugs."

Just a shit load of booze.

No, not anymore.

"Well, maybe you should start. You can come in and share a smoke if you want?"

She took a deep breath and looked him in the eye, her shoulders straight as she tried to convey that she was entirely fucking lucid and that she intended to stay that way. "I need your help."

He frowned, his slight grin turning upside down. "You're serious? There's a monkey in your flat?"

"Yes! Look, there's shit on my leg."

He looked down and then wrinkled his nose. "That's grim."

"Just come and see it for yourself, okay?"

"Yeah, alright." Brandon shook his head and chuckled. Rather than head off to put on shoes or grab keys, he simply stepped out onto the concrete landing barefoot and left his door hanging open behind him. Without a word, he walked over to Cecily's door and waited beside it with his hairy arms folded.

Cecily grunted as she joined him. "You'll see. I'm not crazy. Or high. I'm clean and sober."

"Good for you. Let's just do this quick, okay? The F1's about to come on."

"The what?"

"Formula One? The motor ra– Never mind."

She opened the door and allowed him inside. A flash of anxiety crossed his face as she forced him to go first. Still, being a typical man, he strode down the hallway with his chest puffed out.

The flat was silent.

"Where is it?" Brandon asked, standing in the lounge and looking around with his fists clenched.

"My bedroom."

He turned and wiggled his eyebrows at her. "You want me to go see a monkey in your bedroom? Right..."

She shoved him in the back. "What does that even mean? Just be a decent guy and help me."

"What's in it for me?"

"I won't turn into a mad bitch from across the hall who makes your life a living hell."

"Fair enough."

They turned to face the bedroom. The door was ajar, her unmade bed visible inside.

"I-I closed the door when I left," she said.

"Okay. Well, I don't see anything. Smells pretty bad though."

Cecily leaned sideways and peered through the gap. "M-maybe it's gone back inside the wardrobe. That's where I found it."

"Uh-huh." Brandon was clearly dubious again, but his hands were bunched into fists and he stood on the balls of his feet like he was ready to run.

"Go on, then," Cecily urged. "Go look inside."

"Just go in and catch a monkey, yeah? Like it's the most normal thing in the world? How did the thing even get in your flat?"

"I have no idea. It must have come through the window last night or something. It looks like somebody's pet."

"Yeah, maybe. Okay, right, here goes. Ready? I'm gonna grab your duvet and try to trap it. Sound like a plan?"

She nodded enthusiastically, glad he was taking charge. Until now, it seemed he would be pretty clueless about what to do.

Brandon crossed the threshold into the bedroom and leapt to the foot of her bed. He scooped up the duvet and turned towards the wardrobe, holding it out like a net.

"Where is it?" he yelled. "Where is it?"

"I don't know. I don't know." Spurred into action by his panicked tone, Cecily leapt up beside him and readied herself to usher the monkey into their trap.

But the monkey wasn't there.

She thought for a moment that the animal might have been hiding beneath the messy pile of clothes inside the wardrobe, but it was too shallow to hide a creature that big. The wallpaper at the back had been torn and ripped even more, barely holding onto the wall.

"There's nothing here," Brandon said, tossing the duvet back down on the mattress. "Are you messing with me or what?"

"No, I swear. I..." Scanning every corner of her cramped bedroom. The double divan filled most of the room but sat too low to hide a monkey. She only had one bedside table. On the other side of the bed was a small, empty carpet space between the divan and the wall. Then there was the wardrobe.

Empty. It's totally empty except for my clothes on the floor.

Brandon was staring at her dirty pillows, then he turned to face her. "You been drinking, Cess? You get kind of crazy when you—"

"No." She wanted to punch him in the arm, but she restrained herself. Taking a breath, she shook her head calmly. "I haven't had a drink in three-months, Bran."

"Then, maybe you should go have one." He turned and strode out of her bedroom. "Because you're hallucinating monkeys."

"It was here." She chased after him, catching up to him in the lounge. "I swear."

He stopped and looked at her. "Look, Cess. I don't know you that well, but from what I do know, you're a little... unpredictable."

"What? What does that mean?"

"I used to hear you and Mike arguing at all hours, and the empty bottles in the bin on collection day. You got issues, girl. It's alright, we all do, but get help, yeah? My cousin's bipolar."

She shoved him into the hallway, now wanting him gone. "You don't know anything about me. Don't act like you're better than me. There was a... there was a..."

He smirked, walking backwards. "Yeah, a monkey in your flat. Right. Okay."

"Just fucking go!"

"Come get me if you see it again."

Chuckling, he headed for the door.

"I'll come get anyone but you. Thanks for nothing."

"Charming. You try to help a neighbour."

Cecily slammed the door behind him and turned around to face her flat. Now that she was alone again, she began to consider if Brandon's mockery was warranted.

Maybe I do need help.

I'm seeing monkeys that aren't there.

———

CECILY MADE herself go for that walk, where she had found herself, strangely, longing for a dog. She passed by an all manner of people exercising their various and assorted hounds, and their wagging tails and lolling tongues made her imagine what it might be like having a loyal companion of her own. With Mike gone, she was lonely. But the last thing she needed right now was another boyfriend, so perhaps a dog was the answer, the fresh start she needed.

But I've never owned a dog. What if it hates me?

Could a dog hate a person? Other than house training and walking them, what else was there to do?

The added stress might be more than she could handle right now, however, so she put it out of her mind.

But maybe...

It could be a reward, she told herself, a lightbulb going off. She could set herself a target of six months sober and get herself a cocker spaniel puppy once she made it. They seemed cute and friendly. She would certainly be able to afford a pedigree puppy after all the money she was saving on wine.

One of the few good things about being sober.

She continued to mull it over in front of the television, and then later over a pepperoni pizza she had ordered from *Valentinos* down the road. It was greasy, cheap food, but it hit the spot. Then she went to sleep, falling into a dream easily.

She awoke at 4AM with a dry mouth and a headache. For a moment, she thought she was hungover—and her heart started pounding against her ribs—but then she pushed aside the cobwebs and remembered she hadn't had a drop last night. She was okay. She hadn't failed.

I just feel like regular old shit.

It was a lonely time to be up and about, and the next few hours made her feel like the only human being on earth.

The car site was closed on a Sundays, so this was her second day off. Most of her similar-aged colleagues worked most Saturdays and partied afterwards, but Cecily had always hated working weekends. They were the days for self and family. Her dad had always worked the weekends when she was a kid, and she had always hated it. One day, she might have kids, so she didn't want to get into the habit of working them either. It meant missing out on the biggest day for commission, but Cecily earned enough money to get by without it.

She got up and went into the kitchen, switching on the kettle to make a coffee. For a moment, she didn't even see the monkey sitting on the counter. The sun was yet to fully rise and the light coming from the kick-board LEDs was too weak to dispel the darkness. All she saw at first was an indistinct grey blob.

Then it moved.

"Shit!" Cecily leapt back from the counter and smashed her shoulder against the doorframe. The pain, however, was a distant echo as her consciousness leapt forwards and focused on the fact that a bloody monkey was in her kitchen.

I knew it. I knew it was real.

Something crashed against the floor tiles. Cecily realised it was her *Garfield* coffee mug. It shattered into pieces at her bare feet.

"You little shit. Get out of here. Shoo!"

She took a swipe at the monkey, but it leapt over her arm and right past her face. She heard it come down behind her on the tiles. As she turned, it bolted out into the hallway.

The first thing she did was open the front door to her flat, hoping the critter would see a chance to flee. But it went in the other direction and headed into the living room.

"No, no. Come back here. Get out of my flat."

She raced after the hopping monkey, begging for it to get out, but it leapt up onto the sofa and started digging and scratching at the leather. The sofa was, by no means, in good condition, but there were a couple more years left in it providing it didn't get mauled by a god damn capuchin monkey.

Capuchin! That's it.

"Get out of here, monkey! You don't want to mess with me. I'm bigger and stronger than you."

The monkey leapt up onto the TV cabinet and stared at her. In the dim morning light, its eyes sparkled. Its white face was almost ghostly.

Seeing the animal calm prompted Cecily to pause. She stayed where she was and talked quietly and soothingly. "Have you been here all night? Who's your owner? Because it's not me. Life's hard enough without a monkey to worry about."

The monkey squatted down into a small ball, suddenly looking like something that couldn't possibly be a problem. Cute. Defenceless. Quiet.

Cecily slowly pointed a finger at it. "You just behave, okay? I'm in control here. This is my home. You're not allowed to be here, so I'm going to get somebody to come get you. Someone nice who knows how to deal with animals like you."

The monkey let out a sigh, almost like it was listening to her. Of course, there was no way it could understand what she was saying, but it at least seemed to react to her voice. She became even more certain that this was somebody's pet.

I can't just toss it out. If it gets hit by a car or attacked by a dog, its owner will be devastated.

Its owner who can't even keep track of the bloody thing.

She considered fetching Brandon again, but she knew he wouldn't be awake at this time, and even if she beat at his door, he would probably refuse to wake up. Also, he had been an arsehole yesterday, and she was still mad at him for not believing her.

The monkey hid from him. But how?

"I'm going to call animal services," she said and then headed for the bedroom to grab her mobile. "Just stay there."

Her phone was on the side table, and she groaned when she realised that she'd forgotten to put it on charge. The battery was at 4%.

Huffing, she plugged in her charging cable and left it to get a little more juice. Ten minutes would be enough. She could make a call with it plugged in, of course, but she didn't want to leave the monkey unattended.

Back in the living room, the animal thankfully hadn't moved. That was good, but how long could she rely on it to stay that way? It was only a matter of time before it started acting up again.

So she sat there on the sofa watching it, barely daring to move. Her instinct was to switch on the television and fill the deep silence in the room, but that would likely startle the monkey and reignite the havoc.

Best that she just sit there a few moments longer and wait for her phone to charge.

She made it about five minutes, staring at the monkey and the monkey starting back at her, before she had to go check her battery. She decided 11% would be enough. She took it into the doorway of her bedroom, watching the monkey as it seemed to take a nap.

A quick Google search brought up the number for an animal control service in the next town over, so she dialled the number and waited. Pressing option one to report a dangerous animal on the loose, she let out a laugh at her predicament. She wasn't sure the monkey actually *was* dangerous, but it wasn't no cat stuck up a tree, that was for sure.

Someone answered her call, a woman named Judy. She wasn't particularly polite, but who would be at 5.30AM? She did liven up, however, once she heard Cecily's complaint.

"You have a capuchin monkey on your property? And it's not yours?"

"No, it's not mine! It's clearly someone's pet, but it's got inside my flat."

"It's highly dangerous to own a primate as a pet, ma'am."

Cecily rolled her eyes and sneered. "Okay. Well, it ain't mine, like I said, so can you help me or not?"

"Of course. I'll need your address and telephone number, and then I can send an agent right out to you."

"Make sure it's your best monkey-wrangler, okay?"

"All of our personnel are qualified, ma'am."

Cecily rolled her eyes again, wishing she had come through to a plucky morning person, or at least someone with half-a-sense-of-humour.

She gave her information and the operator promised someone would be with her within the hour. In the meantime, Cecily should place a barrier between herself and the monkey, ideally locking herself in a separate room.

No problem. I'll just let the monkey have my flat to itself, shall I?

Cecily closed the bedroom door and sat down on the bed. Slowly, the darkness lifted as the sky outside turned from dark blue to pastel.

It reminded her she needed to get blackout curtains, as now that she wasn't passing out drunk each night, the rising of the dawn often woke her. Whenever that happened, she spent the rest of the day under a fog. Selling cars was hard enough, but doing it half asleep was even tougher.

Hybrids can deliver up to eighty miles to the gallon. If you have solar panels and a home charger, then running a Tesla can almost work out free. Toyotas might not be the sexiest cars on the road, but nothing is more reliable. Range Rover? Yes, yes, they are fantastic. There's a reason so many rich people drive them!

Yeah, it's called more money than sense. If it doesn't break down on you, then some rotten sod will rob it.

"*Blergh*," she moaned aloud at the thought of work. She had gone straight into sales right from high school, desperate to earn money and be free of her mother. It was never meant to be permanent, but once she had started paying bills and living on her own, escape became impossible. No one was going to help support her while she retrained to do something else. A painful fact of life was that most jobs were boring and unfulfilling. No one loved what they did.

At least no one I ever met.

Best you could do each day was try to snatch a few laughs here and there. And maybe fall in love.

One day, it might happen again.

Mike hadn't been perfect, and them breaking up was for the best, she knew that. As much as he had blamed their constant arguments on her drinking, he had tipped back plenty himself most nights. If she had a problem, then he had enabled it for long enough to own part of the responsibility for it. You couldn't dive off a cliff with someone and then complain when they you got wet.

But I am to blame. I'm not dodging responsibility.

I chose to drink. Until it was no longer my choice at all.

Time passed by slowly, the clock on her phone barely changing.

But eventually, chaos erupted once more.

———

CECILY SPRINTED into the living room just in time to see the TV topple off the stand. She dove to save it—but was too late.

Crash!

Before she could even curse, something clawed at the back of her scalp.

Screaming, she staggered back and forth, slapping at her head as though it were on fire. The monkey shrieked and chattered, digging and clawing harder.

"Get off me! Get off me!"

Blind and panicked, Cecily staggered into the kitchen. She slammed down hard on the tiles, smashing her knees as she sought to escape the vicious creature tearing out her hair. She reached out a hand and yanked open the cupboard beneath the sink, groping in the dark.

Her fingers closed around something heavy and familiar: a bottle. A wine bottle. For a second, Cecily froze.

Of all the things to find right now.

The bottle of wine had been like the body of a loved one hidden beneath her floorboards—a dark whisper, calling out to her at night. For some reason, she had refused to throw it out, and over time it had become some kind of totem—a powerful relic containing all of her willpower and self-determination. If she could abstain from alcohol with a bottle right in her reach, how bad could she be?

And yet, lately, the bottle had been calling out to her more loudly—trying to convince her she was cured. Three-months sober proved she didn't have a problem, and all of the chaos from the past would never happen again. She would make new friends; ones who understood her; and she would find a boyfriend stronger than Mike. She just needed a man who could handle her. No, she didn't have a problem. She was fine.

How good would it feel right now kick back and relax, Cess? It's been a tough week at work, right? You're probably going to get fired.

"Get off my back!"

The monkey leapt away and skittered into the corner by the stainless steel bin she had kept for years.

Cecily clambered to her feet, using the oven handle as support, and kept the wine bottle tucked beneath her armpit. Eyes fixed on the nasty little monkey, she reached up behind herself and switched on the cooker-hood's light.

The monkey's eyes shone white like a demon. But it seemed to have once again calmed down.

Cecily's hands were shaking, the bottle in her left hand growing heavier and heavier. The crisp, golden liquid inside could make all this go away—the pain in her head, the shame in her guts. The loneliness and self-doubt. Fuck, she could probably grab the monkey by the scruff of its neck and toss it out onto the landing with some Dutch courage inside of her.

Her jaw locked, she straightened her shoulders, grabbed the bottle's twist-top in her palm. "Fuck this."

She opened the bottle of wine and held it up in front of her face. Then she turned and poured it down the kitchen sink. It had been stupid to keep it around, but for whatever reason she had done so. Now it was time to say goodbye. No more wine. No more wondering if she could ever go back. If she had been drunk right now, who knows what might have happened? No way could she deal with a nasty little monkey while pissed out of her head.

She dumped the empty bottle in the sink, and grimaced at the chemical stench wafting from the drain. Then she turned around and pointed a finger. "Now look here you little shit..."

Huh?

Cecily looked left and right, left and right, then went and peered into the hallway. The sun had risen outside and the gloom in the living room was gone, but there was no sign of the monkey. Once again, it had gone into hiding.

A knock sounded at the front door. "Animal Services."

Cecily groaned. "Great. How am I gonna explain this?"

———

TONI COVERED her mouth and giggle. "So you had Animal Services here because you thought you had a monkey in your flat?"

Cecily laughed, but it stuck a little in her throat. "I *had* a monkey in my flat. I swear."

Toni leaned over the new Ikea coffee table they'd just finished putting together and sipped her coffee. "Maybe it was a squirrel. Or maybe you're just... still adjusting to, you know, to everything."

"Yeah," Cecily said quietly. "Maybe."

The room was warm, cluttered with half-assembled furniture and takeout wrappers. It smelled of coffee and new beginnings. For a moment, Cecily closed her eyes and simply breathed it in.

"You do look better," Toni said with a smile. "You look like... like you again. How long again?"

"Six months." Cecily tucked her hands between her knees and the sofa. "Feels longer though. Feels like I've lived a hundred different versions of myself in that time. Trying to find peace. Trying to find out who the hell I even am anymore."

"You still beat yourself up too much, Cess."

"Maybe. But beating myself up has kept me alive." Cecily smiled, but it was a small thing, something she barely dared to do in front of the friend she had hurt so badly. "I just wish... I could forget some of the things I did. To you. To everyone. They're like ghosts inside my head."

Toni shrugged, looking older than Cecily remembered. "You can't forget, because that would be letting you off the hook. But it means you know what you did was bad, and the fact you are suffering for it means you don't have to keep beating yourself up even more."

In the corner, Max—her cocker spaniel puppy—slept curled up in a patch of sunlight on the carpet, his paws twitching as he dreamt of whatever dogs do. Right beside him, invisible to all but her, Cecily's monkey lay curled up too. It was smaller now, and far quieter, but not gone. Never gone.

"I forgive you, you know. I wouldn't be here otherwise." Toni asked, following her gaze to the sleeping puppy. "You're trying to be better and I can see that."

Cecily gave another weak smile, but this time it came a little more confidently. "I can't forget the things I'm done or get rid of my demons, but maybe I can learn to live with them. That's the plan anyway."

Toni reached out her hand, and Cecily took hold of it firmly, taking a moment to bask in the feel of someone else's skin against her. A human connection she needed so badly after the last six months. She grinned at her friend and breathed in deeply, ignoring the anxious thrum inside of her head.

She would never be perfect. Never fully healed.

She looked over at her monkey.

But I got this.

THE MAN WHO FOLLOWED ME THROUGH A FIELD IN CONSETT

I always thought it 'were grim oop north,' but it turns out I was wrong. It's beautiful. Like, in a way I didn't even know England *could* be.

We drove all the way from Bristol. Mile by mile, the world opened up wider and wider. The sky was endless, and the hills stretched so far that they could have hidden sleeping gods. I had thought I knew nature, but I didn't.

I thought I knew a lot of things.

It was supposed to be a relaxing getaway with my boyfriend, Reece, but it turned into the worst day of my life. The beauty of the countryside that day only makes my nightmares more surreal.

When the police first interviewed me, they said 'start at the beginning,' but it's hard to latch on to the exact moment when I realised I was in deep shit. It happened gradually, you know? Like my mind was at war with itself, and I had to let go of all my misconceptions before I could truly accept that the horror was real.

Bad things only happened to stupid people who put themselves in danger right? Not me—not smart, dependable Jess.

I didn't think I was doing anything wrong, standing in an empty field with my boyfriend. Where was the danger in that?

I remember Reece shaking his head, a bemused grin on his face as he stared off into the distance. "This is just... wow!"

I understood how he felt. It was breathtaking in every direction. And the air. Wow, the air felt crisper. Purer.

We had rented a little stone cottage in a place called Cornsay, a village so high up we were face-to-face with multiple wind turbines rising from the valleys below. An escape from our busy city lives. A break from studying.

My name is Jess and back then—just a year ago—I was studying Creative Writing and English at Bristol. I wanted—still want—to become a writer. Reece was studying Finance. He wanted to be rich. I think, one day, he might've been. If only he'd got the chance to be brilliant.

This was our first trip together. We wanted to breathe fresh air and go hiking along the Durham coast, collecting sea glass in Seaham and eating fish and chips in Whitley Bay. So far, we had done none of that. It was our first day, and we had stopped at a vast tract of land just past a sleepy little place named Tow Law.

I leaned against Reece, my head on his shoulder, and enjoyed the view for what felt like hours, a watercolour painting come to life. "I think I could move up here forever," I said, and I had truly meant it in that serene, perfect moment.

Reece chuckled. "You would get bored. What would you do without Nando's and a bar to serve you cocktails?"

"Newcastle's right up the road. I honestly like it here. It's not what I expected at all."

"You mean you expected everywhere to be covered in coal dust and the locals to be carrying knives carved from human bones?"

"What? No! Don't make out like I'm... I dunno. What is the *ism* I'm looking for? It's not racism."

He squeezed me, making me feel warm. "We'll just call you a general bigot, cover all the bases, yeah?"

I elbowed him gently in the ribs. "All right, I admit I thought it would be a bit rundown, but it's not that at all. That little village with all the independent shops; it was amazing."

"Is this what we've been dreading?" Reece asked, turning me around to face him. He had a serious expression on his face that filled me with dread. "Is this what is gonna break us? I knew things were going too well."

I frowned, my tummy aflutter. "What are you talking about?"

"You're going to become a bumpkin, aren't you? You're gonna get a flat cap and a red setter and live up here in some dusty old house built by Norman the Conqueror."

"Norman the..." I shook my head and giggled. "And what if I do? You wouldn't come with me? You could get a pipe and slippers."

"I'd rather have a property portfolio in London." He raised a tawny eyebrow. "There's plenty of money around here—we both saw it—but the power is still down south. Always will be."

"What power? Anyway, I'm just enjoying myself and having a little fantasy. Lighten up. You're probably right about it being too rural, though."

"Plus the weather." He pointed into the distance, where a thick mist hung over the horizon. It was another thing I'd never truly seen before. Up in the rolling green hills, you could *see* the weather. When the sun shone, it felt like the world was glowing. When it rained, you could see the water in the air before it reached you.

You could also see anything that moved for miles.

I pointed and gasped. "Oh my god, look!"

"Oh, wow!" Reece grinned. He was a massive animal lover. We both were. "Is that a pheasant or a grouse?"

"I think that's a grouse. Like that bird on the whisky bottles, right?" She adjusted her stance. "But I was pointing over there, babe."

Reece turned his head and saw the deer thirty metres away, a tiny little thing no bigger than a spaniel. It saw us, too, but didn't panic. It just stood there, moving only slightly. Then the slender fawn bounded off into the hedges.

"Oh my god. That was amazing." Reece said, with the cutest look on his face. "It didn't seem bothered by us at all."

"Probably because it knows you wouldn't hurt a fly," I said. "You know you're too soft to make it in the big city with all those investment bankers and lawyers?"

He wrapped his arm around her and chuckled. "Then I guess you'll have to look after me forever."

"I'm just kidding," she said, letting out a slight shiver. "You're going to be successful no matter what you do, Reece. And you won't need to be an arsehole about it."

"Good to know, because the dicks screw the arseholes and the arseholes shit all over the dicks."

I took a moment and then grimaced. "That's gross."

"Yeah, it kinda was. Sorry. Anyway, shall we head back to the car? *If* we can find it, that is."

"I think we came from over there," I said, pointing to a bunch of trees I couldn't name the species of. Specifically, a tall, thin one with whitish bark different from the thicker trunks around it. It seemed familiar.

"I think so too."

I pulled out my phone and checked the time. "It's getting late. We should find somewhere for dinner on the way back."

"Look somewhere up," Reece told me. "I fancy Thai."

I tried searching for restaurants nearby, but failed. "No signal, babe."

Reece turned a circle, waving an arm at all the nothingness. "Really? You should make a complaint to Vodafone."

"They probably won't care, seeing as I'm with EE."

"Aren't they all the same these days? The phone networks are like a bunch of inbred cousins at this point."

I chuckled at the absurdity. Reece always made me laugh. It'd been a fun six months, moving faster than any relationship I'd ever been in. But there were obstacles in our path, and I worried about them constantly—things such as me being from Maidstone and Reece being from Nottingham. Eventually, our degrees were going to end. What then? Would we both move to London? Did I even want to?

But I was in love.

Our possible ending was less than eighteen months away. It hung over me like the mist on the horizon, making every smile strained and every caress of Reece's fingertips a finite treasure.

Our love was a puppy with cancer. All I could do was pet it and love it and pray that it pulled through.

It terrified me.

"You're thinking." Reece pulled a face. "It's not good when you get that glazed over expression. Last time you went on an hour long rant about Meghan Markle. You threw a stapler."

"Sorry." I snapped back to reality, knowing what he meant about my tendency to wind myself up with intrusive thoughts. He always called me a 'dweller.' "I'm good. Come on, before it rains."

We both turned towards the white tree–and we both stumbled backwards in surprise on the moist, uncut grass.

Reece grabbed my hand, almost protectively. "Oh! I wonder who that is?"

The stranger was clambering over a small rock wall at the far end of the field. He almost fell, but made it back to his feet and then started drifting towards us. He wore a white dress shirt with jeans, which was an odd combination for outdoors. Where the hell had he come from? And why was he covered in mud? Those were my first thoughts, but then I worried we were on his land.

Everyone we had met north of Leeds had been friendly and humorous, but there were miserable people everywhere. Maybe we were trespassing on some grumpy old farmer's land. Was he going to threaten to shoot us if we didn't scram?

"Hello?" I shouted, which makes me cringe now. To have done something so utterly pointless. "Is everything okay?"

The stranger didn't respond. He stumbled towards us, his head lowered, his hands grasping.

Reece moved slightly ahead of me, still reaching back and holding my hand. "Is there a problem, pal?"

Still no reply. That was when I felt the first pangs of unease. Whatever this is, it was all fine, right? Nothing bad was going to happen. *It's just a guy. A stranger coming to talk to us. What's to be afraid of?*

But that unease increased, my tummy fluttered with trapped butterflies, like when I was riding Saw at Thorpe Park or approaching the first drop of the log flume.

And things changed forever in that moment. Suddenly, the vast unending wilderness transformed from comforting to menacing. Reece and I were vulnerable, alone in a place we didn't know. City kids in the wilderness. This was not our home. We hadn't been invited. We didn't know the rules.

The stranger got closer. I could hear him grunting now, which both reassured me and horrified me. Was this stranger in need of help? If so, what the hell was wrong with him? And the mud on his shirt...

It wasn't mud.

"Oi," Reece shouted, putting a hand up. "Hold up, will you? Stop there. Hey, what are you doing? I said stop!"

But the stranger didn't stop. He marched forwards, his legs almost failing him. It was as if he were falling forwards rather than walking.

I took a step back, the long grass making the ground beneath my feet feel untrustworthy. Reece stepped back with me, still holding my hand, and squeezing hard enough that I might have cried out if I wasn't so freaked.

The stranger reached out his fingertips bloody. He opened his mouth. Blood spilled down his chin.

That was when we ran—or more accurately, we turned and jogged, the both of us still too safe in our sheltered reality to consider that we were truly in danger. Not intelligent young city-dwellers like us.

We should've run.

We put some distance between us and the stranger before turning back. I'm not sure what we expected, but I was desperate for the man to shout after us, enraged about some transgression we were blind to. To act in a way that at least made some degree of sense.

But the stranger continued to stagger after us in near silence. I could even hear the wind blowing through the long grass.

So we jogged a little more.

The stranger followed.

"The fuck is wrong with you?" I yelled back, suddenly furious. I had a pretty respectable temper back then, but I lost it in that moment and never got it back again. During the last year, I've lost count of the amount of times I've flown off the handle because of this uncontrollable, terrified rage now implanted inside me. One more incident and I'll probably be kicked off my course—not that I'm going to pass anyway. I'll likely have to resit the entire year.

Grief is one hell of a spanner.

I'm not sure how long Reece and I jogged for, but the stranger never gave up his pursuit. Eventually, we were huffing and puffing and had put enough distance between ourselves that our pursuer was a tiny sprite on the horizon.

But when we stopped to take a rest, the sprite got bigger, shambling ever closer.

"He must be on drugs," Reece said, huffing and grabbing at his ribs.

I shook my head. "No. He's a fucking zombie."

I'll never forget that we both laughed at that moment. It's something that should've been impossible, but with Reece next to me, things weren't yet at their absolute worst.

That came shortly after.

"This is messed up," Reece said, one eye on the stranger getting closer. "I promise we're getting out of this. I'll kick this guy's ass if I have to."

"You're not a fighter, Reece." I said it somewhat harshly I realise now. It hurt his pride.

"Just because I've never been in a fight doesn't mean I can't stick up for myself, Jess."

I nodded but gave no reply. I wish I had.

We pushed through some hedges, a grim silence followed us. We were exhausted now and freaked out, but more than anything we were just utterly out of answers. The situation was insane, and I just kept thinking, 'when does this end?' When would we return to a reality where things made sense again? Why was this horrible man following us, and what were we supposed to do about it? Just keep jogging forever, taking rests whenever we could, until we found civilisation again?

God, I missed civilisation.

Again, the vastness of the countryside became oppressive. There were no roads in sight, no houses or villages. The only man-made structures I could see were the distant wind turbines turning languidly in the distance. The endless fields of yellows, greens, and browns were like a patchwork blanket, but the only living thing ensconced within them were the odd gathering of white splotches. Sheep wouldn't help us.

Nothing could help us.

I embraced Reece then, not because I feared I might lose him—even then I was still misguided by own inherent feeling of safety—but because I wanted a moment of peace in his arms. I closed my eyes and blanked my mind. For a moment, everything was normal again.

It didn't last more than a few minutes.

"Come on," he eventually said. "We have to keep moving."

But we were beat. Neither of us were athletes, and the uneven ground was turning my calves to stone. Both my shins felt like they might snap at any moment. We collapsed against a thick trunk of an oak tree and shared a look of despair. A look that said: 'We can't go on.'

The stranger was about thirty metres away, shambling quickly despite barely being able to stay upright.

Reece pushed himself away from the tree.

I reached out and grabbed his arm—the last time I would ever touch him. "Babe?"

"I've had enough of this."

And so had I. I let him go.

Despite being a strong-willed, independent woman, I stood back and allowed Reece to defend me. I just wanted this madness to be over, whatever the consequences.

"What is your fucking problem, you psycho?" I had never heard Reece be so aggressive, but I found it reassuring. Maybe he did know how to handle himself when necessary. "Do you want me to knock your block off or something?"

The stranger picked up speed, closing the distance between them. He let out a moan. Pained. Hungry.

I saw Reece clench his fists.

"Last warning, mate. Fuck off, right now or I'm gonna beat the shit out of you."

The stranger came right at him.

Reece swung his fist awkwardly, but he hit the target. His knuckles *thunked* against the side of the man's jaw and knocked it sideways. Blood and teeth spilled down his white, bloodstained shirt.

That was when I knew it was over.

Despite the firm blow to his jaw, the stranger didn't hesitate. He grabbed Reece's face with both hands and gouged out his eyes with his thumbs.

Hearing my boyfriend's squeals was the worst sound I've ever heard. Something I can't even describe to you. Like his soul was leaking out through his mouth. Pain and misery and fear mixed into a cocktail so thick it could choke you.

I froze.

Maybe I should have done something, but what? Reece's eyes were hanging down on his cheeks, and the stranger had his dirty thumbs buried in the sockets. Can a person survive that?

The answer is obvious now.

Even with several missing teeth, the fucking monster bit into Reece's windpipe and crushed it like a dog's chew toy. The only mercy was that it halted Reece's screams and turned them into barely audible whimpers.

I ran.

For as long as I could.

It was almost night by the time I collapsed in the middle of a yellow field. The flowers or crops that grew there scratched at my arms and made me itch, but I didn't care. I lay down on my back, stoney earth digging into my back, and hoped I had finally put enough distance between me and the psychopath who had just killed my boyfriend to be safe.

Reece.

I was in the middle of nowhere. I hadn't even known it was possible to get lost in England. To me, rural used to mean a few farms and a garden centre between towns, or a stretch of countryside where rich people lived.

I fell asleep.

By the time I opened my eyes again, darkness had arrived. The moon shone with a supernatural aura, bigger and brighter than any I'd seen before. If it hadn't been so bright and clear, I wouldn't have seen a thing. The darkness beneath the trees was so thick you could reach out and touch it.

At some point, I remember screaming at the top of my lungs.

The scuffle of dragging feet. Soft, hungry moans.

I'm not sure how much time had passed, nor did I know how the stranger had found me again, but he had. There were a dozen different directions he could have gone in. I was a needle in a very large haystack, but he was about to seize the needle.

He reached out to grab me.

It seemed to take forever to get to my feet.

Everything felt heavy. My legs ached.

I made it up just in time. The stranger's fingertips snatched at my jumper and almost grabbed hold of me.

Then I was stumbling through an endless grey sea, thorns and bristles tearing at my clothes and biting my hands as I tripped and trudged my way through an overgrown field. The stranger followed in my wake, moving easily through the trampled pathways I was furrowing for him.

My legs grew numb as they fought against the undergrowth. The moaning behind me grew louder. I imagined hands reaching out for the back of my neck.

Seconds seemed like hours. I just wanted this hell to be over.

Every inch was agony. My lungs cried out in tandem with the pulsating ache in my legs. It was like moving underwater.

But then I burst free of the ocean.

I erupted out of the field and immediately picked up speed.

Lights flickered ahead—a lighthouse beckoning me to safety.

Fumbling hands caught the bottom of my jumper.

The sudden jolt caused my legs to give out. I fell.

I knew I was dead.

My screams were almost immediately cut off as the stranger dropped on top of me. His hands went to my neck. His moaning and panting made me wonder if he was going to do terrible things to me. To my body.

That gave me a last burst of energy.

No stranger was going to do this to me. I didn't deserve it. I wouldn't be a victim.

I managed to turn onto my back and throw up my arms, just in time to grab the psychopath by the throat and keep him from biting me. His broken teeth snapped together with a *clack*, and bloody saliva leaked all over my face. I wondered if any of the blood had belonged to Reece.

Reece.

"Fuck off!" I yelled. "Just fucking die, you piece of shit!"

"He's already dead, ma'am."

I tried to look up, but from on my back, I could see nothing but the horrible, blood-stained man on top of me. Then his head exploded.

Chunks of *god-knows-what* hit me in the face, making me blink and splutter and choke. Then I squealed and moaned out for help.

Another stranger was there beside me, and I was pretty sure they had just saved me. When the man on top of me crumpled sideways without a head, I was sure of it.

I pushed the corpse aside and scrambled away in the grass, too exhausted to get up. I smelled smoke in the air, as well as foul odours that must have come from the corpse—and me, because I had wet myself.

"Did he bite ye?"

I looked up and over at an old man standing inside the rim of light given off by the windows of a small house. A smoking shotgun lay folded across his arm. He was wearing a flat cap and wellington boots.

"W-what?"

"Did he take a bit of ye?"

I shook my head. "No. No. I... I..."

He reached out a hand and helped me up. "Let's get you inside, little miss. The wife will put the kettle on. You're okay. Chin up."

"I... I..."

He nodded at me, a compassionate but firm glint in his eyes. "Come now. We'll catch our deaths out here."

I hadn't even realised I was cold, but I was shivering and soaked with blood and sweat. My pissed-soaked legs were like ice. "I don't understand. My boyfriend... He... W-why did this happen?"

My rescuer let out a long, tired sigh. "One thing you have to watch out for oop north: all the bloody zombies."

I said nothing else after that. Not until the police came by an hour later to take me to a hospital in Durham, by which time the farmer who had saved me burned the headless body outside on his compost heap.

"That was one year ago today, Dr Matthews, and six months since my parents forced me to speak to you every week. You've been begging me to open up about what really happened in the northeast, thinking I would admit to killing Reece, but I didn't! You want to know what happened? Well, the answer is a frickin' zombie ate my boyfriend. Do you believe me? Huh? Answer me, Dr Matthews. TELL ME YOU BELIEVE ME!"

RECORDING TERMINATED AT 16:03.

CASSIE

Sunday

"Hip-hip-hooray! Come on sweetheart, blow out the candles." Susanne put a hand on her daughter's back as she sat at the coffee table in the lounge. The cake in front of her was a sponge covered in pink frosting. Susanne had made it for her daughter herself.

Cassie rolled her eyes but couldn't keep from beaming as her family stood around her—cousins Jess and Mikey, Auntie Danielle and Uncle David. Also, her father, Lee. No one had invited him, but he had a track record of turning up whenever it pleased him.

"This is so lame," said Cassie, still smiling as she pulled back her blonde hair and leaned forward to blow out the fourteen candles. It took three attempts—and by the final blow it seemed personal—but she eventually managed it. Satisfied, she collapsed back in her chair and adjusted the white D&G t-shirt she was wearing over ripped jeans. Apparently 'scruffy' was the fashion of the day. The last time Susanne had been fashionable, *Blur* topped the charts.

Lee shook his head and smiled, flashing the gold crown on the left side of his mouth. He'd started shaving his head right down to the scalp after the divorce, something that made him look even more like a thug. "I can't believe you're fourteen," he said. "My little lamb."

"Dad! Don't call me that."

He put a hand over his mouth and feigned abashment. "Sorry. I forgot you're too cool for nicknames now that you're an adult."

"She's *not* an adult," said Susanne, knowing their daughter still snuggled a stuffed Elmo every night and couldn't watch a horror film without screaming.

One minute my little girl, the next she's telling me to fuck off.

"Near enough," Lee said with a shrug. "Me and you were already drinking down pubs at her age."

Cassie gasped, her eyes wide. "Really?"

"The world was a lot safer back then," Susanne said. "And we weren't fourteen. Your dad is exaggerating."

Lee smirked and gave their daughter a look that suggested, *Mum needs to lighten up.*

"Your mum had her moments," said David, Susanne's brother. "But luckily, she had me to watch out for her."

David's wife, Danielle, elbowed him in the ribs and chuckled. "It's a miracle she survived then, if that's the case."

"Hey, I was a good brother."

Susanne raised an eyebrow. "You hit on all my friends, but other than that you were okay, I guess."

David looked sheepishly at his wife. "I don't know what she's talking about. Call my solicitor."

Their young children, Jess and Mikey, started giggling, but not at the conversation. They had wandered over to television and were watching *Bluey.*

"Good thing I came along to take her off your hands," said Lee, winking at David. "I taught her a few things you couldn't, big bro."

"Let's not be crass," said David. "There are children present."

Lee took a swig of beer and placed the glass down on the sideboard, not bothering to use the mats that were right there. "Just having a laugh, mate. Chill out."

"Dad..." Cassie gave him a scathing look. "Be nice."

"Sorry, little lamb."

"Dad!" Despite feigning offence, she laughed. She could never help herself when her dad was around. Susanne hated that; was jealous of it, in fact.

Susanne dug her nails into her palms and forced herself to go into the kitchen. While Lee might not be doing anything wrong—and was actually nice that he was spending time with Cassie—it chafed that he had turned up without an invitation. His presence was like having a turd in the room. You could try to ignore the smell, but it was impossible to truly relax until it was gone.

Since the split three years ago, Lee had slept around more than a gigolo, bounced between a dozen jobs, and often disappeared for weeks at a time. He liked to hurt her, and for a while he had, but eventually she turned numb to his antics. He meant nothing to her now. And that he could barely stand.

Lee's current trick was to pop up out of the blue and play the cheeky, lovable dad for a few hours—always on the side of his mischievous daughter against mean old mum; always spoiling her and telling her whatever she wanted to hear. Meanwhile, Susanne had to be the one to raise Cassie the right way, to make her into a responsible, well-adjusted adult that doesn't always get what she wants. No, Susanne had to play the part of the wicked witch while Lee always got to be the hero.

Susanne leaned over the sink and took some deep breaths. The last thing she wanted was to let Lee know he was winding her up.

"Hey." Her brother, David, entered the small kitchen behind her and put a hand on her shoulder. "She seems happy. For a teenager anyway."

She turned to face him, hands on her hips. "I can't believe she's so grown up. Seems like only yesterday I was pushing her around in a pram."

"You've done a great job with her, sis. She's gonna make us all proud."

That almost brought tears, and Susanne had to suck in a breath and hold it until the fuzzy feeling in her eyes retreated. "I'm already proud of her. It's been tough on her these last few years."

"Tough on you too." David reached out and took both of her hands in his. They looked nothing alike—she a brunette and him a blonde—but their smooth, long-fingered hands were identical. "Don't let Lee bother you. Just tolerate him like you would any other idiot. The world's full of 'em unfortunately. You're the responsible adult in Cassie's life. Lee is just a–"

"Just a what?" Lee entered the cramped kitchen and leaned an elbow on top of the microwave, making the top panel sink inwards. He had a smirk on his face, but beneath was a sliver of anger that Susanne knew only too well.

David stuttered for a moment before straightening up and speaking firmly. He was a smarter, more successful man than Lee, but he was no fighter. "I was talking to my sister, Lee. It doesn't involve you."

"Sounds like it does."

Susanne groaned. "Get lost, Lee. We're not doing this."

Lee feigned offence. "Doing what? I walked into the kitchen and you pair were talking me down."

"We weren't," said David. "You're not that important."

"Oh, look at this one, won't ya?"

Susanne stepped forwards and shoved her ex-husband in the chest– something she once wouldn't have dared to do. "This is my kitchen, Lee, and I'll discuss whatever and whoever I damn well please. You don't like it, leave."

The veil fell from his face. In a low, menacing voice, he said, "It's my daughter's birthday, Sue. I don't need to be invited."

She shoved him again. "My fucking house, Lee. My house."

"Mum!"

"We can hear you arguing," little cousin Jess shouted from in front of the TV, not one for tact at six years old.

Susanne went into the lounge with a sigh. "Lee and I were just winding each other up. It's all good."

Lee entered behind her with his hands up. "Hey, don't blame me. I just wanted to get a glass of water."

"Funny," said David, "because you have a pint of beer over there."

"Don't want to get dehydrated, do I, mate?"

Susanne grunted. "Since when have you ever drank sensibly?"

Cassie shook her head irritably and muttered. "Can we not have one day without you getting at each other? I never even asked for a party. I wanted to go shopping with my friends."

"Honey," Susanne moved towards her with a hand out. "I thought it would be nice to see family. You haven't seen your cousins in weeks."

There was no argument Cassie could make without sounding spiteful—which was something she was not—so she folded her arms and flared her nostrils.

David cleared his throat and moved towards his wife, Danielle. "We should get going anyway."

"You don't have to go," said Cassie, bordering on contrite, but not quite there yet. She loved her auntie and uncle, and she often doted on their younger children, but she apparently wasn't in an affectionate mood today.

David leaned down and kissed her on the cheek. "Happy birthday, Cas. Love you."

"Love you too, Uncle D."

Susanne turned to Lee and nodded towards the door. "You need to leave as well. I won't have you here alone with us."

To her relief, he offered no argument aside from a roll of his eyes. He gave Cassie a kiss on the mouth and whispered something in her ear that made her laugh. Before moving away, she saw him hand over a wad of cash, which Cassie pocketed in her jeans with a rosy-cheeked grin.

Susanne closed her eyes and took a deep breath. Cassie hadn't seen the bruised ribs and arms, or the panic attacks in the middle of the night that her father had caused her mother. All she saw was the cool dad who gave her money and let her think she was an adult.

When everyone had left—and Susanne had locked the front door—she went back into the lounge. Cassie was tapping away at her iPhone. In front of her on the coffee table was a small pile of presents, which she had showed little interest in. David had bought her a second-hand Nintendo Switch, which he had thought would go down well, but it had received only a lukewarm reaction.

She's not a kid anymore. Where did my little girl go?

"So honey? Do you want to watch a film or something? We could try that new one on—"

"I'm going to my room," she said, and got up without even glancing away from her phone. Expertly navigating the room by blind instinct, she went out into the hallway.

"Oh, okay," Susanne called after her. "Do you want me to bring you up a piece of this cake?"

"And eat like a thousand calories? No thanks!"

Susanne watched her daughter stomp up the stairs, feeling a little dazed. "Well, I'll just clean up then, shall I? Happy birthday, Cass."

———

MONDAY

The front door slammed, causing Susanne to almost spill her tea. She got up from the sofa and went to greet Cassie in the hallway, but she was already stomping up the stairs.

"Honey, what's wrong?"

Stomp-stomp. "Nothing." *Stomp-stomp*

"Doesn't sound like nothing. Did something happen at school?"

"No." She went into her room and slammed the door.

Shaking her head, Susanne stood for a moment at the bottom of the stairs, trying to remember being a teenager herself. Had she been this irrational?

Probably.

Not wanting to ignore the situation, Susanne clomped up the stairs and went into her daughter's room. The door jammed halfway, obstructed by a wheeled desk chair.

"Why have you tried to block the door?"

Cassie was sitting on her bed with her feet up on the duvet and her maroon school blazer unbuttoned. "Why do you think, mum? Get out."

"Excuse me, young lady, I will not. You come home from school and storm upstairs without even saying hello. What's got into you?"

"Nothing! I just want to be on my own."

Anger took over her face, but it was a plasticine mask hiding something else underneath. Was she holding back tears?

"Sweetheart..." Susanne sat down on the foot of her daughter's bed, causing Cassie to pull her feet up as if she feared being infected by some disease. "What is it? You can tell me."

"Tell you what?"

"Whatever it is that's wrong. I'm on your side."

Cassie rolled her eyes.

Susanne sighed. "You might not always think it, but you're my world."

"It's nothing."

Susanne nodded, waiting for her daughter to finish, but instead, she let out a huff and said, "I just have a headache, Mum."

"Cassie..."

"Mum! Please, just leave me alone."

"Okay. I'll make you a sandwich."

Cassie nodded, which Susanne decided to take as a minor victory. At least her food was still acceptable to her teenage daughter.

"Brown bread. And no crisps. I'm getting fat."

"Sweetheart. You are nowhere near fat. In fact, you could do with a few extra pounds. Look at those hips." She prodded her daughter's sides, making her squirm. "You need to put corks on them."

"Mum! Mum, stop it!" Her giggling turned to anger and she shoved Susanne away. "I don't like that!"

"You used to love being tickled."

"Not anymore."

"Okay, I'm sorry. I'll leave you to it."

Cassie shrugged and pulled her phone out of her blazer pocket.

Susanne went downstairs and finished her cup of tea, then started preparing a ham sandwich while she listened to the radio. When she heard a discussion about climate change, she groaned and switched to Smooth FM. "I've heard enough about the world ending, thank you very much."

The doorbell chimed.

"What now?"

Susanne went into the hallway and saw an amorphous black blob behind the frosted glass door panel. She opened up to discover two schoolgirls, both wearing blazers the same as Cassie's.

"Hello girls? Can I help you?"

"Yeah," said the brunette on the right, taller and wider than the petite blonde beside her. "Is Cassie there?"

"Um, yeah. Hold on." She turned and called her daughter's name up the stairs. She had to do it twice more before the bedroom door opened.

"What?"

"Some of your friends are here for you."

"Who?" She appeared at the top of the landing, an expectant look on her face that soon turned sour. "Oh, hi Gemma."

The blonde smirked. "Hi, Cass, you coming out?"

"Um, not right now. Thanks."

"Oh come on," said the brunette. "Hang out with us."

Susanne looked up at her daughter and then back at the girls loitering on her doorstep. She didn't understand the vibe here, but she didn't like it. Trusting her instincts, she gave the girls a wide, beaming, utterly fake smile and started to close the door. "Cassie has a headache. You'll have to call on her another day."

Both girls shared a look and then giggled in tandem. Without a goodbye or thank you, they turned and went back down the path, leaning into each other conspiratorially and giggling some more.

Susanne closed the front door and turned to the stairs, but Cassie had already gone back into her room.

Ten minutes later, when she delivered a sandwich, Cassie had her earplugs in and was listening to music. She refused to talk, but Susanne could tell she'd been crying.

Who the hell were those little bitches?

They best not come back.

———

WEDNESDAY

Lee's banged up old van was idling on the curb, giving off fumes. He had brought Cassie home forty minutes later than promised, meaning she would miss having a shower before bed. It was nothing new. If Susanne told Lee the sky was blue, he would fight to the death to prove it was green. If she'd had any sense, she would've asked for Cassie home an hour before she actually needed her to be.

The two of them stood at the end of the path, illuminated by the fringes of the security light. They were chatting about something, oblivious to Susanne standing on the doorstep waiting. Lee had his hands on Cassie's cheeks, looking at her fondly. He then gave her a peck on the lips and rotated her towards the front door, slapping her on the rump and sending her on her way. Cassie giggled, but when she said good night, she didn't turn back to say the same. Was she still in a mood? Since her birthday, she had barely smiled.

As her daughter passed through the door, Susanne rubbed her arm. "How was bowling?"

"Good."

Lee whistled at the end of the path. "Fancy going for a pint, Sue? Old time's sake?"

That didn't even deserve a reply, so she simply shut the door.

Rather than stomp up the stairs, Cassie went through the lounge into the kitchen. There she poured herself a glass of water and gulped at it thirstily. She seemed a little shaky.

"How was your dad?" Susanne asked. "You know, he shouldn't slap you on the butt like that anymore. You're not a little girl now."

"Shut up, mum. He's just messing about."

It wasn't a fight worth picking, so she simply nodded. "Okay. Who won the bowling?"

"Huh?"

"Who won? Your dad used to wipe the floor with me every time."

"Oh, yeah." Cassie gave a thin-lipped smile. "He got like four strikes. Jammy git."

"Yep, that sounds about right. That's the only reason he takes you bowling. He's shit at everything else."

Cassie giggled, which was like music. "I wanted a game of pool, but he said he was too tired. I reckon he knew he would lose."

"He's awful with a pool cue."

Unless he's wrapping it around someone's head at closing time.

"Did he feed you?"

"Yeah, we had pizza."

"Okay, great." She frowned. "Um, did you try to wear the pizza?"

Cassie pulled a face. "Huh?"

"You have muck in your hair." Susanne reached out and grabbed a crusted clump of her daughter's blonde hair. "You best have a late shower, but straight to bed afterwards, okay? It's late."

Cassie grabbed the clump of sticky hair and grimaced. "All right. Night, mum."

Her daughter gave her an unexpected hug. She squeezed back tightly and kissed the top of her head, trying to ignore the scent of her father's cheap supermarket *eau de toilette*.

Cassie went upstairs. The shower hissed a few moments later. A strange, nameless melancholy filled the house.

———

THURSDAY

The school had never called Susanne to come in during a workday like this. Luckily, she worked from home as a part-time law clerk, but it was still inconvenient to have to drop everything.

She could only imagine what her daughter had done. Cassie rarely got in trouble, but her attitude lately...

A receptionist escorted Susanne to an office, where Cassie was sitting with her head down and Mrs Weir, the headteacher, behind a desk.

"Ah, Mrs Clifton, please sit down."

"It's Miss Barry," she corrected. "I updated my records ages ago."

Mrs Weir frowned. "Oh, I apologise. I'll look into that."

"Why did you call me here?" She took a seat beside her daughter, but Cassie wouldn't meet her eye. She had her fists inside her sleeves and her blazer pulled tightly around her. "Are you okay, honey?"

"I'm afraid not," said Mrs Weir. "Something very serious has happened."

Susanne's stomach churned. "What? What's happened?"

"Cassie?" Mrs Weir spoke sympathetically. "Do you want to show your mum what you did? Cassie?"

Cassie still wouldn't look up, so Susanne put a hand on her wrist. "Honey, tell me what—"

Cassie hissed in pain and pulled her arm away.

Susanne glanced at Mrs Weir in confusion, but the other woman simply gave an empathetic smile and nodded at Cassie, as if to say, *it's between the two of you.*

"Cassie, sweetheart? What happened to your arm?"

"Nothing."

"Cassie, show me."

"Go on Cassie," Mrs Weir urged. "There's no hiding from this."

Susanne's stomach juices continued to slosh back and forth like the wave pool at the community centre. Her legs felt drained of blood, which made it fortunate she was sitting or else she might have fallen.

Reluctantly—and painfully slowly—Cassie put out her bare arm.

Susanne gasped at the bloody criss-crosses running up and down the length of her forearm like a roadmap. Some were thin red scrapes, barely noticeable, but others were deeper and thicker, filled with a layer of dried brown blood.

"What... What the hell have you done?"

"Mum. Don't freak out."

"Freak out? Why...Why would you do this to yourself? I-I feel sick." She put her hands on her knees and took a deep breath, leaning forwards. "Jesus."

Mrs Weir cleared her throat, getting Susanne's attention. "Miss Clifton—"

"Barry!"

"Gosh, I do apologise. Please forgive me."

Susanne shook her head, but was too focused on breathing to say anything. She really did fear she might be sick.

"Miss Barry, we take this kind of thing very seriously. In addition to self-harm, Cassie's school performance has dropped dramatically in the last few weeks. Something is clearly going on, but she doesn't want to say what it is."

Susanne tried to look at her daughter's arm again. but couldn't. She put a hand over her mouth. "I... I had no idea."

Mrs Weir nodded and smiled. God love the woman, because she didn't seem to be placing any blame. If she started implying that this was in someway Susanne's fault, it might actually cause her to hyperventilate.

Because it is my fault.

I knew something was wrong.

But Cassie won't talk to me.

She finally turned to her daughter. "Sweetheart, you need to tell me why you did this. Why would you hurt yourself?"

"I dunno," she said.

"You don't know? That's not good enough."

There were tears in Cassie's eyes, but she seemed angry too. Why was she angry? "I just did it, okay? I was messing around and I cut too deep. It was an accident."

Susanne stared at the criss-crosses and instantly knew that some of them were older. "This wasn't an accident, Cass."

Cassie rolled her sleeve back down and turned away. "I don't care what you think, Mum. Whatever."

Susanne opened her mouth to speak, but nothing came out. She didn't know what to do or what to say. She didn't understand why her daughter would do something so stupid. "Things were fine," she muttered. "We were fine."

Mrs Weir cleared her throat again. "Miss Barry, this isn't something that will get solved in this room. Now, you mustn't at all take this as an accusation, but I'm duty bound to contact a social worker. They will assess the situation and work to resolve it."

Susanne looked the woman in the eye. "Resolve it? What do you mean?"

Are they going to take my baby away?

Mrs Weir smiled, still seemingly sympathetic. "It's not my expertise, but I imagine someone will arrange for Cassie to go to counselling. Clearly, she needs to talk to someone."

"She can talk to me! Cassie, tell me what's going on." Cassie turned in her seat even more, like she was trying to get away. "You need to talk to me. I won't accept this. I won't let you hurt yourself."

"Just fuck off, Mum."

Susanne gasped. "I beg your pardon?"

"Miss Barry? Miss Barry?"

Susanne turned to face Mrs Weir, her mouth still hanging open in shock. "What?"

"Cassie has always been a good girl, so I am sure this is something we can quickly get to the bottom of. In the meantime, try not to get angry, and please don't blame yourself."

"How can I not blame myself? I'm her mother."

"There's a lot of pressure on young people today, no matter how much you try to help them. In fact, before you came in, Cassie told me you're the one person she can rely on."

Susanne almost collapsed to the floor. She didn't know if it was relief or sadness. Instead, she turned and put a hand on her daughter's shoulder. "Baby, we will sort this, okay? I love you. Everything is going to be all right."

Cassie started to sob quietly.

"I'm going to suggest you keep Cassie off school for the remainder of this week," said Mrs Weir, although it wasn't a suggestion. "Then we'll be at half term. Perhaps a short break from the pressures of studying will help things settle."

Susanne nodded. "That's absolutely fine, Mrs Weir. Thank you." She turned to Cassie. "Won't that be nice, sweetheart? A few weeks at home to relax?"

Cassie gave no response, so Susanne leaned over and gave her a cuddle. Her daughter trembled in her arms.

What the hell is going on with my little girl?

———

SATURDAY

Susanne had never seen her daughter in a rage before, but that was the only way to describe it.

It started with a feral screech that prompted Susanne to stand up and turn away from the dishwasher she'd just been about to load. For a moment, she thought she'd heard a cat outside, or children playing in the street too wildly, but when she heard Cassie swearing at the top of her lungs, she knew something was wrong.

She ran up the stairs like Usain Bolt and kicked open the bedroom door like Jason Statham.

But Cassie was okay. She wasn't being attacked, nor was she hurting herself again. Thank God.

Since coming home from school on Thursday, Cassie had been quiet and tearful, but had spent most of her time on the sofa where Susanne could keep an eye on her.

But I let her out of my sight and now something has happened.

But what?

Cassie saw her mother standing in the doorway and started hyper-ventilating. Tears soaked her eyes and her lip was slightly bloody. But most concerning, she was dressed only in her bra and knickers.

"Honey, calm down and talk to me. Let me help."

Cassie clenched her fists, opened them, clenched them again. She made a low guttural moan. Susanne stood still and did nothing, acting the same way she would if facing a wild animal. Cautious. Confused. Afraid.

Cassie's eyes glanced off to the side.

Towards her laptop.

From where Susanne stood, it looked like Cassie's social media was open. There were photographs, several of them in a grid.

Susanne took a step towards the laptop.

Cassie pounced, leaping in front of her. "No!"

"Let me look at your computer."

"No."

"Cassie move." She grabbed her daughter's arm and tried to budge her out of the way, but she yelped in shock when Cassie lashed out and shoved her. It sent her staggering backwards into the wall, where she struck the back of her head. It was enough to stun her.

Cassie raced over to her laptop and slammed it shut.

Still stunned, Susanne pushed herself, groggily, away from the wall. "Step aside right now."

Cassie backed away, sheepish and wide-eyed, perhaps shocked by what she'd done.

Susanne lifted the lid on the laptop. It had gone to sleep, so it presented with a black screen at first. Then the password screen loaded.

Damn it.

"Cassie, what's your password? Cassie, tell me right now."

Cassie shook her head, tears streaming down her face.

"Cassie? I'm not playing around. Give me your password."

"No. No, Mum, I can't."

"Why not?"

"I don't want you to see."

Susanne turned away from the screen and studied her half-naked daughter. "See what? Cassie, please? I... I don't know what to do here."

The tears came to them both, and suddenly they were both stood weeping at each other.

"Mum, I'm sorry. I-I didn't mean to push you. Are you okay?"

Susanne nodded.

Cassie's beautiful face contorted in misery. "I'm so sorry."

Susanne nodded. "I know. I know you are, sweetie. Come here."

Cassie hurried forwards into her mother's arms, and they held each other. Her sobs intensified and soon her entire body was shaking. "Just let me help you, sweetheart. Tell me what's wrong."

"I will," she said. "Just not right now."

"Okay. Okay, but you need to let me in. This has to stop. I want my little girl back."

"She's gone."

Susanne moved her daughter back so they could see each other. "No, she's not. You will always be my little girl, do you understand me? Whatever is going on, I love you and I will support you. You're the most beautiful thing in my world, and if anyone hurts you they'll have me to answer to. Do you hear me?"

Cassie nodded. It looked like she was about to say something, but more sobs escaped her, so Susanne just held her again. While she did so, she looked around her daughter's room for some kind of clue as to what was going on. Her clothes were on the floor in a heap. The noodles Susanne had made her an hour ago sat uneaten in a bowl on the side table. Her phone was on the floor under her bed, as if she'd tossed it away in anger. Then there was the laptop.

Even in the safety of her home, Susanne could not keep the world from getting at her daughter. She couldn't protect her–because she didn't even know what she was supposed to be protecting her from.

She rubbed Cassie's back, not wanting to let her go. Not wanting to let anything else upset her little girl. It was the only thing she could think to do as a mother. Just love her little girl. Was that enough to make everything okay?

————

SUNDAY

Usually, Susanne bought her shopping online, but truthfully she had just needed to get out. The house was claustrophobic with her and Cassie constantly at home together.

At least things seemed to have got better after yesterday's outburst. After letting her daughter calm down for an hour, Susanne had ordered a pizza, and then sighed with relief when Cassie ate half of it. Then they watched a comedy on Disney+ together, which had got them both laughing. Before going to bed, close to midnight, Cassie had given her mother a great big hug and apologised for her behaviour. Maybe they had finally reached a turning point. She was still refusing to give up her laptop password, but there was time to come down more firmly on her about that.

Today felt like a good day.

Susanne went into the kitchen with her shopping bags and placed them down on the counter. The breakfast bowls she'd left in the sink were now clean and in the dish rack. "Wow, thank you, daughter. You must be feeling better."

She put the shopping away, daring to whistle a happy tune. Perhaps Cassie would fancy a walk to the park later. A bit of fresh air would do them both good.

She went to the bottom of the stairs. "Cassie? Honey, you up there?"

No answer. Was she sleeping in the middle of the day? She was a teenager, she supposed.

"Cassie?"

When there was still no answer, she crept up the stairs. After all the tension, it was probably a good thing if her daughter was resting, but it suddenly occurred to her that the more likely explanation was that she had her earbuds in listening to music.

But when she opened Cassie's bedroom door, she wasn't in there.

She must have gone out.

Susanne didn't like the thought of her daughter not being home with the way things had been lately, but she was old enough to come and go during the day.

Instinctively, she turned to her daughter's laptop, but it was closed, which meant it would ask for the password again.

There was something on the bed. A slip of paper.

Susanne went and picked it up, and smiled when she saw that Cassie had written her a note.

I love you, Mum. Sorry.

I love you too, honey.

With a sigh of relief, Susanne left the bedroom and closed the door. She was about to head back downstairs when she heard the dripping coming from the bathroom. The bath taps were in need of replacement, which meant they would leak unless you twisted them shut with plenty of elbow grease. Cassie must have had a bath before leaving. Or maybe she was listening to music while having a soak.

"Cassie? Cassie, are you in there?" She rapped the back of her hand against the door. When there was no reply, she tried the handle.

The door was unlocked, so she opened it.

Cassie was lying in the bath, earbuds in and her phone hanging by its wire at the side of the bath.

Susanne's first instinct was to turn away and respect her daughter's modesty (for a year now, Cassie had got mad if Susanne barged in on her naked), but when she realised her daughter was asleep, she decided it was too dangerous not to wake her.

She stepped into the room, feet resting on the purple bath mat.

The water was pink with whatever Cassie had added to it—shampoo or bubble bath?

A near silent drone came from the earbuds, the song unrecognisable.

"Cassie," she reached out and prodded her daughter on the shoulder.

She was ice cold.

Susanne put her fingers into the pink water and gasped to find it tepid. "You'll catch your death in here. Cassie, come on, wake up." She prodded her daughter again—more firmly. "Come on now, stop being silly. Wake up. Cassie. Baby, come on."

Susanne realised her entire body was shaking, and she couldn't remember taking her last breath. When she spoke again, her voice belonged to a high-pitched stranger. "Come on now, young lady. Enough of this. Wake up right now. Do you hear me?"

Cassie's right wrist was lying beneath the water. A dark red cloud flowed around it, contributing to the pinkish hue inside the bath. Cassie herself was a sickly shade of grey.

"Cassie, sweetheart, don't do this, please." She shook her daughter by the shoulders, back and forth. Her head flopped lifelessly. Her wrist rose and fell in the water, releasing a dark red torrent.

Susanne grabbed her daughter and pulled her by the armpits. They were almost the same size now, and Cassie was like a dead weight, but the water helped. She managed to slide her daughter's hip up and over the side of the bath and pull her free from the water. The two of them collapsed in a wet heap on the fluffy purple bath mat.

Eyes blind with tears, Susanne dragged Cassie's limp body onto her lap. Then she stroked her daughter's beautiful blonde hair and tried to warm her up. She was so cold. Too cold.

"What's wrong, Cassie? Just tell me, won't you? Tell me what I can do. Tell me why this is happening. I don't understand. I don't understand. Why won't you tell me?"

Why?

Why?

Why?

"Cassie?"

The Squirrel & the Pants

"Four months," said my wife Sally, the yin to my yang, the Asterix to my Obelix, the lactose free chocolate to my hard-boiled egg.

I swivelled in my chair to look at her–the sunlight hitting her face in such a way that she resembled a young Eddie Murphy. "Four months what?"

"Four months since we moved to Hawthorn Dene."

I shook my head, confused. "My name's Iain. Who's Dean?"

"Hawthorn Dene. As in, where we live now."

"Oh, I thought we moved to Hawthorn. I've been wondering why people have been calling me Dean lately."

She rolled her eyes at me. "What are you up to? The kids said you were in the toilet for almost an hour."

"Someone left a crossword book in there."

"*You* left a crossword book in there."

"Recollections may vary. Anyway, I nearly finished one this time without checking the answers at the back. Can you believe what I got stuck on? Bestselling horror author, eight letters."

Sally looked up and to her right, obviously thinking of an answer. "Um... Oh! Matt Shaw!"

I glared at her, almost falling off my office chair. "Don't you dare." I shook my head and took a moment to compose myself. "John Saul. The answer was John Saul."

"Oh, right. Well, I don't know many horror authors, do I?"

"You're married to one. Some say an extremely talented, a once in a generation voice."

"Who says that?"

"My mom says that. She said it this morning on the telephone."

Sally leaned forwards and gave me a hug. "Don't work too hard, honey, okay? You look a little tired."

"Sleeping is for mortal men. Not creative titans, like me."

With a wink, she looked me up and down and purred. "You're a titan in more ways than one, baby. To think that God made a man as smart and as athletic at you, all in one package."

I took her hands in mine and gazed at her, knowing her words to be heartfelt and true. "Thank you. Thank you for realising that about me."

She frowned. "Realising what?"

"Huh? I..."

"I think you were daydreaming, honey." She put a hand on my shoulder and gave me a gentle shake. "Like I said, don't work too hard."

"I never do."

"Ain't that the truth." She turned to leave my writer's lair, almost knocking my signed Katy Perry poster off the wall with a clumsy shoulder as she slipped out the door.

I turned and went back to my 2011 MacBook Pro, fingertips hovering over the worn, naked keys. It was only my preternatural typing skills that allowed me to operate a keyboard lacking half its symbols, but after so many years—and a gazillion words—the laptop and I had become one. I was a warrior. It was my sword. I was a missile. It was my payload. I was a McDonalds drive-thru. It was my BigMac. Synergy. Marriage. Perfection.

I closed down a few dozen penis enlargement pop-up ads and opened up my internet browser. Immediately, I checked the horror book charts, barely containing myself when I saw so many of my adversaries looking down at me. My clenched fist waved in the air. "I'll get you one day, Stephen. Mark my words."

My latest masterpiece was already halfway done. Forty-thousand words about a serial killer named Nugget who killed vegans and made them into popcorn chicken. It was a guaranteed crowd-pleaser. But right now was not a good time for writing. My fingers hovered over the keys again, but they did not strike. For whatever reason, the creative juices weren't flowing today. I needed to take a break. Perhaps another trip to the toilet?

To reset my eyes, I looked up over my laptop's screen and peered out of the window into the garden. The artificial lawn was ugly, but it was maintenance free and a great place for Dave to do his business.

"Ah, Dave..." I took in a wistful breath. "The most wonderful pug in the world." I could hear him snoring at my feet beneath the desk. He hadn't farted in hours. A good boy.

Having moved to the paradise of the greater Sunderland area, my new garden was a sanctuary. European Starlings perched atop the fence panels, ready to take off and blacken the sky like a biblical plague, while the hedges were full of field mice and shrews, each set upon a nightly quest to illegally enter my home and claim squatter's rights.

A red squirrel stared at me from the middle of the fake lawn.

Red squirrels no longer existed in many places. The mighty grey squirrel had long ago made cucks of them. The last time I had ever seen one in my forty distinguished years was at Blackgang Chine on the Isle of Wight. It had been a great day for the people of the island to host me, and I could tell it meant a lot to them. One person even went so far as to tell me, "I was a real piece of work." Lovely.

The squirrel was still staring at me. At first it was cute, even prompting me to wave, but then it became somewhat impertinent. "Shoo!" I said, waving a hand in front of the window. "Be off with you! I'm trying to work."

The squirrel didn't move. Its beady eyes pierced me through the glass, seeing into my soul. Its bushy tail waved back and forth, a gesture I knew was meant to taunt me.

After telling the creature to scram several more times, I chuckled to myself. Obviously, it couldn't understand me. This was a Sunderland squirrel—a beast from the North East. I was speaking the wrong dialect as I was originally from the West Midlands.

"Ha-way, Squirrel. Get gan. There's nay scran round 'ere, pet."

The squirrel's bushy red tail swished, but the rest of its body remained stone still.

I stood from my desk and put my hands on my hips. "Right! Don't say I didn't warn you."

To get to the kitchen, I had to leave my office in the East Wing and head into the West Wing. It took twelve whole steps. Success was a heady cocktail.

I entered the kitchen and found my kids lying naked and upside down on the leather sofa with their iPads in the air. *Bluey* playing on one. *Wednesday* on the other.

"Why are you two not dressed?" I demanded. "It's past noon."

Jack craned his head backwards and looked at me upside down. "You're naked too."

Looking down at myself, I had to disagree. "I'm wearing underpants. I have been nearly all week."

"Don't know where my clothes are," Molly said without looking at me.

"Did you try your wardrobe?"

"Nope!"

"Well, that's where I'd start. Come on, both of you, go get dressed. The postman won't come here anymore because of you two."

With a huff, both my progeny got up and headed out of the kitchen. Their eyes remained glued to their tablets as they navigated with the same spatial awareness of a blind person—deftly avoiding furniture and door frames without looking up for even a split second. It was actually impressive.

I shook my head, worried that humanity was evolving in some very strange ways. Like my extra stretchy cheeks. What purpose did that serve? Was I advancing towards some kind of human-flying squirrel hybrid? Would my future bloodline swoop down from trees, riding the winds with their rubbery jowls?

Returning to my task, I headed to the kitchen's French doors and threw them both open at once. "Right, you fluffy, nut-stealing bastard, it's time to meet your..."

The squirrel was gone. No sign it had ever even been there.

"That's what I thought!" I raised a fist in the air. "And don't come back, you hear me? Don't mess with me. I'm an author. I'm Iain Rob Wright!"

From atop the fence, the starlings alighted, drenching the lawn in a thick black shadow.

———

I HAD NEVER BEEN a good sleeper—my genius mind was always too filled to bursting with monstrous ideas to thrill and entertain the masses—but most nights I could eventually start drifting towards the smoky abyss of slumber. Tonight, however, I had been tossing an awful lot. Eventually, it annoyed Sally enough that she yelled at me. "Will you stop it? You keep knocking me with your elbows."

I removed my hands from my prestigious todger and apologised. "I can't settle."

"Why not?"

"It's nothing."

She turned to face me in bed, lifting up her sleep mask like a motorcycle cop lifting his visor in some American movie. In the silvery moonlight spilling through a gap in the curtains, she looked just like a young Burt Reynolds. "Honey," she said. "It's two in the morning and you're wide awake. For both our sanities, just tell me what's on your mind. You'll feel better if you let it out."

"Some things are better left in my brain. They're too hard to put into words."

She sighed. "Last time you couldn't sleep, it was because you couldn't figure out why they trained miners to become astronauts in Armageddon."

I couldn't keep the irritated hiss from escaping my lips. "Well, answer me this, Sal. Is it is easier to become an astronaut or is it easier to become a miner?"

"I don't know."

"It takes *way* more training to become an astronaut, and the candidates would also be much smarter on average, so why, oh why, my dear, didn't they train the astronauts to become miners instead of training a bunch of oddball miners to become astronauts? It makes no sense. No sense at all." I realised I was breathing rapidly, getting het up about it all over again.

Sal reached out and put a hand on my naked, manly chest. "What's on your mind, honey? Why can't you sleep?"

"It's nothing."

"Iain? You have three seconds to tell me or I'm going to make you sleep in the spare room."

I grunted and folded my arms. "Squirrel."

For a moment, she just peered at me in the near darkness. "Squirrel? As in, the little animals that live in trees and eat nuts?"

"They're arboreal rodents," I said, "and they can take a baby's face off."

"I'm pretty sure they can't, honey. Anyway, why do you have squirrels on your mind? Are they part of the WEF's evil schemes?"

"Everything is a part of the WEF's evil schemes, but it's not that. And it's not squirrels. It's squirrel. Singular."

"Okay?"

"It was looking at me, Sal. In the garden."

Slowly, a smirk crossed my wife's face. A moment later, she was chuckling and jiggling under the covers. "That's why you can't sleep? Because a squirrel was looking at you?"

"You weren't there. He kept staring at me. I told him to stop, but he ignored me."

Sally took a breath and held it, trying not to laugh anymore. "I honestly don't know what I can say to you right now," she said. "Is this going to keep you up all night, because if so, it might be time for the doctor to up your crazy pills."

"I'm already on the maximum dose. They said it's the same amount Amber Heard takes."

"Get up and make yourself a cup of tea," she said, her patience clearly thinning. "Maybe it'll relax you enough to sleep later."

"Maybe you're right." With a resigned exhalation from my nostrils,

I took Sally's advice and got out of bed. My bare feet sank into the carpet and I crept onto the landing, being careful not to wake my two snoring offspring in their palatial bedrooms as I passed. Them kids had it way better than I did at their age.

Dave followed me out of the bedroom and down the stairs, almost bowling me over as he raced ahead. Sometimes, I was certain the little pug was trying to kill me.

The kickboard spotlights in the kitchen were on, but I decided not to turn on the main light. Darkness was where I did my best work, the place my true heart dwelled. Like a creature of the night, the moon empowered me while the sunlight revealed my flaws—such as the fact I was balding.

I switched on the kettle and waited for it to boil. When it was done, I made myself a cup of Yorkshire Tea and sat down at the dining table. There, I thought about the existence of the universe and if I could ever capture its true meaning on the page. It was the eternal quest of all great writers to capture and express the deeper truths of life.

Dave farted at my feet, setting my teeth on edge and making me shudder. "Wow," I said encouragingly to my beloved pug. "That's... meaty."

Dave wagged his curly tail, his exposed anus twitching like a deadly spore.

A yawn escaped my lips, and I imitated a Tarzan-like wail for fun. Hopefully, Sally didn't hear it and come tell me off.

She didn't.

To add to the highjinks, I beat at my chest like a gorilla.

Then I sipped my tea as Dave farted again, the air in the room growing thick and slightly intoxicating. When he cracked out a third trump, I could take no more. Standing up, I went over to the kitchen counter and cracked a window.

The squirrel stared right at me, illuminated by the solar powered security light on the rear fence. It was as if it had known I would eventually come and stare out this kitchen window in the middle of the night.

I put down my tea and glared right back at the impertinent little critter, determined not to be the first one to look away. "You don't know who you're messing with, buddy."

Minutes went by.

The kitchen was cold and dark, but inside I was a burning fire. My heart thudded, pulse pounding in my temples. Without noticing, I had clenched my fists and locked my jaw. Did I want to fight this thing?

Yes, I wanted to fight this thing. The cheeky bleeder wouldn't stop staring at me. In my own home. How dare he? How dare he?

I was being ridiculous.

Breathing through my nose, I forced myself to calm down. My fists loosened. My jaw unclenched.

The squirrel hadn't moved an inch. Its stare was unbroken, impenetrable. A terracotta warrior standing sentinel.

But it was just a squirrel.

"And I'm a man," I said out loud. "I won't have a barney with you, Mr Squirrel. I'm better than that. You hear me?"

I finished off my tea and wrinkled my nose. Dave had fallen asleep beneath the table, but the moment I started back up the stairs, he woke up and raced ahead of me, almost bowling me over.

Fifty-fifty, the dog was trying to kill me.

———

I MUST HAVE GRABBED a few hours of sleep because I didn't notice Sally getting out of bed. Patting the warm, empty side of the mattress, I let out a yawn of bad breath. Feta and olives, which was strange because I had eaten neither.

"Alexa," I mumbled. "What time is it?"

Playing Follow me *by* Uncle Kracker.

I groaned. "Alexa, stop. Idiot."

With great effort, I brought my wrist up in front of my face and checked my watch. It was five-past-ten. "Jesus, I'm up early."

I considered going back to sleep but didn't feel tired enough, so I got up. My belly rumbled, begging for a Pot Noodle or a ham sandwich. Normal breakfast things. I was thirsty too.

After getting dressed in jeans and an only slightly baggy XXL T-shirt, I went downstairs, where I found my gorgeous family sitting in the living room playing Mario Kart. To my chagrin, I noticed Jack was playing as Luigi, which was a big no-no. Luigi was my guy. Still, it was 2023, and you had to allow children a little leeway, so I let it go. For now.

"Who's winning?" I asked.

"Mummy," Sally said. "Obviously."

I pointed at the screen. "Toss a turt, Molly. She's right ahead of you."

Molly pulled the trigger on a red turt and sent it right up Princess Peach's backside.

I stuck my tongue out at my wife and smirked, "Now you're second."

"Charming," she said, rolling her eyes. "I made you a coffee in the kitchen."

"You're the most wonderful, beautiful woman in the world," I told her.

She purred. "And you are the most masculine, perfectly sculpted stallion God ever created."

"Thank you," I said. "Thank you for noticing that."

Sally frowned at me. "Honey, are you okay? I think you're still half-asleep."

I rubbed at my eyes and blinked. "Yeah. I'll, um, go get my coffee."

As I shuffled into the kitchen, I rubbed at my face. When had I last shaved? It felt like my stubble grew faster when I was tired. The worse I felt, the hairier I got. "Need to get my act together. Matt Shaw isn't going to beat himself in the charts."

Gotta get a new book out. And then another. And then another...

I rose a fist at the ceiling and bellowed. "When will it end? When?"

Sally yelled at me from the living room to keep it down. "Stop being dramatic. It's a Sunday."

I lowered my fist and grumbled. "Sorry, honey."

My favourite Katy Perry mug was steaming on the counter, and the lovely addictive scent of coffee drifted into my nose. Like a cartoon dog floating towards a cartoon pie, I travelled across the kitchen tiles on the tips of my toes.

The first sip was perfection, evoking crisp Amazon rains and the wet, earthy tang of fertile soil. The heady blend was so smooth that it was almost chocolaty. You couldn't beat Aldi's freeze dried coffee grounds. I lifted my mug and held it next to my cheek, enjoying the radiating warmth. "Because I'm worth it."

"Who are you talking to?" Jack asked as he entered the kitchen in boy's pyjamas, an old lady's wig, and fake boobs. I'd learned not to ask questions.

"Oh, I was just pretending to be in a TV advert."

He frowned at me, as if I were the weird one. "Why?"

"Why not? I could be a star of the screen one day, a member of the Mitchell family in Eastenders or something. Sky's the limit."

Jack nodded, somehow seeming to pity me at just nine years old. "Mum says that with your face, it's lucky you became an author."

"I will be talking to your mother later. She'll be sorry she said that."

"Why what are you going to do?"

"Sulk," I said. "She hates it when I sulk."

"We all do, Dad." With that, my young son went into the fridge and helped himself to a Peperami. "Come play Mario Kart. Mum gets really annoying when she wins."

I nodded. "Two minutes and I'll be in to beat her. I assume you'll be playing as Baby Mario as per usual?"

It concerned me when he left the room without providing an answer. Everyone knew Luigi was my guy!

Shaking my head, I muttered under my breath and turned around, sipping my coffee. "I hope he understands how much I—"

That goddamn motherclucking, beady-eyed rat was staring at me again. Right there again. Same patch of fake grass. Same death stare. Had the thing even moved?

If not for the gentle swaying of its bushy tail, I might have thought the squirrel was a garden ornament. An intricately detailed, brightly coloured statue of an impertinent tree rat.

I was barefoot, and it looked like it'd been raining, so I stomped off to get my clogs from the porch. Sally must have heard me huffing and puffing because she called out to me as I passed by the lounge. "What's wrong?"

"That bloody squirrel is staring at me again."

"What?"

"The squirrel. He's got it in for me, I swear."

I tried to get inside the porch, but the door was locked. "Babe? Where are the house keys?"

"In my handbag?"

"Which of your ten handbags are you talking about?"

I heard her huff, and a moment later she appeared in the hallway. Underneath the glare of the LED spotlights, she reminded me of a Ghost-era Whoopi Goldberg.

"Iain, what is going on with you and this squirrel? Do you need me to go chase it away?"

"No, that's not going to..." I shrugged. "Would you?"

"Come on." She took my hand and led me back into the kitchen. "I'll handle it."

"He's really trying to upset me, babe. I don't know why he keeps looking at me."

"I'll ask him," she said.

When we reached the kitchen, I let go of her hand and hurried over to the kitchen window to point the little bugger out to her. My finger scanned left and right, trying to pinpoint the target.

My mouth fell open.

Sally joined me and put a hand over her eyebrows to see through the glare. "Where is he, babe? You point him out to me and I'll go sort him out."

"He's gone," I said, shaking my head in utter disgust. "He's doing this on purpose, Sal. I came down last night and he was here. I wake up this morning and he's here. Soon as I go to get help, he runs off to make me look stupid. This is a hate crime."

"How is it?"

"Because I hate that squirrel."

"It's just a squirrel, honey." She put her hands on my elbows and turned me to face her. "I know this year's been tough, but everything is okay. You're just under a lot of stress."

I nodded. "Sales are down, and last month there was that whole thing with the garden gnome."

She put a finger against my lips and shushed me. "Don't bring up the gnome. We all love you, Iain. Everything is okay. Okay?"

"Yeah, okay."

"So, are you going to let this squirrel thing go?"

"I'll try. Maybe I'm nuts."

She gave me a smirk. "That would explain why there's a squirrel after you."

With a throaty grumbled, I put my hands to my face. "Not funny, honey. Not funny at all."

———

SAL TOOK the kids out to get ice cream while I cleaned up after our roast dinner. Periodically, as I loaded the dishwasher, I glanced out of the window. The squirrel had been gone since disappearing that morning, and slowly I started to see the funny side of things. My mind, however, remained fixated. It was impossible to rest, knowing that squirrel was still out there somewhere; lurking; biding its time. Why had it been so interested in me?

It didn't make any sense.

Turning around, I looked over at the Katy Perry calendar I had fought so hard to place on the wall beside the fridge. "Oh, Katy, am I going mad? Is this how you felt when you cut off all your hair and dyed it blonde? How did you bounce back after getting so low?"

As always, Katy's wise eyes stared back at me and told me all I needed to know. Her candy cane dress might as well have been a scholar's cloak.

Face your fears, Iain. And buy my next album.

"Will do, Katy. Will do."

Knowing there was only one solution, I went and slipped into my *crocs* and headed out into the garden. It was cold and damp, with slimy leaves around the edges of the fake lawn, but the brisk northern air was like a tonic. It grounded me, and refocused my mind. "I'm sorry for being rude, Mr Squirrel. I've been under a lot of pressure lately with sales, and putting on weight, and that whole thing last month with the garden gnome. Anyway, you live here too and I had no right to shoo you away. You are very welcome in my garden. Look out for Dave, though; he might eat you."

There was the slightest movement to my right. I turned and saw the red squirrel sitting atop the fence. Its bushy tail shook, dislodging twigs and leaves. This time, when it stared at me, there was something different in its eyes. A new understanding passed between the two of us. A war had been averted. Like Taylor Swift and Kanye, we had chosen peace.

"It's nice to meet you," I said. "My name's Iain Rob Wright, best-selling author."

The squirrel tilted its head at me inquisitively.

I cleared my throat and chuckled. "You probably haven't heard of me, but if you read horror, then you definitely would have."

The squirrel stared at me.

"Anyway, like I said, my name's Iain. Pleased to meet you." I extended a hand and strode towards the fence.

The squirrel rose up on its hind legs, its front ones extended out in a friendly gesture, much like an invitation to hug.

Then the furry bastard leapt right at me.

I yelped in surprise as the airborne rodent landed on my face, and I screamed as I was suddenly blind. For a moment, I feared my eyes had been clawed to pulp, but quickly I realised I had merely closed them.

A fuzzy pair of squirrel bollocks rubbed against the bridge of my nose.

"Smells like Nutella," I mumbled as I staggered and flailed across the garden. I spun and twisted desperately, trying to dislodge the furry face hugger, but before I could succeed, my foot came down on wet, slimy leaves—or one of Dave's pug packages—and I went cartwheeling backwards through the air.

The fake lawn cushioned my fall, but the compacted sand beneath knocked the wind right out of me.

The squirrel leapt off my face. I didn't see where it went. I saw only stars.

I was aware of something lying across my leg. It was a short length of flat wood from one of the fence panels. I had no idea where it had come from, but it had ended up balanced precariously across my thigh like a seesaw.

The squirrel stood upright on the lawn, two-feet beyond the bottoms of my shoes. From my skewed vantage point, the animal seemed twice its normal size, and the look in its eyes was oddly human. It saw me as a man, as an enemy. As its bitch.

"Are you working for my enemies?" I asked in a trembling voice.

Instead of answering, the squirrel hopped up onto my ankle. I yelped in horror, my entire body frozen in fear, but the bastard showed no mercy.

Beady eyes locked onto mine as the squirrel crept up my leg, placing one scratchy, clawed foot in front of the other. Moving up, inch by terrifying inch.

My bladder released itself, soaking the plastic lawn beneath me and draining into the sand. Somehow, I knew the squirrel was drinking in my fear. I saw the delighted sparkle in its eyes.

"I have a family," I muttered, and the thought of them gave me strength. "Jack, Molly, Sally. They mean everything to me."

The squirrel kept its gaze upon me, continuing its slow ascent up my leg. It was about to step up onto the wooden board, which was still balanced across my thigh. It might be the only chance I got, the only weapon I had with which to defend myself.

I moved an arm, intending to reach for the wood.

The squirrel hopped forwards, landing on the plank and keeping me from grabbing it. Its weight was surprisingly heavy and pinned the wood against my leg.

I saw my chance.

"You done fucked up, Red."

The squirrel was perched slightly to one side of the plank, causing the other end to rise up slightly. Balling up my fist, I smashed down on the wood, using the fulcrum of my thigh to catapult the squirrel into the air.

But instead of launching the rodent, the plank snapped in the middle.

The squirrel tumbled into the gap between my legs.

Then I felt something clamp down hard on my testicles.

A steam train could not have squealed louder than I in that moment. The sharp, white-hot agony launched me like a firework and I immediately started pinwheeling around the garden, trying to yank the squirrel off my nuts. Its bushy tail swished in the air like the propeller of a Spitfire. Its little arms and legs fanned out like it was having a whale of a time.

I wailed in misery,

"Somebody help me! Please! I might want to have another child. Get it off, get it off!"

I span around, faster and faster, but the wicked little shit sank its teeth in deeper and deeper into my funsack. This was how I was going to die. Talented author found dead in garden. Red Squirrel suspected of impertinence and murder.

I wailed even louder, wishing I had neighbours to hear me, but I was too rich to have any.

My consciousness began to pack its bags.

"H-help me!" I staggered woozily. "Anyone?"

"Honey? Jesus, oh my God! What is happening?"

I turned to see Sally and the kids standing in the open French doors. Their faces turned pale in horror.

My wife leapt out onto the sandstone patio and pointed at my crotch. "Iain, what is that?"

"Squirrel. I told you. Told you it was out to get me."

Thankfully, Sally asked no other questions. She leapt forwards and grabbed the squirrel's bushy tail with both hands. "Oh, so soft," she said, digging her heels in and yanking as hard as she could. "Like a snuggle blanket."

"Not now, honey. Just... Just..." I doubled over and vomited. Then I looked up at her and begged. "Help me."

"I'm trying." She yanked even harder. "It won't let go of your nuts."

Out of breath and rapidly fading, I reached out and grabbed my wife by the shoulders. The squirrel remained attached to my balls. "Tell people I died fighting an angry badger, not... not a squirrel. Not a..."

Collapsing backwards like an ironing board, I landed on my back and passed out. I didn't know if I would ever wake up again.

---

1 year later.

    Guardian Newspaper Excerpt.

*"Celebrated author and proud eunuch Iain Rob Wright finally finds success with latest chiller novel–***Nugget, the blood-soaked squirrel***. Stephen King immediately retires, claiming torch to have finally been passed."*

'I told you I was the best,' Iain Rob Wright told our interviewer in his signature high-pitched tone. 'I win. Yeah, I win!'"

ALSO, pants.

House of 1000 Tiny Babies

"Shit! Oh shit, oh shit!" Colin jammed his index finger in his mouth, the coppery tang of blood flooding his tongue. Served him right, trying to get fancy with breakfast. Chopped strawberries in his granola? Who did he think he was? The Queen of Sheba?

He didn't know how bad the cut was, but the sharp spike of pain had been enough to make him cry out in shock. Gingerly, he pulled his finger out of his mouth and inspected it.

"Oh!"

He teetered on the spot, hip pressed up against the kitchen counter to support his weight. Blood always made him woozy, and there was a lot now, flooding from a thin, straight line along the side of his index finger. When he pressed at the flesh around the wound, it puckered like a kissing mouth.

He took a deep breath and held it. It wasn't as bad as his thudding heartbeat told him it was, he knew that. Just a cut. Not like his fingertip was hanging off or anything.

"Needs a plaster," he said to himself soothingly. "No biggie."

His stomach sloshed as a wave of nausea washed over him, but he was able to stumble over to the fridge and grab the tin of medical supplies from the cupboard above. It was mostly filled with paracetamol and constipation remedies—but there must be a plaster or two in there.

He set the tin down on the counter, and then struggled to open it one-handed. Once he succeeded, he was relieved to find a strip of beige plasters. He used his teeth to open one.

Wrapping the plaster around his finger was an exercise in frustration, and it hit him with a pang of loneliness. Back when he'd been married, Lisa would always bandage his booboos—not that he ever got many as an accountant. Still, it had been a nice thing to have someone tend to your wounds. Now, he was two years divorced and obliged to take care of himself.

A little shaken, Colin stood aimlessly in the centre of the kitchen. For a moment, he couldn't decide what to do. He felt oddly emotional— even a little teary. Probably best he distract himself.

"I'll call Tess," he said out loud to fill the silence.

Tess was his daughter. Twenty-five now, and a full-time maths teacher (she had his head for numbers). Soon, she would likely be married with children of her own, thus repeating the circle of life. Colin just hoped her marriage lasted till the end—or ended early enough to still have a life ahead of her. The problem with getting divorced at fifty-four was that starting again was an utterly daunting prospect. Would he ever find another partner to share meals with? Did he even want one?

Who could ever live up to Lisa? I spent my life with her.

Until I drove her up the wall.

Colin was under no illusion that he was hard to live with. While he'd never been officially diagnosed or given a label, he had, at the very least, OCD. A bumbling mess of anxiety and neurosis, he was, and age had only made him worse.

Some people are better off being alone.

At least for the sake of other *people.*

Not a day passed by that Colin didn't miss having his house full of heartbeats. Yet, when he had lived with Tess, Lisa, and his son— David— it had been a constant cause of stress for him. Being constantly surrounded by the mess, the noise, the complaining. His family loved him, but he knew that sometimes they couldn't stand him.

He wasn't a big fan of himself either.

Emotions still awash, Colin retrieved his mobile phone from where he'd left it on top of the microwave and called Tess. It took her several rings to answer.

"Dad?"

"Hi honey, are you okay?"

"Yeah, what's up?"

"Oh, nothing much. I just cut my finger making breakfast. Silly sod, aren't I?"

"Are you okay? Does it need stitches?"

He chuckled. "No, no, it's fine. I put a plaster on it."

"Okay. Was there anything else? I'm really busy right now."

"Oh, I didn't mean to interrupt. I'll let you get back to it."

She sighed down the phone. "You sure you're okay, Dad?"

"I'm fine."

"I'll see you next Sunday for lunch, right? Is David coming?"

"I don't think he can make it. Something to do with work."

"Alright, Dad. I'll see you soon, then."

He gripped the phone for a moment, not wanting to say goodbye. "Okay, honey. Have a good day."

"You too." She ended the call.

For almost a full minute, Colin stood there in the kitchen, staring out the window at the back garden. Then he poured himself a glass of water to rinse the taste of blood from his mouth.

The silence was total until the sudden trill of the doorbell broke it. He flinched, his stomach sloshing once more. The doorbell rarely rang.

It was little surprise when it turned out to be the postman with a parcel that wasn't even for Colin. The young lad, with shoulder-length blonde hair, gave him a casual wink as he asked, "Can you take a parcel for next door, mate?"

"Yes." Colin nodded. "Of course. Number four?"

"Yep. I knocked, but no one answered."

"Think they're actually on holiday. I saw them loading luggage into the boot yesterday morning."

The postman raised an eyebrow. "Wish I were off somewhere nice right now. Could use a break."

"Early mornings getting to you?" Colin crossed his arms and hid his wounded finger under his armpit. He wasn't sure why it embarrassed him. "I couldn't do what you do. Up at the crack of dawn."

"Eh, you get used to it. Mondays are the worst because I go out on a Saturday night, don't I?"

Colin chuckled, actually enjoying the brief exchange. "You'll have to stop the partying, young man."

"Or find another job, eh? Anyway, here you go. Cheers."

Colin took the small square parcel and turned to place it on the side table beside the door. When he twisted back around to continue chatting, the postman was already trotting back down the driveway.

Colin closed the door and went back into the kitchen to finish off the last of his water. Once again, he stared out at the garden. A bright, sunny day, with the grass so green it was almost emerald. His hard work last summer had paid off and early spring saw his little slice of nature blooming with life. All he needed to do now was turn the flower beds, ready for some seeds. While most of his plants were perennial, he kept a row at the back for some colourful plug plants, like begonias and geraniums. It was the one part of his garden he changed every year for variety, keeping everything else exactly the same. This week, he might even get some petunias.

Now there's a thought.

With nothing planned for the day (he was a semi-retired, self-employed accountant working from home) he decided to go get those flower beds turned over now. If he worked up a sweat, he could reward himself with a nice cool bath and a good book. He was halfway through the most recent Brandon Sanderson doorstop novel, and he couldn't get enough of Kaladin Stormblessed. A loner turned popular hero. If only.

Even though it was sunny, Colin felt a chill as he went out via the laundry room. Try as it might, spring was not summer, even if it sometimes wore the same clothes.

Rather than a shed, Colin had only a small grey storage cupboard made of plastic set against the back wall of the house. He opened its door and pulled his neon green trowel off its hook. To keep from hurting his bad finger, he also put on his padded gardening gloves. Last thing he wanted was a bunch of soil inside his cut.

Not with next door's cat constantly doing its business in my borders.

Feeling a little lighter, he went and knelt at the rear of his modest lawn. The grass was soft beneath his knees, even more inviting than his old mattress upstairs (the same one he had once shared with Lisa).

I really should change it. I need something firmer. My back isn't getting any younger.

Colin got to work turning the soil, enjoying the succulent darkness rising to cover the faded, brittle top grains. Few things were more pleasing than a perfectly dug flowerbed.

Every time he scooped, he picked out tiny rocks and weeds, tossing them under a nearby fern. It was an easy job, thanks to yesterday's heavy rainfall. April showers gave life to a garden. In fact, he dug for an entire hour without getting tired.

He felt the trowel hit a rock and held it up to inspect. He picked at a small chunk of yellowy stone peeking through the soil.

No, that isn't a stone.

"Huh..." Colin wore a bemused expression as he examined the strange, tiny object buried in the mud on his trowel. Blue eyes, blonde hair; it was a tiny little plastic baby. "Now, how on earth did you get here, buddy?"

———

COLIN TOOK off his shoes and called Tess again, not remembering she was busy until it was too late.

She answered. "Dad? What now?"

"Oh sorry, I forgot you were busy. I just..." He examined the tiny little baby in the palm of his left hand and groaned. "Don't worry about it. I shouldn't have called."

"Well, you did, so what is it?"

"I found a little plastic baby in the garden. I was wondering if you buried it as a kid."

"What?"

"A tiny plastic baby. I just dug it up while I was weeding. Thought maybe you'd buried it to find later. Like a time capsule type of thing. But a plastic baby."

"Dad, what are you talking about? I have no idea about any plastic babies. Are you going senile?"

He chuckled. "Maybe. Sorry. I shouldn't have called."

"No, it's fine. I'm between meetings. How are you doing?"

"Just pottering around as usual."

"You need to get out, Dad. Go talk to people. Get yourself a girl-friend. Move on, like mum has."

He felt sick. "Yeah. I will."

She sighed. "Life doesn't need to stop, you know? Get out of the house. It'll do you good."

"You're probably right, Tess."

Silence.

"Okay then," she said. "I'll see you next Sunday, yeah?"

"Next Sunday. Love you."

"You too." She ended the call.

Colin put his phone down on the kitchen counter and examined the plastic baby. It was the size of a two-pence piece; a hard chunk of resin formed into a chubby torso, a fat head, and dinky little arms and legs. It was cute, making him think of Tess and David when they were babies. He remembered only a few things that far back, but he could still picture them toddling around in their nappies like it was yesterday. Further back, he could even see Lisa with her swollen belly, carrying David. They had been so happy. Once.

Colin's fastidiousness had been bearable back when he was a younger man, even desirable in many ways. It had helped him run a successful business and amass a decent fortune, and it wasn't really until he had semi-retired and started working from home five years ago that things had taken a bad turn. His marriage had been far healthier when he had worked fifty hours a week in an office, instead of at home where his anxiety and OCD became untamed ogres.

He sat down at the tiny breakfast bar beneath the kitchen's wall-mounted television and placed the baby down in front of him. He stared at it for a good ten minutes. When you were ageing and lonely, you sometimes passed the time simply by doing nothing. It was too much to embrace every long, drawn out minute. Afternoon naps were vital. Mental hibernation.

It was only eleven-thirty, but his belly rumbled. After cutting his finger, his strawberries and granola had gone unmade. In fact, the offending strawberry that had led to him slicing his finger was still sitting next to the punnet on a small plastic cutting board. He cleared up and wiped down the surfaces.

From inside the pantry cupboard, he grabbed a green Pot Noodle and put the kettle on. A couple of times a week, he forced himself to make a proper lunch–sandwiches or a salad–but most days he survived on Pot Noodles, crisps, and microwave meals. He didn't smoke or drink alcohol, so he figured a diet high in sodium wasn't the end of the world. What did he need to live to a hundred for? The last thing he wanted was to end up in a nursing home and spend all of his capital on keeping himself alive instead of dying with dignity and leaving his money to Tess and David.

At least the half that Lisa didn't take.

At least she let me have the house. My OCD lair, she called it.

It was true that Colin's home was an extension of his neurosis. Every ornament sat perfectly on their regularly dusted shelves. The lounge television, sofa, and other furniture were all ancient but familiar. The only things that changed inside his home were the fresh flowers in the vases. He found comfort in stasis. Change was just another word for stress.

Life is less stressful when you know what to expect.

He stabbed a fork into his softening noodles and took them into the lounge. The carpet was fifteen-years old, but had been expensive once, so its creamy fibres had remained plush and vibrant. He enjoyed the way they felt beneath his socked feet. Equally, he enjoyed the enveloping gulp of the old, brown sofa when he sat down on it. It would be another three whole minutes before his noodles were ready, so he leaned over to pop the container on the side table.

He froze.

A tiny baby stared back at him, lying on its side atop the weathered oak surface.

"How did *you* get there?"

The baby had green eyes, but Colin had been sure they were blue earlier. Perhaps it was a trick of the light. Green and blue weren't worlds apart.

He picked up the tiny baby between his thumb and forefinger and studied it. There was no way it could've got there by itself. He had left it on the breakfast bar. He was certain.

Am I going senile?

Come on, I'm not that old.

He took the tiny plastic baby into the kitchen...

...where he found the blue-eyed baby looking back at him.

The green-eyed baby was still pinched between his thumb and forefinger. He placed it down with its sibling.

"I'm losing my mind," he said, shaking his head. "I must be."

He was unsure what to do, so after standing for a moment, he decided the best course of action was to make a cup of tea.

Grabbing the milk from the fridge, he poured it into his favourite mug—a large, orange Garfield one that had come with an Easter egg Tess had brought him with the money from her first job at the local newsagents. He'd held onto it for almost a decade.

While he waited for the kettle to boil, he grabbed a teaspoon and lifted the lid on the sugar pot next to the sink. When he looked inside, he gasped.

A tiny, brown plastic baby stared up at him.

———

THE TINY PLASTIC babies had gone multi-cultural. He now had two little white ones and a black one. Each was different, be it eye colour or some other feature. The brown baby had thicker eyelashes.

Colin picked the small doll up and placed it with the other two. His strange little family.

"What the hell is going on?"

Someone was messing with him. What other explanation was there?

But who? Who would want to play a prank on me?

Colin had never been much of a joker, and neither had his children.

Lisa had a great sense of humour, but she would've found this kind of thing silly.

But there was no one else in his life who would bother to wind him up. He had no friends, no coworkers. His Facebook was full of past acquaintances, but he didn't desire the real life company of anyone except his family. Netflix, the Internet, and a good book or two were enough to keep him sane, even if Tess was always on at him to get a life. Was this her doing? Was she trying to lighten up his existence with a surreal joke?

I don't dare call her, though. If I interrupt her at work again, she might get mad. Then she might not come visit on Sunday, and it will be almost a month since I saw her last.

Almost three months since I saw David.

He sent a text. Hopefully, that wouldn't be too intrusive.

> Found another 2 plastic babies. Are you playing a prank on me? X

If Tess was busy, it might be a while before she texted back, so he put down his phone and continued making his cup of tea. The three babies sat on the breakfast bar, unmoving.

Of course, they're unmoving. They're not alive, Colin.

They're just multiplying.

With a shudder, he poured hot water into his favourite mug and sat down in the lounge again.

He spent the afternoon and early evening trying to keep his anxious mind occupied by reading his book and doing crosswords via an app on his phone. While he was usually okay with not having answers, this mystery was driving him mad. He checked the front door, and every window, but all were locked. It was impossible that someone had crept inside the house to plant the babies.

So how the hell did they get here?

Looking at his watch, he saw that it was now eight o'clock in the evening. The day had flown by and, at the same time, had crawled along at a snail's pace. Frequently throughout the day, he checked on the trio of plastic babies and was relieved to see them where he'd left them. He checked every cupboard, cubbyhole, and shelf for more. There were none.

Three random plastic babies in my house.

His mood fell and his mind was full of chatter. When he got like this, he was at risk of obsessing—running over something again and again in his mind until he made himself ill. The only way to stop it was to go to bed and wipe the mental slate clean. Although early, he was eager to put this day behind him.

Checking the three tiny babies one last time, Colin grabbed his mobile phone and went upstairs to bed. The covers were unmade, but he had changed them two days ago, so they were perfectly inviting. Before he slid into bed, though, he filled his bedside glass with water from the bathroom. Then he closed the curtains and got undressed.

Wearing only his boxer shorts, he climbed into bed.

Strangely, despite the early hour, he was exhausted. He didn't even want to read and nod off like he usually did. Instead, he shuffled down and reached over to the bedside cabinet to plug his phone in to charge.

A tiny plastic baby stared back at him. This one had brown eyes and a smiling face.

———

COLIN LEAPT out of bed and paced the entire house. It had gone dark outside, and with his neighbours away, he felt utterly alone—a victim of a surreal, unexplainable nightmare that no one would believe.

What could he do?

He couldn't call the police over four tiny plastic babies. Could he?

They'll just laugh at me.

Nor could he call Tess or David. They would think he was getting ready for the old people's home. Perhaps he was.

No one who would take his plight seriously. He wasn't sure he took it seriously himself. It was absurd. Stupid.

But as freaked out as he was, he wasn't in danger, was he? What could a few chunks of plastic do to him?

I'm more worried about who put them here. Who has been inside my home?

Sleep was an unobtainable, distant cloud. Yet, at some point towards dawn, Colin's disordered mind managed to shut down for a couple of hours and gave him a blessed break.

Then came the dreams. He was walking through a never-ending concrete underpass, his footsteps echoing off the walls. It was icy cold. The air smelled stale.

Along with the sound of his footsteps was something else. A *chittering* noise. Like ants marching over a microphone.

Movement ahead.

Colin turned around. Movement behind him too.

The *chittering* grew louder as a horde of babies shuffled towards him on stiff, unmoving legs. More noise came from behind him. *Chitter-chitter-chitter.*

He woke up with a startled yell right as the first dozen babies started nipping at the exposed flesh of his forearms. For a moment, his mind refused to establish a grip on reality. Instinctively, he reached out to grab his phone and see what the time was. Four plastic babies stared at him from the bedside table.

He leapt out of bed, screaming.

Grabbing his phone, he raced out of the bedroom and downstairs. Inside the kitchen, he found the other four plastic, still where he'd left them. That made eight in total now.

They keep coming.

He checked his phone, hoping to find a message from Tess, admitting that this was all a joke. But there was nothing. It was a little before nine in the morning. She would already be back at work by now.

When he called, she didn't answer.

He called David next, but got his voicemail.

I need to talk to someone.

Anyone.

Lisa? No, not her. I can't let her know what a mess I am.

He picked up his phone and googled: *Need to talk to someone.*

The number for the *Samaritans* came up.

Colin had never imagined calling a helpline, but that was what he did. He pressed the numbers and called.

"Hello there, friend. This is the Samaritans. My name is Imran. How are you doing this morning?"

"Not so good."

"I'm sorry to hear that. Can I ask your name?"

"C-Colin."

"You sound a little stressed out, Colin. Has something happened? Can I help?"

"Yes."

"I'm listening. Tell me how you're doing, Colin."

Colin swallowed a lump in his throat, his words momentarily stuck. "I-I'm not sure how to."

"That's okay. We can talk about something else if you'd like? Where about are you from?"

"Portsmouth, originally. Exeter for most of my life."

"Exeter? Nice place. Good shopping there, right?"

"It's okay. Where are you?"

There was a brief pause before the man answered. "I'm up north. Harrogate. You know it?"

"Yorkshire? I've never been, but it's supposed to be nice."

"It's lovely. You should arrange to take a holiday here. The fresh air is wonderful, and the landscape is beautiful. Do you live alone, Colin?"

"Yes. I-I'm divorced. My kids are all grown up."

"Does that get lonely sometimes?"

"I suppose so. It's okay. I'm better off alone, trust me."

"Why do you say that, Colin? You sound like a nice man."

Colin shrugged, even though Imran couldn't see the gesture. "I have strange ways."

"How so?"

"I'm a neat freak, among other things."

"That's very common. I can't stand it if my house is untidy, but my wife would happily live in filth." Imran chuckled. "We're all made differently. That's the way it's supposed to be. Do your children visit often?"

"Yes, they come and see me. Well, not as much as I'd like."

"I understand. Colin, I can tell you that so many parents are in the same situation. Kids grow up and get wrapped up in their own lives. It's nothing you've done wrong."

"I know that. They're just busy."

"I understand. It's nice to chat with you, Colin, so feel free to choose a different subject."

"I... I think I might be losing the plot."

Imran cleared his throat down the line. "What do you mean?"

"I'm going mad. Or, at least, something mad is *happening* to me."

"Talk to me about it, Colin."

"There are these tiny plastic babies. They keep turning up all over the house. More and more of them."

"I'm sorry, Colin. I didn't catch that fully. Can you say it again, please?"

"Tiny plastic babies. They keep turning up."

"Plastic babies? I'm not sure I understand. Can you explain it to me?"

Colin grunted. "That's the problem. It makes no sense. I dug up a little tiny baby in my garden yesterday afternoon, and when I brought it inside, I found two more. Then there were others in my bedroom. I have eight of them now."

"Eight babies?"

"Tiny plastic babies."

A moment stretched by, long and silent.

"Colin? I'm really sorry to ask this, but are you having me on? Because if you're calling just to–"

"What? No, I'm not *having you on.*"

"What exactly are you telling me, then?"

Colin squeezed the phone and tutted. "I'm telling you someone or something is trying to drive me mad. They keep putting tiny plastic babies in my home so that I find them. I don't know exactly how they're doing it, or... or maybe it's me and I just don't know I'm doing it. Is fifty-six too young to get dementia?"

"I'm not sure. Do you need me to send help, Colin? If you're in distress, then I can–"

"No, don't send help. I'll end up in the loony bin."

"But if you're having trouble with reality."

"I'm not having trouble with reality. The tiny babies are real."

"Colin, I need you to tell me your address. Let me send someone who can work this out with you."

The man thinks I'm insane.

Exactly what he had been afraid of.

"I have to go, Imran."

"No, hold on a mo—"

Colin ended the call and paced the kitchen, his heart thundering in his chest. He wanted to cry and scream. He called Tess and David again, but both were still busy.

I need to calm down. I'm getting worked up. Just take a breath.

Colin headed into the lounge to watch television as a distraction. The silence was only making things worse.

He cried out loud when his bare foot came down on something sharp. When he looked down, he saw another tiny plastic baby—this one pale skinned with a thatch of painted blonde hair.

"No! No, please stop this. Enough of this!"

Something caught his eye. He glanced towards the lounge's only window, spotting something beneath the Venetian blinds. As he approached, he saw a conga line of babies stretching across the sill.

Screaming, he ran back into the kitchen, only to find more tiny babies scattered about the counters. Colin clutched at his hair and pulled, his vision swirling.

He felt something in his hands. Something hard and tiny and buried in his hair.

———

THE DOORBELL RANG, and Colin screamed again, tossing the tiny brown baby he had found in his hair onto the floor. He raced to answer the door.

It's Tess! Or David!

They're going to be standing there, laughing. What a prank they played on their poor old dad.

The rascals. The bloody sods.

The postman was wearing shades, despite the morning being overcast. He smiled at Colin and shook his head. "Number 4 again, mate. I reckon they're trying to keep Amazon in business."

Colin stared at the large flat parcel like it was an alien object. "W-what?"

The postman frowned. "You all right, mate? You look a little out of it."

"C-come in. Please, come in."

"What? Why?"

"I need you to see something. Please."

The postman lowered the parcel and shifted uncomfortably. "I-Is everything okay?"

Colin shook his head. "I think I'm losing my mind. Come inside and tell me if you see what I see."

"God, this is proper weird, mate. But all right, I'll come in. This best not be anything 'orrible, though."

"Just come into the lounge."

The postman stepped inside, leaving the door open—probably to aid a quick getaway. He folded his hands around his parcel as Colin led him into the lounge.

"Look, can you see the...?"

There was nothing there. No tiny plastic babies. No conga line on the windowsill.

"What am I supposed to be looking at, mate?"

Colin shook his head, over and over again. "No. This doesn't make any sense."

The postman backed off towards the door, although he seemed sympathetic. "Are you okay?"

"Come into the kitchen."

"Why?"

"Because there are more babies in there."

"Babies? Mate, you're freaking me out now."

"Please, just take a look in the kitchen and then you can go."

The postman nodded and allowed himself to be led again, although he looked ready to throw a punch at the first sign of danger.

Colin hurried into the kitchen and looked at the breakfast bar.

It was empty.

There were no tiny plastic babies in the room at all.

"They're gone," Colin muttered.

The postman shook his head sadly. "I think you need help. Can you call someone to come over?"

Colin rubbed at his eyes and looked at the breakfast bar again. When he was sure there were no babies, he looked at the postman and tried to nod confidently. "Yes. Yes, I'll call my kids. I'm fine. I... I just had a fright."

"Well, relax and stay calm, yeah? Everything seems fine." He turned to leave the kitchen, but then he looked back. "You sure you're going to be all right?"

Colin nodded and waved a hand. "Don't worry about me. Sure, I'll see you tomorrow with another parcel for number 4."

"Ha! Yeah, I'll leave this in your hallway with the other one."

"Thanks." Colin remained in the kitchen, listening as the front door slammed shut a moment later.

Alone again.

Where did the babies go?

He went back into the lounge, wanting to watch the postman through the window, to see if the man got on his phone and called for the men in white coats.

But as soon as Colin entered the room, he froze.

The cream carpet was littered with tiny plastic babies. Hundreds of them. More of them perched atop picture frames and peeked out from behind various ornaments. The room was infested with them.

Colin began to cry. It was all too much.

He couldn't cope with any more of this.

He went and got his phone. Called Lisa, his ex-wife. Something he hadn't done in a long time.

"Col? Is everything all right?"

He smiled, unexpectedly glad to hear his ex-wife's voice. For a moment, he couldn't speak. "I... I just... just wanted to check in."

"Really? We haven't spoken in a year."

"I heard about the wedding. I just wanted to say... congratulations.

"You don't have to be happy for me, Colin. But thank you."

"I'm sorry I was so hard to live with, Leese. I hope you've found someone who makes you happy."

"*You* made me happy, Colin. For a long time, you did. Things just ran their course. That's life. We move on."

"I suppose we do. Well, anyway, it's good to hear your voice. Maybe I'll even come to the wedding."

Silence.

"Or not."

"It's not a good idea, is it?"

"No. What was I thinking?"

Lisa cleared her throat, obviously wanting to end the call now that he had made it awkward. "You're seeing Tess on Sunday?"

"For dinner, yes."

"Give her my love, won't you?"

"Will do. Goodbye, Lisa."

"Goodbye, Colin. Take care of yourself, okay?"

He smiled down the phone, feeling a little more at peace. "I'm going to."

The call ended, and he went to make himself a cup of tea, ignoring the hundreds of tiny plastic babies surrounding him. It didn't matter where they came from. The question didn't need an answer.

———

"DAD?" Tess shouted, entering the hallway. "Hello? You didn't come to the door, so I let myself in." She waved a hand in front of her face. Her dad had never been much of a cook, but the smell in the house gave her cause for concern. They were supposed to be having roast pork, but it smelled more like some kind of gamey stew. Perhaps he had changed his mind about the menu.

"Dad? Where are you?"

She went into the lounge to find the television switched off, which was unusual as he liked to keep it on for the company (the only company he could bear to have in his home for more than a few hours). As a child, this house had been like a prison. Leave a thing out of place and her dad would throw a fit.

It wasn't his fault. He was ill. Or different, if you want to be kind.

Still... I hate being here. This place never felt like home.

"I'm sorry I never text you back in the week," she said. "Work has been hectic." She looked towards the kitchen, listening for clanking pots and pans, but heard nothing. "Mum said you called. That was nice of you. She still cares about you, you know? Dad, can you answer me, please?"

Where the hell is he?

Tess marched into the kitchen, frustrated. Was he out in the garden? Half her memories of her dad involved him being outside, planting his flowers and plants. If only he had cared as much about–

She froze in her tracks, halfway through the kitchen door.

Her dad had yanked a thick zip tie around his neck and sat himself down at the breakfast bar while he strangled to death. There was a note in front of him along with a pen. He must've written it moments before...

Before he killed himself.

"Oh Dad, you son of a bitch."

The tears came fast and fierce, but Tess was enough in control of herself to creep forward and take the note with a shaking hand.

Don't miss me. I want you to be happy.
Like I used to be.
Love, Dad.

Tess let the note drift back down to the table as she shook her head and sobbed. Despite the horror of seeing her dad dead, she couldn't help but reach out and take his clammy grey hand as it rested on the table. It was shockingly firm. His fingers moved stiffly, clutching something small pressed into his palm.

Tess had to use both hands to straighten her dad's finger and see what it was he had been holding as he died.

"What the hell?"

It was a tiny plastic baby with blue eyes.

The one he said he found buried in the garden.

Shit, I remember this now. I do.

"I did bury it, Dad," she said out loud, almost as an apology. Why hadn't she remembered it before? She must've been six or seven and had planted it in some strange hope that it would grow into another little girl to keep her company and have tea parties with. Stupid. David had still been a toddler, and she hadn't liked him at the time— not that they had grown any closer since. Theirs was a family of loners.

Of the lonely.

She shook her head and sighed. "Why didn't you tell me you were feeling like this? Why didn't you ask for my help?"

She dropped the tiny plastic baby down on the table and called the police, wondering if there was anything she could've done to prevent this.

If only there had been some kind of warning sign.

The Manuscript

To Louis, Drendale Tower was little more than half a stone wall and a big pile of rubble, but the brown road sign meant it must have mattered to someone. It was an historic landmark, the remnants of a small border fort built in the fourteenth century to keep the mad Scots on their side of the border. The only reason he and Robbie went there, though, was because girls could sometimes be found, drinking cider or sharing vapes.

Not today, though.

Today, Drendale Tower was just an abandoned ruin lying in the centre of misty parkland beneath an overcast sky promising rain. A depressing Sunday made even gloomier by its lonely melancholy.

"I might go in," Louis's best friend, Robbie, said, and he dropped down from the top of the stunted stone wall. He landed amongst the crumpled beer cans and mouldy dog ends that the drunks and druggies left here at night. Like Louis, he was obviously bored.

The two of them lived in the Edward Street terraces about a twenty-minute walk away. People called them the 'benefit boxes,' because the houses were so pokey and most of the people who lived there were unemployed. Louis's mam, however, was one of the few exceptions. She worked overnight at the big Asda on the ring road. It was the best job she'd ever had, and sometimes she got to bring back free food that was going to get thrown out.

"Yeah, let's call it," Louis agreed, hopping down off the wall too. "Lacey Turner ain't gonna show up now, is she?"

Robbie patted him on the back. "Sorry, bro. I really thought she'd be here. Calum French said she was planning to hang out here with some of her friends."

"She don't like me, anyway. Darren Kennedy said he had her from behind down Lowby Park, and she's been in love with him ever since."

"Darren Kennedy is full of shit, man." Robbie rolled his eyes. "Don't you remember the time he said his dad was a coach at Newcastle United? Then everyone found out he's just a manager at Screwfix?"

Louis guffawed. "Yeah, that was proper funny. He got roasted for like a month. *The Screwfix kid. Ask him for a screw.*"

"You'll get her, man. You're a canny lad. How could she resist?"

When Louis saw his friend smirking, he pointed a finger and raised his eyebrows. "Eh, you're no Bobby Dazzler yourself, man."

Robbie put his arms out defensively. "Hey, I'm as serious as a heart attack. I reckon you got a chance, bro."

"Really?" He scrutinised his friend's face, waiting for his serious expression to crack and reveal the lie. But it didn't crack. "All right, fair play, then. Cheers."

Robbie chuckled and then looked up at the grey sky. "Come on. I don't want to get soaked if it rains."

Louis realised that the clouds had darkened substantially, rain almost a certainty now. So they got moving, leaving the broken-down wall everyone called 'the Tower' behind them. As he did so, his foot struck something hard, which at first he assumed to be nothing more than rubbish. But when he looked down, he saw a big wad of paper stacked in a neat pile. "What the hell?"

Robbie was a few feet behind, but he moved up to join him. "Did someone come up here to do their taxes or summit?"

Louis crouched and studied the top sheet of paper. There were just three words written on it in red handwriting, scrawled in the very centre of the page. He read them aloud. "Invite the Wolf." Then, with a frown, he added, "It's a story, I think. Like, what do they call it?"

Robbie took a step back, gasping. "Yo! You mean a manuscript?"

"Yeah. That's it! I think this is a manuscript." He picked the pile of papers up and marvelled at how crisp and white they were. Left out here in the dirt, they should have been wet and soiled, but they were spotless. "Doesn't say who wrote it. That's weird, right? It would usually say '*by*' someone. The author."

"Louis, put that thing down, man! Don't touch it no more."

"What? Why?" He stood up, still holding the manuscript. The paper seemed to vibrate gently in his hands, but he must have been imagining it. "You're acting weird, Robbie."

"No, man, I'm not. That thing, it's one of *them*." He pointed his finger and stepped back further. "It's one of the cursed manuscripts."

Louis examined the top page again, still seeing nothing except for the handwritten title. "What are you talking about?"

"The Cursed Manuscripts. The Cursed Manuscripts. How do you *not* know what I'm talking about? Shit, this is bad."

Louis moved back to the wall and sat down on the lowest part of it. His stomach was fluttering, the slightest morsel of dread being picked over by a moth inside his gut. Why was Robbie so worried?

"I have no idea what you're talking about, man. Why are you freaking out?"

Robbie had gone as white as a sheet, and he looked like he was about to sprint away across the fields. Slowly, however, he seemed to calm down. Eventually, he walked over to join Louis, although he didn't sit down.

"You know that website I like to go on–*Splatt!?*"

Louis nodded. "The one with all the spooky stuff?"

"Yeah, it's a bit like if the X-Files was an ad-supported website instead of a law enforcement agency."

"Or a made up show..."

"Whatever. Anyway, about three years ago, they posted this article called *The Devil's Fiction*, and it was all about these weird manuscripts turning up all over the world in random places."

Louis flexed the manuscript in his hands, feeling the weight of it and testing its realness. It really was an odd thing to find out here in the dirt. "Alright, go on."

"Well, these manuscripts are evil, bro. The article said they're all written in blood, and anyone who reads one dies a horrible death."

Despite his unease, Louis couldn't help but laugh. "Ha'way, man, you expect me to believe that? It's just a bunch of papers, Robbie."

"What colour is the ink? Huh?"

"It's red. So what? You can buy red pens. For all I know, the other pages are blank. Look!"

Robbie covered his face with his arm. "Don't! I don't wanna look, man!"

"Oh shit." Louis examined the other pages, leafing through them carefully while trying not to drop the entire thick bundle. The words were all written in the same red scrawl as the title page, but complete sheets of it, line after line after line. Messy handwriting from margin to margin in a dark, uneven red.

Compelled, Louis read aloud a paragraph from one of the beginning pages. "*He saw nothing inside the back of the van except an unmoving darkness that reminded him of the under-stairs cupboard at home. He always shivered whenever he passed it, worried he might get trapped inside, unable to escape the dark, with no one to hear his cries.*"

"Stop! Louis, don't do that. Don't fucking read it."

His friend's urgency and volume caused him to fumble the stack and drop the papers on the ground.

The manuscript landed unnaturally, the pages staying perfectly together.

"I told you, man," Robbie said. "I told you not to read it. People die when they read the Cursed Manuscripts."

Louis froze, his legs turning leaden and his blood icing up. Then, once again, he laughed. "Stop it, Robbie. You're freaking me out. This is a stupid prank, right? People don't die because they read words."

But Robbie wasn't laughing, and after being friends for four years, Louis knew him pretty well. Well enough to know when he was being serious. He truly believed what he was saying.

"Okay, tell me more about what you read in that article." Louis looked down at the manuscript on the floor. "Why would reading this thing kill me?"

Robbie put his hands to his face, like he wanted to cry. "Shit, I don't remember. Um... it was something to do with a curse."

"Kind of in the name, man."

"They're written by the devil or something. The Vatican has been collecting them and storing them in a vault. If they were all to be read, it would kick off the end of the world."

"And each one is a story? How many are there?"

"I don't know, I don't know. Loads of them. Hundreds. They've been trying to cover it all up, but people have been dying all over the world after finding these things. Each one is a different story, and the guy who wrote the article said they're like warnings to humanity. Like, there was this one about a vampire apocalypse starting because some guy pricked himself with a needle and made a deal with a demon. Then, there was this one about kids going online and doing a ritual that brought back the dead."

"Wait!" Louis wagged a finger, his eyes widening. "I remember that. There were all these videos online of kids freaking out or getting attacked on camera. They were everywhere for like one week. Then they were all gone. Norman's Ritual, right?"

"It's all cover ups, man. There's so much shit going down that they don't want us to know about."

"Okay, all right, can we just think this through for a minute? Are you really saying that I, a fifteen-year-old kid from some random shit-hole in England, am going to die because I read a few words written on some paper? Are you really telling me that this thing on the ground is actually a cursed manuscript written by the Devil? My mum can't win three quid on the scratchies, but I'm lucky enough—out of billions of people—to find one of these things?"

"Unlucky, bro. You're unlucky."

"Whatever. It's insane either way."

Robbie just stared at him for a moment, and Louis could almost see the cogs spinning in his head. "I'm only telling you what I read."

"On the Internet, on a site that gets clicks by freaking people out."

"Then why the hell is it out here, Louis? Why would a handwritten manuscript be sitting out here in the middle of nowhere?"

"Because someone put it here, obviously. Probably someone who read the same article you did. It's like when everyone kept dressing up as clowns and chasing people. It's a trend."

Robbie let out a tiny chuckle. "You really think so? You think this is all just a prank?"

"It has to be. Otherwise we're saying that the Devil is real and God knows what else."

It started to rain; just a spatter, but its light touch brought Louis back to reality. "And now we're gonna get soaked. Come on, I'm done with this. You've freaked me the hell out, but I don't believe it."

Robbie chuckled louder and then shook his head in shame. "Yeah, bro, sorry. My imagination got the best of me."

"Nay worries. Anyway, if I'm dying then so are you. You were listening when I read the words out, right?"

"Yo, what the hell, man?" Robbie started walking away. "I'm not gonna sleep for a week now, thanks to y—*shit*!"

Louis saw his friend's foot come down on a discarded beer can.

It shouldn't have been cause for alarm.

Yet Robbie's ankle folded and he fell sideways like a pushed ladder. The sound of his temple striking the solid stones of the broken-down wall sounded like rotten fruit splatting on kitchen tiles. The impact sent Robbie's body into a spin and he tumbled onto his back. His head was the wrong shape by the time his body settled.

Louis screamed, but there was no one to hear. He dropped beside his friend and shook him—his head flopped lifelessly. Blood trickled out of his eye sockets and both ears. "No, no, no. Robbie? Robbie, man, no."

The wind died. A sudden chill.

Robbie opened his eyes.

Louis gasped, his bladder immediately releasing piss down his thigh. His friend's head was pulp, but he was alive and awake. In fact, he was talking.

"Read the words. Give your soul. Read the words. Give your soul."

The voice was not Robbie's. It sounded like crunching glass and came from far away. Nor were they his friend's eyes staring back at him. They were cold black voids, deeper than the deepest of wells.

Louis screamed again, but when he attempted to get away, the thing inside Robbie's corpse grabbed him by the collar and yanked him forwards with incredible force. Louis saw the jagged, broken stones of the Drendale Tower rushing towards his face as he hurtled forwards.

And then all was black.

———

VATICAN INVENTORY LOG - CM91679
Secrecy a priority. Papal code section: 16.92

Manuscript 13.24-07, discovered May 2024 in Drendon-Le–Dale, County Durham, by teenagers Robbie Mitchell and Louis Owens. Both were discovered dead after catastrophic head injuries sustained at local landmark Drendale Tower. The circumstance of their deaths is unknown.

DRONE

"Put that back!" Debbie tapped Millie's hand to keep her from plucking the *Cadbury Creme Egg* from the carton beside the till. "I already told you we're not getting any snacks. You haven't stopped eating all day!"

Her nine-year-old daughter sulked, which yanked at Debbie's heartstrings of course, but Millie was starting to get a little belly from too many crisps and too much chocolate.

I don't want her to go through life struggling with her weight all the time.

I don't want her to be like me.

The line moved up and Debbie put her items on the conveyor belt. Just a few things for dinner–spaghetti, marinara sauce, mushrooms, garlic bread. Truthfully, the quick trip to *Morrisons* had been mostly to get some fresh air and time away from the house. Three weeks into the six-week Summer holiday and Millie was already climbing the walls.

If Debbie had the money, she would have happily planned a bunch of days out for them both, but money was tight and only seemed to be getting tighter. So Millie had been stuck at home every day, except on the odd occasions when she went to play over at a friend's house.

"Can we go to the park after this?" Millie asked, leaning against the conveyor belt and risking her purple sleeve getting caught in the edge.

"I thought you were too old for the park? That's what you told me."

She shrugged, more like a teenager lately than a nine-year-old. "I know, but it's better than doing nothing. There could be people from school there."

Debbie went to say no, almost by default, but she reconsidered and saw no real reason to object. She had accountancy work to be getting on with at home, but she didn't mind working a little into the evening. "Okay, honey. If you want to. Let's just get this stuff in the boot."

Millie bagged up while Debbie paid the cashier, tapping her card against the terminal and then tensing up while she waited for it to be approved. With the way money seemed to fly out of her account day after day, she always fretted about her card being declined.

Having to stand there, all embarrassed. God, it would be awful

The payment was successful. The cashier dismissed her with a quick smile before moving on to the next customer.

Debbie reached to grab the shopping bag, but Millie hoisted it first. They began walking. "Thank you, honey."

"No problem."

She's a good kid.

Wish her deadbeat dad would realise that. Maybe then he would help me out and take her more than once a week.

Debbie realised her mood was falling, so she forced herself to smile. She had read somewhere that the physical act of grinning could actually trick the mind into feeling more positive. Probably nonsense, but it seemed to work a little.

"So what film should we watch tonight, honey?" she asked as they headed out through the first set of automatic glass doors.

"Dunno. How about we start the Harry Potter films again?"

They passed through the second set of doors and headed out into the balmy summer air.

"Sounds good," Debbie said, but inside she was groaning. It would be the third time watching the Harry Potter films from start to finish. By this point, she wanted to punch the mop-headed little brat right in the mouth.

Briefly forgetting where she had parked, Debbie looked around until she spotted her shiny silver *Hyundai* near one of the trolley shelters right in the middle of the car park. She always chose an easy space over a close space. Parking wasn't her greatest skill.

"Ah, over here." She changed direction and slowed until Millie caught up. Her daughter was almost as tall as her now, which wasn't saying much at five-foot-three, but still...

As they neared the car, walking side by side, both of them flinched at the sudden sound of breaking glass.

Millie turned her head. "What was that?"

"I don't know." Debbie turned too, slightly out of breath from the march across the car park.

Several people were standing around the car park, searching for the source of the sudden loud noise.

Debbie thought she heard a faint *zip* sound, like fingernails scratching a dashboard.

One of the people standing around suddenly fell backwards—an old lady in blue. It was like a switch had suddenly flipped inside her brain and rendered her body useless.

A heart attack? An aneurysm?

The old lady just lay there on the concrete, unmoving in the sunshine.

Debbie put a hand across her mouth and gasped. "We need to call an ambulance."

Millie covered her mouth too, perhaps unconsciously mimicking her mother.

Startled bystanders rushed to help the woman, but Debbie stood still and pulled out her old iPhone. For a moment, she saw her own chubby, pale face reflected back at her in the unlit screen, but then the device woke and tried to battle the sun with its failing back light.

She brought up the keypad and typed in 9-9-.

The phone exploded in her hand; a cloud of glass and plastic.

A hot, throbbing pain swelled within her.

Millie was staring at her, her eyes wide and terrified. "M-Mum, what is it? What's happening?"

Debbie stared at her palm in disbelief. She could see right through it—a bloody hole in the fleshy pad beneath her thumb. "I... I'm hurt, honey."

Then she screamed.

But no one noticed.

Because lots of other people were screaming too, an entire chorus of wailing.

A young man who was trying to help the fallen old lady suddenly collapsed right beside her. A fine mist sprayed out from the side of his head.

The bonnet of a bright red *Alfa Romeo* buckled inwards and its alarm started blaring. The windshield of a rusted *Saab* shattered into a thousand pieces.

Debbie struggled to stop screaming as she continued staring at the hole in her hand. The wound was leaking blood—it flowed hotly down both sides of her wrist. "S-someone's shooting at us."

Millie turned pale. She'd been watching the escalating chaos around them, but she clearly didn't understand it. "Mum?"

Despite the agony seizing up her entire left arm, and the dizziness washing over her, Debbie grabbed her daughter by the wrist and yanked her backwards. Just as a chunk of tarmac exploded at her feet.

"Oh my God," Debbie yelled. "Oh my God. Help! Help us!"

Millie started wailing. The sight of her daughter's distress forced Debbie into action and she dragged them both across the car park. She made a beeline for their car.

More tarmac exploded, half-a-metre in front of them.

They were going to die. There was no way they'd reach the car in time.

Cover was their only salvation. They had to find some.

Debbie yanked on Millie again. "Get down."

They leapt into a gap between a white transit van and a blue Jaguar SUV. The two of them ducked down between the high-sided vehicles and covered their heads, whimpering and pressing against each other.

More screaming. It seemed to come from everywhere.

Debbie couldn't help herself. She peeked around the rear of the van to see what was happening.

People were racing to get back inside the supermarket, but several of them fell before they could make it. Their heads oozed blood onto the pavement.

Bodies littered the car park. One man had slumped forwards into his trolley, his legs now pointed up in the air.

A dozen dead, at least.

Debbie heard more of those *zip* sounds, every one a bullet flying towards its target. More windshields shattered. More people screamed. Screaming strangers sprinted past Millie and Debbie's hiding spot, desperate to find safety of their own. One man collapsed just out of sight, only the bottoms of his trainers visible from where Debbie hid.

"Mum, what's happening?" Millie was trembling like a leaf, more than Debbie had ever seen a person shake.

She hugged her daughter. "It's okay. Just stay down. Th-there's a shooter?"

"What? Like in America?"

"Maybe it's a terrorist attack. Just stay down."

Millie couldn't go much lower, already on her knees with her head lowered almost to the ground, but Debbie pushed her down a few more inches. It felt safe where they were hiding, sandwiched between two high-sided vehicles, so she decided the best thing to do was stay put and pray for rescue.

Where's the shooter, though? Can he see us hiding here?

Debbie was trembling so badly that it was difficult to continue peeking carefully out from cover. The longer she poked her head out from the side of the van, the more she risked getting her face blown off. But she was desperate to see where the danger was, desperate to know if her daughter was safe where she was hiding.

Millie made an awful sound behind her.

Debbie ducked back into cover and turned around. Her daughter was choking, about to be sick from absolute shock and terror.

Debbie rubbed Millie's back as she vomited against the Jaguar's front tyre, chunks of hot dog splattering against the intricately shaped alloys.

"It's okay, honey. We're going to just stay here and take deep breaths. That's it."

"I... I don't understand." She spat stringy saliva and groaned. "Why is this happening?"

What answer could Debbie give? What would even make sense to a nine-year-old? "It doesn't matter right now, sweetheart. We just need to stay hidden until help arrives."

"Is help coming?"

"Yes."

They crouched in silence for the next few minutes. Debbie held her wounded hand against her abdomen and bit down on her lip. The only thing that had ever hurt even close to this was when she had given birth to Millie—a nine-pound bundle of hurt and stretch-marks.

I can't let anything happen to her.

The screaming died down. The shattering of windscreens had stopped altogether. Did that mean the danger was over? Had the gunman been taken down? Tackled by some brave bystander? Or had he fled the scene?

Debbie had never seen a gun in real life, so being shot at was something she'd never worried about before. Getting mugged at knifepoint or even sexually assaulted, sure, but not shot at by a madman. It wasn't something that was supposed to happen.

Debbie heard another *zip*, followed by a thud that she now knew was a body hitting the ground. The threat wasn't gone.

"Mum, I want to go home."

"I know, sweetheart. This will all be over soon."

Another *zip*. Another thud. Another body.

How many were dead now?

A pained moan erupted from nearby, somebody injured but not killed.

Like me.

Debbie realised how lucky she was to only have a mutilated hand. Even if the doctors had to chop it off, she still had her life. She still got to be a mother and enjoy popcorn nights in front of the telly.

But what if the gunman is walking the car park, rooting out people hiding? What if he appears any minute and points his rifle at me? Or Millie? What do I do then?

Debbie suddenly felt less safe. Maybe it was smarter to keep on running, to make it to the car or even the main road. They could zigzag, dodge in and out between cars...

The Jaguar bounced on its springs, a bullet striking its bonnet.

Millie screamed. Debbie did too. Her wounded hand went to her mouth and she tasted blood.

A second shot blew out the van's side window.

Squealing, Debbie realised with mortal terror that the shooter knew they were hiding there. But how? How did he see her crouched down between the two vehicles?

Millie yelped and looked up at the sky.

Debbie looked up, too, just in time to see the danger and throw herself down on top of her daughter.

Another menacing *zip* sounded, followed by a metallic thud as a bullet cut right through the Jaguar's driver side door and left a ragged hole. The shot had been aimed at Millie.

The drone tilted to-and-fro ten feet overhead. From the way it flitted about erratically, it resembled some kind of giant insect. A green light flashed rhythmically on its underside while a sleek black turret rotated on its belly like a wasp's stinger.

Debbie gathered up her daughter and screamed. "Run!"

Thank God fear had not frozen either of them as they bolted from cover at the same time.

Now that she knew where the threat was coming from, Debbie's ears detected the soft *brrr* of the drone's rotors. It sounded like a swarm of angry bees.

Millie made it inside one of the car park's perspex trolley shelters. She immediately shoved herself into a gap between two rows of stacked trolleys and lay on the concrete between the wheels. She then turned her head and peered at her mother. Debbie knew the drone was right overhead from her from the way her daughter's eyes darted frantically.

I'm going to die. I'm going to get sho–

All of a sudden, she was tumbling to the ground. If a bullet had struck her, she didn't feel it. Her pulse roared like thunder in her ears. Sweat soaked her back beneath her blouse. Her legs cramped up, and she feared she might never get back up.

I don't care what happens to me. Please, God, just get my daughter out of here.

Debbie didn't think she'd been shot. Her legs had simply abandoned her and sent her sprawling. She was lying on the ground right beside a dead man, her arm stretched out in a puddle of his blood. All around her, tins of beer and snack food littered the ground. Whoever the poor man was, he'd been planning on having a good time.

Killed for no reason. His life snuffed out.

One of the beer cans exploded and skated across the tarmac, foamy liquid fizzing out of its side. Then a second bullet hit the ground right beside Debbie's head. She was lying on her tummy, but she pushed up now with the last of the strength she had left, making it back to her feet and leaning into a run. Millie's pleading stare filled her with a surging desire to live.

She made it into the shelter and shoved as many trolleys in front of them both, hoping it would be enough to create a shield.

The drone whizzed back and forth outside the shelter, a predator trying to invade the entrance of a defenceless creature's lair. Debbie stared right into its blinking green light, wondering who was looking back at her through some screen somewhere. Some heartless monster who didn't care about taking innocent lives.

A monster who had shot at her nine-year-old daughter.

The drone tilted and then zipped across the car park. A moment later, a stranger screamed in despair as someone they cared about died and hit the ground. Two seconds later, the screamer died too.

Debbie crouched down with Millie, pushing them both deeper into the cavern of trolleys that were scattered all around them. The drone had gone after easier prey, but would it be back?

"Where are the police, Mum? Why isn't anyone here?"

Debbie swallowed a lump in her throat and felt it stick in her windpipe. She ignored the sharp pain and held her daughter with both arms. "They're coming, honey. They're on their way."

"How do you know?"

"Because they have to be on their way."

"I don't want to die, Mum."

The sight of Millie's terror brought tears to Debbie's eyes. "I know, honey. Me either."

"You're bleeding."

Debbie held her hand up and actually chuckled. "Yeah, it hurts a bit."

Millie hugged her, no longer trembling but ice cold. Debbie was red hot, leaking sweat from every pore. Exertion had turned her into a wheezing ghoul.

"Sweetheart, I love you so much. I'm so sorry if I haven't been the best mum. I've always done my best, but I should have done better. Maybe if I–"

"Mum, don't. Please."

She nodded, realising she was saying goodbye, and that meant she was giving up. "I love you, honey. We're going to be okay."

If those are my last words, they'll do.

Everything appeared blurry through the Perspex dome of the shelter, but Debbie spotted the drone back in the sky above them–a shadow whizzing back and forth.

Picking people off like it's a goddamn video game.

I hope they catch the monster who's done this. I hope they catch him and throw him in a pitch black cell.

Debbie watched the whizzing black blob a moment longer, then let out a trapped breath. "I-I think we're safe. It's ignoring us."

"Mum, how is that thing shooting people?"

"It's a drone. Somebody fitted a gun to it. My God, all those people."

"When will it run out of bullets?"

Debbie looked at her daughter and reached out to wipe a tear from her cheek. "I don't know anything about guns, honey. We just need to sit tight, okay? Help will come soo–"

"You keep saying that! Where are the police?"

"I don't know."

The two of them lay on the ground beneath the trolleys, both of them trembling. Millie was still cold, Debbie still hot. Her hand hurt, but it was a background pain now. The worst discomfort came from her hip pressing against the hard concrete.

The car park went silent. No screaming, no more frightened chatter. She might have assumed the drone was gone, but something deep in her guts knew that wasn't true. She knew what the silence truly meant.

We're the last ones left.

Everybody's dead.

The drone reappeared overhead, its blurry shape still visible through the perspex shelter.

The shelter shook as a bullet ricocheted off its roof panel. Then one of the side walls fractured, a spiderweb of cracks spreading from top to bottom.

"Mum! Mum, it's going to get us!"

"Stay down, honey. We have to stay covered."

More bullets hit the shelter. The plastic sheeting cracked and bent. It looked like it might hold, but then the drone started shooting at the edges and knocking pieces loose from the metal fasteners. The cracked panel leaned inwards, barely holding on to its steel supports.

The drone zipped around the shelter, moving in front of the entrance. A bullet pinged off a trolley and embedded in the concrete, not more than a few feet from Debbie's face.

Millie screamed.

Another bullet struck a trolley, knocking it into its neighbour.

Millie scrambled to get her feet beneath her.

"Millie, no!"

Debbie grabbed at her daughter, but she was too frantic—and stronger than she looked. Kicking out hysterically, she caught Debbie right in the jaw and knocked her silly. Millie leapt up and crashed her way through the maze of trolleys.

Then she was out, back in the open.

The drone zipped through the sky. Its turret rotated.

"Millie!" Debbie screamed. "Get back here."

But Millie didn't listen. She sprinted like a screaming gazelle across the car park.

I have to save her. I have to do something.

Debbie pushed herself up off her belly and crashed her way out of the shelter.

Millie was already thirty metres ahead. The drone flew right behind her.

"Come get me," Debbie yelled. "You hear me, you sad little man playing with his joystick? You come deal with me!"

The drone almost seemed to skid in mid air. It had no front or back, so it didn't turn around, as such; it simply changed direction.

It headed towards Debbie.

It's going to shoot me.

But if it gives Millie enough time to make it inside the supermarket.

Debbie didn't want to die, but running was pointless. She was too slow and out of shape. Any stamina she had left would barely take her ten steps.

The drone raced towards her as Millie raced for safety.

Debbie grabbed a pair of beer cans off the ground next to the dead man. She wasn't much of a drinker, but right now she would love to be safe and sound at home with a bottle of wine.

"Fuck you," she yelled. "You evil monster."

Her injured hand screamed with pain, but she pushed through it and hurled one of the beer cans into the air. It sailed harmlessly past the drone, which zigzagged out of the way almost mockingly.

"They're going to catch you," she shouted. "Whoever you are. They'll get you and expose you for the spineless coward you are."

The drone stopped in mid-air, hovering just ahead of her, so close she could've whacked it with a broom if she'd had one. The little turret on its belly rotated to point at her. Its green light flashed.

Debbie glared and bellowed angrily. "Fuck off!"

She hurled the other can of beer, feeling a rage she'd never experienced before. A car park of atrocity. How dare someone commit such wickedness? How dare someone come and take her life, as if it were their right to do so.

The drone tilted to avoid the incoming beer can.

But it was too slow.

The can smashed right into the drone's rotor on one side, making it inside the protective guard that ringed each of the four quadrants. Rather than bounce or ricochet, the beer can wedged in place, held tightly by the stalled propeller blades.

The drone dropped like a rock and clattered to the ground.

Another deadly *zip* sounded.

The bullet struck the radiator of a BMW parked right behind Debbie. A plume of steam emerged from the newly dug hole.

The drone skittered on the ground like a fly with a missing wing. Try as it might, it could not get airborne again. Debbie stood and watched it, hating the thing even though it was just a machine—a toy. At the edges of her vision, she saw Millie make it safely inside the supermarket.

My daughter's alive.

And so am I.

Debbie limped forwards, her body shattered, her adrenaline ebbing. The drone was much smaller than it had seemed up in the sky. A pathetic thing, really. Three of its four rotors were still spinning, but the weight of the jammed beer can kept the machine grounded.

Dozens of innocent dead because of this thing.

Debbie sneered at the blinking green light. "I might be a middle-aged, out of shape single mother, but I beat you. I beat you."

She raised a foot and brought it down hard on the centre of the drone, on the block of plastic housing its electronic innards. It shattered easily, but the rotors kept spinning. Two more stomps finished it off. By then, the only part still working was the blinking green light. It seemed to look at her pleadingly, an insectoid eye attached to a diseased brain.

"They'll find you," she said. "They always find people like you."

A vehicle screeched to a halt twenty metres behind Debbie and made her turn around. She was so numb she barely even flinched.

The police car evoked nothing but a resigned sigh from her.

Two officers leapt out of the car and immediately surveyed the carnage in aghast horror. There might have been three dozen people dead in the car park, their bodies scattered everywhere. Glass and debris littered the ground, torn open shopping bags and discarded belongings, like a war zone.

No. A massacre.

"You're too late." Debbie yelled at the police officers. "Everyone's dead. You should have been here sooner."

One officer, a man seemingly in his fifties, stepped forwards to meet her. He was still surveying the bloody carnage, but he brought his eyes up to look at her. "I'm sorry. We came as quickly as we could, but..."

Debbie shook her head. "But what? Why didn't you come sooner?"

"Because this is happening everywhere, ma'am." The officer seemed sick to his stomach as he said it. "All over the country."

Debbie almost fell down. It took a sheer force of will to remain standing. "W-what do you mean?"

"I mean..." the officer shook his head and sighed. He looked past her at the fallen drone and pointed. "I mean we're under attack. There are drones like this everywhere, shooting at people. It's a national emergency."

Debbie wanted to say something, but words failed her, so she just stood there, wondering whether she might be sick.

The police officer started mumbling, and then swearing. Debbie blinked, shook herself, and then followed his gaze until she saw what was causing a slow panic to rise up in him.

"Oh no," she muttered. "Please, God, no."

A black cloud headed towards them—a dozen drones or more.

Death from above.

"We need to get inside," Debbie said. "I have to protect my daughter."

The police officer nodded and called for his colleague. Then the three of them sprinted for the supermarket, yelling out warnings to those already inside.

Debbie found Millie just inside the entrance. Thirty or forty people stood with her like a group of refugees, cow-eyed and shell-shocked.

Millie was crying as an old woman was trying to soothe her, but she beamed when she saw her mother enter with two police officers. "Mum! You're okay. Is it over?"

"No." Debbie grabbed her daughter and raced deeper into the supermarket. "It's only just beginning."

Zip.

Zip.

Zip.

RESOLUTIONS

Heather needed to control her drinking. In fact, she was going to make it one of her New Year's resolutions. Crazy nights out were taking a heavier and heavier toll as she neared her thirtieth birthday. Tonight, she had sunk a double vodka and coke for each single that her bestie, Ava, had drunk.

Maybe I'll do Dry January. It might help me shift this flab on my belly, too.

She shook her fuzzy head and licked her dry lips, feeling increasingly worse for wear as the alcoholic high wore off. The overground train from London took forty minutes to reach Beaconsfield, at which point she would get a taxi home and pass out in bed. Tomorrow morning would be fun time.

Not.

The train carriage's rhythmic swaying was both comforting and nauseating. The breeze from the open slat window was a gentle palm on her cheek.

Heather texted Ava, letting her friend know she was safely on her way home.

On train now.

Ava lived in London, but Heather found the city frightening—especially in recent years. It was a frantic, intimidating place—even if it was also exciting and full of life.

Despite her incoming hangover, Heather had to admit that tonight had been a pretty great New Year's celebration. The fireworks above the Thames had been amazing, set in time to modern pop and classic rock. She'd almost teared up when the Beatles' *Yesterday* rang out as pride-inducing images of Britain's past were projected onto the Houses of Parliament. Midwives of the early NHS. Weary soldiers returning home from World War 2. Families reuniting after the Covid lockdowns. For the first time in quite a while, Heather felt positive about her country's future. Tonight had reminded her that most people just wanted to be happy.

Leaning back in her seat, Heather peered around the carriage. She was the only person sitting inside, which was odd. The city had been packed tonight, yet it appeared no one else was heading home. It was only half-past-twelve, though, which was early, she supposed. The celebrations in the pubs and clubs would likely go on for several more hours. Even now, colourful explosions peppered the horizon of the night sky.

The carriage's overhead LEDs flickered for a moment. The train's brakes squealed as they slowed down for the next station. Through the long windows on both sides of the carriage, Heather saw street lamps and headlights blurring together like orange paint on the surface of a puddle.

Maybe I should have stayed out later. Ava wasn't ready to call it a night. God, why am I so uptight?

The train came to a shuddering stop. The doors at either end of the carriage slid open and let in a draught.

A single man staggered inside from the cold. His erratic, wobbling gait made it obvious he was drunk. Hardly surprising, seeing as half the country most likely had been drinking tonight, but neither was it comforting. Being female and alone on a train with a drunken man was not a pleasant scenario.

This is not what I need.

Heather peered up at the ceiling and let out a sigh of relief when she spotted the distinctive black domes of two CCTV cameras, one at either end of the carriage. Did that mean the driver could see her? If anything happened, would he or she come to the rescue?

Thankfully, the drunken man slumped onto a bench several rows ahead and didn't even seem to notice she was there. He leaned forwards and let out a groan. His hair was uncut and greasy, a tangled mess. A puffy blue jacket and a red-checked lumberjack shirt beneath. Jeans, trainers, and a chunky gold bracelet.

And he smelled.

Heather put a finger underneath her nose and winced. Even at the best of times, she had a squeamish gut, but tonight she was trying to keep down half a dozen vodkas. She let out a groan as her gorge rose and her throat bulged, to combat it she tucked her nose inside her blouse and breathed in her own scent rather than that of the horrible, unwashed man.

"Nev a gan," the stranger muttered, his words slurred. "Nev again."

Heather felt her skin tighten—an instinctual reaction, as if her very flesh itself were trying to retreat.

Great! The guy's off his rocker.

Just keep your head down and hopefully he'll fall asleep.

"Kill me."

Heather glanced back and forth. The carriage doors were still open, but before she could even contemplate leaving, they hissed shut and the train lurched forwards. She could enter another carriage and hope there would be other people on them—normal people.

The front carriage was usually the busiest.

Heather rose in her seat, halfway between standing and plopping back down.

A growling, demonic sound escaped the stranger, followed by the spatter of foul liquid on the scuffed plastic floor.

The smell in the cabin worsened, acidity mixing with the cloying stench of body odour.

Heather leapt up, unable to remain there any longer, worried she might vomit herself if she didn't find fresher air.

"Somebody, help me. Please."

Heather stepped into the aisle and turned to leave, but instead of walking to the back of the carriage, she froze. "Damn it," she muttered. What kind of person would she be if she walked away from someone begging for help?

Come on, Heather. He's probably a homeless drug-addict. Don't get involved. Don't...

"Help me. I need help."

Heather put her hands to her face and felt like sobbing. As much as she didn't want to approach this horrible-smelling man, she knew the guilt she would feel if she abandoned him.

What if something happens to him and I could have helped?

Guilt lasts longer than revulsion.

She turned back and headed for the front of the carriage. The drunken man was now slumped across the bench on his side. He retched and heaved, more vomit hitting the floor. His miserable groans sounded like a cow giving birth.

"Hey, are you okay?"

Obviously not.

"Never again," he moaned. "No more."

"Yeah, I'm feeling a bit like that myself. How much did you drink?"

"Never again."

Heather took the last few steps to position herself beside the bench. The stench was so strong that it settled on the surface of her eyes and made them burn. Despite her disgust, she reached out a hand to comfort the man. When her fingers met his shoulder she shuddered, but all she felt was a mild warmth beneath the coarse fabric of his shirt.

"Stop!" The stranger bolted upright, and then lurched forwards as more yellow-and-green liquid spewed from his mouth, creating a gruesome pond that spread across the floor like an oil slick. Heather leapt back to avoid it touching the toes of her wedged heels. She gagged, unable to help it, and her mouth filled with stale vodka and garlic bread.

She stumbled back against the bench on the opposite side of the aisle. The drunken man stared at her, his eyes so bloodshot they were like squished cherries. His scraggly brown beard was wet with bile, while a slug of snot stretched sideways onto his bright red cheek.

"Jesus!" Heather didn't mean to pass judgement, but the state of the man surprised her. As bad as he smelled, he looked even worse. Like a walking plague. Instinctively, she backed away, a hand moving up over her mouth.

"Help me!" he yelled, getting up from the bench and stumbling into the aisle. He reached out a hand to her. "Help me stop!"

"I-I'll get the driver," she said, both as a threat and as an offer to get someone who might actually be able to do something. "Just stay here."

But he didn't stay. He stumbled after her like a zombie.

"Stop!" Heather turned on her heel and hurried for the connecting door at the rear of the carriage, the drunken man stumbling after her. Thank God he was incapable of running.

Heather pressed the *OPEN* button. The door slid open. A fetid gust hit her in the face. Somebody was coming the other way, entering the carriage. Had they heard the commotion and come to investigate?

The newcomer was a woman. She stepped towards Heather as if she didn't see her, forcing her back into the aisle.

"I need help," Heather said, glancing back over her shoulder. "There's a man who—"

"I can't," the woman moaned. "No more. Get it away."

"What? What are you?" Heather stumbled back a step, realising there was something wrong with the woman. She couldn't get through the opening. Her body was too wide and thick.

The moaning woman was wedged in the doorway, reaching out a puffy white hand. "Help me! I need help!"

Heather gasped in horror, her heart drumming in time to the fireworks she could still hear popping in the distance. She thought she heard cheers and laughter, too, but she couldn't fully focus. The woman in front of her was so *fat* that her eyes were barely visible behind her swollen cheeks. Her jowls were like two jiggling sacks on either side of her face. When she opened her mouth to moan, her teeth were rotten and brown.

Heather spun around, too frightened to do anything now except run. But the stumbling drunk was standing right behind her. He reached out and grabbed her face, his foul-tasting thumb slipping past her lips and into her mouth. Before she could let out a scream, his entire body bucked as a stream of hot vomit hit her face and spilled inside the neck of her sparkly blue blouse.

No!

She gagged and threw up the contents of her own stomach, turning her face and spitting out the man's disgusting thumb. She stumbled, but the large woman stuck in the door grabbed her hair and yanked.

Heather squirmed. "Let go of me! Let go of me!"

The woman pulled Heather's hair into her mouth and started chomping on it. Adrenaline and fear gave Heather the strength to yank her head forwards aggressively enough to free herself, although some of her hair ripped free from her scalp.

Angry now, as much as she was terrified and revolted, Heather shoved the drunk aside, knocking him onto the nearest bench. He immediately rolled onto his side and vomited. Meanwhile, Heather wiped puke from her face and neck with a miserable wail. It was like cold rice pudding. The sensation made her gag again.

"I can't stop," cried the woman behind her. "I need help."

"Help me," said the puking man. "Save me."

Heather hopped away from them both, sneering and shaking her head. "What the fuck is wrong with you both? What the fuck is wrong with you?"

She raced down the aisle and stumbled as the train came to a sudden stop.

The doors hissed open.

"Thank you, God."

They had reached the next station. It didn't matter where it was, Heather just needed to get the fuck off this train.

Someone entered the carriage ahead, stepping in from the platform. For a moment, Heather feared it might be another freak—another monster with no self-control. Another New Year's freak. She threw her head back in relief when it turned out to be a normal, attractive young man in a tracksuit.

"Careful," she cried out. "There're drunk people in this carriage. It's not safe."

The man raised an eyebrow and tilted his head at her. She didn't blame him for being confused.

But then he did something that confused Heather.

He sprinted at her full tilt, head forward and arms pumping. Rather than try to dodge him in the cramped aisle, Heather put her arms out and screamed. He was coming too fast to avoid.

At the last moment, the sprinter leapt sideways up on to a bench, and then clambered over the carpeted backrest before leaping onto the chairs behind. Absurdly, he then proceeded to hurdle down the carriage, bench by bench.

The drunk man and the large woman moaned and reached out for the newcomer with both arms, like he was an old friend they wanted to hug. He bounded right past them, even as they clawed at his top. They yanked it up to reveal a skeletal ribcage beneath.

"Holy shit!" Heather wondered how the man was even alive. He looked like a desiccated corpse.

"Got to keep going," the skinny maniac cried out breathlessly. "Got to shift it. Healthy. Be healthy. Look good."

Heather shuffled backwards and felt a breeze at her back. When she turned, she saw the doors were still open. The dark night beckoned, offering a release from this madness.

"Fuck this!" Heather legged it for the opening, head down in the refreshing breeze that fought back the stench inside the carriage. New Year's Eve was a crazy night, full of drunks, criminals, and weirdos, but this took the freaking biscuit. If the driver was watching on the cameras, then he clearly didn't give a shit enough to help her.

She reached the doorway just as it began closing—*beep, beep, beep*.

No no no.

Heather leapt through the shrinking gap just in time, struck her elbow and half-spun around as she stumbled out onto the platform. She yelled for help.

People started heading towards her from the direction of the station.

Yes! Somebody get me the hell out of here.

Panting, she bent over and reached out a hand. "Th-there are crazy people on the train. I-I think I'm gonna faint."

"It's okay. It's all okay. Everything is going to be okay."

Heather was relieved to hear the words—words from someone who was going to help her instead of act insane.

"No more meat for me."

Heather's heart stopped. "W-what?"

She straightened up slowly, sensing a stranger only a few feet away from her. What she saw was hard to describe—a sweaty, middle-aged woman with what looked like a pair of mouldy lettuces mushed in her hands as she shoved them against her open mouth.

"No mwore mweat. No more mweat. New me."

Heather backed up as she realised the platform was full of odd, strangely vacant people, all of them stumbling around and muttering various phrases.

Drink more water.

No more weed.

Got to stop the cake.

Couch to 5k. Couch to 5k.

Only drink at the weekends.

Heather turned to run the other way, but a line of people approached from the other side. The man near the front had his pants around his ankles as he shuffled towards her like a mental patient. He clutched his penis, pulling at it furiously. "I'm disgusting. Got to stop. I'm disgusting. Got to stop."

Her world spinning, and the night sky mocking her with joyful flashes of red, white, and green, Heather had no choice but to scream at the top of her lungs, internally praying that someone normal—*anyone* normal—would reach her before the two groups of demented strangers did.

The train's carriage doors reopened.

Heather turned just in time to see the original, drunken man lunge off the train towards her. He grappled with her a moment before throwing himself on top of her and tripping her to the ground. She opened her mouth to scream, but immediately found it filled with chunky vomit as the vile man puked all over her face.

She choked, unable to breathe, her throat clogged by another person's stomach contents. Her arms were pinned to her sides. She couldn't see. Couldn't breathe.

Somebody please help me. I need help.

All around Heather, strangers echoed her thoughts, muttering in miserable tones.

"Help me. Please. I can't do it by myself."

"Got to lose weight."

"No more porn. No more wanking."

"I'm disgusting."

"New year, new me."

"No more one-night stands."

"Help me. Help me. Help me."

Heather felt a pressure inside her skull that threatened to push out her eyeballs. Her throat bulged with foreign vomit. Both eyes burned, covered with half-digested food.

I'm going to die. I'm going to die.

On New Year's Day...

———

HEATHER BOLTED UPRIGHT, gasping for breath and clawing at her throat. "Get off me! Get off me!"

"Whoa, whoa. It's alright babe." A familiar voice soothed her as a hand stroked her hair. "Calm down."

"She alright back there, love? I need to pull over if she's going to chuck her guts up."

Heather blinked and rubbed at her eyes. She could see again, breathe again. But where was she?

Ava was peering down at her, her coffee-coloured skin darkened by shadow. Her eyes crinkled as she gave a small chuckle. "It's okay, Hev. You just had too much to drink."

"W-what?" Heather looked around and saw the back of a man's head.

A taxi. I'm in a taxi.

"My train..."

"You missed it," Ava said. "You're coming to crash on my sofa. Remember?"

Heather shook her head. She was resting on Ava's lap, and sweating with the warmth coming off of her friend's thighs. Slowly, she raised herself upright. London rushed by outside, lights, cars, and people. While some of the bars were still open, many more were shuttered. "What time is it?"

"Twenty-past-three. We partied pretty hard, babes. You were fine one minute, but then you'd obviously had enough. My fault. You wanted to leave at midnight."

"No... No, it was fun. I think. I... I had an awful dream."

Ava put a hand on her thigh and squeezed. "Well, don't let it bother you. It's 2025. It's gonna be a great year, I can feel it."

Heather thought about the train in her dreams, filled with desperate, tortured souls. "Yeah, I hope so. God, I'm so glad you were looking after me tonight. Thank you."

"No probs. Ride or die, right?"

Heather felt horrendous, but when she smiled at her friend, she felt a warmth inside of her. She might be single, living pay cheque to pay cheque, and six pounds overweight, but she had a wonderful bestie. "You're right. We're going to have a great year, you and me."

Ava nodded emphatically. "Damn right. Got any new year's resolutions?"

More images flashed through Heather's mind. Of drunken men and emaciated lunatics. Of public masturbators and overeaters. "God no," she said, almost barking the words. "New year's resolutions drive you insane. Let's not make any, please."

Ava flinched, clearly startled by her overreaction. "Okay, okay. No resolutions. Let's just see where life takes us. Destination unknown."

Heather chuckled, now feeling silly that a dream had disturbed her so much. "Long as we don't take a train there, we'll be fine."

Ava could only frown in confusion as the taxi took them home.

THE DANDELION

The sun beat down on Darren as he strolled along the pavement outside his ground-floor flat and headed for the nearby bus stop. He'd landed himself a job as a bakery assistant in Tesco, which was a pretty poor position for a twenty-nine year old, but it was only to keep him going until something better came along. He'd given up a better job as a mechanic back home in Stratford, but he had wanted a completely clean start in a nice little town called Evesham. A place where he had an almost zero chance of bumping into his ex, Megan.

The bus stop was in front of a small patch of grass where children sometimes played football after school. It was quiet now.

He sat down on the bench inside the plexiglass shelter and let out a yawn. This week he was working two-till-ten shifts, which saw him staying up late to relax once he got home. It played havoc with his body clock and he was half-asleep most the day. Again, it was hopefully temporary while he looked for another job in the car industry.

The bus wouldn't arrive for another ten minutes, but Darren had a phobia of tardiness, harkening back to his childhood, when his single mum always delivered him to school late. Almost every morning he had had to walk into a class already in session.

"Afternoon," said an elderly gentleman strolling down the pavement from the opposite direction. Darren assumed he was going to sit for the bus too, but instead the old man moved behind the shelter and went over to the small patch of grass. His back was so curved he looked like he was hiding a beach ball under his dull, grey jacket

For some reason, he was holding a small steel watering can.

What is he doing? Why's he on the grass?

The patch of greenery was devoid of anything in the way of flowers or plants. It was a simple grass square surrounded by some bushes–the type of unused space you found in most housing estates.

The old man bent over, causing his back to bulge even more. He proceeded to water the grass.

No, not the grass.

A dandelion?

There, at the old man's feet, was the unmistakable yellow mane of a dandelion. It was large and vibrant, but still just a weed.

Darren watched in utter confusion as the old man emptied his watering can, turned, and then walked away without a second glance. Quite clearly, he had come specifically to water that dandelion.

"What the actual hell? That was... weird."

The bus came five minutes early. Darren thought about the old man all day.

———

DISASTER AVERTED yesterday afternoon after a Boeing 747 passenger jet was forced to make an emergency landing in the English Channel. Rescue boats were immediately on hand, and there have been no recorded casualties.

"Jeez!" Darren swallowed the last of his cereal. "I would have liked to have seen that. What a splash."

It was another warm day, so he decided against wearing a jacket. It meant his supermarket uniform was on full display, which was embarrassing, but he didn't want to arrive to work sweaty.

He exited his flat and started down the pavement towards the bus stop, passing by a neighbour walking her dog. He offered a thin-lipped smile and when she returned it, a tiny jolt of adrenaline hit his stomach. It hadn't yet dawned on him that he was once again able to pursue other women. Megan had been so jealous that he hadn't dared even look before.

Despite everything, he still missed his ex. He missed their wild love making and nights in front of the telly drinking wine, but he didn't miss her checking his phone or blaming him for things he hadn't done, or removing all his friends from his life. She had taken him back to square one. He had nothing and no one, and when it had finally ended, she had smirked at his misery. If she couldn't have him, then she seemed perfectly happy to see him destroyed. Moving town had seemed like the best option.

He had been afraid of how it might end if he didn't escape.

Darren sat down inside the bus shelter, again ten minutes early. While his mood was okay, he wasn't looking forwards to another boring shift in the bakery. Cutting bread, sweeping up crumbs—it was mindless work. At least working in a garage, you were sometimes faced with puzzles. A clunking in the engine, a mysterious electrical problem, a strange smell—every day was a little different. But with bread, nothing ever changed. Even the delicious scent of sweet pastries was starting to bug him.

"Afternoon." The old man appeared on the pavement, just like he had yesterday. Once again, he held a small steel watering can.

"H-hello." Darren shook his head in confusion.

He's not, is he?

Is he watering that damn dandelion again?

Sure enough, the humped-backed old man plodded onto the grass and proceeded to water the solitary weed. It made no sense. There were no other weeds in the small field which made the dandelion stand out a little, but no one would mistake it for a flower. Strangely, it seemed to flicker slightly, despite there being no breeze.

"Um..." Darren stood up and went around to the back of the bus shelter. "Why are you doing that, exactly?"

The old man looked over his rounded shoulder. "Sorry, young man?"

"Why are you watering that dandelion?"

"Oh," he looked aside sheepishly. "No reason. I just like to help nature."

"It's a weed."

"A label we've given it, because it's strong and hardy and keeps the weaker plants from thriving. A bit like people, wouldn't you say?"

Darren frowned, but slowly, his expression lifted. "Wow, dude, that's deep."

"See you tomorrow." The old man tottered off without looking back.

"What the hell?" Darren asked himself. "What the actual hell?"

———

DARREN HAD CHANGED his number when he moved, but he had left it with a couple of remaining friends, the ones who had forgiven him for ghosting them. Somehow, Megan had got a hold of it.

Hey, babe. Been thinking about you lately. Do you still think about me? xx

Darren was awash with panic as he read the text message over and over. Why was she contacting him? It'd been months.

I'm not getting drawn in. She's not doing this to me.

Before their final split, he and Megan had broken up several times already. They would stop talking for a few weeks before one of them gave in and drunkenly text the other. It was a cycle of extended misery, an addiction to each other—and like any addiction, the longer it went on, the more damage it caused.

Like cirrhosis of the heart.

Their relationship had never worked, but it took effort to willingly accept loneliness. Darren was proud of himself for moving away, but now this text message...

He felt vulnerable. Weak. Confused.

Suddenly, all the hope and strength he had been working to gain went away. His thumbs tapped the touchscreen. *I'm okay. Why are you—*

In a panic, he deleted the words on his screen and then deleted the text message from Megan. He didn't want contact with her, not even to tell her to go away. She couldn't make him respond.

What if she finds out where I'm living?

Feeling unwell, Darren wanted to get some air. He was due to catch his bus in twenty minutes, but there was no reason he couldn't leave early.

He hit the pavement and headed for the bus shelter. This time, when he reached it, he stepped onto the grass. Peering down, he examined the dandelion. As far as he cared to think about little yellow weeds, he decided it might just be the most bright and healthy dandelion he had ever seen. It was like an oversaturated computer image, the yellow almost seeming to bleed off the petals and stain the air around it. "Huh, maybe watering you *has* helped."

Realising he would probably look very strange to any passersby, Darren went and sat inside the bus stop.

The woman with the dog came along again. This time she said hello and smiled a little brighter. It helped Darren retrieve some of his mojo, and it reinforced his desire to never ever speak to Megan ever again. You couldn't keep banging your head against the same wall hoping it would suddenly stop hurting. One day he would meet a new woman, one who made him happy. The prospect excited him.

Movement in the periphery of his vision caused him to turn his head. He expected a bus, but it was the old man again, carrying his water can.

The geezer's insane.

Darren stood up to speak with the old man. Concerned that he might be a lonely widower or suffering with some kind of dementia. "Hi again. Watering your dandelion?"

The old man looked at him through rheumy eyes and seemed to blush. "It's my little ritual. It may seem silly but it's important that I do it."

"Why?"

"It just is."

"No, really? Why?" Darren smiled. "I want to know. Maybe I can help."

"Really? You mean you could water it too?"

Darren chuckled. That wasn't what he had meant at all, but he didn't see the harm in it. "Yeah, sure, why not?"

"I must admit, this is getting harder and harder. The walk takes me almost an hour here and back."

"Well, I live two minutes away in the Terry Street flats. It would be easy for me to come water this dandelion, but you need to let me know why first."

The old man looked down at the weed and licked his dry, cracked lips. "You won't believe me if I tell you."

"I promise, I will. Why do you need to keep watering this dandelion every day?"

"Because if I don't, the world will end."

———

"WHAT DO YOU MEAN, *the world will end?*"

The old man sighed. "See, I knew you wouldn't believe me."

"I didn't say that." Darren cleared his throat. "I just, um, wasn't expecting you to say that. Explain it to me."

"Well, I'm not sure that I can." The old man looked down at the dandelion and seemed to think for a moment. "What's your name, friend?"

"Darren."

"I'm Fred."

"Pleased to meet you, Fred."

This guy needs help.

"Pleased to meet you, too, Darren. So here it is. My wife, Sue, was a fortune teller, you see? Not a professional, but she would sometimes perform seances for friends—read their palms, that kind of thing. She also had dreams. They were never wrong."

Darren narrowed his eyes. "She dreamt things and they happened?"

"Yes. All through our marriage, she made these predictions. Once she dreamt that we should avoid the motorway on a trip we were taking. Ten minutes later, a lorry overturned and caused a pile up. People died. We might have died. Another time, she dreamt we were going to get burgled. We stayed up that night, and at 3AM we scared the robber away when he tried to force open our window. Then there were the little things, like she always knew when a family member would pass away, or when the phone was going to ring. It was just her gift. She never made a big deal of it, but I learned to always trust her instincts."

Darren smiled kindly. *What a load of bollocks.* "My mum believes in all that kind of stuff. She's really superstitious."

"It's not superstition, young man. There are things in this world that get overlooked. Science has replaced the human soul."

"But it also gave us microwave dinners." Darren tittered, then realised his joke was probably misplaced.

To his relief, Fred gave a small chuckle. "I must admit, it's not all bad. Still, nothing beats human intuition."

"Your wife, she's...?"

Fred nodded. "She passed three years ago. Forty-six years, we were married. Tell you the truth, I'm just waiting to join her."

Darren felt a twinge in his stomach as he imagined the old man's loneliness. Life was a beautiful and cruel thing, and being alone made everything harder.

"It must be tough, Fred."

"You have no idea, young man, and I'm glad for that. Anyway, in the months before Sue left me, she kept having the same dream about this very dandelion. She woke up each morning saying it needed to be watered, and that if she failed to do it, something terrible would happen."

Darren kept a straight face, not wanting to betray his disbelief. "Did she say *what* would happen, exactly?"

"No, but at night when she had these dreams, she would say the same thing over and over in her sleep. *Yggdrasil.*"

"E-drazzle? What does that mean?"

"*Yggdrasil.* She wrote it down once—Y.G.G.D.R.A.S.I.L—and I looked it up on the internet. It's the tree of life, connecting this world to the next. It's what the norsemen believed in."

"As in the vikings?"

Fred smiled. "Yes, the vikings. They believed that Heaven and Hell and the earth and all other places were connected via the tree of life, and that its life-force was the essence of creation. If it were to ever die..."

Darren couldn't help it. He laughed. "Wait, are you saying..." He looked down at the little yellow weed. "You're telling me you think this dandelion is the tree of life?"

"No." Fred shook his head. "I'm telling you that my wife thought so, and she was never wrong. If I don't water this dandelion, something terrible will befall the earth."

"You truly believe that?"

"Without a shred of doubt. I've been watering this dandelion for three years. It never wilts, it never loses its leaves, and it never shrivels, not even in the winter."

"That's impossible."

"And yet it's true. If you don't want to help me, that's fine. I'll keep on as long as I can."

"And then what? What about when you can't come to water it any more?"

The old man shivered. "Then I'll pray for us all."

———

WEEKS WENT BY. The old man never missed a day watering the dandelion. Darren spoke to him regularly, chatting about life and love, loss and heartache. It was good to share his pain about Megan, and it was nice to have Fred's reassuring input that he had been brave to move away. "Love shouldn't swallow you up," he would say. "It should lift you up and make you feel lighter than air. It sets you free. When you find it, you'll know it."

The old man never missed a day.

Until he did.

Darren waited at the bus stop and didn't see Fred. He went to work, and worried about the man all day. Then, at home, he worried some more. At twenty-to-midnight, he was half-asleep in front of the telly, watching the news.

An unexpected storm front has gathered to the UK's north-west this evening and is feared to be even worse than the one in 1987 when several people died. Experts are currently uncertain if this extreme weather front will reach the British mainland, but all maritime traffic has been put on high alert.

Darren yawned, only one eye on the telly. The weather lately had been lovely and sunny, with just a gentle breeze. Could there really be a deadly storm on its way—a monster hiding out of sight?

It's the dandelion. Fred didn't water it today.

Don't be stupid.

Darren closed his eyes and tried to nod off on the sofa.

But he couldn't.

What if the crazy old coot is right? What if something bad happens?

Don't be stupid. It's insane.

But what will it hurt for me to go out and water it?

"No. No, I'm not taking on Fred's delusions. It's just a weed. A stupid weed."

Darren stood up to go to bed.

Instead, he filled up a pint glass with water and put on his shoes.

"I can't believe I'm doing this," he said as he went outside in the dark. The moon overhead was full, which seemed to suit the situation. He was playing out the scenes of a weird short story.

All the lights in the nearby buildings were off. He felt like the last man on earth. At least no one could see what he was doing. The men in white coats would probably come to drag him off otherwise.

He reached the dandelion, finding it easily, and marvelling at its brightness, even in the dark. "Don't tell anyone I'm doing this," he ordered the weed.

And then he upended the pint glass and watered it.

He went back to his flat, laughing at himself, but also feeling a sudden sense of relief.

———

THE FEARED STORM FRONT, nicknamed Bertha, failed to materialise during the night, breaking apart in the Atlantic Ocean and failing to make landfall. Experts say it was a near miss, and that it could very easily been a cataclysmic display of climate change in action.

Darren stared at the telly in disbelief. "I did that," he said. "I made the storm go away. Because I watered the dandelion."

Come on, really? That can't be true.

He didn't have work today, so he'd slept in a little. Now, however, he found himself very much awake.

It needs watering every day.

Filling up another pint of water, Darren hurried outside and headed for the bus stop.

The dandelion was still there, of course, almost as if it were waiting for him. Without delay, he upended the pint of water onto its roots. "There you go. Hey, wait, does this count? Does each day reset at midnight or is it a twenty-four-hour period?"

He shook his head, his mind a mess of fear and confusion and embarrassment.

"Um, excuse me? Are you Darren?"

Darren spun around and yelped. "Oh, wow, you startled me. Um, yeah, I'm Darren. Who are you?"

"I'm Fred Wheatley's solicitor. He left an envelope and instructions at my office a couple of weeks ago. I'm to give it to you in event of—"

"Fred's death?" Darren sighed miserably.

"Um, no, not at all. I am afraid Fred has suffered a stroke. His health has been poor for some time, ever since his wife died."

"Sure, yeah. It's been rough on him."

"Anyway, I don't know the contents, but this is for you." The man stepped onto the grass and frowned when he saw the empty pint glass in Darren's hand. He handed over an envelope and then left him standing there alone.

Darren opened the envelope and pulled out a sheet of paper with unsteady handwriting on it.

Hello, Darren. If you're reading this, then I'm dead, or injured, or demented. Thank you for the company these last weeks and months. It's given me something to look forward to each day on my daily mission.

Needless to say, you'll have to take over now. You must water the dandelion every day or something awful will happen.

Please do this.

Your old friend, Fred.

P.S. I'll be back with my Sue, so don't feel sad for me.

DARREN FOLDED the paper and put it in his pocket. He shook his head. "So, what? I have to water this bloody thing for the rest of my life now?"

He hated that the only answer seemed to be *yes*.

————

THREE WEEKS. Three weeks of watering a weed, with no hope of ever stopping. Every day, Darren dared himself to leave the dandelion to go thirsty, but every day his fear forced him outside with a pint glass. The woman who walked her dog now thought he was insane. The kids, now off school for the Summer, thought he was a weirdo.

I am a weirdo.

It was due to rain tomorrow, which left him wondering if that would allow him a day off. Did he have to water the dandelion himself, or would any source of nourishment do? Without knowing, he knew he would be forced to play it safe and do it himself.

Why did I agree to do this? It's lunacy.

But what if it's not? Can I risk the fate of the world?

This is my life now.

He was already running late for work, so he didn't rush as he poured water into his pint glass and took it outside. He now had to wear a backpack to keep the glass safe at work as he didn't have time to take it home before catching the bus.

When he stepped outside his front door, Megan was there, smiling at the sight of him. "Babe, I have missed you so much."

It felt like a punch in the guts. "W-what are you doing here, Meg?"

"I wanted to talk to you. You moved away!"

"I wanted a fresh start."

She nodded as if she understood. "Things got pretty bad between us, but I still love you, Darren."

He hated that he still loved her too. She was the beautiful brunette that had turned his life upside down in the best and worst ways. A part of who he was and would always be.

"I have to get to work, Megan. I don't want to do this. We don't make each other happy."

"It can be different this time," she pleaded. "I know I can be jealous, but I promise I'll deal with my shit. You weren't perfect either."

"Not saying I was. Look, I can't do this, all right?"

She noticed then that he was holding a pint glass full of water. "What are you doing with that?"

"Huh? Oh, nothing. I'll text you later, Meg. I have work."

"Skip it. For me."

"No, I can't. It's my job!"

"So what? Pull a sicky." She reached out and held his hand. Looking into his eyes, she said, "Let me show you how much I've missed you."

He broke away and started walking. "Don't do this, Megan, please."

Never being able to back down easily, she followed after him. "Darren, just hear me out. I promise you, we can make this work. We're meant to be together."

"Is that what you thought when you posted all over Facebook that I cheated on you?"

"I thought you had."

"You always thought I was cheating on you. I couldn't even look at other women without you going mad."

He picked up his pace, his heart pounding. It was then that he realised his ex actually provoked a physical response in him. His hands were trembling.

"Are you seeing someone else?"

"What? No!"

"Then what's wrong? Why can't we can go back to your flat and let off some steam? I haven't been with anyone either."

"I don't care." He reached the bus stop. Mercifully, a bus was approaching.

But I need to water the dandelion. If I get stuck working late...

Sometimes his bosses made him work till midnight. He couldn't risk that happening and being unable to water the dandelion.

He stepped onto the grass and approached the weed.

"Darren? Stop and listen to me."

Out of nowhere, Megan shoved him. The glass went flying out of his hand and landed in the grass. Its water drained away into the earth.

"No! What are you doing?"

"What are *you* doing?"

"Nothing, I just..." He huffed. "Now I have to go back home."

"To fill up your glass? Why?" The look on her face was mean, like a witch eyeing up a child. It made him shudder to think how many times he had seen that expression.

"Just go, Megan, please. I don't want to see you."

"You don't mean that." She grabbed him and pulled him into a hug. It knocked him a little off balance and they staggered together.

The dandelion.

"Stop!" He grabbed her arm and pulled her away. "Be careful."

She frowned at him, looking at the ground. "What? Is there dog shit?"

"No, it's the dand—" He stopped himself. He didn't want to share this with her.

But it was too late.

She studied the ground until her eyes located the bright, healthy dandelion. "Dandelion? What about it? It's just a stupid weed." She bent down to pick it.

"No! Don't! Please, just leave it."

She straightened up and folded her arms. "Why? I don't understand."

"You don't need to understand. Please, just leave it alone."

"Fine. Can we go back to yours and talk, then? It's taken me ages to find your address. The least you can do is hear me out."

It sounded so reasonable, but he knew where it would lead. The same old cycle of making up and fighting and slowly getting too intense for sanity.

He reached out and took her by the hands. "I care about you, Megan—I always will do—but I don't want to be with you, okay? All we do is hurt each other. It was making me ill. You can find someone better than me, someone who truly makes you happy."

"*You* make me happy."

"I don't."

"You do!"

He nodded, feeling stronger as he spoke his truth. "Okay, fine, then you don't make me happy, Megan. You don't lift me up, you pull me down and swallow me up. I moved away to start again, and that's what I'm going to do. Don't contact me again."

Her face fell, a dark veil moving across her eyes. "Are you serious right now? What the fuck? Why are you being like this?"

"I'm just being honest. We're over, Megan, and that's not the end of the world. Things will take time, but we'll both be happier for it."

"Don't patronise me, you twat!" She shoved him in the chest, snarling like a feral cat. Megan hated not getting her own way. She always lashed out.

Darren saw what happened next in slow motion. He watched Megan turn back and forth, her hands clenched in fury. She was looking for something to destroy, but in that empty patch of grass, there was only one thing.

"Nooo!"

Megan kicked the dandelion as if it were a soccer ball, tearing it right out of the ground along with a divot of earth. It twirled in the air. Darren was sure he saw the colour fade from its petals.

A pain struck his chest and he staggered back on his heels, gasping for breath. "What have you done? What the fuck have you done?"

She sneered at him, flashing her perfect white teeth. "What the hell is wrong with you?"

The air went still. The warmth of the sun seemed to disappear.

But nothing happened.

"Well?" Megan demanded, glaring at him and shaking her head. "What the fuck is your problem? Have you lost the plot or something?"

"I..." He blinked, trying to awake from a bad dream. "I don't know. Maybe I have. Fred... He convinced me."

"Who's Fred?"

"It doesn't matter."

She stepped towards him. "Look, I know you're upset, but I really have changed. Let's just talk back at your flat."

You'll know love when you find it.

This isn't it.

"Goodbye, Megan. It's over."

"No, no I won't accept that. I won't−"

She stumbled, and instinctively, he reached out to steady her. Then he was stumbling too as the ground shook beneath their feet.

"It's happening," he said, gasping. "Something bad is coming."

Megan just looked at him, confused.

Darren studied the ground where the dandelion had been rooted and saw a deep black hole. Then a light emerged from the darkness, like the sun returning after an eclipse. It grew brighter and brighter until he couldn't bear to look.

The ground quaked. Megan and Darren fell to their knees.

Megan reached out to him, and in that moment he saw no reason to deny her, so he wrapped his arms around the woman who had made him miserable and forgave her. It didn't matter anymore. It was over.

It's all over.

"What's happening?" she asked him as she trembled on the ground beside him.

"You broke my heart," he said, "and now you broke the world."

"What? I don't understand."

"I know. Just close your eyes." He held her close as the ground opened up and swallowed them whole.

After that, it swallowed everything else.

UNCLE JACK'S ARCADE

"I can't believe you brought me here," Jessica said as they ambled along the promenade. It was a mild spring afternoon with a pleasant breeze, but Richard had to admit the town was true to its reputation. It was a complete and utter dive.

The entire seafront was an echo, a fading Polaroid. Three decades ago, the rickety pier would have been a place of simple joys. Now, it was half abandoned and littered with coin-operated toddler rides and vending machines. The cafe had probably done good business before the days of *Greggs* and *McDonalds*, but now it looked as if it could barely afford to keep its doors open. The only good thing about Boole was the beach. Unspoiled and litter-free, nothing like the crowded beaches of Brighton Richard was used to.

He squeezed Jessica's hand. "I know it's seen better days, honey, but don't you think there's something quaint about a place like this? It's real, right? Authentic."

"It's full of poor people," she said, wrinkling her nose. Of course, she was being facetious, and her wry smile confirmed it, and yet...

She can't enjoy things unless they cost a fortune.

Some people have nothing. We used to have nothing.

Besides old ladies, pulling trolleys behind them, and gouty old men zooming back and forth on scooters, the streets of Boole were mostly occupied by hooded teenagers and day-drinking adults. Not to mention migrants of many colours. No one offered a friendly glance as they passed, and some eyed up Jessica openly without fear of reproach. Maybe if Richard had been a larger man, they might have kept their leers to themselves, but as it was, he inspired little reason to be afraid– at least not based upon appearances alone.

Try me in the boardroom and I'm a lion.

Richard had made his first million almost five years ago to this day. That had been the hardest one to make. The following eleven had come quickly and easily, and he was now richer than he ever thought possible. Spending money was a chore though, now that he had so much of it, which was why he left it mainly to Jessica. She had picked their house, their car, their staff, and had transformed herself from a demure brunette into a fake-breasted blonde bombshell.

Richard's company had grown with a simple premise of putting experts in touch with businesses that wanted to hire them. It was like *Fiverr* but for highly paid professionals. The idea had come to him after growing tired of losing out to marketing jobs by Filipinos and Bangladeshis who couldn't do the job even half as well as him.

"I want to go back to the hotel," said Jessica, pouting. "We can look online and find somewhere nice to eat tonight."

"We will in a little bit," he said. "I want to show you something first."

She rolled her eyes behind her fake lashes. "I swear to God, Richard, if we end up eating at that crappy little chip shop back there, I'll kill you."

He let go of her hand and linked arms instead. "Oh come on. Wouldn't it take you back? Fish and chips used to be a treat when we were kids. Don't you ever miss the days when we were poor? Not everything has to cost a fortune."

She let out a sigh. "I'm a stuck-up bitch, aren't I?"

"No comment."

She elbowed him in the ribs. "Watch it, you. I might be spoiled, but..." She shrugged. "I hope you know I'm proud of you. You've come so far."

He turned to look at her, taken by surprise. "Um, yeah, I know that. Nice to hear you say it, though."

"I always thought you would make it far, even back when we had nothing, but I never thought we would end up as multi-millionaires."

He blushed and scratched the back of his head. "Yeah, not quite sure how I pulled that off."

"Because you're a sociopath when it comes to business," she said. "I've seen you make grown men cry."

"All's fair in love and war. It's a competition and everyone is playing to win. Just look at this place." He waved an arm, highlighting the shuttered shop fronts and a scruffy man drinking super-strength lager on a bench. "This is what happens when you lose."

"Exactly," Jessica said, "so why are we here?"

"I told you. I want to show you something. One of the guys at the lodge told me about it. Said it's right opposite the entrance to this pier. In fact, I think we've found it."

Jessica frowned, then glanced ahead. "Uncle Jacks Arcade?"

Richard beamed, glad that it hadn't all been a wind-up. The guys at the lodge liked to play jokes on each other, so he had half expected to find a brothel or a vape shop.

But no. It was exactly as described.

"Uncle Jack's Arcade," Richard repeated, letting the words out slowly.

Jessica was still pulling a face. "You brought me to stand on a sticky carpet and play the 2p machines?"

He took a moment to enjoy her beauty. At thirty-four, her skin wasn't quite as flawless as it had once been, and her collagen-filled lips didn't appeal to him as much as her natural ones had, but her light green eyes sparkled with the same intensity they had held twenty. The way her nose wrinkled with every expression still filled his tummy with butterflies. Richard wasn't the kindest man, or even the most handsome, but his loyalty to Jessica had never faltered. In fourteen years, he had never even looked at another woman. The guys down the lodge made cheating on their wives a sport, but he never took part. Jessica was the love of his life, and as in business, he never took his eye off the prize.

"Like I said, Jess, not everything has to cost a fortune. Let's just slum it for a couple of hours, okay? Maybe I can win you a teddy bear from the grabbers."

"Those things are fixed. Not like when we were kids. I still remember how my dad used to bring me home from holiday with a carrier bag full of stuffed toys. He would win almost every time. Nowadays..."

"The world has become cynical," he admitted. "Everyone's out for themselves. It's horrible, really."

She moved closer to him and shivered, despite the weather being mild. "At least we have each other. Us against the world, right? Same as it's always been."

"And always will be." He kissed the top of her head. "I never would have got anywhere without your support."

"Behind every great man..." She winked at him.

"Come on," he said. "I hear this place closes at seven, so we best make the most of it."

She groaned, but allowed him to lead her forwards. "You want to hang around here for two more hours? God help me."

"We're slumming it, remember?"

They trotted along the gum-stained pavement, still linking arms. Then they headed into the arcade's open-sided entrance.

Chirps, whistles, and flashing lights of a dozen gaudy colours met them.

Few people occupied the arcade, but it wasn't totally empty. Kids and old ladies stood entranced by the penny pushers, teenagers and men by the blinking fruit machines. All Richard saw was people throwing money away.

But he was planning to do the same, so he tried not to judge.

Jessica pointed and grinned. "Oh my god, Rich, look! They have *Mad Dog McCree*. We used to play that all the time when we went down the bowling alley. Do you remember?"

Richard gasped. "Christ, I'm surprised that thing's still working. It should be in a museum."

They both took a moment to watch the cowboys dodging around the screen, drawling and spitting and hitting every cliche. It was like looking through a portal into the past. He pictured himself and a young Jessica giggling side by side as they took shots at the bad guys. He also remembered the frustration of her always winning. She had a killer instinct, a desperation to win.

She always knew how to take down a no good varmint.

"You want to play?" she asked him.

He went to say *yes*, but instead shook his head. "It would only disappoint us. Let it remain a happy memory."

"You're right. Life is for new experiences, not old ones."

"Exactly. Follow me."

She raised a sculpted eyebrow at him, but did as he asked, following him across the arcade. They passed by dozens of machines, new and old, but the only other ones he recognised from his past were a *Daytona* cabinet and a four-player *The Simpsons* game. If he had spotted a *Mortal Kombat* machine, he might have actually reached for his spare change.

Flawless victory.

Richard went and stopped in front of the cashier's booth. An old woman sat inside, with wispy grey hair collected in a ponytail. Her eyes were two giant planets behind her thick spectacles. "Yes, sir?"

Richard reached into the inside pocket of his Ralph Lauren quilted jacket and pulled out a cardboard ticket. It said very little on it except for: A GUEST OF JACK'S.

The woman took it and eyed him up for several seconds. Then she made a phone call from a handset inside the booth.

"What is this?" Jessica asked, realising that something was up.

He shushed her and continued to wait. The more time that went by, the faster his heart beat in his chest. Once again, he feared that the guys at the lodge were playing a prank on him.

But then the old lady put down the phone and offered Richard a tight-lipped smile. From underneath the desk, she produced a single brass key attached to a red plastic tag. She handed it over and said, "Use this on the staff entrance next to the *Splatterhouse* machine. Enjoy your time at Jack's."

Richard took the key with a polite nod. "Thank you, ma'am. You have a good day."

"Uh-huh."

He linked arms with Jessica and led her away, moving to the edge of the arcade and searching for the machine the woman had mentioned.

"Are you going to tell me what this is all about?" Jessica asked him. "What did you hand that woman? A ticket?"

"A very special VIP ticket."

"VIP? For what?"

"I'm not quite sure, other than it's a one of a kind experience available only to the extremely wealthy. Ten-mil net worth to be eligible."

Jessica groaned. "Oh, Rich, it's not going to be some stuffy old boys nonsense, is it? I still have nightmares about that shooting weekend. The women you left me with barely had a brain cell between them."

"I promise, this won't be like that. The guys told me it will blow our minds."

"Fine. But if it's dreadful, I get to choose where we eat tonight."

"You just want lobster. Don't you ever get sick of it?"

"Never. I was born to eat lobster."

They both chuckled and searched the periphery of the arcade, passing but an adult's only section full of fruit machines, and then ambling by a bank of *Deal or No Deal* machines.

Then John saw it.

Splatterhouse. The machine was emblazoned with a machete-wielding, solid little ox of a man wearing a hockey mask. Immediately to its right was a green door with a red and white sign: STAFF ONLY. There was no door handle, but there was a keyhole.

Richard went over to the door and aimed the key. It took him two stabs, but eventually he got it in the hole. "We're in," he said.

"Now you just need to give it a good twist," she said with a wink.

Smiling, Richard turned the lock. He then pushed open the door. Inside was a short, blind corridor with a bend to the right. The two of them stepped inside and let the door close behind them. Despite the old-fashioned key, it audibly relocked behind them. A shiver ran up Richard's spine.

I actually have almost zero idea about what I'm about to see.

All the guys told me was that I would need to be okay with seeing blood.

Richard's best guess was bareknuckle boxing or dogfighting. He knew Jessica would enjoy the former, but he dreaded her reaction if it were the second. They both cared little for people, but dogs were an elevated species. No spite or jealousy in a dog. You could let your guard down around a well-trained spaniel in a way you never could around people. People took advantage if you showed them your soul.

They turned the corner to the right and encountered a staircase. The bottom was unlit.

"Richard, are you sure about this? We're heading into a basement."

He swallowed a lump in his throat and hoped she didn't see it. "It's fine. It's just hidden from the public, that's all. That's the whole point. It's an exclusive experience."

"That we know nothing about."

"I know it's for rich people only. That should appeal to you."

"You have a point." She grunted. "Fine, let's get this over with."

Richard took the first step and headed down. Jessica followed behind him. They left the light of the upper landing and entered the gloom below.

A plain doorway punctuated the end of a short corridor. A red light shone above the door, offering a minimal amount of light.

"Just open it." Jessica huffed. "I'm going to wet myself otherwise."

Richard had to will himself to move, suddenly feeling like he was somewhere he shouldn't be. Fortunately, fighting back his nerves was a skill he had perfected long ago, so he steeled himself and walked over to the door. It was unlocked. He opened it.

A bald-headed man in a suit immediately met them. He gave a quick bow and bid them welcome. "Mr and Mrs Roth, please enter."

Richard exchanged a glance with Jessica and was unsure whether he felt relief or more anxiety.

Jessica nudged him in the back, prompting him to step inside, and he found himself inside a large basement area with a cement floor and four windowless walls. Filling the space were a dozen or so arcade games.

But with a difference.

Jessica stepped up beside Richard and shook her head. "W-what is this?"

"I'm not sure."

The bald man moved in front of them and bowed again. "Welcome to Jack's basement. The games here are one of a kind. Your payment has been received and you are free to indulge as you wish."

"How much did this cost?" Jessica asked Richard, an accusatory tone.

He shrugged. "A mil."

"You paid a million quid for something you know nothing about? Why?"

"Money buys connections and connections buy power. The guys at the lodge promised me this would be worth the cost and more."

"I don't understand. What is this? Why would you make a decision like this without me?"

Richard was unsure of the answers, but his stomach was uneasy and he was feeling unsure. It had been a long time since anything had unsettled him.

So many terrified eyes looked at him from around the room. So many young men and women bound and gagged. Jessica had asked the right question: What the hell was this?

"My name is Brown," said the bald assistant–slash–bouncer or whatever he was. "Would you like me to explain things for you?"

"Y-yes, please," Richard said. Jessica took his hand and squeezed it.

"Very well." Brown swept a hand around the room, gesturing to what was on display. "This country, and the town of Boole-on-sea specifically, has a migrant crisis. An illegal migrant crisis. These people you see before you have crossed our channel illegally, therefore they are foreign invaders without rights or entitlements. We picked them up from the beaches as soon as they landed and took them immediately to our holding facility. They do not exist." He gave a smile. "Except for your enjoyment."

Jessica put a hand over her mouth. "These people are refugees? They come here to escape wars, don't they?"

Brown's friendly expression faltered for a moment, his eyebrows raising ever so slightly. "Sometimes, yes. We do our very best to extract reliable information from these people when housed in our care. Those who are genuinely fleeing danger are released. Those who we find to be of a criminal persuasion, or are simply here to exploit our generous welfare system, are judged appropriately and brought here.

"To do what?" asked Jessica.

"First things first." Brown turned and picked up a pair of clipboards from a desk by the door. He handed them one each. "Standard NDAs. Please sign."

Jessica looked at Richard. He was there because of his friends at the lodge, and all members were obliged to look out for one another. They wouldn't do anything to land him in an unpleasant situation. He gave Jessica a nod and then signed the form. She copied him, but scrawled her name reluctantly.

"Wonderful," said Brown, "and now there's one last thing. I'm afraid it's a tad unpleasant."

Jessica groaned. "What is it?"

He turned again and took something else from the table. This time it was a slender metal pole with a small flat piece attached to the end. For a second, Richard feared it was a brand, but nothing about it suggested it was hot.

"What is that?" he asked.

"It's a tool for etching flesh, Mr Roth. It's laced with a highly corrosive acid. Don't worry, it's a negligible amount—just enough to get the job done."

"Fuck that," said Jessica, stepping back.

Brown blinked slowly. "Ma'am, this brand is known only to a select few people. By wearing it, you will gain access to the upper echelons of society. Merely by being invited here, you have proven yourselves to be people of great worth and potential, but without the mark, it is meaningless."

Richard took a breath and held it. Then he let it out, rolled up the sleeve of his jacket, and thrust out his arm. "I'm assuming it only hurts for a little while."

"It hurts very little. More of an itching, burning sensation really. Much better than the old way of using hot iron."

Richard grimaced as Brown shoved the acid plate against the inside of his forearm. Jessica groaned beside him, fearful of taking her own turn, but truthfully it wasn't so bad.

"The scar will be quite faint," said Brown, "which is by design. Don't want to advertise it to the masses now, do we?"

"No, of course not." Richard smiled, the slight pain knocking away some of his anxiety.

Jessica shook herself for a moment and let out a long sigh. She pulled up the sleeve of her blouse and offered her slender white arm. "Get it over with."

She squealed when the acid hit, but quickly got a hold of herself.

"You okay?" Richard asked her.

"That was rotten," she said.

Brown gave them another bald-headed bow. "Apologies. I must admit, it's nice to have a young lady here. We get so few."

Jessica eyed the prisoners around the room and shook her head. "Are you going to hurt these people?"

"That's up to you."

"What do you mean?" asked Richard.

"I mean, these people are here for your enjoyment. Play the games and have some fun."

Richard shook his head. "This seems like a bad idea."

"I assure you that everything that happens in Jack's basement is entirely confidential. There are no cameras, no witnesses, and no reprisals."

"And what if we refuse?" Jessica folded her arms and winced as her burn brushed against her chest.

Brown offered a smile, but his eyes narrowed slightly. "Then you would be free to leave, one-million-pounds poorer and with this door forever closed to you. Also know that the amount of influence the members of this club wield is beyond comprehension. There are basements like this throughout the world, and not one has ever—or will ever—come to light. So long as you never discuss what you have seen here, then we wish you the very best. We will, of course, have to remove your mark. I would simply etch over the top of it with a square shape. Harmless, I assure you."

Richard nodded to show he understood. He knew the world was

run by a powerful elite, and that connections were the key to success, but he was in way deeper than he had expected to be. The guys at the lodge ranged from owners of successful construction firms to high court judges, but until now he had always felt himself on equal footing. Now he felt small and naïve.

And a little excited.

Brown stepped back over to the door, giving an unspoken message that they were now free to do as they pleased.

Jessica clung to him as he went deeper into the basement.

There were such sights to see.

The first game was a coconut shy, except the coconuts were brown faces held in place by some kind of headgear. Piled up in a series of buckets were several dozen fist-sized rocks. Pretty clear what the game was: hit the coconuts.

"This is sick," said Jessica. "We're not actually going to do this, are we?"

He looked at her and immediately hated the judgemental look on her face. The only opinion that actually mattered to him was hers. "Do you think these people will be let go if we walk away? Of course not. They're dead, whatever we do. But if we walk away, then we lose whatever power this place can afford us. This is it, Jess. This is the shadowy entrance to true power. You love the house we have now, right? How about a dozen of them all over the world?"

She shook her head, seeming sad. "It's not about that. It's about whether we are actually going to murder people for fun. Are we those people, Richard?"

"People die all the time for far less. That Prada coat you're wearing? You don't think blood went into making it somewhere along the line? What about your Tesla? We both know what goes into making car batteries. This is the price of admission, babe, whether we like it or not. The poor suffer so that we don't have to. At least this is honest."

She nodded. "Honest? I suppose it is."

"And look at them," he added. "These aren't women or children. They're young men. What the hell do they think they're doing here? Who knows what they planned to get up to? This is their punishment."

Jessica sighed, and then, to his surprise, she picked up a rock. She held it to her side, but didn't throw it. She seemed to be thinking.

The four heads peering at them from the shelf trembled from side to side. Their eyes bulged in terror as they moaned around their cloth gags.

Jessica flung the rock.

Like with most things, she was naturally skilled, and the hard chunk struck one of the faces right on the forehead. A trickle of blood spilled down his brow. His moaning turned to squealing and he struggled to pull his head out of the harness.

Jessica took a shuddering breath. All colour left her face as she turned to Richard. "Y-Your turn."

"What? Oh, um, yeah, okay." He reached into the bucket and realised his hand was shaking. The cold kiss of the rock against his palm made him shudder.

Am I really about to do this?

I have to. No backing down; especially not in business. And this is business. The oldest kind.

Richard eyed up the four terrified faces staring at him through bulging eyes. Which one should he aim at? The one who Jessica had hit was still conscious, but in obvious pain. Blood had run all down the left side of his face.

Should I put him out of his misery? That would be the kindest thing to do.

"Okay, here we go." He lifted the rock and held it out to his side. Then he lifted a knee and rotated himself into a throw, flinging the rock as hard as he could.

Direct hit.

"Whoa!" said Jessica. "Good shot!"

Richard couldn't deny feeling proud.

The rock had struck the bleeding man right between the eyes, shattering his nose with an audible *crack*. The sounds he was making now were more animal than human.

Jessica put her hands to her ears. "God, make it stop. That noise. It's like fingernails on a blackboard."

"Hold on." For a moment, Richard didn't know what to do, but then he grabbed another rock and flung it. It missed the mark. Instead, he clipped another man in the ear and his moaning joined the brain-damaged squeals of his colleague.

"Damn it," said Jessica, and she grabbed another rock for herself, letting it fly. It struck the bleeding man again, right in the centre of his forehead.

The noise stopped.

The three remaining heads stared at Richard and Jessica in terror. It was intoxicating. He had never seen fear like it. So pure. So powerless. And all because of him.

I'm a predator. I am dominant.

Jessica staggered back a step, turned away, and vomited onto the concrete floor.

"Shit," said Richard, and he turned to Brown, who had already approached from the doorway. He was pushing a mop bucket with him, which appeared very odd considering his expensive suit.

Jessica groaned and wiped at her mouth. "I'm... I'm so sorry."

"Not at all, ma'am. It happens to the best of us. Especially the first time. I hope you're enjoying yourselves, nonetheless. Please help yourselves to champagne from the back of the room. It helps one to take a brief rest between playing. The adrenaline can get a little too intense."

Richard nodded and had to fight down his own stomach juices as they threatened to leap into his throat. He concentrated on Jessica, putting a hand on her back and rubbing as he guided her away from the human coconut shy. He spotted a buffet table at the rear of the basement.

The spread was impressive. Caviar and king prawns on ice, fine cheeses and freshly baked bread. It was the champagne that got his attention, though. Hands shaking almost uncontrollably, he poured the fizzing liquid into two long-stemmed glasses and gave one to Jessica, who immediately spilled twenty-quids worth. It didn't matter a jot. He had more than paid for this.

Jessica downed the drink in one and then immediately poured herself another. She, too, was trembling. "We just killed that man," she said. "I... I killed him."

"We did it together."

She shook her head like he was mad. "Yeah, it was a real bonding experience, darling."

He put a hand on her shoulder and looked her in the eye. "Okay, okay, let's just debrief. A guy is dead. A stranger who came here illegally and who was probably a criminal. It doesn't affect us at all. We're safe, we're healthy, and we're protected. There's no reason to panic, so let's take a deep breath."

She downed half her champagne, gasped, and then nodded. "You're right. Everything's fine. That was..."

Kind of horrifying?

"...an experience, to say the least. Transcendent even."

Richard sipped his champagne until it was gone and then placed the empty flute down on the table. When he turned around, Brown was standing right there.

"Mr and Mrs Roth, is everything to your satisfaction?"

Richard nodded. "Yes, thank you."

"Will you be playing another game?"

"I..."

"Yes," said Jessica. "Maybe one more before we go."

"Marvellous. Then may I suggest you peruse the area a little first and pick wisely."

Richard and Jessica watched Brown lumber away. He was the strangest gentleman Richard had ever met. Deadly—no doubt about it—but very polite indeed.

"Okay," said Jessica. "We should take a look around like he said."

Richard took a few breaths to keep his nervous system under control and then nodded. He linked arms with his wife and strolled forwards.

The first machine they saw was like the basketball machines upstairs, except instead of basketballs, you threw six-pound bowling balls into a net placed above a young man's head. Jessica didn't want to lose a nail, so they skipped that one.

Next was a machine set up like a Skee Ball–Arabian Derby combination, where you rolled balls up a ramp and tried to land them in holes for various amounts of points. The points then translated into moving a camel jockey along a race track at the top. At the finish line were four terrified brown faces. Because at the front of each camel was a stiletto blade pointed directly ahead. The winning rider would pierce the skull of whichever victim was unlucky enough to receive the winning jockey.

They continued onward, unsure which game they wanted to play. Which stranger they wanted to kill.

This is surreal. Richard shook his head. He had always suspected the existence of a seedy underworld, open only to the uber rich, but this went beyond his wildest imagination. An arcade of people. The poor and destitute really were disposable. Their lives meant nothing.

These people are criminals. They made their choices.

They headed towards the back of the arcade where there was one more game. This one was larger than the others, and from what Richard could work out at first glance, it was some sort of giant whack-a-mole machine.

You apparently accessed the game by climbing a short set of wooden steps to one side. There, you would encounter a large platform with holes in. Beneath the platform was a dozen young men fixed to vertical poles attached to some kind of piston engine. As the engine rotated, the various poles would move up and down, forcing their heads up through the holes above. The platform was big enough to walk around on between the gaps.

Jessica climbed the steps first, stopping halfway to look back at Richard. "You coming?"

He licked his lips and nodded, joined her at the top. They were about eight feet off the ground, enough to feel a little dizzy. From beneath his feet, Richard heard moaning. The platform rattled slightly as the 'moles' struggled to get free.

Mr Brown appeared below, standing next to a large red button affixed to a post. "Are you ready to begin? Your mallets are just behind you, there."

Richard turned and saw a wooden rack with four baseball bats slotted inside. He took one and raised it up, shocked by how weighty it was. How good it felt in his hands.

Jessica grabbed one, too, a slightly smaller bat from the right-hand side. She also seemed to enjoy the weight of it, swinging it gently back and forth while wiggling her shapely hips. After a moment, she looked Richard in the eye. "You ready for this?"

"Yeah."

There was no backing out now. They had already killed a man, and just seeing this place was a point of no return. If they left now, Richard would probably be allowed to keep his mark and join the secret world of the elite, but if you were going to do something, best to go all in. He didn't want rumours floating around of him backing out on only his second game. For all he knew, the guys at the lodge had played every game here multiple times.

No, got to play at least one more. Show them the first game didn't upset me too much to continue.

I don't know if I'm enjoying this or not.

"Here we go, folks," said Brown, and he smashed his fist against the big red button.

A jaunty tune played. LEDs embedded in the platform lit up and began to flash in sequence.

The first head came up through a hole. It was an African-looking man, with a large scar across the top of his shaven head. He moaned and mumbled, but was facing away from them. No pleading stares from him.

Jessica leapt forwards and swung her bat.

She missed.

The head popped back down a split-second before she made contact.

A second head popped up. This one was a man with dirty-coloured skin, more white than brown, but still foreign.

What am I thinking? A third of my staff are people of colour. Do I really think this is okay?

Jessica swung again, almost like she was hitting a golf ball, and this time she made contact. The bat smashed into the man's temple and shut off his moaning. The *whomp* of it was sickening.

"Come on," said Jessica, already gasping from exertion. "You're not even trying."

He realised she was enjoying this just as he realised he wasn't. But if Jessica was having fun, then it must be okay. She was his barometer of human behaviour. Everything he'd achieved in life was due to her support and guidance. She had never let him down.

Another head popped up out of the hole. Richard brought his bat down like he was chopping wood and scored a direct hit. The head went back down into the hole, sporting a huge divot.

"One all," cried Mr Brown. "Very good."

Another head came up. Richard swung and missed.

Jessica got the next one, smashing a young man right in his eye socket and exploding his face. It didn't kill him, though, and he moaned like a gutted dog about to be put to sleep.

Another head rose. This one a woman. She had somehow managed to spit out part of her gag and was mumbling words at Richard as he stared down at her. "Pwease! I hwave cwildrun."

Richard gasped. "What?"

"I assure you she does not," said Mr Brown, rolling his eyes.

"Hit her," said Jessica. "Quick!"

Richard lifted his bat...

...but he couldn't follow through.

The woman appeared Eastern European–Romanian or Hungarian. Her dark brown eyes were full of life–and they were fixated on *him*. "My swon's name is Bogdi. My dwaughter's name is–"

"Hit her," Jessica said again.

But it was too late. The woman's head went back down into the hole.

Jessica grunted, and then swung at the next head to come up. She smashed the man's skull so hard it imploded like a half-filled mouldy pumpkin.

"Three one to Mrs Roth."

To Richard's horror, the young woman came up again. "Please," she begged clearly, having spat out the rest of her gag. "I was kidnapped and brought here to be a whore. I just want to go back to my country, back to my children. My home."

She doesn't want to be here. She's not a foreign invader here to take advantage. This woman is a victim.

Do I care?

Yes!

"I... I don't want to play this anymore," said Richard, tossing aside his bat. "This isn't fun."

"Oh, how disappointing," said Brown. "But as you wish."

"No," said Jessica. "I'm not done." She swung her bat and smashed the young woman in the forehead, cracking open her skull like an egg. Her eyes rolled back in her head. Dead. If she really did have kids, they were never going to see her again.

Richard staggered, almost falling into one of the holes. Jessica grabbed him by the arm and steadied him. The look she gave him was unkind. "What the hell is wrong with you?"

"She didn't want to be here, Jess. They snatched an innocent woman."

"So what? What difference does it make to us? God, you look like a ghost."

Brown cleared his throat. "Is everything okay, Mr Roth?"

"Y-yes, thank you. I just..." He leaned in and whispered to Jessica. "I screwed up. I thought I wanted to step behind the curtain, but I don't. This place is sick."

She shushed him. "Keep your voice down. What if they hear you?"

"I don't care," he cried. "I don't need this. We became successful all by ourselves. This isn't us, Jess. We used to be ordinary people. When did we lose our souls?"

"Quiet," she said, glaring at him. "What the hell has got into you?"

It was like a floodgate opening. At first, he'd been numb, playing the games without accepting reality, but now the weight of his actions washed over him. "We're murderers, Jess. We can't ever undo that. There's blood on our hands."

"Mr Roth, do you need assistance?"

"No. Just shut up."

"As you wish."

"Stop it." Jessica was frowning and shaking her head. "You're gonna make trouble for us."

Richard gritted his teeth. "The guys at the lodge can go fuck themselves. I don't want to be a part of this world." He looked at her pleadingly, taking solace in those green eyes that always looked upon him with love. His one true ally in this cruel world. "Can we just be us again, the way we used to be?"

She smiled at him.

And then said, "No fucking way."

Richard gasped and was too shocked to move as Jessica swung her baseball bat at the side of his head. It hit him so hard that he felt the impact all down his spine. Suddenly, the world turned sideways then upside down—as he went plummeting through one of the mole holes. He crashed at the bottom, hearing a loud snap. Then he couldn't move. In front of him, the young dead woman slumped against her pole, her bleeding head hanging in front of her.

What... What is happening?

"Mrs Roth? What on earth have you done?" He heard Brown's voice above.

"He isn't cut out for this," said Jessica. It sounded like she was descending the stairs. "I know Richard. He would have freaked out about this and caused a problem. Without me, he never would have made anything of himself, but I knew he would crumble eventually. He's always been so emotional. This place would have broken him completely and undone all the work I put in."

"Apologies, Mrs Roth, but why on earth would you kill your husband?"

"Because I just made ten million quid with a swing of a bat. Not to mention the controlling shares in a fast-growing company, a property portfolio, and one thing worth more than all."

"What is that, Mrs Roth?"

"I just gained access to some very powerful people, right?"

Brown chuckled. "Indeed. As I said, Mrs Roth, it's wonderful to see a powerful young lady here. We are sorely lacking."

"Well, you just added one to your ranks. First, though, we need to dispose of a weak man who's been a thorn in my side for far too long."

Richard tried to moan, but he couldn't. *She means me. She hates me. I can hear it in her voice.*

"Oh, Mrs Roth, you don't have to worry about that. You are a woman of influence now. You don't need to dirty your hands. I'll have our people take care of everything. I'm just sure we can achieve wonderful things together. You're an impressive woman."

"You have no idea," she said. "Now, is there somewhere I can get cleaned up? Oh, and can you recommend a good restaurant? I'd like to eat lobster tonight."

"Of course, Mrs Roth. Right this way."

What? Why is this happening?

All's fair in love and war.

Richard lay in the dark for more than an hour. Then a pair of unfriendly looking men in suits arrived and slit his throat.

BENEATH THE BED

"Mam! Mam!"

Natalie slid her sleep mask up onto her forehead and wiped drool from the corner of her mouth. She half-rose in bed, staring blindly into the darkness and trying to come to. The alarm clock on the bedside table read: **3:12**.

"Mam!"

Groaning, she threw aside her duvet and rotated her hips until her feet touched down on the carpet. The third time this week Jordan had woken up screaming. She thought the sleepless nights ended with toddlerhood, but apparently age eight came with its own set of nightmares.

Half-zombie, half-concerned mother, Natalie staggered across her bedroom and stepped out onto the landing. Jordan had stopped calling out and was now simply whimpering. She already knew what the problem would be. It was the same every night.

When she pushed his door open and stepped into the soft glowing circle of his nightlight, Jordan flinched. He was drenched with sweat and his lower lip was quivering. When he looked at her, it was like he was peering right through her.

"Honey?" The sight of him sent her grogginess away and she drifted quickly over to his bed. "Oh, sweetheart. Have you had another nightmare?"

He reached out with both arms as she sat down on the edge of the mattress and gave him a cuddle. "It spoke to me again, Mam."

"The monster under your bed?"

"Yes."

She kissed the top of his head, his thin blonde hair damp. Several strands of it stuck to her cheek as she pulled away. "It's just you and me, honey. There's nothing that can hurt you. This is our home."

"But he wakes me up and says mean things."

She eased him back so she could look him in the eyes. He was trembling and pale. Did he have a fever? "What mean things?"

"He says I'm horrible and that I should be the one stuck under the bed. He wants to get out."

Natalie placed the back of her hand against his forehead. It felt cold, not hot, but that might have been the sweat. "I think you might be coming down with something, sweetheart. Our minds can imagine all sorts of things when we're poorly. Are you feeling okay?"

"Just hot. Can I take my pyjamas off?"

"Sure, but I want you underneath the covers. It's a chilly night."

She helped him to get undressed and tucked him back up in bed. She used his rolled-up pyjamas to pat down his glistening brow and then tossed them into the corner. In the orange glow of the nightlight, he appeared cherubic—not at all like his father.

How did something so precious come from something so hard and callous?

"Do you want your lullabies on, sweetheart?" She nodded towards the little Alexa on his nightstand. He had stopped asking for his night-time music lately—perhaps he thought it was too babyish—but now he smiled, clearly comforted by the suggestion.

She stood up from the bed and asked the device to play Jordan's sleep playlist. After the third attempt, the increasingly obstinate AI lady did as requested.

I swear Alexa is getting more and more stupid.

"Okay, honey. I'm going back to bed. If you need me, wake me up, but everything is okay, okay?" She leaned down and kissed him on the cheek. They exchanged *I love yous* and she left him alone.

Natalie's bed called to her, and it embraced her with a heavenly warmth when she slid back beneath its covers. Thankfully, tomorrow was Saturday, which meant no morning school run. Just a blessed, but most likely brief, lie in.

Please don't wake up too early, Jordan. Let Mammy sleep.

———

JORDAN WAS NOT himself at breakfast. He barely touched his cornflakes—even with extra sugar—and he drank only sips of water. Natalie grew more and more certain that he was under the weather. If it continued into tomorrow, she would get an appointment at the doctor's. For the most part, he seemed okay, though, if a little quiet.

It's probably just tiredness. Three nights of broken sleep takes its toll.

They spent the day together, cuddling on the settee and watching episodes of *The Simpsons*. She could barely believe the programme was still going after all these years; could remember watching it when *she'd* been a kid.

Why have the characters not aged? Bart has been a kid for decades. It's weird.

When evening arrived and bedtime approached, Jordan grew visibly unsettled. He twitched and scratched at himself, so much so that the skin on his arms reddened. He started gulping at his water, which would do him no good if he woke up with a full bladder. Eventually, she had to refuse to refill his glass.

"Would you like a biscuit before bed?" she asked. "You haven't eaten a lot today. It's no good going to bed hungry."

He shrugged, which again was a strange gesture for him. Natalie couldn't remember him ever being indifferent about a biscuit. Deciding for him, she went and fetched three shortbreads and a small glass of milk. "Okay," she said, "eat them quick. You need to catch up on the sleep you didn't get last night."

"What if the monster wakes me up again?" His voice jittered as he spoke. "What if he tries to make me live under the bed?"

"Honey..." She sat beside him on the settee but didn't hug him. She was frustrated and wondering how long this saga would go on for.

"There's no monster under your bed, Jordan. I check every night, don't I? It's all in your head."

"Then why does it wake me up?"

"I'm not sure, but if you go to bed worried about it, it'll keep happening, won't it?"

He clutched at the fabric of his soft blue shorts. "How do I not worry about it?"

"By..." She let out an exasperated sigh. "By thinking about something else. Something nice."

Finally, a beaming smile settled on her son's face. "Like going to Spain with Daddy?"

It hit her like a pair of punches, the first being from the mere mention of that man, but the second—much harder punch—coming from the fact Jordan had chosen his father as an example of a happy memory.

She wanted to argue, to tell him it was almost two years ago now that his father had taken him on holiday—or perhaps mention that Jordan hadn't seen his dad for six weeks now that he had found himself another woman—but all she did was offer back a forced smile. "Let's go brush our teeth and get into our jammies, okay? I'm going to have an early night, too."

"Yay!" Jordan always liked it when they went to bed at the same time, comforted that she was on the same floor while he drifted off. He really was such a nervous child.

They went upstairs and took turns over the bathroom sink with their toothbrushes. Hers was an electric one, but she hadn't charged it up, so she ended up using it like a manual brush. Something so simple, and yet she was too disorganised to handle it.

I need to get my act together. I'm barely coping.

When was the last time I cooked a nice meal instead of throwing something quick in the oven?

Natalie hated missing Chris, and she had to keep reminding herself that it wasn't really him she missed but the convenience of being in a relationship. To have someone helping her raise Jordan, to pay some of the bills...

But it isn't worth the black eyes and the constant abuse.

"Mam, are you okay?"

Natalie lowered her toothbrush and turned to Jordan. He was watching her curiously, as if she was an animal at the zoo. Unnerved, she checked herself over, trying to see if she had suddenly grown a third breast. "I'm fine, honey. Why?"

He shrugged his little shoulders. "You look sad."

She rinsed off her toothbrush and smiled. "Just shattered. Hope we both get a good night's sleep tonight."

"Me too. But what if the—"

She placed a finger over his lips. "Nice thoughts only, remember? Think about your favourite movies."

"*Minions.*"

Another forced smile at the mention of the chronically unfunny banana people. "Yes, think about minions."

"And not the monster under my bed."

She rolled her eyes and put a hand on his bony back. "Jammies on and into bed. I want you asleep in ten minutes."

And please don't wake up tonight.

———

"MAM!"

Natalie snapped awake. Somehow, her sleeping body must have been expecting it, because her eyes opened wide and her vision adjusted quickly to the gloom. Before Jordan managed to call out again, she was already on her feet and marching across the landing.

Her patience was thin, her exhaustion thick.

"Honey, you've got to stop this. Everything is fine. You're safe."

"Mam! Mam, the monster broke my bed."

Natalie switched on the room's main light and rubbed at her eyes. Once the black spots left her vision, she realised Jordan's bed was damaged. One of the wooden legs at the bottom had snapped, the splintered remains like a vampire hunter's stake.

God, I've got monsters on the brain.

"What on earth happened?"

Jordan was sitting up in bed, shaking his head over and over. "The monster! He's trying to escape. He's trying to get me."

Natalie groaned. There were fewer than a dozen inches between the bed's white-painted wooden side boards and the carpet, so any monster would have to be pretty small or squashed very flat to be hiding underneath.

Am I seriously contemplating the logistics?

"It's just an old bed," she muttered, licking her dry lips. "This is why I shouted at you all those times for bouncing."

"I can't sleep upside down," he said. "Call Daddy. I'll have to sleep at his house."

Yeah, good luck with that. He hasn't replied to my last dozen texts.

"I'll sort something out for now, honey. Then maybe I can find some money to get you a nice new bedframe."

"A big bed," he said, a demand not a request. "One high up by the ceiling."

"A cabin bed? We'll see, okay? Let's just sort this one for now."

She scanned the room, studying the cheap wooden furniture—a chest of drawers that had once been hers and a bunch of *Ikea* storage cubes. It upset her that her son had so little in the way of new things, yet she also knew there were kids far worse off than her son. She loved him, which was all she really had control over, and all he really needed.

From the top drawer of the dresser, she gathered a handful of hard-back books—the *Very Hungry Caterpillar, Elmer, Barney Goes the Carnival...*

"We need to clear some of these out," she said, more to herself than Jordan. "You had most of these as a baby."

"But I like them," he complained, still sitting up in bed. "I still read them."

She raised an eyebrow. "Really? Well, for now, they're going to be propping up your bed."

Gathering a handful more of the stiffest books she could find, she formed a pile of an appropriate size and went over to the bed. She knelt, placed a hand underneath the broken corner. But she found it heavier than expected and had to complain at Jordan to get him out of the bed while she lifted it.

"I don't want to get out, mam. What if the monster grabs my foot?"

"Jordan! I'm literally down here on the ground. There's nothing under your bed."

"But he's been whispering to me all night, telling me he's going to get out and hurt me. Telling me I'm evil."

She gasped and let go of the bed. "Evil? Where did you even learn that word?"

"From the monster."

"I don't want you using horrible words like that, okay? You're not *evil*."

Jordan pouted, like he was deciding whether to cry. "What does it mean?"

"It means *not very nice*, and you shouldn't say it."

"Is it a swear?"

She shrugged. "I'm saying you can't say it, so *yes*."

"Okay, mam. Sorry."

"It's fine. Let's just get your bed sorted."

Gritting her teeth, she lifted the bed with him still on it and managed to wedge the stack of books underneath the broken corner. It was pretty solid, pretty secure.

While I'm down here, I should check under the bed.

What? Why? It's not like there's an actual monster under there.

"Mam?"

She rose up on her knees, pressing down on the bed to test its stability. "Yes, honey?"

"If my bed breaks again, can I come sleep with you?"

Natalie had a strict *no co-sleeping* rule—except for when Jordan was ill—but she supposed a broken bed was an exceptional circumstance. "As long as you don't do anything to break it yourself, then yes. Please, though, try to go back to sleep. Mammy's really tired."

He flopped back against his pillows and unironically let out a yawn.

She kissed his cheek and tucked him in before stumbling wearily back to bed.

I'm gonna kill *that goddamn monster under the bed.* She rubbed at her eyes and groaned. *Or it's going to kill me.*

———

NATALIE DIDN'T EVEN MAKE it until morning.

"Mam! Mam! Mam!"

"Jesus Christ!" She leapt out of bed, angry now. So on edge was she, so anxious about being awoken, that she had not fully gone back to sleep. The bedside alarm clock read: **4:48**. She thanked God it was Sunday. But she was still desperately tired, so much that she wanted to scream.

She stomped across the landing, her son's cries like high-pitched bird squawks. As she went to throw open his door, she stopped herself and took a breath.

Getting angry won't do anything. Jordan already has one angry parent.

She pushed open her son's door and forced herself to smile as she entered. Unexpectedly, it was dark, the nightlight switched off.

Has there been a power cut?

"Jordan? Are you okay?"

"Mam? It's dark. My light."

She crept into the room, trying to navigate in the sliver of moonlight coming through the gaps in the curtains. Her hand located the squishy, mushroom shaped nightlight, and she fiddled until she found the switch on its base. The light came right back on. No obvious reason for it to have been off.

She blinked as her eyes adjusted, and she focused on her son's pale, sweaty face. "Jordan, did you switch this off?"

"No. It was the monster. The other boy under the bed."

"The what? What other boy?"

"Mam, we have to kill him. He wants to get out. He wants to hurt me."

Natalie tried to keep her temper, but it came loose too suddenly. "There's nothing under your goddamn bed, Jordan. I'm sick to death of this. You're just being naughty now. Nothing bad will ever happen to you while I'm around, so just close your eyes and go back to–"

"*Mammy.*"

"What? What is it?" She glared at her son, and he stared back at her with wide, terrified eyes. For a moment, she thought he was frightened by her tone, but then, for some reason, she got the sense it hadn't been him who had spoken.

"Mammy..."

Jordan continued to stare at her, not even blinking. His lips hadn't moved. The voice had come from under the bed.

"Mammy!"

Slowly, knowing she had no choice but to check—to make sure that there was nothing in the room that could harm her son—Natalie lowered herself to the carpet, going down and down and down until her cheek was pressed against the rough, worn fibres.

She stared into a familiar set of eyes.

Jordan's eyes.

The face peering out of the shadows beneath the bed spoke in a trembling whisper. "Mammy, there's a monster in my bed. He trapped me down here and I want to come out now."

"Sweetheart?"

"It hurts down here, Mammy. There's no room. I want to get out. Please."

Natalie felt her heart stop beating, and it was replaced by a jagged crystal that snagged her flesh from the inside. She tried to speak, but her stinging stomach acids leapt up into her throat and gagged her. As slowly as she had descended, she began to rise. Rise and rise until she was up on her knees and staring across at a little boy in her son's bed.

But the little boy was gone, replaced by a slender creature with a mangled skull full of teeth.

Natalie let out a scream, but it did nothing to stop the beast from biting into her face. Did nothing to free Jordan from his prison beneath the bed. In fact, as her life ebbed away, she found herself lying on the floor right next to her little boy. His terrified eyes looked into hers as she drifted away into oblivion, leaving him alone with the terrible monster in his bed.

"Mammy, I want to get out."

LIVING SPACE

Scott Khan woke shivering on a cold, hard surface. Pain bloomed in his back and shoulders. A groan escaped his lips.

He pushed himself into a sitting position.

"The hell am I?"

He blinked once, twice, and tried to make sense of what he was seeing. Instead of waking up in his nice warm bed in his Cheshire flat, he had awoken in some sort of warehouse or storage area.

No—more like a large cupboard, maybe ten feet across.

A single dim light hummed overhead, a stubby fluorescent strip. The walls were shiny—possibly metallic—but completely featureless, like the doors on the stainless steel refrigerator he had at home.

As Scott's confusion worsened, it dragged up a swelling fear inside of him. Nothing about his sudden awakening made any sense, but something was clearly wrong.

He clambered to his feet and turned a full circle. It was then he noticed he was still wearing his work clothes—trousers, blue suit-jacket, and open-collared shirt. The same thing he'd been wearing—

Yesterday? This morning?

What time is it?

Where am I?

Things dawned on him gradually.

"You want money, huh?" He yelled it at the walls; all four of them identical and with no doors or windows of any kind. "You kidnapped me, hoping I'd pay you for my freedom? Well, fuck you. I ain't paying you a goddamn penny. If you seriously bel—"

The stubby light went out, engulfing him in darkness.

"Ha! You think I'm afraid of the dark? You better let me go, or else you're gonna end up floating in the goddamn canal. Do you know who you're messing with? I can buy and sell your entire bloodline. I'll make it so your great grandkids owe me money. Do you hear me?" He probed his way forwards until he was banging on the solid walls. "Do you hear me?"

No reply.

Not willing to accept this bullshit, Scott searched for a door, running his hands over the smooth surfaces and feeling for a crack or seam. There must have been a way in and out of this room.

A voice came from the ceiling, a slight crackle betraying that it was coming from a speaker. "If you want light, pay."

"Fuck you."

The voice did not speak again.

Hours went by.

———

MORE HOURS WENT BY.

Scott killed some time yelling threats and kicking at the walls, but it appeared no one was listening. The longer his pitch-black imprisonment continued, the less it felt like he was in a room and the more it felt like he was in a box. A sleek, silver box with no escape. Whoever was responsible had put a lot of thought into this. How long had they been planning on this kidnapping?

Is this about me? Or is it random? Did I piss someone off?

Probably.

Scott tried to think who could be behind his predicament. He had over a dozen tenants in his properties, most of whom liked to whinge and complain about the tiniest things. *We need new windows, the kitchen needs replacing.* But could any of them actually hate him enough to do something like this? Something so utterly stupid?

It has to be someone who owes me money. Or a business rival trying to shaft me.

"Who are you?" Scott demanded. "Come on! Have the balls to tell me. You got a problem with me; be a man about it. Turn the light back on and face me."

"If you want light, you must pay."

"We're going to be here a long time if you're hoping to break me."

But the truth was the dark was starting to get to him. It wasn't the usual kind of darkness—that solid grey morass that still let you see the shape of things. It was a total absence of light.

And sound.

And senses.

The only thing existing inside the room—besides himself—was the cold, hard floor.

"Just out of interest, how much do you think you can get out of me?"

"If you want the lights on, pay."

"How much?"

"Five-hundred pounds."

He let out a laugh. "Five-hundred? All this for five-hundred quid?"

"To turn the lights on."

"Fine. Go on, then. You can have five-hundred quid, you desperate wanker."

Something hit the ground inches from where he was sitting. He flinched and shuffled sideways along the wall. It wasn't until he saw a soft glow that he reached out tentatively to grab the object. Was this the light he had just bought? What about the ceiling bulb?

He reached out and felt a silky texture, some kind of blanket or scarf. The glow was coming from within the bundle, and when he pulled it closer, the fabric unfolded. He discovered something familiar wrapped inside.

"My phone," he muttered, recognising the screensaver—a picture of his orange cat, Lucky. The pet had belonged to his ex. She had left. The cat had stayed.

Something was stuck to the back of the phone's protective case—a strip of paper. Scott peeled it off and studied it. In the light of the screen, he made out two sets of numbers. A bank account number and a sort code.

"If you want light, pay."

"No thanks." Instead of doing as his captor asked, Scott dialled 999.

There was no dial tone at all.

"How do you expect me to pay you if I have no signal?"

"You can connect to the Wi-Fi. The password is *rent*. Any data traffic beyond that sent by your banking apps will be blocked."

Scott took a moment to consider. Were they bluffing? Could they restrict his phone in such a way? He didn't know.

He searched for Wi-Fi and found a single access point. It was named: LIFE. He put in the password—R-E-N-T—and connected. Immediately, he tried to send a text message to his secretary, Heather. It failed to deliver.

Over the following hour, he tried several things—emailing the police, making a Zoom call—but all failed. He couldn't even browse the internet. Finally, he tried one last thing. He transferred five-hundred pounds to the account written on the slip of paper.

The transfer went through.

A minute later, the dim fluorescent light flickered to life, bright enough that it made his eyes ache for a few seconds while his pupils adjusted.

"I paid you, okay? Now, let me out of this fucking box."

No reply.

Several hours went by.

———

SCOTT MUST HAVE NODDED off and woken himself snoring. His mouth was dry, and the sinuses at the back of his nose were sore like he had the beginnings of a cold. When he licked his lips, they were sticky.

"W-water," he said. "I need a drink."

A barely detectable crackle followed by that voice from above. "Water costs money."

Scott growled. "How much?"

"Two-thousand pounds."

He shifted his position, and the base of his spine tingled as he took the weight off his rump. How long had he been sitting on this horrible floor?

"Two-grand? Or else, what? You'll let me die of thirst? What would be the sense in that?"

"You wish for water? Water costs money."

Scott shook his head and sneered. Fine. They could have their money. Whatever it took to get out of there. Once he was free, he would find out who these fuckers were and make them pay.

With interest.

He sent two-thousand pounds to the mystery bank account. It wasn't even international, so would be easy to trace if he went to the police. But that wasn't the way he liked to deal with things.

The last time he'd relied on the courts, he had been stuck with a delinquent tenant for nine months, losing money the whole time. Eventually, he had had to pay a couple guys he knew from the local mosque to break in and remove the woman and her toddler forcibly. Once she was out, Scott had changed the locks and claimed complete ignorance of the two men who had visited her. Luckily for him, the woman had been too afraid to push things any further.

No, the police were good for nothing.

I'll deal with this my own way. I'll make it balance.

"Okay, I paid you," he grunted. "Water."

Movement overhead, part of the black ceiling shifting. Then something fell.

A water bottle bounced in the centre of the room, then spun around in a circle as if Scott were playing spin the bottle with someone. He snatched at the bottle quickly, worried it might split open and spill its expensive contents. With it firmly in hand, he wrenched off the cap and gulped thirstily.

The water was gone in two deep swigs.

Wiping his mouth and gasping, he demanded more.

"Two-thousand pounds."

"What? Fuck you. I paid you already. Give me more water."

"You must pay again."

"Pay to not die of thirst? Are you sick in the head or something? I can't pay two-thousand pounds every time I need a drink."

No reply.

Hours went by. Eventually, Scott paid the two-thousand pounds.

———

THE BATTERY on his phone was half dead, so he switched it off until he could put together a plan of escape. It was his only lifeline. Whoever was blocking his calls would have to sleep eventually. Maybe then he would be able to get a call through or fire off a message.

And say what? I have no idea where I am.

"Why are you doing this?" he asked. "Is it just for the money? If so, give me your final number and we can get this over with."

"Rent is due."

"What are you talking about? Tell me how much you want and let me go."

"Rent is ten-thousand pound."

"Fine." He switched his phone back on and went into his banking app. There was sixty-thousand in his current account, but he could transfer more from his shares account or use his credit card if needed. "There, I sent it. Let me go."

"Rent is due every twenty-four hours."

"Your ain't keeping me here for twenty-four hours, mate."

No reply.

"Yo! Do you hear me? Let me the fuck out."

Hours went by but nobody came.

———

SCOTT LOST TRACK OF TIME. After sleeping for some time, he came awake shivering. The temperature inside the room had fallen. The floor was like ice. Teeth chattering, he laughed humourlessly. "L-let me guess; heating costs money?"

"Correct."

"How much?"

"Six-thousand."

He sent the money and rubbed his shoulders until the chill went away. After that, his body reminded him of other concerns.

"Food. How much?"

"Five-thousand pounds."

"Fuck sake. Why are you doing this?" He shook his head in disgust and tapped at his phone. "There, I sent it."

The hatch in the ceiling opened. A plastic tub fell through and landed in the middle of the room. Scott ripped off the lid and winced at the smell. "Fucking dog food? What the fuck are you playing at? Give me human food, not this processed garbage."

"This is the food you can afford. It is bad for you."

"No shit. I need vegetables, fruit, some meat. And it needs to be halal. Come on, you can at least respect my beliefs."

"This is what you must eat. Anything better will cost you more."

"How much?"

"Fifty-thousand pounds."

Scott grimaced. "I don't have enough left in my account. I would have to sell some of my stocks and shares, but that takes twenty-four hours."

"Then you must eat what you can afford."

"Screw you, bitch. I'll give you everything in my account, but you need to let me go, okay? I can't give you what I don't have."

"You have no choice in this matter. Pay to live. Or die and someone else will take your place."

Scott dragged himself up off the floor. He was hurting, his joints creaking. His armpits smelled. The last of his deodorant and expensive cologne had long faded. "What do you mean, someone else? This is about me, right? What do you want?"

"Rent."

"Rent?"

"You must pay your landlord. You must pay to eat. You must pay to live."

"You're insane. I only have so much money to give. Take it and let me go."

There was a soft scraping sound, backed by a low rumble.

Scott looked around, blinking in the low light. What's happening? What is that sound?"

He pawed at the walls, and jumped at the ceiling—but the ceiling was fifteen feet up and the walls had seams only at the corners where they met. The scraping continued.

Scott gasped. "Stop! Stop it!"

"Rent is due in twelve hours. Pay or you will be evicted."

"Evicted?"

There was no reply, but Scott had an idea of what that meant. The rumbling and scraping noises were the sounds of the walls closing in.

———

AFTER TAKING a piss in the corner, Scott spent the next void of time thinking heavily. It was the only thing he could do. Think or go insane. Probably both, eventually. The smell of the dog food sitting in the middle of the room made him feel both sick and ashamedly hungry.

He thought once again about who might be doing this. Maybe it was the woman and her toddler. Maybe it was a current tenant. Mr Greenwood had sent him an abusive email just last week about mould in his daughter's bedroom. Scott had ignored it, knowing the property was fine and just needed to be kept warm. Mr Greenwood would have to accept having to put the heating on more. There was also his ex, Lexi, who he had kicked to the ground in front of her friends when she had come home sloppy and drunk. The humiliation had caused her to leave, but he had quickened her out the door with some words he probably shouldn't have said. It wasn't something he was proud of.

I should have tried to fix things.

Maybe he wasn't a good man. But he wasn't evil. He didn't deserve this.

I'm just a businessman. It's not wrong to be successful.

He was sure this couldn't be the work of a tenant, so he rested upon the notion that this was about nothing more than money. It was always about money, in the end. Underneath every care or concern, every moral code and ethic, people always wanted money.

Instead of trying to find a way out of his cell, or beg his captors for mercy, Scott slowly fell into a half-asleep stupor. His mind shut off after so much thinking and the time passed by more easily. He had no idea how long it had been when the walls started moving again.

———

HE LEAPT TO HIS FEET, yelling. "Hey! Hey, stop! Why are you moving the walls again? Why are you making it smaller in here? I need room."

"You have enough room. Rent is due."

"What? Okay, stop. I-I'll send you another ten-thousand. Let me check my phone. Just stop."

"Fifteen-thousand."

"What? It was ten before."

"Costs have risen. Pay or someone else will."

"Fine. Wait. I'll use my credit card. For fuck's sake..."

He made the payment, using up half his credit limit in one fell swoop. This was going to financially ruin him, his working capital almost gone.

No. None of this is legal. As soon as I get out of here, I'll make it right. I'll get every penny back. Maybe I will go to the police.

"Alright. Stop moving the walls.

The scraping and whirring came to a slow stop. The room was half the size it had started out at, barely wide enough to lie down.

Heart thudding in his chest, Scott slid down the wall and slumped into a sitting position. Then he realised he needed to go to the bathroom.

"This isn't just about money," he said. "If it was, you would want to get this over with fast. This is torture, which means it's personal. So why me? Why are you doing this to me? What the fuck did I do to anybody?"

"It's just business."

"Right. Business is about being a man and doing what needs to be done. Let me go now and we'll forget all about it. I can take the hit."

"Business is never personal. There are merely winners and losers."

Scott took a deep breath in and held it a moment. "Look. I'm starving, I need a wash, and whatever lesson I'm supposed to learn, let's just assume I've learned it, okay? Just tell me who you are so we can work this out. I know that's not your real voice. You're using a device, right? Then there's this motorised cell. You're obviously a tech guy. Respect to that. This is all top-tier stuff. Maybe we can make some money together after all this is through."

The lights went out.

"Your bill is due."

"Nah, man. I'm done, right? I ain't playing your games anymore. It's over."

He shuffled out of his suit jacket and draped it across his legs. If this was a game of willpower, then he wouldn't be the one to lose. Screw it, he'd close his eyes and snooze for however long it took for the other asshole to get bored.

Scott kept up the defiant act for what felt like a few hours until he began to shiver again. Another bill due in this sick little game, but he wasn't about to hand over any more of his hard earned money. Why the hell should he?

Pulling his suit jacket around himself, he tried not to shiver—unwilling to show his tormentors he was suffering. His need of a toilet grew urgent, and his stomach cramped almost constantly, but he didn't let it show.

What do I do if I can't hold it in any longer?

The walls moved again, forcing him to shuffle along the ground. This time, instead of crying out, he said nothing, calling his captor's bluff. What was their end goal? If it was to kill him, then what could he do about it? If it was to humiliate and torture him, then he wouldn't give them what they wanted.

The walls stopped closing in, leaving him just enough space to lie on his side, but not enough to spread out the other way. His once square room was now a narrow corridor.

"Rent is due. Your heating and lighting are overdue. You now owe fifty thousand pounds."

"I don't have it. All my cash is locked up in investments and savings. It's over, okay? You can't get blood out of a stone.

Silence.

The lights went out. It grew colder.

————

HOURS WENT by and Scott finally had no choice but to take a shit at one end of his narrow space. In such tight confines, the smell was overpowering, and his inability to clean himself left him unsettled. Somehow, this act of self-humiliation was what broke him. He felt the arrival of tears.

When the walls began to move, he let out a wail. "Stop. Please, let me go. I'm sorry, okay?"

The walls stopped moving, leaving him wedged, knees and back against the hard surfaces.

"Sorry for what?"

"For everything. Whatever I did. Throwing mothers out on the street. Putting prices up every year. Refusing to make repairs. I'm a shitty landlord, right? Is that what this is about? Please, just tell me."

"It's just business."

The walls closed in. So tightly that Scott could barely breathe as his body contorted into a twisted pretzel. His knees and elbows screamed in agony. He squealed in pain.

"P-please. I-I can't get... can't get... air."

"Air isn't free. You must pay one-hundred thousand pounds."

"Air is... free. Air is... free."

"Not anymore. One-hundred-thousand."

"Can't."

The walls clamped shut and Scott's remains mixed with his shit and the canned dog food. The room would be cleaned, ready for its next tenant.

It wasn't personal. Just business.

FATHERHOOD

John had never imagined being in a position like this–covered in another man's blood. He didn't relish it, but he couldn't deny his shock at how capable of torture he was.

Anger was the key. The burning spark inside his chest consumed all other emotions besides rage. The only other feeling in the room was fear–but that wasn't coming from him.

He struck Adam across the face again, his knuckles stinging as they thudded against cheekbone. Adam whimpered, already spitting blood from the previous round of beating. One of the younger man's teeth glistened on the ground at their feet. His ankles were cable tied securely to the chair legs, his arms behind his back.

A cellar would have been handy for this kind of thing, but instead John was forced to make do with the office at the back of his warehouse. It was Sunday, so his three staff weren't in yet, and the adjacent businesses in the tiny industrial estate were closed too.

"Why? Why are you doing this, man?" Adam's lips were swollen, his words slurred. "You're a psychopath."

John gritted his teeth, nearly overtaken by rage. "You know why, and the sooner you admit it, the sooner this will all be over."

Adam could barely keep his head up, but he nodded towards the video camera set up on a tripod in the corner of the room. It was old–a relic from the days before twenty-megapixel camera phones–but it still did the job. John couldn't count the hours of family footage he had captured with the thing. Almost all of Polly and Daphne's childhoods, starting with the first car trip home from the hospital with Daphne wrapped in a knitted pink blanket gifted from his mother.

Adam moaned. "You want some kind of confession? For what? What do you think I did?"

John clenched his bloody fists, ready to inflict more fury upon this young man. He was surprised the kid hadn't caved yet. His terror was palpable; had been from the moment John had pretended to be a dejected delivery man asking for a push start. When Adam had left his parents' driveway to help push the nondescript white van from behind, John had pounced, tapping him on the back of the head with a hammer to stun him, before bundling him inside and tying him up. It had been a bold abduction, but all had gone to plan.

John didn't care if he got caught. Just so long as Adam got what he deserved.

"Look at that camera and admit what you did."

Adam shook his head, his blonde hair parted at the back by a bulbous lump where the hammer had hit. The lad hadn't lost consciousness during the assault, which was good. Brain damage wasn't part of the plan. He needed to be awake and aware for every part of this.

"Fuck you!" Adam shed his fear long enough to fight against his restraints. The wheeled office chair began to rock back and forth, but its wide pedestal kept it from toppling. "Let me go or I'll fucking kill you."

John smiled. "That's it! That's the real you I want to see. No more playing games. I know what you are, Adam."

"I don't know what you're talking about, you bloody nutcase. Let me go or I swear to God–"

"What?" John leaned forward and lowered his head enough to meet Adam's eye line. "What will you do to me? Leave me for dead in an underpass?"

Adam winced.

John knew the boy was trying to act tough, but he saw the fear in his eyes. Just a little more work—another few bouts of *unpleasantness*—and the truth would come out.

Then she'll be here and see what I've done for her. She'll finally have peace. Soon. So very soon.

John turned to the office desk behind him and picked up the thin slice of steel he had placed there. Shaped like an angular U, and with several bore-holes for screws and bolts, it was a piece used in the construction of escalators. The supermarket contract made up a full thirty percent of the company's business, which made simple components out of sheet metal. It was a dirty job that left a man's fingers permanently covered in nicks and cuts, but it paid the bills. It paid for Polly to keep a horse at the local stables and attend stage school at the weekends, and for Daphne to attend Warwick University to study law. Every hour of boredom was worth it to see his girls happy.

But Polly wasn't happy anymore. Her smile was gone. Her spirit had been brutalised.

John paced around Adam, circling behind him then returning to the front. He took his time, soaking in the whimpers of his enemy.

Then he struck. He dragged the razor-thin steel component down the side of Adam's nose, opening up a bright red gash along the bridge that immediately gushed with blood.

Adam struggled and squealed, then spat blood as it ran into his mouth. His knees knocked back and forth as he tried to free his ankles, his wrists straining against the cable ties and scraping away flesh.

"How does it feel?" John demanded with a sneer. "Huh?"

"Please. Please, stop this."

"Not until you admit to what you did."

Adam lifted his head, a trail of blood running down the middle of his handsome, twenty-year-old face. He looked John in the eye, not so much desperate as confused. "I don't understand."

John could play this game all day. He wasn't going to be beaten. Not by this monster. "You're a bit of a lady's man, Adam? Is that right?"

He shrugged. "I suppose so."

"One of the fixtures at the *Oubliette Lounge?*"

"My uncle built it."

John nodded appreciatively. "Wow. That must make you the big man. Free drinks? VIP access?"

"So what? I like to party. What's the crime?"

"How many young girls have you sweet talked into alleyways and toilets, Adam? How many young girls have you used and abused?"

Adam spat blood. He clearly tried to hit John, but missed as he was standing halfway behind him. "A fuck load more than you ever have, prick. Now let me go."

John raised the bloody shard of metal. Adam flinched. "I suggest you watch your mouth, lad, or I'll slice your lips off. See how many girls want to kiss you, then."

Adam shook his head and sneered, but he kept quiet. Eventually, he looked up at John and spoke again. "Is that what this is about? Did I shag your missus or summin'? Or sleep with some old tart you were hoping to bang? Tell me who and I might be able to remember the details for you. You can wank off while I tell you."

John erupted. Leaping forwards, he sawed the metal shard back and forth against Adam's flesh.

Like carving sirloin.

It was surprisingly easy to get the whole ear off, and when John showed it to Adam, the young lad screamed in horror. His screams quickly turned to guttural yells for help.

"No one is coming to save you." John wiggled the ear back and forth before tossing it onto the carpet. "Just like no one came to help Polly."

Adam's eyes went wide. "P-Polly?"

"Yes, Polly Macintosh. My daughter."

John watched Adam for some kind of give-away, a flicker in his eyes that betrayed his guilt, but the only thing on display was panic and fear. And shock.

"Y-your Polly's dad?"

"Yes!"

"I-I-I'm sorry."

"You should be. Real sorry."

John snarled and took Adam's other ear. This time, he stuffed the appendage into Adam's screaming throat, pushing it down until he was forced to swallow it with a choking sob.

"P-please stop. Please. I want to go home. I want my mum."

"Did Polly beg? Did she beg when you forced yourself on her?"

"What? I didn't!"

"You did! She told me."

"I didn't!"

Why wouldn't he admit it? How much pain did John need to inflict?

He was going to find out.

———

JOHN HADN'T PLANNED on using the welding torch. In fact, it was used so rarely that he had forgotten all about it until he found it at the back of the tool cupboard. The oxygen cylinder was half empty, but the flame ignited with hissing fury.

He started with Adam's feet.

Next, he cooked the lad's fingertips until they crackled like sausages in a pan. By the time John was done, Adam had shrieked himself into unconsciousness. Blood, snot, and tears stained his face, but beneath his cheeks were the pallid colour of chalk.

John leaned back against his desk, a bloody hand pressed over his mouth. Thin slices from the metal shard covered his fingers, and his right thumb was pale and blistered from an accident with the torch. He wasn't coming out of this unscathed.

Physically or mentally.

What have I done?

There's no going back.

Something had snapped inside of John. It had happened quickly, almost as soon as the torture had begun. For a moment, he'd been horrified by his actions, but once he pushed through, the ordeal became *exhilarating*. Adam's screams were like primal music, torn loose by unimaginable pain.

Pain that John was inflicting.

Inflicting because this monster had hurt his little girl. There was no room for mercy. He was a righteous weapon delivering justice.

He was a broken father.

John pulled out his phone and checked his messages. There was one from Sandra, his wife, asking what he wanted for tea. He couldn't speak to her right now—not while he was like this.

He sent off a single message. To Polly.

———

ADAM WOKE up about thirty-minutes later. The pain returned first, several seconds before comprehension did. It took a further moment for his damaged mind to fully refocus on reality, but once it did, he wailed like a madman.

John shut him up by stamping on his blackened left foot.

Adam howled, but managed to shut himself up enough to merely hyperventilate.

"This is it," said John. "Act Three. Time to decide how this ends."

"J-j-just kill me. P-please. No more."

John shook his head, eyes fixed on the younger man. "Admit what you did and I'll call an ambulance. Look right into this camera and say it. You can live through this."

Adam's eyes fluttered, his consciousness fading in and out. "All right. I-I'll say it."

Finally.

John placed the welding torch down on his desk and folded his arms. "Go on."

"What do you want me to say?"

John sneered. "I want to own what you did to Polly. What you did to my daughter. You raped her. You chatted her up, got her drunk, and when she tried to slow things down, you found it unacceptable. Not used to hearing the word *no*, are you?"

Adam shook his head, his eyes rolling up into his skull for a second. "W-will you get me help? If I admit to it?"

"Yes. I don't care what happens next. I just want a confession."

"Fine, I'll say it. Just get help... I... I did something. I hurt her."

John nodded triumphantly. "When? Where?"

"At the club. I chatted her up, just like you said, but she wasn't up for it, so I lost my temper. I was drunk, I'm sorry."

"You're sorry?" John's bloody hands squeezed tight. Somehow, hearing Adam apologise, as if he had merely made a mistake, infuriated him all over again. There was no saying sorry for this. There was no forgiveness or understanding.

John grabbed the welding torch back off his desk and reignited the flame.

Adam screamed, thrashing at the cable ties. Veins and sinew bulged in his neck. "You promised! You promised you'd call an ambulance."

"When did I promise?" John shoved the lit end of the torch into Adam's face, burning both eyeballs until they popped like overripe grapes. The younger man blacked out again. Vomit trickled from his mouth down his chest.

Adam let out a high-pitched whistle from his throat and then began to seize, his limbs stiffening and his jaws clamping. Then, just as suddenly, his entire body went limp in the chair. His chest continued to rise and fall, but only barely.

"D-Dad?"

His daughter's voice echoed in the warehouse, right outside of his office. His text had bid her to come meet him here. She always worked on a Sunday, running the tills at the nearby Co-op, so he knew she would be up and dressed.

"In the office," he shouted. "Don't be shocked, okay? I did this for you."

"What? Dad, what are you talking about?" She opened the door slowly, peeking inside. The office was well lit by a fluorescent tube light, so it took her only a second to spot Adam in the corner of the room, slumped in the chair and covered in blood. Both his eyeballs were oozing down his blackened cheeks.

John looked at his daughter and frowned. "Shit! Oh, it's you, Daphne. I... I was expecting your sister. Try not to panic, okay? This–this is a good thing."

Fortunately, Daphne didn't panic. She had always been the strongest of his daughters; less emotional than Polly. Shaking her head, she reached into her pocket and pulled out her phone. "I know you texted Polly. I have her old sim in my phone, remember? People still message her occasionally, those who don't know what happened. But she's gone, Dad. You know that, right?"

He flinched and then grimaced in disgust. "What? Daphne, what on earth are you talking about?"

Daphne stepped further into the room. Her eyes went from John to Adam and back again. She seemed to swallow a lump in her throat, one so big that it caused her to wince. "Is he dead, Dad?"

John looked at Adam and then frowned at his daughter. "Blind for life, but still alive for now. I got a confession, though. He admitted what he did to Polly. Maybe now she'll be able to sleep at night."

Daphne noticed the camera in the corner of the room and let out a sigh. "You can't keep doing this, Dad. You said you were better. You promised Mum that the last time was the last time."

He stepped towards her and she flinched—his own daughter. "Daphne, I know this is shocking, but I made a vow to punish the monster who hurt your sister."

"You did! Two years ago, Dad. You got the guy who did it. Don't you remember? Mum found him hacked to pieces inside the back of your van. You left the body there so long it was infested with flies."

John tried to find words, but he was too confused. "What? I don't..."

"Brett Gaffney," Daphne yelled. "The owner of the *Oubliette* night-club, where... where it happened. You got him. You punished him. It should be over.

John rubbed at his forehead, trying to make sense of why his daughter would try to confuse him like this. "That... that makes no sense."

"Is that Adam in the chair?" Daphne put her hands over her face and moaned, sounding like she was going to be sick. "Brett Gaffney's nephew? Jesus, Dad. Polly was friends with him. She liked Adam. He's a good guy. What have you done?"

John put a hand to his forehead, feeling a migraine coming on. "H-he got what he deserved."

Didn't he?

"Deserved?" Daphne said angrily. "Like the other two men you butchered out of delusion? At least this time you got someone vaguely related to the culprit. We..." She put a hand to the back of her head, grasping her ponytail like she was trying to hold on to her own skull. "We can't cover for you anymore, Dad. It's sick. *You're* sick." As if to prove her point, she turned and vomited all over the carpet.

Adam murmured. His leg shook sporadically. Even if they called for help, it was probably too late for him.

He was a monster who deserved to die. Polly named him. Spoke about him all the time.

Because they were friends.

Jesus...

A sudden spike of pain hit John's brain. He doubled over and almost fell. He saw Daphne rushing towards him and tried to palm her away, but she was insistent and kept urging him to listen, until she was able to shove something in his face.

Her phone.

On it was a BBC news article. The headline read:

Popular Redditch teen found dead in underpass. Town's third murder this year. Witnesses needed.

"This is the fourth time you've done this, Dad. You can't stop yourself. *We* can't stop you. I miss Polly, too, but this is so wrong."

The floor began to tilt and John collapsed against his desk. Although appearing concerned, Daphne made no move to help him. In fact, she looked at Adam with far more sympathy.

It all came flooding back. John's knees buckled as the story he'd been telling himself crumbled. He remembered it all clearly. The nightmare gripped him.

Getting the call at four AM from the police. Being asked to come take a look at the body to confirm it was Polly. The months of investigation that led nowhere, prompting John to hit the streets himself, threatening local scumbags until he finally got the truth of it. Hesitant whispers had eventually, but unanimously, named local club owner Brett Gaffney as the man who had violated and murdered his beloved youngest daughter. It wasn't the first bad thing the man had done. He had deserved to die.

John looked at Adam and saw the ruins of a young boy. His mind and body could never heal. Any life he might have hoped to have lived would now be a nightmare of trauma and misery.

I've ruined him. Just like his uncle ruined my daughter.

John took the bloody shard of metal from his desk and slit Adam's throat. The boy didn't even wake up.

Daphne groaned in horror. John hated the fear in her eyes.

"I'm crazy," he said, a statement of fact.

Daphne nodded and lifted her phone slightly. She was trying to secretly make a call.

Calling the police.

He stepped towards her, and when she flinched he wrapped his arms around her. "It's okay," he said. "You can call them. Just tell your mother I love her, okay? I love all my girls."

John turned and went over to Adam, looking down at the younger man as blood pumped from his neck. Maybe the kid hadn't deserved to die. But neither had Polly.

The world was cruel.

Lonely and confusing.

Madness was comforting.

John lifted the bloody shard of metal one last time and sliced his own neck. As he fell, he saw his only living daughter screaming, but he couldn't help but notice the relief on her face as well.

He hoped Polly would be happy to see him, and that she would forgive him for what he had done. Because he had done it for her.

Madness was comforting—so was death.

GEMINUS

E than had never been a bad-looking man, but as he stared in the ensuite mirror, he saw the beginnings of old age—slight creases at the corner of his eyes and grey hair at the temples. Was thirty-five the age—the age when everything started breaking down? His knees didn't quite have the same springiness and his neck rotated with a noticeable *crunch*.

But it wasn't all over yet. He was still slim and toned thanks to a three-day split at the gym, and so far he had lost no hair from his head. Women still looked his way from time to time, which was fortunate, because he had found himself single and childless as he fast approached middle age. The only money to his name was the forty grand equity in his two-bedroom Sunderland flat.

He prodded at his cheeks, pulling down his eyelids and wrinkling his nose. His reflection copied him—of course—and he found it strangely mesmerising as he studied himself down to his individual pores.

"Six years wasted," he muttered, referring to his shattered relationship with Claire. Things had ended three months ago, after she had disappeared for two nights, partying with her friends. It wasn't the first occasion, and by the time Ethan finally ended it, he had been living constantly on edge, waiting for the next uncontrollable bender that would leave Claire recovering for days. He had tried to help her–to convince her that their wild youth was now behind them–but eventually, the heated disagreements had become enraged arguments. Claire wasn't ready to grow old and die. Life was for living.

He missed her.

She had always felt like *the one*, ever since asking for her number at the coffeehouse where she had worked as a waitress. They had fallen in love quickly, and Ethan soon pictured the two of them growing old together.

Now he had no clue what the future held.

And it felt like time was running out.

His pupils dilated as he continued to stare into the mirror. The bathroom's orange ceiling light flickering behind him, the bulb on its last legs. Dinnertime had come and gone, but he wasn't sure he could be bothered to cook. Ironically, he'd been drinking a lot the last few weeks to make his nights feel less lonely, so all he really fancied right now was a beer.

I wonder if Claire is drinking right now? Is she out on the town?

Turning away from the mirror, Ethan wondered if...

What...?

He turned back again, studying his reflection. Strange. Something had seemed slightly off, as if his image had lagged for a split-second.

Again, wrinkling his nose, Ethan observed himself for a moment longer. Then, with a chuckle, he moved away, feeling stupid.

"I'm going crazy," he told himself before putting the strange moment down to dizziness. For the first night in a while, he decided not to have a beer.

The unfettered loneliness was unpleasant.

———

ETHAN AWOKE fresh and vibrant in his double bed. Monday–his day off along with Sunday. He was Head Chef at *Italiano Gardenia* in town, and it took a full two days to be free from the smell of garlic which clung to him like cologne.

This morning, he felt light instead of heavy. Although his thoughts turned, as usual, to Claire, they didn't burn quite as hot. Despite the rough ride of the last few years, he still missed her company and sense of humour—and especially missed their passionate lovemaking that had somehow never suffered even during their worst times—but most of all, he missed not being alone in the world. It was frightening to suddenly find yourself without support after coming to rely on it being there.

But today things felt a little less glum. The dark clouds over his life had parted and he could see a patch of blue sky.

"Life finds a way," he said, hearing Jeff Goldblum's voice in his head.

As he often did upon waking, he headed directly into the lounge and switched on the television before making himself a mug of instant coffee in the kitchen. As the kettle boiled, he leaned on the counter and stared out the window at the allotments across the road. No one was there yet—the green and brown grids lifeless—but around lunchtime, the oldies would appear and start pottering around. That was about all the activity this quiet street ever saw besides traffic.

Before Claire left, they would sometimes go out for lunch on a Monday, followed by a walk in the park. Now he spent his off days doing nothing. He needed to get a hobby.

"Don't think I'm ready for the bowls club yet," he told himself. "Maybe I should take up fishing."

The kettle clicked. Ethan reached out to lift it from its base.

He paused.

In the corner of his eye, a flicker of movement. His reflection in the double-glazed window.

Once again, that same strange sensation washed over Ethan. Like something was out of balance. A subtle thing, almost instinctual, like the way you could feel the tiniest blister on the roof of your mouth with your tongue.

Like a crazy person, he raised one hand and watched as his reflection copied him precisely. Then he blinked, testing himself for dizziness, of which he was sure he had none. He couldn't even put it down to a hangover. It was the first morning he'd awoken without a bad head in a long time.

With a sigh, Ethan turned back to grab the kettle again.

"There!" He shot a look back at his reflection, and this time he was sure it had moved too slowly. Just the slightest delay, barely perceptible, but wrong enough to give him goosebumps. "What the hell?"

He moved back and forth, waved his hands, and almost ended up dancing like a lunatic. His reflection behaved as it should, mimicking him precisely.

"What is going on inside my head? I'm losing it."

Ethan sagged against the counter, wondering if he needed to go see a doctor and get tested. Of course, his reflection wasn't playing him up. That would be crazy.

So why was he so sure it hadn't moved right?

———

THE NEXT FEW days crawled by. His sleep each night had been disturbed, and a wracking cold had caused him to call off work. He got the suspicion Mr Tuliman knew about his recent drinking and was mistrustful of his absence, but the truth was that Ethan had drunk only a few beers each night and was genuinely feeling unwell.

It had to be because of his reflection. He was now, more than ever, sure it was misbehaving. The slight movement delays had grown more severe, and this afternoon, when he had waved at himself in the bathroom mirror, his reflection had done so sluggishly. No more doubting it—or himself.

Something was messed up with his reflection.

But he didn't know what to do about it. Did he call someone to come check it out? Show somebody else what was happening?

But what if they saw nothing?

All the better reason to call someone.

But who? His dad was long dead, and his mother lived with his sister on the south coast six hours away. They barely spoke. His entire world consisted only of...

Claire.

No, that wasn't true. He had friends, people he worked with and the lads at the gym. Going for a drink was usually an option with someone or another. And yet...

"There's no one I trust."

Even my own reflection is betraying me.

His bundle of tissues on the coffee table were caked with snot, so he went into the bathroom to grab another roll. It was impossible not to look in the mirror above the sink as he passed by.

The sight of his reflection froze him stiff.

He was smiling at himself.

Ethan, startled, faltered backwards. His legs almost folded beneath him, but he caught his balance and blinked. Then he stared, wide-eyed, at his reflection.

His smiling, *disobedient* reflection.

The image in the mirror was untethered–a separate being following its own will. As it continued to smile, it lifted a hand and waved.

Ethan screamed.

———

ETHAN WENT IMMEDIATELY to the doctor, not even making an appointment. After arguing with the receptionist to the point of being arrested, a Dr Mulgutty had agreed to see him. The diminutive, smartly dressed woman was clearly doubtful of his claims that his reflection was betraying him.

"The stress of your recent breakup, exacerbated by alcohol, has probably caused you to have a nervous breakdown," she said without emotion. "Its severity can be managed in several ways. Light exercise, a healthy diet, and try to relax as much as possible. To help you, I'm going to prescribe a course of beta blockers. Take them whenever you feel like things are getting too much. It'll help keep you calm."

"That's all it is? Stress?"

"Let's assume so for now. Do you have any other symptoms? Headaches? Vomiting? Fever?"

"No. Just... the problem with my reflection."

The doctor nodded and smiled. "I'm going to book you another appointment, one week from today. We'll see where we're at then."

So he'd taken his prescription and caught the bus home, reassured by a professional telling him not to worry, but equally concerned that she hadn't taken him particularly seriously.

Seeing things made a person crazy, right? Like, schizophrenic or something?

Is that something you can just get? One minute you're normal and the next... poof! *You're a fruitcake.*

During the ride, Ethan saw his reflection in the bus window. But rather than focus on it, he looked through it at the tired Sunderland streets passing by as he approached the Wearmouth Bridge. The sight of the river was calming, but then he remembered that water could be a mirror too. What would happen if he stood on the banks and peered at its reflective surface?

He popped his first pill from the foil packet and swallowed it dry, flexing his neck like a gulping swan. It was probably all in his head, but he felt calmer already—a little less buzzing in his skull. It left him unprepared when the bus stopped at a set of traffic lights outside a large-fronted butcher's shop.

At first, he saw several of the other passengers captured in the shop's large plate-glass window, almost like an alternate reality where doppelgängers existed and lived identical lives. The various heads faced forwards in a line, all uninterested by the world beyond their window.

One face peered directly back at Ethan. His own. Of course, that made sense because he was staring at the butcher shop's window, but his reflection was doing more than just staring.

Ethan's reflection put its thumbs in its ears and waggled its fingers while sticking out its tongue. Dumbfounded, Ethan placed his hands over his mouth, scared he might have gone insane. But his mouth was clamped shut. No tongue sticking out.

"No... I took the pill."

He turned his head to an older man with wispy grey hair sitting on the bench behind him. Was he seeing this too? No, he was reading a newspaper. Ethan thought about asking for his help, but what could he even say? Then the lights turned green, and the bus got moving again.

Ethan caught one last glimpse of his reflection in the Butcher shop window. It was normal.

But I'm not. I'm not normal.

———

ETHAN SPENT the day in the living room, watching movies and trying to keep his mind from wandering. He was trembling constantly, despite the beta blockers, and he kept fighting the urge to cry. Never in his life had he felt so little trust over his own mind and body. Never before had he felt so alone.

Texting Claire was probably a bad idea.

But it was his only idea.

Been going a little crazy lately, he typed. *Hope you're okay. X*

The kiss was a mistake, he knew it, but the message had sent.

———

AFTER A DOZEN small bottles of beer, Ethan must have passed out, because he awoke in pitch-darkness. The TV was on, but had loaded up its screensaver—a small red square moving around the screen. It wasn't as spooky as in the old movies when a person would awake to static, but it still felt slightly otherworldly.

As he blinked his grogginess away, Ethan saw his face reflected in the television screen, barely visible. He reached for the remote and woke the TV up. The main menu was a bright blue and bathed the room with light.

Ethan took a few shallow breaths and stood up. Unsteady on his feet, he could not ignore his aching bladder and had to rush to the bathroom right away. As he stood over the toilet and released an almighty stream, he was unhappily aware of the mirror at his back. It had all started with that damned mirror. The madness. The doubting of his own sanity. Was it a cursed piece of glass? A portal to hell?

No, it was just a cheap round mirror Claire had bought at a charity shop two years ago. It was mundane.

So what is going on with me? Am I ill?

Hexed? Maybe Claire's taken up witchcraft and put a spell on me as revenge for dumping her. She always did have a temper.

Does she even think about me at all?

He shook off the last of his stream, then squeezed to eject those last few drops that were always ready to slip out and wet his underwear. Turning around, he dared look in the mirror, determined not to be cowed by something so ordinary.

A reflection with a life of its own was unnatural. Unwanted. Perverse.

Impossible

Yet it persisted.

His reflection blinked and smiled, then waved. It didn't keep still for a single second. All the while, Ethan stood statuesque, not even breathing. This reflection was no longer a figment of his mind or a symptom of illness—it was his *enemy*.

"What the fuck do you want?" he demanded of himself, glaring at his own unruly image. "Why are you doing this to me?"

The reflection shrugged, speechless like a mime artist. It even made exaggerated faces. One minute sad, the next laughing.

"Fuck you!" Ethan leaned over the sink, his nose almost touching the glass. He glared into his own eyes, but saw swirling black pools that had a sinister essence of their own. This thing was not him. It was something else. Something bad. "Leave me alone. Leave me alone or... or..."

Ethan reeled back, raising his fist. He was about to punch the glass and break it...

But his reflection had returned to normal.

Ethan saw only his own weary and exhausted self in the mirror. "I won't lose myself," he muttered. "Even if I don't like what's looking back at me, you won't take my reflection from me. It's mine. My image. My life."

He leaned forwards again, this time not quite so close. "Do you understand me? Whatever you are, I won't let you have it. I won't let you drive me crazy."

His reflection stared back at him.

"Good. That's sorted, then."

I really am crazy. Talking to my own reflection.

Ethan studied himself, seeing not a pore out of place. Was it over? Had his brief insanity ended? Had the pills finally kicked in? He waited for his reflection to mock him, but it didn't. No inane smiles. No mocking, silent laughter. Just a lonely, pathetic man that Ethan hated to look at.

But not as much as I hate the other guy.

The mirror suddenly shattered, cracking from corner to corner and exploding outwards.

Ethan didn't have time to throw his hands up as two pairs of hands grabbed his face and squeezed. Some of the glass shards remained glued to the mirror's backboard. Reflected in them, he saw himself laughing.

———

CLAIRE WAS WORRIED ABOUT ETHAN, which she knew was ironic. If she had worried about him more when they had been together, they might still be a couple.

"But I'm ready to make up for it now," she said, as she climbed the familiar steps up to the flat she had so recently lived in. She couldn't blame Ethan for ignoring her calls and texts over the last few days, but it hurt her all the same. He also wouldn't be out of order if he refused ever to speak to her again. She'd lost count of the amount of times she had cheated on him, or lost her phone while she partied with her pals. Pals who she had finally realised were toxic.

"I'm toxic too," she said, reaching the landing. Years of drinking and drug taking had warped her mind to where she had lacked a conscience, but she was determined to fight and regain the person she had once been. Losing Ethan had been the wake up call she had needed.

Two months without a sip or swallow of anything bad. That was the time limit she had set for herself. *Sort your shit out and then go back and beg Ethan for another chance.* She had only one shot at this, so the wait had been necessary in order to give herself the best chance. It'd been the hardest thing she'd ever done, but she had pushed the bad away and now realised that Ethan had been the only good in her life.

He might not take her back—a terrifying thought—but she owed it to herself to try. She might let him down... She might fail...

But she might not.

She and Ethan were meant to grow old together. She felt it in her veins. The moment he had walked into the coffee shop where she had worked, the moment their eyes met as he slid a chair out and sat down gently—like he was in a quiet library and not a busy cafe—she had felt it. Felt *him*.

Just like she felt something was wrong right now.

The plan had been to visit Ethan Saturday night, knowing he had Sundays off. That would allow them to thrash things out long into the night if need be—and for Claire to say all the things she needed to say. As well as hear all the things she needed to hear.

And now she was standing right outside his door.

Our door.

It felt bizarre to knock—she had once held a set of keys—but she accepted the discomfort and took a moment to breathe. She took responsibility for it, instead of apportioning blame.

When there was no answer to her knock, an icy shudder ran across Claire's shoulders. She tried the door handle and found it unlocked.

The television's quiet muttering drifted into the hallway from the lounge as she stepped inside. *Loose women* or some windbag chefs—the only things that could be on at this time of day.

The lounge was empty. Drained beer bottles littered the carpet. The air smelled stale. Ethan had never been a massive drinker—thank God—but he'd clearly taken up the habit since their break up. Did that mean he missed her? Wanted her back, even?

Is he hurting?

But before Claire even approached that bridge, she needed to make sure he was okay. "Ethan? It's Claire. I wanted to see you. Ethan, are you here?"

God, what's happened? This doesn't feel right.

She went into the bedroom, hoping to find her ex-lover sleeping, but the bed was crumpled, unmade, and empty. The window was open, letting in a breeze that had turned the room chilly.

"Ethan? It's Claire. I... I want to talk things out. I'm sober now. And I still love you. Where... where are you?"

She considered he might have gone out on a bender—he had seen her do so often enough to know the signs—but it didn't seem like something he would do. It was something *she* would do.

Just drink yourself into oblivion until you have no choice but to collapse into some loser's bed or onto a friend's couch.

Am I crazy for thinking he might possibly forgive me?

Ethan...

After checking the kitchen and finding only dirty coffee mugs piled up in the sink, she decided to check the last place left—the bathroom. Voices in her head whispered unkindly, telling her it was a private place where she was no longer welcome. But she had to find Ethan.

She padded across the hallway and stopped outside the bathroom door. The carpet there was damp. Had there been a flood? Was the bath overflowing? Perhaps Ethan had fallen asleep or passed out.

"Ethan," she called out softly through the door, and when there was no answer, she opened it and stepped inside slowly. The air was damp.

A fly buzzed from one side to the other.

Broken glass crunched beneath her feet.

Ethan stared back at her from the bathtub. She saw her own reflection in his eyes.

Then her phone buzzed with a message:

> Been going a little crazy lately, he typed. Hope you're okay. Eth X

SELFIE

Glenda was exhausted after such a wonderful day. She gave her eldest daughter, Carol, one last hug and said goodbye. As soon as the front door closed, she put her back against it and deflated. Birthdays were lovely, but at seventy years old, the parties were draining as much as they were fun.

It's a big one, though. Seven-zero. Seven decades. Wow!

Glenda had experienced a lot in her time on earth, with two husbands and three children, but the past had started to feel surreal lately. *The Beatles* had released their first single during her childhood, something she remembered like it was *yesterday*–excuse the pun–but it was also so incredibly distant from her current self that it now felt as if it had happened to somebody else. Half *The Beatles* were in their graves, and the world had become a whizzing, whirling, sleepless place of beeping electronics and blinking lights. While she loved her *Netflix* and *Facebook*, she yearned to go back to the days when folks had chatted on the doorstep and baked cakes for one another.

"Oh, come on now, Glenda," she told herself. "Let's not get maudlin. The world moves on and that's a good thing."

Talking to herself was a habit that came both with living alone and being old. If not for herself, she'd have no company at all.

She went into the kitchen to make herself a cup of tea and readjust back to solitude. Twelve people had just occupied her three-bed semi, offering gifts and singing *Happy Birthday*. Now that they had gone, the house felt disconcertingly quiet.

She switched on the small television on the kitchen counter and hit the plastic lever to boil the kettle.

Loose Women came on—four sour-faced ladies complaining about the state of the world. Usually, she would switch the channel to something a little cheerier, but the background chatter was comforting, so she left it on.

She poured her tea and sat down at the small breakfast table pushed up against the back wall. There, she picked up her favourite gift of the day, given to her jointly by her three daughters. It was a new mobile phone, to replace the sluggish antique she'd been using for the past six years. Carol had set it up all for her before leaving.

Glenda marvelled as she lifted the sleek, cold glass and metal handset in front of her face, and she delighted when it unlocked automatically after recognising her face.

"What will they think up next?"

The phone operated more or less the same way as her old one, but it was so much faster and brighter and bigger. It was going to take up a lot of room in her handbag on Bingo nights, but at least it wasn't too heavy.

"Let's check out the camera, shall we?"

Carol said all her old photos would be on the new phone, and that any fresh ones would look extra fantastic. Glenda could hardly wait to take some snaps with it.

And that's what she decided to do. Despite sitting in her kitchen, with nothing in the way of inspiration, she opened the camera app and panned around the room. It was immediately clear how much better the quality was, and when she zoomed in on the kettle, framing it in the centre of the screen, she could make out the limescale on the spout. Holding the phone with her left hand, she tapped the white dot with her right index finger and took a picture.

"Wow, look at that quality. Ha! I'm a professional photographer." She giggled, proud of herself for keeping up with modern technology.

Computers might still be a mystery to her, but smartphones were easy.

"I should take a selfie," she announced, "and send it to the girls so they know I'm using my gift already."

Her finger hovered, searching for the right button to press to switch to the front camera. Once she located it, she gave it a tap and was greeted by her own face.

"Oh dear. What a state."

She adjusted her hair and wiped a cake crumb off her cheek, then tried on a smile. It was as good as she was going to look at this stage in her life, so she moved herself into focus and took the picture. "*Cheese!*"

She checked the picture out in the gallery a moment later and grunted. "Not bad. Bit dark, though."

Glenda stood and turned around to capture a selfie from the opposite angle. Perhaps the light would be better over by the doorway into the living room.

Once again, she gave a grin and said, "*Cheese!*"

She checked the latest picture and was once again disappointed. There was a shadow all the way behind her on the living room wall. It was probably her own silhouette, as it resembled a head and shoulders, but it darkened the picture and made her look grey.

But when she turned to face the living room, there was no shadow on the far wall. In fact, she located her short silhouette against the door frame and it went no further.

She took another picture. The shadow was still there in the living room.

"Huh, am I doing something wrong?"

The imperfect picture was fantastic quality—the colours were bright, and she could make out the individual pores around her nose—but the background was taken over by a black smear. She decided to send it in a group message to her daughters.

> Keep getting a shadowy spot when I take pictures. Could it be a fault?

A few minutes later, her middle daughter, Sharon, replied.

> Oh, mum, that's a shame. We'll have to take it back to the shop.

Carol replied after.

> I'll come by tomorrow and take a look. Sorry, mum xx

As usual, her youngest—Fiona—didn't answer.

Always too busy, that one, Glenda thought. *She never sits still.*

"Oh well." She went and picked up her cup of tea from the kitchen table and raised it up. "Here's to me, and to seventy more years. Ha! I should be so lucky."

She went into the lounge and sat down in her comfy armchair before promptly falling asleep.

———

GLENDA AWOKE A SHORT WHILE LATER, her naps rarely lasting longer than forty minutes. In fact, sleep became less of a concern with every passing year, as if her body now expelled so little energy during the day that a few hours each night and a nap in the afternoon were more than enough to keep her clock ticking. Although, she had to admit, this time she didn't feel refreshed by the brief shut eye. It was a struggle to get out of her chair.

Luckily, the weariness soon went away, and she headed into the kitchen to prepare herself some dinner. Cooking for one was a downside of being twice divorced, but at least tonight she could take advantage of the leftovers from the party. Carol and Sharon had stayed behind to help clear up, so the mess was all gone, but they had put the remaining buffet items in the fridge.

"What do we have here, then?" Glenda rooted around, tongue sticking out, until she brought out some coleslaw and potato salad. She accompanied it with some cajun prawns, mini samosas, and a pair of triangular tuna sandwiches.

Yum!

She had herself a bizarre but acceptable spread, and sat down at the kitchen table to eat. Before she took a bite, though, she picked up her new phone and took a quick snap of her plate.

> Leftovers are the best xx

Carol replied right away.

> Ooh, I'm cooking spaghetti. Still stuffed from this afternoon.

Glenda chortled and typed back:

> Not me. You know how much I like my food.

> Yes! You could eat a pony, mum. It's actually impressive xx

Glenda put the phone down on the table, but then picked it up again. With a frown, she decided to check out the selfie camera once more. She saw herself on the screen, and there was no strange shadow behind her. Just the white kitchen wall and the refrigerator.

"Huh? Maybe it's fixed." She took a picture of herself smiling and immediately checked out the results in the gallery. A hiss escaped her lips as she shook her head. "Nope. Still there."

The odd shadow once again spoiled the background of the picture. This time, it was cast against the stainless steel refrigerator in the corner. Closer than before, it looked even more like a head and shoulders. As if a shadowy figure was standing behind her.

"Well, that's terrifying." She studied the photograph closer, to reassure herself, then let out a chuckle. She took another three pictures from various angles. The shadow was in every one of them, always a similar distance behind her, as if floating in midair. Clearly, there was a fault with the lens.

Turning the phone, Glenda examined the three small glass circles that she knew were the various cameras her new phone possessed. There was no problem with those, so she turned the phone back around and squinted at the little device underneath the top section of the screen. She wiped it with her thumb, wondering if there was a speck of dirt needing to be dislodged.

When she took another picture, the shadow was still there, looming right behind her.

"Jesus!" She leapt up out of her chair and spun around. Of course, there was nothing behind her, yet she shivered all the same.

She knew she was being silly, but the sudden urge to leave the kitchen overwhelmed her. It felt like there was a ghost in the room. Once she made it back into the living room, she gave herself a telling off. "Seventy is too young to be going senile. Stop scaring yourself, Glenda."

It wasn't the worst time she had ever freaked herself out. Living alone—and being female—made it easy to conjure up frightening scenarios. A creaking floorboard in the night was a robber coming to hurt her. A ticking sound coming from the boiler was a gas explosion waiting to happen. Smudges on a camera lens were ghosts.

"Dear oh me."

She forced herself back into the kitchen to eat her dinner. As she sat down and resumed, she deliberately refused to pick up her phone. The shadow would still be there, she knew, because the camera was obviously faulty.

Carol would be by in the morning. She could take it back to the shop to get it exchanged. Such a shame, though, because she really had been delighted with the thoughtful and expensive gift. It sure beat the shoulder massager the girls had bought her last year. The bloody thing had been taking up space in the cupboard ever since.

After she finished dinner, Glenda rinsed off her plate and left it on the drainer to dry. It was a Thursday night, so there would be little to watch on television, but she could find something most likely. Probably a rerun of *CSI,* or even an episode of *Glee!* She loved nothing more than a trip to the theatre, so a show about show tunes and musical numbers had been right up her street when she had discovered it a few years ago.

As it turned out, she had no luck at all, ending up with a

programme about life at a Midlands zoo. Still, most days she would take animals over people, so it wasn't all bad.

By nine o'clock, Glenda was exhausted. Her usual bedtime was a little after ten, but today had been a busy day, so the batteries had drained early. She could have spent the entire day cleaning and would have been less tired.

"I'm going to sleep well tonight," she said. "As soon as my head touches that pillow."

Once again sluggish, Glenda clambered out of her armchair. She had brought her phone in from the kitchen already, but she decided to check it before she went to bed. The camera might be broken, but it still worked otherwise.

There were a couple of messages from her daughters—and one from Sue Cartwright, her Bingo buddy—but none warranted a reply. So, she switched off the television, the lights, and headed for bed.

As she climbed halfway up the stairs, she felt a breeze on the back of her neck, and a tingling in her chest. Suddenly, she struggled to take another step. Her body deserted her, like it wasn't really there.

S-something's wrong. It doesn't feel right.

She didn't know why, but she raised her phone and opened up the front-facing camera. She saw nothing behind her except near total darkness, broken only by the dim light coming from the lamppost on the footpath outside. To combat the gloom, she hit the flash icon, which caused the screen to go bright white as soon as she thumbed the button to take a picture—so bright that it startled her and almost sent her falling backwards down the stairs.

Her heart drummed in her chest, faster and faster.

She went into the phone's gallery and opened up the most recent picture. Her heart stopped drumming. Then it leapt into her throat.

The shadowy figure was right behind her, two pairs of eyes glowing red as they captured the light of her phone.

"Oh my... No, no."

Hands shaking, Glenda took another picture. Then another. And another. Flash. Flash. Flash.

She flicked through the photos, one after the other. The shadowy figure moved slightly in each one, until it was leaning right over her shoulder and staring into the camera with its face right next to hers. A definite face. Two definite red eyes.

For a second, Glenda thought she imagined hands wrapped around her throat, but when she realised she couldn't breathe at all, the truth became horrifyingly clear. Her chest caved in and her throat bulged shut as she dropped the phone and let it bounce down the stairs.

She clutched at her throat.

She tried to scream. Her lungs were empty.

Help. Please, somebody help me.

The house was silent. She was utterly alone.

———

SOMETIMES CAROL HATED BEING the responsible daughter. Even with Sharon and Fiona both being in their mid-thirties, they were unreliable and selfish–especially since starting families of their own. They seemed to forget that Mum had raised them almost single-handedly after Dad had left. Carol knew the courage and compassion that hid behind her mother's placid exterior, and it frustrated her that her sisters didn't.

And as usual, I'm having to rush around on my lunch break to sort out the phone that Sharon and Fiona didn't even want to chip in for. I'm surprised they even came to the party yesterday.

Carol used her spare key to quietly open the door to her childhood home and then called out. "Hello."

Mum was usually up at the crack of dawn, but often took a short nap during the day. Carol didn't want to startle her.

"Mum? I text you to say I was on my way, but you haven't read the message. Mum?"

She opened the door wider and stepped inside. When she saw a body at the bottom of the stairs, she screamed.

"Oh no, oh no." She dropped down beside her mum, who was lying on her back with her feet partly up the stairs. She had a rictus grin on her face, her dentures hanging half out of her mouth. Both hands were wrapped around her own neck, like she had been choking.

As soon as Carol wrapped her hand around her mother's wrist, she knew she was dead. So she sat and sobbed quietly for five or ten minutes while she recovered from the shock. Then she called an ambulance, so that people could come and pronounce her mother dead.

I can't believe it. I saw her yesterday. She was fine.

Carol called her sisters. Fiona didn't answer—no surprise—and Sharon did so testily. "What is it, Caz?"

"It's mum."

"What about her?"

"She's dead."

Silence on the phone. Then a sharp intake of breath. "W-what?"

"I came to fix her phone and found her at the bottom of the stairs. She must have had a heart attack or something. An ambulance is on the way. I called them."

"Are you sure she—"

"She's cold, Sharon. She's gone."

"I ... I'll be right there. Does Fiona know?"

"No. She won't answer."

Sharon huffed into the speaker. "Okay, I'll get a hold of her. I'm sorry, Carol. I'm sorry you found her."

Carol rubbed the back of her mother's cold, stiff hand.

"I'm not sorry. She needs me with her right now."

"Um, just stay put, okay? I'll be there in twenty minutes."

Carol ended the call and tossed her phone down on the carpet. It was then that she spotted her mother's new phone lying near her body. She had been so pleased with it.

"You were so happy yesterday, Mum. Maybe it was a good day to end it on, but why did it have to be so soon? I love you. Hope you know that."

She picked up her mum's phone and stared at the screen. Carol had set herself up with *Face ID* when she'd set it up, so it unlocked with a quick chirp. Her mother's face came up on the screen, startled and pained. Had she accidentally taken a selfie when she was having a heart attack? Had she been trying to call someone for help?

Did she try to call me? Did she call out for me? Oh God.

The picture looked like it had been taken on the stairs, with only darkness behind her mother. Carol swiped through several similar photos all taken at the same time, and then several random ones in the kitchen that had obviously been taken earlier. They were good pictures. And in a cruel irony, there was no shadowy mark in any of them except for the very first one she had taken and shared in the group chat. It appeared as if there wasn't a problem with the camera after all. Her mum had obviously been confused.

But if she hadn't have thought something was wrong with the phone, I wouldn't be here. She might have been lying here alone all by herself.

"Thank God we got you a new phone," she said, and wiped away her tears. "I just wish you'd been given longer to use it."

TIFF'S TRINKETS

The buzz from Dave's morning drinking session had worn off and left him with a bad head. His skull was a cantaloupe squeezed by giant hands.

Keith's fault. If he didn't blow half his benefits on cigarettes, he could afford to get more lagers in. How many times do I need to tell him to switch to vaping?

Dave was skint, but that wasn't new. In fact, he'd caught a bus into town that afternoon specifically to earn some beer money. Problem was, his face was known all over town by now. *Tesco* wouldn't even let him through the doors.

Trying to keep people from surviving. Massive companies owe a debt to those at the bottom like me. Not as if a crate of beer is going to affect their profit line.

The sky was blue, not a cloud in sight. Dave could even feel the sun on his back as he trotted down Sedgwick Hill. If not for his banging headache, it would've been a *bosting* day. The sooner he got home and back on the lager, the better.

Perhaps he could hit a store on the fringes of the town centre. Some charity shops had jewellery and video games–and the old biddies who worked there were blind and senile. He could even sneak a hand in the till.

Dave shook his head and chuckled as he continued down the hill, passing by a line of taxis parked along the kerb. Each one had an Asian driver behind the wheel, something he'd always been curious about. Why did Pakistanis or Muslims or whatever always drive the taxis around town?

Probably 'cus it's a cash business. Everyone knows Muslims don't pay tax. Bloody spongers.

Dave saw a teenaged girl coming up the hill towards him and gave her shapely legs a quick glance before smiling at her. She averted her eyes and looked away so quickly her brown hair swished over her shoulder.

Damn, am I getting old or summin'?

Nah, I'm only twenty-eight. Plenty of time left to pull the odd teenager.

He rubbed at his unshaven chin and grunted at the painful pulsations inside his skull. Perhaps if he'd been born with a better brain, he would take better care of it. Intelligence wasn't something he was blessed with, but he'd trained as a mechanic after leaving school and had been good at it. If not for the wankers in charge, he'd still be there now, making good money.

But what was the point of working fifty hours a week for someone else's gain? You only got one life. He wasn't going to waste *his* working himself to the bone.

Sod that!

He reached the bottom of Sedgwick Hill and looked across the road. The *Heart Foundation* was shuttered up—shite luck—and *Primrose* was gone altogether, replaced by yet another curry house. A small chemist open, but it was too narrow to work in—plus pharmacists were like meerkats behind their little counters. Soon as you stepped in, they were up on their tippy toes, watching you.

Why do you want plasters, sir? Are they for yourself? Do you have any allergies?

They're bleedin' plasters, mate!

Dave stopped walking and took a moment to strategise. Despite the sunshine, he shivered. Probably the booze in his system. He always got chilly after a sesh. Usually, he'd pass out in his flat beneath the thick, snuggly blanket his mum had got him last Christmas. She used to buy him a big bottle of voddie every year, but it'd been a while since she'd done that. Now, he got presents like blankets and lava lamps.

She drinks more than I do, bloody hypocrite. Three cans of Special Brew *every night since I can remember. Used to call me all sorts as a kid, she did. Then she'd spend all the next day with a hangover watching* Murder She Wrote. *Stupid bint.*

Dave flinched, strangely on edge as a black cat emerged from a shadowy recess to his left. It had slunk out of a narrow alleyway that he hadn't even known was there.

Wonder where it leads?

Dave liked alleyways. Sometimes they led to loading bays and stockrooms. If the timing was right, you could come across an open fire escape and snatch a box full of whatever from the stockroom. Once, he had swiped a box full of prescriptions spectacles from the back of the opticians. There'd been Ray-Bans, Oakleys, and loads of other designer frames. He'd netted almost a grand that week.

It was worth a punt, so he turned sideways and shuffled into the alleyway. It smelled of piss. "Animals. Who wizzes out in the street?"

The alleyway was only twenty feet long, and it exited into an enclosed courtyard with a square of weed-covered paving slabs. No loading bays or open back doors. *Bollocks.*

But there *was*, however, a single *front* door. A shop entrance.

What the hell is a shop doing back here? Must have the worst footfall in town.

A cheery pink sign hung above the door. It read: *Tiff's Trinkets.* Below the name was a bright red rose.

Probably one of them soap shops, selling fancy bath bombs and hand creams. Not for me, all that tat.

Although, that stuff was pretty easy to pinch and was easy to sell. Stuff a few bath bombs into the front of his hoodie, make small talk with the cashier, then make a casual exit. Piece of piss.

Even if I can't flog 'em, I can give 'em to Sarah next door and get in her good books. A few too many tats for my liking, but she washes up well on a Friday night. Plus, she has a job at Halfords, which is handy.

"Fuck it. Let's 'ave a butchers."

Dave shouldered his way inside the tiny shop, wincing when a bell sounded above the door. He hated those things. Drew attention to you before you'd even made it inside.

Sure enough, a young woman looked up from behind a counter at the back. She was cute, but probably out of his league. There was a genuine warmness to her smile that caused Dave, inexplicably, to smile and wave back at her. "Hey," he said, looking around. The shop was bigger than it looked from the outside, with three separate aisles leading to the counter.

The young woman beamed and waved back. "Well, come on in, why dontcha! I'm Tiff. Welcome to my trinket store."

Dave raised an eyebrow. This weren't no soap shop.

———

"WHAT IS THIS PLACE?" David asked.

The woman continued to smile, her cheeks rosy and freckled. "Clue's in the name, honey. It's a trinket store."

Dave nodded. "Um, okay, so, like antiques and stuff?"

The young woman thrust out her bare arms and fanned them dramatically. "Stuff of all kinds. If something is of interest, there's a chance of it ending up here on my shelves. You never know what you'll find."

"Um, okay, then. Mind if I have a browse?"

The shelves were cluttered with an insane mixture of odds and ends. Ornaments and old electronics. Clocks, pots, and walking sticks. A bizarre assortment. Some of it had to be worth something.

"Of course you can browse, honey. Feel free to touch, feel, smell, and deal. But you can't steal."

"What?" Dave's shoulders stiffened. "Why would you say that? Bit judgemental, ain't it, love?"

That disarming smile remained on her face, seemingly cemented in place. It should've been annoying, but... "Oh, all men steal," she said cheerily. "It's what built the world. I mean no offence. Just wanted to inform you that you can't steal anything here."

We'll see about that, darling.

"I have money, so don't worry. I'm just gonna take a look around. My mum's birthday is coming up."

"Oh, how lovely! I have just the thing for her."

Dave nodded. *Here's my chance.* "Got summin' special in the back, 'ave ya?"

"No, no. Right there, next to your foot."

Dave looked down and realised the shop was so stuffed full of stock that it even littered the floor beneath the shelves. His foot was pressed lightly against a cardboard box. He reached down and slid the box into view.

"What the...?" He was shocked by what he saw. It looked like the complete collection of *Murder She Wrote* on DVD—a dozen fat-spined cases containing three of four discs each.

"About 60-odd discs in there," said Tiff. "That'll keep her busy for months. Plus, those mysteries never get old."

Dave glanced up at the young woman and shook his head. "My mum loves this programme, but how did you know that?"

"It's a classic. I guessed right, huh?"

"Yeah, you did." He then asked a stupid question. "How much?"

He had no money, so her answer didn't matter, but it still surprised him when she told him she only wanted a fiver.

"Five quid? For all these discs?"

She shrugged. "No one wants DVDs any more. They're just taking up space. You want them?"

"Um... yeah. I'll pop back later and get them."

Or steal them as soon as your back is turned. I can get twenty quid for these, easy. Or maybe I should give them to mum. It would make her day.

Tiff leaned over the counter and put her hands together in a steeple. Every one of her fingernails was a different colour. Her blonde hair was streaked with pink and purple. "I thought you said you had money."

"I do." He bristled. "Just don't want to carry this box around with me right now. I'll come back and get it before I drive home."

"You can pay now and I'll hold them for you."

"Yeah, but I might not make it back before you close. I got a lot of stuff to do."

She nodded her head slowly. "Ah, okay. No worries. I'll make sure nobody else buys them today. Yours, if you want them."

"Thanks. So, like, what else you got around here? Any jewellery? I love a bit of gold."

"I have bracelets and bangles, necklaces and dangles. Whatever you're looking for, I probably have it. Look over there. Do you see that wristwatch?"

Dave did see the wrist watch. It seemed to call out to him from the shelf it was sitting on. Its rectangular housing appeared to be gold, but it had an aged leather strap, which was disappointing. All the same, its simple old-fashioned face—with only a pair of analogue clock hands—cried out *expensive*. It wasn't trying to pose or impress. It was just old, well-made, and heavy. Dave held it in his hand and purred at the weightiness of it.

I want this.

"Bit old fashioned," he said.

"Of course," said Tiff, leaning further over the desk like she was trying to get off her feet. "It's a *Tavannes*. One of the oldest brands in the world. That piece was made in 1930 and belonged to an American Captain named Ernest Nachtnebel who came to Britain after the United States entered World War 2. He came from old money and could actually trace his ancestry back to German aristocracy, which obviously made for some awkward moments around the allied campfire."

Dave actually sympathised. His grandfather had been German, and while the old man had died when Dave was only twelve, he still remembered the cheeky pound coins shoved in his palm or the plateful of biscuits that would always be waiting whenever he visited. "That must have been tough for the poor sod. Where did his loyalties lie?"

"He never got to find out. Ernest was found dead in his barracks at Aldershot, strangled with his own belt. At first it looked like suicide, but a fellow officer noticed his watch was missing—a gift from his wife that he never took off."

Dave nodded. "Greed makes people nasty."

"It does indeed," said Tiff, lifting a finger and giving him a confirming waggle. "They found the watch in the footlocker of a corporal from the wrong side of the tracks. Nigel McAdams."

"Huh," Dave frowned. "That's weird. My mum's surname is McAdams. My dad's name was Weber, but they never married."

Why am I sharing this?

Tiff's face lit up, her freckles seeming to glow. "My word! I wonder if there's any relation."

"What? Am I related to a murderer and a thief, do you mean?"

She chuckled. "Oh dear, I'm sorry, I wasn't suggesting that."

"So what happened to this McAdam's bloke?"

"The Army shipped McAdam's off to war. His crimes only got worse with a rifle in his hands, but fortunately he was killed somewhere in France nine months before the end of the war. Shot through the throat, if I remember correctly. His possessions, including that watch, were brought home by a staff sergeant who handed them to his mother. Eventually, the watch ended up in my store."

Dave frowned. "How do you know all that?"

"World War 2 is the most documented era of human history. You can find out just about anything about anyone if you know where to look." She leaned forwards a little more, almost lying flat on the counter now. "Hey, do you want to hear something spooky?"

"Sure."

"They say the watch is haunted. In addition to Ernest and McAdams, three other owners of the watch have died under suspicious circumstances. The last victim was twelve years ago—an investment banker who wore it during a trip on a helicopter that crashed into the Thames."

"Shit..." Dave squinted, his mind whirring. "I remember that. I saw it on the news."

Tiff gave him a crooked grin and wrinkled her cute little nose. "They say Captain Nachtnebel's spirit haunts the watch, killing everyone who wears it, still angered by its original theft."

"Bullshit," Dave spluttered, and then he blushed. He didn't usually care about manners, but this woman was so friendly, so *delicate*... It felt wrong to swear. "Sorry. I just don't believe in none of that stuff. It's just a watch. Not a—"

"Spirit totem?" she said. "A magnet for paranormal energy?"

"Yeah, all that barmy stuff."

"Oh, Mr Weber. You're so very wrong. There are objects of influence all around us. Some we can see, others we can't. Do you know, even the Vatican has a secret hoard of dangerous objects? They have these bizarre manuscripts, you see, and they–"

"I don't buy it," he snapped, feeling a creeping sensation the back of his neck that he didn't like at all. "Anyway, I should probably leave you to it." This wasn't going to work. She wouldn't take her eyes off of him, so it was time to try somewhere else.

But he really wanted the watch. It sat perfectly in his palm.

Tiff blushed, like she'd flicked a switch to make her entire face red. "I got carried away, didn't I? I always do that. You wanted to look around, so I should just let you. Go ahead, Dave."

Dave nodded. There might still be a slim chance of grabbing the watch. Haunted or not, it must've been worth a bomb. History had a price tag. "Okay, I can spend another five minutes looking–Hey!"

Tiff tilted her head at him, an inquisitive cocker spaniel. "Is something the matter?"

"Yeah! I never told you my name."

"Of course you did, Dave."

"No, I never. I mentioned my dad's surname, but not my first name. How do you know me?" His fists clenched at his sides. Suddenly, he felt threatened. Suddenly, Tiff's warm smile seemed a mockery.

She held her hands up in surrender. "You're a known shoplifter." She pulled a face and spoke in an awful Texan drawl. "Wanted dead or alive around these parts."

Dave shook his head and took a step back towards the door. "Why have you been chatting shit with me, if you knew that? Why not just ask me to leave?"

She shrugged. "You've done nothing to hurt me, have you? It would be wrong to judge you off the say so of somebody else. Maybe you're innocent."

He shook his head. "I'm not."

"Oh, well, no matter. I already told you, you can't steal from my shop, so there's no problem, right?"

"Just because you told me not to steal, doesn't mean I won't."

She slid backwards off the counter and finally stood up straight again. She folded her arms and let her smile fall away. She looked odd without it. "Go on, then. Try and steal."

"What? No, you'll call the police. You know who I am."

"I won't call the police, I promise. Whatever happens, I won't tell anyone. It'll be between us. You like that watch? Take it."

"This is a trick."

She shrugged, still serious, almost stern. "If you have to try to steal it, then go ahead and get it out of your system. I won't judge you. People are just people at the end of the day. No one's perfect."

You are, he found himself thinking. *Why do I want to stay here and keep talking to you? What is it about you that's so different? So... beautiful?*

"Fuck it." Dave looked at the watch in his hand and fell in love with it even more. Then he turned and ran for the door.

TIFF MADE NO SOUND, nor did anything to try to stop Dave from leaving with the watch. He yanked open the door and stared out into the strange, empty courtyard.

I'm out of here, you crazy, beautiful lady.

Dave struck his head, rattling his already painfully hungover brain. The blow sent him backwards onto his butt and he landed in the aisle, staring at the cardboard box full of *Murder She Wrote* DVDs.

What the hell?

His vision was spinning, but he managed to clamber back to his feet. This time, he approached the open doorway cautiously, clueless as to what he'd struck his head on.

Tiff still did nothing to stop him. She stood behind the counter patiently.

The courtyard was right there in front of Dave. He put an arm up and felt the air inside the doorway. There was no glass barrier or anything else that might have caused him to rebound painfully to the floor. It was inexplicable.

Maybe I'm still wankered from last night's sesh?

Slowly, Dave took a step forwards. Then another. He passed through the door without incident, one foot already in the courtyard, and he looked back triumphantly.

Tiff was smiling again, her chin placed on her hands as she leaned on the counter. "Good luck," she chirped.

Dave shook his head in confusion. She was an odd one. He almost felt bad for robbing her.

But she literally asked for it.

Dave took off.

And almost ripped his arm off at the shoulder. He rebounded back into the shop, dragged by his right hand that was clutching the old wristwatch.

He had been free and clear until the watch had reached the threshold.

Dave had managed to stay on his feet, barely, but his whole body was now aching. He turned to face Tiff, angered by her cheeriness. "What the fuck is this? Some kind of trick?"

"What trick?" She appeared hurt. "I told you, quite explicitly, that you *can't* steal from my store. Where's the trick?"

"What? You meant I literally *can't* steal?"

"I am often literal, Dave. And yes, it is impossible to steal any of my trinkets. They are mine. If you want them, you must pay for them. Or I can choose to give them to you."

Dave marched over to the counter, snarling. As he neared the strange woman, he smelled flowers. He didn't let it distract him. "Then give me the watch or I'll hurt you."

"You can't hurt me either."

"Want to bet?"

"No. It would be unfair to bet on an outcome of which I'm certain."

Dave thought about throwing a punch, but he knew it would leave him feeling wretched. He was a thief, sure, but he took no pleasure in hurting anyone. Violence had always been a last resort for him—and hardly ever against a woman. So he shook his head in defeat. "What is going on? Why couldn't I steal the watch?"

"Because it belongs to me."

"That doesn't answer my question."

"It does. All the things inside this store are under my protection. My job is to keep them safe."

"Why run a shop if you don't want to sell anything?"

"I didn't say that. I am more than happy to sell certain things to certain people once they understand the risks. Trinkets need to change hands, from time to time, in order to remain in their current state. If an object of influence is allowed to stagnate for too long, its power will eventually rot and turn bad. Then it'll spill out and go someplace else. Someplace it can't be tracked."

"So, you'd be willing to sell me this watch? A watch you think kills anyone who wears it?"

"Yes, of course. If you really wanted it."

He put his hands on the counter and deflated. This was the strangest conversation he'd ever had. His head was pounding, and he would have done anything to take another drink. "Wouldn't that make you a murderer?"

"If I sold you a tiger, and it ripped your throat out, would that make me a murderer? As long as you know the risks, then the consequences are down to you."

"So, if, like, a nun came in and wanted the watch. You would sell it to her? How about a kid?"

Tiff reached under the counter and placed a small sheet of paper down on the surface. It was a black and white mugshot, taken of Dave when security had snatched him in *Primark*. His name was printed underneath his picture. "You're far more handsome in the flesh, Dave."

"Answer my question."

"I just did. Children and hypothetical nuns would never find my shop, so I could never sell them any of my trinkets. I serve a *specific* clientele."

Dave remained slumped against the counter for a moment. The woman might claim to be literal, but she was also vague as hell. "Wait... are you saying that you only sell to–what?–bad people? Are you saying I'm a bad person? Who the fuck are *you* to judge *me*?" He no longer cared about swearing. This woman was playing games with him.

"I don't think you're a bad person, Dave, and even if I did, my judgement counts for nothing. You do, however, have black spots upon your soul. My shop calls out to people like you."

He rolled his eyes and snickered. "Oh really? Why is that, then?"

She drummed her fingers over the top of his mugshot and gave him a lopsided smile. "It's different for everyone. Every soul that finds their way here has a different set of circumstances. Perhaps you're here to see your great grandfather's watch."

"What? That German Captain was my great grandad?"

"No, silly. Corporal McAdams was—the man who stole the watch. He was your mother's grandfather. Ironically, the German side of your family was peasant. They never would have mixed with Ernest Nacht-nebel's kin."

"Story of my life. I was born a peasant and I'll die a peasant."

"Yes."

He glared at her. "Oi!"

"Most of the population are peasants. The word holds little meaning in this century."

"Look, I don't know what your deal is, but I reckon you must be mental, so I'm going now."

"I'm afraid it's too late for that."

"What? I'm leaving."

She shook her head. "I'm sorry, Dave. The shop has decided. You can't leave. Maybe not ever."

"Get your prescription refilled, love."

He turned and marched back across the store. This time, he placed the watch back on the shelf before doing so. Whatever game she was playing, it had somehow kept him from stealing, so he would have to accept the failure and live to fight another day. There were always other places to hit.

Although, they all had his name and face now because of that sodding poster. How was he going to earn now?

I'll have to drag Keith on a bus. I can distract the security guards while he does the lifting. He won't like it, but tough shit.

Eager to be away and earn some beer money before the afternoon ended, he yanked open the shop door again. He didn't remember it closing, but who cared? This whole place made no—

Dave stared out into a featureless black void. It was as if the store was floating in space.

"Like I told you," Tiff said behind him. "The store won't let you leave."

––––––

DAVE THOUGHT ONCE AGAIN about committing violence, but he was too afraid. If he beat up Tiff, then he'd be alone in this fucked up shop. What if she was the only one who could help him?

Who the hell is she?

A witch?

"I'm not a witch," said Tiff, somehow reading his mind. She squinted, as if it were coming through to her on a bad line. "Although, I have many friends who are. They have an awful lot of lesbian sex, you know? Too much, if you ask me. It can start to chafe after a while."

"What are you talking about? Why are you doing this to me? I've done nothing wrong."

Tiff stepped out from behind the counter. She was wearing a long, wide-bottomed skirt dyed every colour of the rainbow. "Now, that's not true, is it, Dave? You've done a lot of naughty things. Take a look around you, don't you see?"

He frowned. "See what?"

"Open your eyes."

Dave looked around at the various shelves. He saw leather wallets, old trainers, jewellery, DVDs, video game equipment, a crystal ballerina–

Hey! I recognise that.

Tiff smiled. "It's beautiful, isn't it?"

"The ballerina? I... I stole it."

"Yes. From an old lady in a bungalow named Nancy. You pretended to be selling tea towels for the probation service. She let you in. Poor lady."

Dave shrugged. "She was doing okay by the looks of it."

"Yes, she had plenty of money to see her through, but only one crystal ballerina. It was a birthday gift from her granddaughter. Poor girl got run over by a bus two weeks before her ninth birthday. The crystal ballerina, along with some photographs, was all Nancy had of her.

"I didn't know that, did I? It wasn't even worth anything."

Tiff seemed to ignore him and carried on. "It was worth more than you know. When you took it, Nancy's poor heart broke. The embarrassment of having been tricked and robbed raised her blood pressure and contributed to the stroke that killed her. Your betrayal was one of the last interactions of her life. She died with you on her mind, Dave. Now she sits inside the ballerina, angry and alone."

Dave examined the glass statue and shook his head. "What are you talking about?"

"The pawn shop you sold the ballerina to passed it on to a single mother named Mandy. After Mandy placed it inside her house, she became cursed with the most terrible clumsiness. Everything fragile around her would break. Mugs would crack in the dishwasher. Vases would fall off the shelves. It eventually caused her such a mighty depression that, in a desperate haze, she cleared her home of everything that could break. Thus, the ballerina ended up in my care."

Dave put a hand to his head and moaned. "A clumsiness curse? That's not exactly *evil*, is it?"

"Who said anything about evil? We're just talking about power-natural energy and unconfined emotions. Anger is the strongest force of all."

Dave glanced back towards the doorway and saw the void still there, an all-consuming maw ready to swallow existence itself. "Th-this is real, isn't it?"

"Oh yes." Tiff gave her bright, flowing skirt a little flourish. "You're exactly where you deserve to be, Dave. The shop wanted you here."

"Because I'm this horrible monster, huh? I didn't know that ballerina meant so much to the old lady. Shit happens. You think anyone ever gave a crap about me? My dad stopped having anything to do with me when I was six years old. I grew up on a council estate surrounded by druggies and psychopaths. What chance did I ever have of a good life? The entire game is rigged. Without poor people like me, there would be no rich wankers hoarding everything for themselves."

Tiff nodded. "You have anger. I feel it. Your truth is real to you, and I understand that. But others have their own truth. Hurting people out of anger is not okay. It has a price, and you must pay it."

"So, what? Am I in hell? Is that where I'm going? Well, tell Lucifer he can kiss my arse."

"I don't know about hell, honey." She looked him in the eye and gave him a pitying smile. "There are many places a soul can go, but I'm outside of those things. What I *do* know is that what we do in one place matters in another. Our sins follow us until the end. They stain us. Mark us out."

"I'm screwed then. Can't do anything about it now, can I? I can't *unsteal* the ballerina."

"No, you can't unmake wounds, but you *can* heal them."

"How?" He looked around at the cluttered shelves, then back out at the impossible, black void. "This has to be a joke. This isn't real."

"You should keep looking around, Dave."

With a sigh, he did what he was told. It was all so confusing that it left him numb. When he thought about what was happening, a panic rose in his guts. He focused on the shelves, trying to make sense of it, of any of the things he saw.

A box of dinosaur *Top Trumps*.

My god, I recognise them.

He had stolen them from a friend's house as a kid, sneaking them into his sleeve as his mum had called from the doorstep that it was time to go home.

There was a silver pendant he had snatched from a charity shop and given to the girl to whom he had lost his virginity.

Every item in the store had a story attached to it, but for the first time, he understood the stories weren't his alone. Had his friend missed the *Top Trumps*? Had he gone mad trying to find them? By stealing the pendant, had he kept money from the pockets of someone who had truly needed it? Maybe his were minor sins, but like with Nancy's stroke, each one had contributed to another person's misery.

No, screw that. I'm not that bad. It's not my fault the world is so messed up. People have to do what they have to do in order to survive.

"I won't steal again," he said. "I get it, okay?"

Tiff smiled. She looked up at the ceiling as if hearing a voice. After a moment, she lowered her gaze and sighed. "Oh, Dave. Honesty, please."

"What do you want from me?"

"Nothing. This isn't about me."

Dave decided things had reached a last resort. He lunged at Tiff, grabbed the strap of her dress, and shoved her back against the counter. "Enough of this bullshit. Let me out."

Her eyes filled with sadness, so much that it hurt him to look at her. Tiff's voice was like strands of silk in his ear. "I understand your anger, my love, but I'm not the one keeping you here."

"Then who the fuck is? Who is keeping me here?"

"They are." Tiff nodded over his shoulder.

Dave kept his hand on Tiff's shoulder strap as he turned his head, but he quickly let go and gasped. "No! No, this isn't real. It can't be."

———

DAVE DIDN'T BELIEVE in ghosts, which was why what he saw standing in the aisles caused him to malfunction. His beliefs clashed with reality and broke the machinery in his dehydrated brain.

"They are the only ones who can judge you," said Tiff. Her voice was full of compassion, like she was going through the horror right with him and guiding him through it.

Dave glanced from face to face. Most he did not recognise, but others...

Nancy had been a harmless old lady in life, but standing in front of him now, she was a feral, rage-filled abomination. She snarled at him, flashing glistening brown teeth. In her hand, she clutched a photograph of a young girl.

"She had that in her hand when she died," explained Tiff. "She's stuck, unable to move on."

Beside Nancy stood a middle-aged man in an army uniform. Dave didn't know enough to recognise much about it, but the USA flag on the arm gave him a clue about who was wearing it. "Captain Nachtnebel?"

The dead man immediately saluted. There was a white suntan line on his right wrist where a watch had once been.

"He always wore it on the wrong wrist," said Tiff, chuckling sadly. "Used to get really ratty when people told him to put it on his left."

Dave nodded, unsure why she was telling him this. What good did it do?

"I... I didn't do anything to this man."

"No," said Tiff. "It's not really fair, is it? The sins of our fathers and all that. The captain had no heirs. Your bloodline ended his."

Dave realised he wasn't breathing, so he forced himself to inhale. There was a lump in his throat and he couldn't get it to budge, so he spoke in a croaky voice. "What do they want from me?"

Tiff moved away from the counter and placed a hand on his shoulder. She was ice cold. "Only they know. You're here because they wanted you to face them. The shop granted their wishes."

Dave looked up at the ceiling and saw only darkness. He hadn't noticed it until now. "What is this place?"

"It's a place between places. A place where ordinary rules get replaced by another set of rules. A meeting point for souls. I never know who's coming until the moment they arrive, but then..."

He turned to her. "But then *what*?"

"But then I know them well. I know all about them. Dave, I understand your anger, your pain, but you are a virus. You pass your pain on to others and it spreads. Over there, do you see that old man?"

Dave nodded. He didn't know who the black man was, but he looked a little like the guy with the deep voice in all those films. His black hair was frosted white, giving him an air of distinction. "Who is he?"

"Bernard Jones. You stole the locksmithing tools from the back of his van. Insurance replaced them, but for three weeks he couldn't work or earn any money. It was right before Christmas, so he couldn't get his grandchildren the things they wanted. Your anger passed into him, leading him to drink too much whisky. He got behind the wheel of his van and crashed against the entrance to a stone bridge. The van flipped into the water and he drowned. Bernard's grandchildren will never forget their worst Christmas ever. Because of *you*."

"What? No, that's... How could I have known?"

Tiff looked him in the eye, gazing right inside of him. "The world doesn't owe you, Dave. We're all alone if we don't embrace each other. There's a war inside all men, and you're helping the wrong side to win."

He nodded, and he realised there were tears in his eyes for the first time in many many years. "I-ithurts too much to give a shit," he said. "Being angry—it makes things easier. If I can blame the world, then..." He shook his head and sighed.

"Then you don't have to blame yourself? I understand. But, Dave?"

"What?"

"*They* blame you. To them, you're not the government, or the rich, or the fortunate. You're just a remorseless monster who stole from them. The only person responsible for their pain is *you*."

"I... I'm sorry."

She stepped forwards, right up against him now.

Christ, she's beautiful. I don't even think she's human. At least, not anymore.

"Are you truly sorry, Dave?"

A tear spilled down his cheek. "Yes! I understand what I've done. I think I always have, but I just didn't care." He looked at Nancy, saw the utter hatred in the old woman's eyes—hatred for *him*. It reflected the way he felt about himself deep down. He was a drunk and a dead-beat—and everything people always warned him he end up being. "I can't make this right, but I *am* sorry."

Tiff sighed and gave a gentle nod. "I believe you. But it's too late."

Dave frowned. He sensed a swelling rage inside the room. It was going to devour him, he knew it. The dead were there to torture him until his soul bled. He wasn't getting away.

I deserve it. I fucking hate it, but it's true. What argument can I make? None. This is my fault.

Dave noticed something glinting to his left. He reached out and took the watch, offering it out to Captain Nachtnebel. "I'm sorry that my great granddad killed you and took this. Please, take it back, and then do what you need to do. I accept your anger."

The captain had still been saluting, but he lowered his arm now with a look of confusion on his skeletal face. Tentatively, he reached out and took the watch with both hands, gazing at it so intently that he looked entranced. It was clearly precious to him. Even in death.

"And this!" said Dave, turning and taking the glass ballerina. He handed it to Nancy, who snatched it from his hands. "I'm sorry you lost your granddaughter. I hope you get to see her again. What I did to you was wrong, but it's because I was angry and sad and..." He let out a sigh. "Lonely. It's lonely when you can't stand to be around yourself."

Nancy clutched the ballerina against her chest and snarled, as if she feared he might try to take it again.

Dave looked around at the spirits in the room. Each one glared at him with dark, lifeless eyes. "I'm sorry that I stole from all of you. I'm truly sorry. If I could take it back, I would. If... If you forgive me, I'll do better. I will. I swear it."

I mean it. After all this, how could I ever go back to who I was? I'll change. But it's too late.

Nancy nodded slowly, her eyes fixed upon him. She still seemed furious, but that anger began to fade. And then, so did she.

"She forgives you," said Tiff, smiling softly. "She was a kind soul in life, and that kindness passed on with her."

The captain saluted again, this time wearing his watch. He, too, started to fade.

"He is a man of honour, and accepting an enemy's surrender is honourable."

Dave sighed. "I'll make it right. I won't waste the second chance. All these people, their forgiveness, it's something I'll never forget."

Tiff gave Dave a sad smile. She put both hands on his shoulders and kissed him on the cheek. "Oh, Dave."

He shook his head. "What? Have I not done what they wanted? Nancy and the captain, they've gone. They've forgiven me."

"Yes, they have, but the others have not. Every soul here has a right to judge you for your sins, and like I said, it's too late. At least for some."

Dave turned and saw some of the ghosts had faded away, but others remained, including the old black man whose tools he had stolen.

Morgan Freeman. That's the name of the actor.

"People are all different," said Tiff. "Some forgive, some forget, but others demand justice."

"So... what now?"

"They have spared your life, Dave. They want you to live. But..."

"But what? What is it?" His heart was hammering in his chest. His head pounded worse than ever. It reminded him he was alive. That he *wanted*, so desperately, to live.

"You took things from them," said Tiff, "so now they want to take something from you."

Dave shook his head. He could barely speak. "What? What do you mean? What are they going to do to me?"

"I'm sorry," said Tiff. "Truly, I am." She turned and picked up his mugshot from the counter. "This really is a terrible picture of you. You really are very handsome."

Dave moaned as the faces of the dead glared hungrily upon him. He felt their anger piercing his veins.

What are they going to do to me?

―――――

STACEY WAS MORE than a little irritated. She'd caught a bus and hurried through town to catch her double lecture at college, only to find out they had cancelled it at short notice. Now she had two hours to kill and nothing to do. She'd already spent her part-time wages from her job at *Burger King*, and her best friends all studied different subjects. Only *she* had chosen to do Art A level, and the other students in her class were not yet at the 'hang-out' level of familiarity.

She considered missing her 4PM lecture, too, and just going home. Her parents would give her grief, but it was better than loitering around town for two hours like a loser. Most of the cool shops had all gone bust. Young people shopped online. Only benefit scroungers and old-age pensioners hung around town during the day.

Like that guy earlier who winked at me. Gross.

As if.

She headed back down Sedgwick Hill. She could catch a bus from the stop at the bottom, which was quicker than heading back up to the bus station.

A black cat was licking its bits at the side of the road, with a taxi driver hanging out his window and trying to shoo it away. The wet silhouette on the car door must have come from a cocked feline leg.

Stacey chuckled. It wasn't such a bad day. At least the sun was shining. Maybe she would sunbathe in the garden at home and do some reading. There was a new Blake Crouch novel on her bedside table that she still needed to get into. She loved a bit of sci-fi, despite being what her friends called *arty farty*.

A man stepped out of an alleyway ahead. To Stacey's astonishment, it was the same drunk from earlier. He still had the telltale dark circles beneath his eyes, and he was staggering even more than before. In fact, he seemed totally out of it. He was muttering to himself like a nutter. "They took them from me," he said. "They took them."

Stacey slowly came to a halt, her calves aching from the march down the hill. A shiver ran up her spine as something instinctual told her that something was wrong.

He's not drunk. He needs help.

The man was shaking his head and sobbing, clutching his arms against his stomach like he was in pain. He kept on muttering the same thing over and over again. "They took them from me."

"Sir, are you okay?"

He flinched, which in turn caused her to flinch. Then he turned to face her, his expression dazed like he'd just been in an accident and didn't know where he was. *Shellshocked*, was the word she would've used. He was also covered in blood. It soaked the front of his light blue t-shirt. "They took from me," he said again. "It didn't matter that I was sorry."

Stacey shook her head. By this time, the nearby taxi drivers had realised something was wrong as well. A couple of them were making their way over. But Stacey still didn't know what was wrong with the man.

"Sir, what happened to you?"

He shook his head at her like she was mad. Ironically, the only madness was coming from *him*—from his vacant, far-off gaze and delirious chatter. "They took from me," he said again, and then he did something that shocked Stacey rigid.

He pulled both arms away from his stomach and held them up. Both hands were missing, replaced by bloody stumps.

What the hell happened to him? I saw him thirty minutes ago and he was fine. He was fine.

She took a step back, relieved when the taxi drivers took over. One of them grabbed the injured man and lowered him to the ground, while another called for an ambulance on his mobile phone.

What happened to him in that alleyway?

Stacey examined the buildings at the side of the road and tried to find the gap he had slipped out of–but there was nothing there. Just shop fronts and doorways.

But I saw it. He staggered out of an alleyway.

"They took from me," the man shouted deliriously as the taxi driver tried to calm him down. "They took from me because I took from *them*."

Blood was everywhere, staining the pavement.

Stacey swallowed a mouthful of bile and started running. She reached the bottom of the hill and leapt on a bus one second before it closed its doors and departed. It was empty except for a single, beautiful young woman sitting at the back. She wore a fabulously colourful skirt that most people would never dare to attempt to pull off. When she saw Stacey staring, she smiled and waved. "You look like you've seen a ghost, sweetheart."

Stacey shook her head. "No, not a ghost. It was... I'm not really sure."

"Well, whatever it was, don't let it bother you. It's a lovely day, and you have your whole life ahead of you."

Stacey nodded. "Thanks. I, um, like your skirt."

"I used to like it, too," she said, "but things get less pretty when you can't take them off."

"Um, sorry?"

The woman waved a hand and chuckled. "Oh, don't mind me. I'm a little loopy. Happens at my age."

Stacey frowned. The woman looked no older than thirty. Maybe she had a few screws loose. Best not to engage.

Stacey turned back to face the front of the bus. All she wanted was get home and put this day behind her. The experience with the man on the hill would likely stay with her forever. Had he been in an accident? Or had someone done that to him?

Cut off his hands? Yikes.

The world was a scary place. Thieves on every corner. Rapists hiding in the shadows. And crazy people everywhere. Speaking of which, Stacey looked back to check on the odd woman in the brightly coloured skirt.

But the woman was gone.

BLOBSAC

DAY 6

Alone in a lab and with minimal funding, Dr Charles Hendrix had finally succeeded. A self-replicating life form created from non-living matter, already growing and evolving at an accelerated rate. The science had come off the back of sixty years of genetic and biological research, and it was so complex that he would struggle to explain it to a majority of PhDs.

A Nobel Prize was all but assured. He had recreated the miracle that had first occurred almost four-billion years ago, when a barren earth had birthed the first rudimentary lifeforms from inorganic material. *Abiogenesis*. Life from nothing.

Charles looked, once again, through his microscope, marvelling at the spongy life form he had created from carbon-based protocells inside his proprietary catalytic incubator. It flittered about, its form nebulous and ever-moving. It was like watching a drop of mayonnaise floating inside a jar full of water.

The creature was six times the size and three times the complexity it had been yesterday—an evolutionary change that would take millions of years to occur naturally.

"For now, I shall call you *Blobsac*, because you're a little blobby sac."

Charles laughed out loud, able to do so as his assistant, Danielle, was currently out getting coffee. Their modest lab was set up inside what was formerly a bakery and warehouse in the small village of Alcester. Funding came directly from a medical investment group who wanted to grow human organs for transplant—and profit, of course. It was a feat all but accomplished across the world, which was why Charles had expanded the scope of his research. He wouldn't merely grow organs, he would grow new life.

And the result was *Blobsac*. A creature with no mouth, or any other sensory organs, but was growing and evolving.

Time to type up the daily report. Charles moved away from the incubator and went over to his workstation, where he opened up his laptop and loaded up his reporting software. A blank box came up along with today's date.

His fingers found the keys.

ORIGIN-ONE (NOW NICKNAMED Blobsac) has grown by a factor of six since the same time yesterday, and it has developed the beginnings of a rudimentary siphon, which I believe will aid in the formation of a basic respiratory system. At its current rate of growth, Blobsac should be visible to the naked human eye as early as next week. Its current evolutionary path appears similar to Cambrian-era molluscs.

CHARLES SAVED the entry and closed his laptop, trembling with a constant and ever-present excitement about the new world he had just created.

DAY 7

Danielle arrived at the lab before Charles, which was to be expected, seeing as he had retired late last night, unable to calm himself to sleep with so much on his mind. It took only one glance at her face to know something was wrong.

"What is it, Danielle? Why is your face like that?"

She cleared her throat and just stood there for a moment. Then she coughed into her fist and pointed behind her. "It's Origin-One. It's grown again."

"Well, of course it has. The incubator is rapidly accelerating the ... evolutionary..." His words trailed off as Danielle stepped aside and revealed the lab behind her. The incubator was almost full, a grey-white mass trembling inside of it. It looked like expectorate from a flu-patient, except it was the size of a football.

"This isn't possible." He clasped a hand over his mouth. "Blobsac was microscopic last night. To be this size, he must have grown at a rate of... of... we're talking a growth factor of a hundred times or more. It's incredible."

Danielle nodded, as white as a sheet. Once again, she coughed into her hand. "It's developed a proboscis too."

Charles stepped up to the glass incubator and marvelled at what he saw inside. What could only be seen through a microscope yesterday was now a creature the size of a cat. Upon its central, bulbous mass hung a thin, rope-like appendage with a sucker on the end to absorb nutrients.

"Danielle, prepare some protein paste. I want to see if Blobsac can consume solid matter."

"Is that what we're calling it now? Blobsac? Cute."

"Get the paste."

Danielle rushed into the kitchen and returned one minute later with a thin protein paste spread across a stainless steel plate. She went over to the incubator, but then hesitated. "Um, I don't want to stick my hand in there."

Charles tutted. "It's a barely evolved organism. What on earth are you afraid of? Just give it to me. I'll place it inside."

She handed him the small metal plate with the spread. He took it over to Blobsac. The thing quivered at his presence, almost as if it were excited. There was no way it could see him, though, for it lacked eyes. It didn't appear to have any basic auditory organs either.

Charles opened the top hatch of the incubator and lowered the plate down on a small section of floor not currently occupied by Blob-sac. The creature never stayed still, the embodiment of a wave in the ocean. Was it wrong not to show caution? While it was certainly too unevolved to pose a direct threat, might its flesh cause an allergic response? An entirely new life form, as primordial as anything in existence—how would his immune system view such a thing?

And then he felt Blobsac brush against the back of his hand.

Charles dropped the steel trail and yanked his arm back with a yelp.

"What?" Daniella said, clearly alarmed. "Did it bite you?"

He turned to her. "What? Bite me? No... of course not. It just touched me for a brief moment. I wasn't expecting it."

"What did it feel like?"

"Huh?" He frowned, and then considered the question. "Oh, well, I suppose it was... warm. Hot, in fact."

She nodded knowingly. "With the energy expenditure from such rapid growth, it makes sense that Origin-One—um, Blobsac—would run hot."

He adjusted his lab coat, resisting the urge to run and wash his hands. "I agree. The chain reactions going on must be explosive. The fact it's been completely starved of anything besides air is confounding."

"It should be impossible," she said. "It's like an alien."

He chuckled, wishing he still had the whimsy of a thirty-year-old medical researcher instead of the aching back of a sixty-year-old. "An alien is only an alien until you meet it. Say hello to our child, Danielle. Say hello to Blobsac."

Danielle waved a hand awkwardly. "Hey, Blobs."

BLOBSAC'S GROWTH is unlike anything ever witnessed in human history, possibly in the history of the cosmos. Such a thing should not be possible under the current laws of science. With no caloric input or energy absorption, Origin-One has increased its size exponentially. Its arrival is more akin to the formation of a planet than the birth of a life form. I anxiously await tomorrow.

DAY 8

The incubator was cracked wide open, which was something

Charles had anticipated. There had been no way to remove Blobsac yesterday, as the creature had grown too large to exit through the hatch, so he had made the unpalatable decision to leave the organism entombed and hope for the best.

The best had happened. The incubator was shattered, but Blobsac was intact.

Its growth was far less today than yesterday, but still noticeable. It was now the size of a typical dog—a cocker spaniel or beagle. Currently, it was slithering around the laboratory floor, and appeared to be hoovering up the shards of glass from the incubator's broken panels. No signs of injury. No blood or bodily fluids. In fact, Blobsac appeared perfectly healthy, seeming to vibrate with vitality.

Danielle stepped into the lab a moment after Charles, and she immediately screamed at the sight of their creation on the loose. "W- what do we do? We need to get it in a cage."

"We don't have a cage big enough," Charles said. "We never antici- pated anything like this. Look, its proboscis is shorter now, and it has teeth!"

"Great." Danielle groaned. "So it can bite us now?"

"Perhaps. It will also be able to see us soon. Do you see those black masses about six inches apart? I believe those are the foundations of ocular organs."

Danielle backed off until she was over by her work desk. She slumped down in her chair and took some deep breaths. "We need to report this, Doc. I mean, this is insane, right? We created our own Pokemon. They're going to want to put this thing in a zoo."

"We tell no one. At least not today. With current conventions, Blobsac will be euthanised, dissected, and studied. You and I might even face prosecution. The laws about this are... *blurry*."

"Surely there are no laws about this at all, Doc? Nobody has ever done anything like this."

"Correct, but still... I would like to wait one more day and see where it takes us. If the situation becomes untenable, then we will contact the proper authorities and hand over our research."

She shook her head, legs dangling from her chair. "What if it's dangerous?"

"Science *is* dangerous, Danielle. The risk will be worth it, though. Once we go public with what we have, we'll be on talk shows all over the globe. Every biotech company on earth will be begging us to work for them. One more day will give us a little extra leverage and give us even more valuable data."

Danielle rubbed at her eyes, as if it were night and not morning. "I'm gonna regret this. I know I am."

"Regardless, our names will be remembered forever, and your Phd is now a formality. Heck, they'll probably give you two."

BLOBSAC IS NOW *a giant mollusc-like creature with the ability to move and feed. While it shows no signs of intelligence, it is merely a matter of time before it begins to exhibit higher function- ing, especially now that basic sensory organs are beginning to form. Tomorrow will most likely be the end of our experiment. To continue further would be reckless and unethical. For now, I will content myself to having replicated the beginning of life on earth. Life from non-living material.*

DAY 119

My folly is without end. The entirety of the United Kingdom has now been enveloped by the gelatinous mass of a creature I once fondly referred to as Blobsac. This morning, Danielle hurled herself from the top railings of the HMS Courage, disappearing into the icy depths of the Atlantic below rather than face another second of guilt. The ocean is now twenty metres lower than six months ago—when Origin-One started absorbed every molecule of water it comes into contact with. While the creature began life without nourishment, it now devours devours devours. What I didn't realise during that first, fateful week, was that the creature I created was pulling the moisture out of the very air and using it to grow. Now it pulls in everything and continuously adds to its gargantuan mass. Soon, it will be as large as the continent of Europe—and Europe will be no more.

All attempts to terminate Origin-One have failed. Explosions cause ruptures that immediately heal. Ballistic ammunitions are absorbed into the creature's mass. Chemicals simply cannot penetrate the mucosal layer covering its thick hide. *The last time I had full sight of Blobsac, it resembled a mammoth cancer—a veiny mass of unstable cells and mutating flesh. A monster.*

If only I hadn't given it that extra day to grow, I might have prevented all this. Perhaps I could have received my Nobel Prize and been content with a lesser achievement. But I had to play God.

I still think about that morning. The morning I expected to come in to find Blobsac the size of a horse and with new sensory organs and appendages. I expected to marvel and gasp before finally reporting my work to the proper authorities and euthanising my creation. It could all have been averted if I had ended things one day sooner.

Instead, I returned to the laboratory to find the windows shattered and bulging, and the roof tiles raining down into the car park. Locals had gathered to point and chatter at the jelly-like substance pushing through sections of the building's brickwork. They must have thought it some kind of hazardous substance—certainly not a living creature that would soon devour the world.

Eighteen days. That's what wiser men than me have predicted. Eighteen more days before Origin-One encompasses the entire globe. By then, there'll be nothing left. No water, no animals, no humans. Just Blobsac.

If the world wasn't ending, I would face trial and be executed, but instead I have been perversely forgiven in order to find a solution, because the biggest expert on my work is, of course, me. This is my problem to solve.

But I have failed.

And my failure has killed the world.

The only decision I have left to make now is whether to follow Danielle into the ocean or whether to wait until the very end and face my folly head on. From the way the Navy men have been eyeballing me, perhaps the choice will soon be taken away from me.

Eighteen days.

TOOTH & CLAW

J ulie peeked through the curtains, a habit she'd taken to performing every ten minutes. Two days had passed since anyone had egged or graffitied her home, but the online hatred was still thriving, and she dared not step foot outside. A prisoner in her own home.

And for what? Daring to have an opinion?

For the last six years, Julie had been the morning show host for *Birmingham High FM*, but a week ago her bosses had suspended her pending a formal review. Somehow, her suitability for the role was suddenly in question, because she had views that *did not align with current brand values*. The truth was that she worked for a bunch of cowards. Money over integrity. Profit over courage.

And the men with control of the purse strings want me gone.

Swinging between weary, apathetic, and downright angry, Julie went and sat down on the sofa in the living room. The TV was off because she enjoyed the silence. It would also allow her to hear if any more of those alphabet lunatics came onto her property. In the last two weeks, they had painted obscene messages on her doors and windows, bricked the rear windowscreen of her Jaguar, and put dog shit through her letterbox. It was insane. These people were *insane*.

And to think I have spoken up for gay rights my entire life. Thirty years on the radio, an exemplary career, and it's all ruined because I refused to kowtow to the cult-like madness.

Julia gasped as a sudden weight came down on her lap. It was Mutley, her highland Terrier. She stroked the wiry mop on his head and chuckled. "You're going to break a bone one of these days, you little monster."

Mutley licked fleetingly at her face, tasting only air as she flinched away. Then he nestled down on her lap and wagged his tail while she continued to pet him. He'd been with her eight years, a gift to herself after the divorce. A new companion for a new chapter in her life. The carpet wetting and shoe chewing had almost sent her over the edge at first, but once the pup became a dog, he'd cemented himself as her best friend. Mutley never judged her or chastised her. She didn't have to watch her words around him.

Mutley wasn't her only pet. She also had Shelby the Siamese cat, who was currently curled up on the living room's leather armchair. There was also her tropical fish tank in the corner, fifty-gallons sitting upon a sleek black stand. Inside was the requisite pleco, a school of neons, several rasboras, two rams, and a boisterous weather loach. She had also recently kept dwarf frogs, but something had caused them to die one week apart from each other. She hadn't got around to replacing them yet. That was it, her little zoo. Her home. Her family. Who knew if having kids would have been better, but it was the life she had chosen, and one which she was at peace with. Truthfully, once her divorce was several years behind her, Julie's life had turned out pretty darn good.

Until things went to pot.

Julie felt herself tense up. Mutley must have sensed it because he glanced up at her face. An affectionate pet, he was often in tune with her emotions, but the look he gave her now was unusual. He appeared dark-eyed and unresponsive. No playful tilt of his head or wiggle of his butt. She smiled at him and smoothed down his tussled forehead, but his tail did not wag. "You okay, honey? Are you worried about the bad people?"

Mutley was no guard dog, but he always tried his best to bark out of the living room window when someone came up her short driveway. Lately, with so many people attacking her house, her little dog had been stressed out and on high alert.

Julie put Mutley on the cushion next to her and went over to the window. She peeked out of the curtains again and saw a trio of young people sitting on the brick wall surrounding her property. It was best to ignore them. She had started the week yelling at intruders to clear off, but it had ended up in a slanging match every time. These teens wanted a reaction—she wouldn't give them one.

One of the teens turned their head, almost like they could sense Julie watching them. She dodged behind the curtain, her heart skipping a beat.

"Scared in my own home," she muttered. "Because of a bunch of deluded lunatics who don't like hearing things they disagree with."

She reached down towards the leather armchair and rubbed a finger underneath Shelby's chin, but her cat did not extend her neck and purr like normal. In the same way as Mutley, she appeared strangely vacant. Stiff.

"Huh, I'll leave you alone then, shall I, madam?"

Shelby just looked at her, her sparkling blue eyes a little duller than usual.

Searching for a pet who would love her, Julie went over to her fish tank. As usual, her proximity caused the fish to congregate at the front of the glass. Even the shy pleco came to say hello with its goofy, sucking mouth.

Julie took the tub of flakes from atop the tank's lid and pushed open the feeding portal. She sprinkled the food into the water and watched as the multi-coloured flakes spread across the shimmering surface.

The lid fell off the tub. Flakes went everywhere.

"Damn it!"

That much food would pollute the water. She would have to fish it out. So, she rolled up the sleeve of her blouse and reached into the water. The fish were not scared of her, so she felt their slimy bodies brush against the back of her hand as they fussed around her. Sometimes, the weather loach even let her stroke it.

"Ouch!"

She yanked back her hand, water dripping all over the carpet. Something had bitten her. In fact, she was bleeding from a tiny cut on the bottom knuckle of her index finger. She shook her hand and swore, confused. Did any of her fish even have teeth?

Then she saw the pleco, attached to the glass, its sucking mouth was wide open and a small set of tiny teeth on display. Had it bitten her? It had never done so before. Was it going for the food and simply caught her by accident?

But why was it now sucking at the glass so aggressively, as though it were trying to break out of the tank and get to her? In fact, all the fish were staring at her through the glass, their lidless eyes like a collection of dull sequins.

"What is wrong with you all?"

Julie flinched as water sprayed her face and something leapt out of the tank's feeding portal. It arced through the air and missed her face by only half-an-inch. She jumped aside and watched the fish land on the carpet.

It was the weather loach. Its shimmering, eel-like body flip-flopped towards her. Julie instinctively went to retrieve it and place it back inside the tank, but before she could Shelby leapt off the armchair and pounced on it.

"Shelby! Shelby, you put that down right now."

Shelby growled, something she rarely did, and tore the poor fish apart, its blood staining the cream carpet.

"Oh, Shelby, no!"

A scream erupted outside. Bloodcurdling. Terrified.

Julie ran to the window and looked out through the curtains. She could scarcely believe what she saw.

The three teenagers outside were yelling and causing a ruckus. It took a moment to work out, but they appeared to be fending off a large dog. The hound's jaws were clamped around a screaming girl's arm, its head thrashing back and forth. Blood stained the pavement, covered the dog's muzzle.

The girl's screams were like a sharp knife against a wet plate.

Julie needed to go and help the girl.

What? Help the girl who's been sitting outside my house to terrorise me. All because I said transgenderism is a mental disorder.

Julie had lost her job.

Her security.

Her happiness.

But she wasn't about to let them take her humanity.

She raced out of the living room and into the hallway. She could still hear the girl's screaming, as well as the desperate cries of her friends.

Julie unlocked her front door and raced out onto the driveway. The sunlight hit her eyes and it took a moment to refocus. Once she did, she saw that the dog had the young girl on the ground, and was ripping and tearing at her throat. She was still alive, but her arms and legs flopped like a rag doll's. The girl's friends, to their credit, hadn't fled, and they kicked at the dog and tried to shove it away. But the compact, muscular beast would not let go.

Then a second dog appeared, this one a sprightly Beagle. It wagged its tail, head down and sniffing the ground. The two girls didn't see it coming.

The beagle leapt at one of the other girls, grabbing her by the ankle and yanking her off of her feet. She began to scream and kick, but the animal was possessed, and no matter how many strikes she landed about its head, the dog would not let go, only chomping down harder and thrashing even more ferociously.

Just as the remaining girl realised what was happening, the original dog let go of the now dead girl and leapt at her. She fell to the ground, screaming beside her friend.

Julie stood on her driveway, shaking her head in utter confusion until a shadow caught her attention and caused her to look up at the bright blue sky.

She ducked just in time to avoid a plump pigeon that attempted to dive bomb her head. It let out a squawk and swooped back into the sky, No question, it was circling around for another attack.

Something moved at Julie's feet. She yelped and hopped backwards as a rat rose up on its back legs and glared at her with evil red eyes.

"What the hell?" She hopped forwards and booted the rodent as hard as she could. She was no football player, but she sent the rat flying four-feet into the air and right across the road.

An almighty crash sounded close by.

A bright red *Post Office* van had collided with the bus shelter on the corner. The uniformed driver was now staggering in the road, with what looked like a pair of squirrels setting about his face and neck.

What the hell was happening?

Julie saw yet more movement down the street, a pack of three foxes chasing a woman with a pram. As she concentrated on fleeing the bushy red menaces, she didn't spot the massive owl swooping down into the pram.

The infant's screams chilled Julie's blood.

She wanted to help the mother, but the foxes caught up with her, circling and snapping at her legs. More blood soon spilled onto the pavement. The baby's screams stopped.

"I... I need to call the police. I need to get help."

The sky darkened, more birds circling overhead in ever-growing numbers. Julie turned and ran back up her driveway. In the distance, she heard more people screaming and crying out for help.

Once back inside the house, she slammed the door and locked it immediately. Panting, she placed her back against the wood and waited, expecting to feel the blows of rabid animals hitting the other side. Something bad had happened. Some kind of attack or disaster.

One that makes wildlife attack?

Impossible.

"It's fucking impossible," she roared. "What the fuck is going on?"

Her phone was in the living room. Other people had probably already dialled 999, but she didn't know what else to do. Nor did she know what to say when they answered. Were the three girls across the road all dead? Was the postman okay?

That poor poor baby...

999 was engaged. She didn't even know that could happen.

An automated message played, stating that a high number of calls were being handled. It then stated, almost aggressively, that all callers should remain inside their homes or seek refuge in the case of an emergency.

"This is it," she said. "The bloody world's ending."

A series of *plopping* sounds alerted her, and when she looked across the room, she saw her fish leaping out of their tank and landing on the carpet. The iridescent neons flopped towards her in a group. The pleco flopped along on its belly.

Her fish wanted to kill her.

She shook her head as something terrible dawned on her. But before she could put her thoughts together, she was alerted by a low, guttural growl and a slightly higher-pitched whining alongside it.

Julie turned to face the sofa. Mutley and Shelby glared at her, no longer her loving pets. They were predators. Killers.

Animals.

Julie screamed as her beloved companions leapt at her with their jaws wide and dripping with saliva. As she stumbled backwards, her heel came down on the beached pleco and she slipped. Falling to the carpet, she didn't even have time to throw her arms up and defend herself as two sets of dagger-like teeth sank into her neck.

The worst part of it all, Julie thought as she bled out, was that she was a fucking vegan.

THE VIEWING

A bbie opened the front door to 19 Kent Street with a great big smile on her face. The man standing on the driveway was handsome and dark-featured in that Mediterranean kind of way. Greek maybe? Or Turkish? He wore smart grey trousers with an open-collared white shirt rolled up to his elbows. He was twenty minutes early, but she had just finished with the previous viewer of the property, so it worked out just as well that he was here now. Maybe she could get finished early on this fine Thursday afternoon and go for an early dinner somewhere nice.

"You must be Mr Clark?" she said, stepping out and offering a handshake. "I'm Abbie. Did you find it okay?"

He frowned at her momentarily, but then took her hand and smiled warmly. "Huh? Oh, yes. I know this area quite well."

"And is it a house in this area that specifically you're looking for?"

"Yes. Yes, I like this area. I like this house." He placed his hands on his hips and looked up towards the second-floor windows. "I would like to see inside."

"Of course. Come on in and we'll take a look around."

She stood aside while Mr Clark moved past her, and then she closed the front door. The rushing drone of the nearby highway disappeared and the house became silent thanks to the triple glazing. She proceeded to speak, to keep things energised, because the worst thing you wanted was to leave a client to think too much. They might open a rickety cupboard or stare harder at the rusty light fitting. No, you had to keep things moving, you had to keep things positive—pointing out the newly fitted downstairs toilet and the lovely bay window in the dining-room. At the same time, you had to position yourself in front of the slight patch of damp on the master bedroom's east wall—and you didn't turn the lights on in the main bathroom because they flickered. Fortunately, this house had very few problems to disguise.

"Right this way," she said, placing a hand on Mr Clark's elbow to gently lead him down the hallway while also ingratiating herself via gentle body contact.

They went into the kitchen, the largest room of the house, and the one most likely to create a positive opening impression.

"Wow," Mr Clark said as he looked up at the ceiling spotlights and then at the floor-to-ceiling cupboards that spanned the far wall. "That's quite a lot of storage space, no?"

He spoke with a slight accent, an almost lisping singsong of a voice. Pleasant. Exotic. Not all foreign clients were fun to deal with—in fact some of them caused nothing but headaches—yet some could be golden gooses. Some foreigners had surprising wealth—often liquid—and once they found something they wanted, they got on with acquiring it. She hoped Mr Clark was a goose.

"It's a wonderful kitchen for hosting," Abbie said, motioning towards the breakfast bar, "be it friends or family. Do you have children, Mr Clark?"

"I love children," he said, which was an odd response, suggesting he had misheard the question. "Are *you* married, Miss Abbie?"

She chuckled. At twenty-six, the thought of being married felt a little absurd—or at least painfully far away. "I don't even have a boyfriend. Poor, lonely me." She chuckled again and looked him in the eye. Some clients liked to flirt—especially middle-aged married men and aging widows. If she could manage to be saucy with *them*, she could certainly manage it with this young, well-dressed businessman.

Mr Clark returned her gaze. The two of them said nothing for a moment, and Abbie felt the back of her neck prickle. Eventually, she realised she was allowing silence to settle in.

"So," she said, "shall we go see the living room?"

He gave her a slight nod, barely moving his head, but it was enough to convey he was ready to continue.

She led him through the home's dining area, with white floor tiles and a thick marble slab of a table, and then they headed through an archway into the lounge. One wall was entirely taken up by a media wall—a massive TV above an electric fireplace. "Perfect for Netflix," she said. "If that's your thing?"

He ran his fingers over the smooth LCD screen and grunted. "I don't spend a lot of time relaxing. I like to keep moving, like a shark."

"A shark? Um, what line of business are you in, Mr Clark?"

He shrugged. "Importing and selling. How long have you been doing this for, Abbie? You are good, very friendly. I like you."

She felt herself blush, and it was awful. Mr Clark was unusually direct, and there was a hard to define strangeness about him that was both alluring and unnerving. In a world full of increasingly soft men, here was an old-style male. A man who felt no shame in undressing her with his eyes. A man who probably gleefully ate red meat while vegans protested outside a restaurant. His confidence was undeniable in the way he carried himself—in the way he stood erect and didn't fidget, every movement deliberate.

Abbie considered flirting with Mr Clark for real.

"Shall we go take a look upstairs?" she said, licking her lips and playing with her hair. "There are three bedrooms, all of a decent size, and the master has an ensuite."

"Yes, I would like to see the bedroom," he said. "Show me, please, Abbie."

She liked it when he said her name.

They went back out into the hallway, where she briefly showed him the downstairs toilet and the small laundry room, before moving on to the stairs. This house was bigger on the bottom than the top, having originally been a bungalow. The previous owners had brought it almost derelict before going on to refurbish the entire property. No doubt, they would be fetching a pretty penny upon its sale. One day, Abbie hoped to buy and sell properties herself, but her saving goals weren't even halfway complete. Each time it felt like she was getting ahead, prices for being alive increased. Every breakfast roll or lunchtime salad cost a few more pennies than it had last week. The only things that didn't go up were her wages and commission.

They headed up the carpeted staircase. Abbie pointed out the modern glass stair rail, but Mr Clark didn't seem particularly impressed. Who knew what his own personal tastes were?

"This here is the main bathroom," she said, opening a door and pointing inside. "As you can see, you have a separate bath and shower to enjoy. The bath also has jets, which is lovely after a hard day's work. Does your wife prefer a bath or a shower, Mr Clark?"

"I am a single man," he said. "I live alone."

Jackpot, Abbie thought. *I should ask him out. I bet he eats at some nice places. Probably drives a Bentley.*

Or a beat up Citroen. You know nothing about this man, Abbie.

So why do I want to see him naked?

Abbie smiled, more genuinely than she had thus far. "Well, this is certainly a lot of house for a single man. The ladies will be throwing themselves at you."

He chuckled—a short, raspy sound. "That is the dream, no? The single man dream?"

"No thoughts of settling down?"

"Hmm, there are many women. How to find the right one?"

She brushed a lock of blonde hair out of her face and gave him a lopsided grin. "You just have to try a few. That's the fun of dating, right? Dinner, nice conversation, and..." She diverted her eyes coyly. "And then you see where the night takes you."

He nodded, but then wandered off towards the master bedroom. Abbie, completely unlike her, had a brief fantasy flash through her head—the image of throwing Mr Clark down on the kingsize bed and having her way with him. Or letting him have his way with her. Mr Clark did not seem like the type to submit.

Shaking herself out of her inappropriate thoughts, she hurried along the landing to join Mr Clark in the main bedroom. He was looking out of the window at the driveway below, his strong hands clamped around his slender hips. "This is a quiet area," he noted. "Are there many break-ins?"

"Not that I'm aware of," she lied, happening to know that crime had recently increased in the area. But so had it everywhere else. "The house doesn't have CCTV, which means it probably hasn't been a concern for the current owners."

He pointed. "The house opposite doesn't have cameras either. Must be a safe street, but people can never be too careful, you know? If I owned a house, I would want to make sure it was secure."

"You don't own a house currently, then? Are you renting?"

"No." He moved away from the window and pushed down on the bed, its mattress springing back up as soon as he removed his hand. Was he thinking the same kind of thoughts she was?

Stop being silly, Abbie.

All she should be focusing on was selling this house and getting her commission. This wasn't *50 Shades of Grey*. Excitement didn't exist in her life–only property surveys and energy certificates. The occasional one-night stand after a drunken night down the *Kentish Bull* was the best she ever got.

"So, what are your thoughts, Mr Clarke?" In other words, *what are your objections? Tell me so that I can overcome them.*

She licked her lips as she looked at him. His dark eyes narrowed and seem to look right beneath her skin, like he was trying to see what her soul looked like. Or maybe just her underwear. He was welcome to see it.

Abbie, seriously. Calm yourself, girl.

"I am thinking you seem nervous, Abbie. I can see the hairs on your arms. Little pricks, you see?" He stepped up to her and took her hand, raising it up so she could see the goosebumps all up and down her arm. "What is wrong, my darling lady?"

"Oh, n-nothing. You're just very handsome." She chuckled like a loon and hated the sound of it. "Must be the effect you have on women. I'm fine, though. Is there anything you would like to know about the house? Would you be interested in making an offer? I know the owners would be willing to wiggle a little on price."

He leant in closer, his face almost touching hers. Their eyes were like magnets, pulling towards each other. "I am afraid I cannot buy this house, Abbie."

"Oh, that's disappointing to hear. Can I ask why?"

"Yes, of course. I cannot buy this house because someone died here."

Taken completely by surprise, she opened her mouth to talk, but she didn't have a response. What was he talking about? Her notes said nothing about any deaths.

When her phone rang in the breast pocket of her blazer, Abbie flinched. It left her embarrassed, and her cheeks flushed with blood. "E-excuse me, I'll just tell them I'm with a client." She answered the call and asked who was calling.

"Oh hi, is this Abbie? It's Mr Clark. I have a viewing booked with you in ten minutes. I'm afraid I'm going to have to reschedule. Is it possible if..."

"M-Mr Clark? You haven't arrived yet?"

"No. My wife and I are unable to make it today, so if we could—"

Mr Clark—or whoever this man standing in the bedroom really was—stepped forwards and removed the phone from her hand. He ended the call, the phone giving a single bleep, and then tossed it onto the bed. Once again, he moved closer, staring into her eyes. "Someone died in this house," he said again. "It is a bad house."

"W-who died? When?"

He smiled—still handsome, but now clearly dangerous. How had she mistaken it for sexual attraction? It wasn't lust—it was hunger. Hunger of a beast. "You died," he said softly. "In about twenty minutes. After we finish playing."

Abbie tried to scream, but a hand clamped over her mouth.

If only she had checked who she was letting into the house.

When the dark-eyed stranger was finally done with her, the property values in the area were about to fall massively.

THE SHRIEKING SHAFT

Nina stuffed her hands in the pocket of her jeans and groaned. Waiting in line sucked. Theme parks, in general, sucked. *Waiting around most the day for a few minutes of fun here and there. Why couldn't we have gone zip lining?*

Allan must have seen her sullen expression, because he grinned sheepishly and rubbed her arm. "I really didn't think it would be this busy. February's usually quiet."

She didn't want to piss on his parade, so she smiled back. Still, she couldn't keep herself from shaking her head a little and sighing. "It's fine. I know you love this. I just hope it's worth it."

"It will. I promise." He turned back to face the queue. The line of people snaked inside a building up ahead, one made to look like an old American hotel named *The Elvira*. Inside was a brand new ride called the *Shrieking Shaft*. Allan had been wanting to ride it all year.

The line moved, people shuffling like cattle. Then they stopped to await the next bout of forward progress.

Allan had told her the shaft had two ride vehicles, holding twelve people each. They worked in tandem, so each time the queue moved, twenty-four people got put out of their misery.

Allan tucked his floppy brown hair behind his ears as a light breeze took hold. He looked at her. "So, what do you want to do tonight for dinner? Your choice."

"I'll probably be too tired to go out," she said, "so maybe we can order takeaway? Pizza?"

Allan wasn't a great fan of pizza, but he could make a sacrifice today. He obviously thought so, too, because he nodded happily. "Sounds good. *Valentinos?*"

"Nah, let's splash out on *Dominos.*"

He glanced at his smart watch, causing it to light up. "Okay, after this, I reckon we have time for the *Kingdom Boat Adventure Ride* and *Castle Splash.*"

Nina let out another groan. "Do they get you wet? It's too cold to get wet."

Again, he grinned at her sheepishly. "Only a little bit, and that's why I've left them until last. *Castle Splash* is the only log flume in the world with a sideways drop. And the boat adventure ride is tame. It's just a bunch of animatronics and stuff. Hey, do you know the elephant robot at the beginning was originally built for Disneyland Paris, but it got sold off when plans for a *Dumbo* ride changed?"

She shook her head and chuckled. "You're such a nerd. How come you love this stuff so much?"

He blushed and looked down at his fidgeting hands. "I just do. Maybe it's because I remember how much my mum used to enjoy taking me to *Drayton Manor* as a kid. We would ride the *Buffalo* again and again. I don't have that many memories of her, but..."

She nodded and put her head against his shoulder and hugged him. "It's nice. Almost like you're honouring her."

Allan had lost his mother at eight-years of age due to breast cancer. Fortunately, he had a decent father who loved him, so he had grown up to be pretty well-adjusted. She noticed his sadness sometimes, though.

I don't know how he ended up being such a positive person. Most people would be angry after losing a parent so young.

"She would be proud of you, Allan. You're a good guy."

He looked away. Nina thought she saw his brown eyes tear up. It didn't take much to make him cry. He was different to the other guys she'd gone out with. She'd known it on their very first date when he had taken her to an aquarium.

That was ten years ago now. I'll be thirty in a few months.

Where did my life go?

The line shuffled forward again. They were getting quite close to the front now. Plain metal barriers formed the beginning of the switchback, but this section was bordered by stone walls covered in lichen and moss. The floor transitioned from plain concrete to uneven cobbles.

Increased theming means we're getting close, right? Allan told me that.

She felt a dose of relief, seeing light at the end of this mind-numbingly boring tunnel.

"Can we get an ice cream after this?" she asked. "If your schedule allows it."

"Of course, we should have plenty of time. I reckon we'll get on this after the next few groups. From what I saw on the internet, things are about to get good."

She rolled her eyes. Their definitions of the word *good* were different.

Twenty feet ahead, a crooked archway rose spanned an entryway. A big fat crow perched on its apex, turning its head back and forth. At first, she thought it was an animatronic, but then it took flight with a sudden, sharp *caw*. It swept right overhead, causing several queuers to duck.

Caw-Caw!

"The size of that thing," she said. "It must be a raven or something."

"Probably not," Allan said as he watched the bird fly off into some nearby trees. "Ravens are pretty rare."

"Well, it was as big as a freakin' cat."

"Maybe it's an omen." He spoke in a spooky voice and waggled his fingers at her. "Impending doom."

"Don't!" She punched his arm. "You know I'm terrified of dying on one of these rickety deathtraps."

He wrapped an arm around her. "Do you know how many fail safes modern rides have? The chances of everything failing at once are one in a billion."

"What about that thing in Florida? Where the kid fell out?"

"It was operator error. Shouldn't have happened."

She folded her arms and grimaced at him. "But it did!"

He bit his lip and paused for a moment, and then he said, "Okay, good point, but there's never been a death at *Crawley Castle*. This place has a perfect track record. You're more likely to die on the motorway."

"You mean the motorway we have to take to get home? Great!"

"Sorry. We can take the B roads home, if it'll make you feel better."

"Are they safer?"

"Um... No, not really."

She punched him in the arm again and shook her head. The best way to avoid freaking out about something was to just not think about it. "Come on, we're moving again."

The line shuffled inside the entryway, and things finally became interesting. The theming was impressive. Cobwebs hung in clumps from the ceiling, while fake stone columns rose towards a thirty-foot-high vaulted ceiling. The stonework walls were cracked in several places, making the entire place seem ancient, despite it not having even existed a year ago.

Straight ahead was a gigantic stained glass window with the colourful image of a devil thrusting a pitchfork into a screaming angel.

"Wow!" she said, still looking around in awe. "Wow."

Allan nudged her playfully, his hair falling in front of his face and causing him to tuck it back behind his ears. "I know, right? Universal Studios would be proud of this. Nothing else like it in the UK."

Nina yelp as the noise of a howling wind started up, a sound effect piped in from somewhere. It was convincing enough to make her shiver.

The line shuffled forwards.

When Nina and Allen came to a stop, they had rounded a corner, allowing them to see dual sets of lift doors. Set on a vertical pillar between them was a strip of copper-coloured buttons. Only one of the buttons was lit up—it was marked with a 'B'.

The basement.

She heard a faint whisper floating through the crowd. *Going dooooown.*

Nina shivered again, but this time it wasn't from the cold. "This is going to be horrible, isn't it?"

Allan shook his head. "It's just a drop tower, except we start at the top instead of at the bottom. You've been on far worse. Remember *Apocalypse* at *Drayton Manor*?"

"Yeah, I hated it."

"Well... this won't be as bad. It's enclosed, so you can't see how high you are."

The line moved forwards again. Now they were right at the front. Each lift had a staff member in front of it, dressed in old-fashioned porter uniforms with fez-shaped hats. Their expressions were glum, almost vacant—an impressive display of acting as both men mindlessly focused on the singular task of ushering guests into the two lifts.

Allan glanced at her. "You ready?"

Her mouth filled with ashes, her stomach hot embers, but she nodded. "Let's just get this over with."

Both sets of lifts opened their doors to reveal they were now empty, their previous riders gone—they had obviously exited onto a hidden platform somewhere.

The usher standing by the lift on the left waved a hand lethargically at Allan, causing him to giggle and step forward. Nina smiled and said thank you to the man as she passed, but he didn't respond.

They stepped inside the lift along with ten strangers—a mixture of nervous and excited guests, including two children. A teenaged boy shuffled up beside Nina as she sat down on one of the wooden benches inside, and he turned to his girlfriend beside him and said, "This is gonna be a right laugh."

Nina groaned, failing to agree as piped-in whispers exclaimed, *You'll never leave.*

The bench had no seatbelts, but they were moulded in such a way that her hips were prevented from sliding left and right. In front of her was a metal railing, which she gripped tightly with both hands. The solidness of it calmed her nerves a little. What frightened her most about thrill rides wasn't the experience itself, but the possibility of something going wrong. She'd once ridden a spinning mouse coaster at the fair that she'd been certain was going to come right off the tracks. It had traumatised her. She'd had a fear of theme parks ever since.

So why the hell do I keep letting Allan drag me on these things?

Because I love him, and I love seeing him smile.

With the benches full, the lift doors closed. A single light on the ceiling flickered, casting an orange glow.

"I really appreciate today," said Allan, rubbing her leg with a chilly hand. "I've wanted to ride this since the minute it opened."

"How big is the drop?" was all she could say.

"One-hundred-and-fifty-feet," he said proudly. "Bigger than *Tower of Terror* in *Disney World*."

Remain in your seats at all times, came a voice from some embedded wall speakers. *Place your belongings at your feet and do not stand up until told to do so. Your destination is down.*

The lights flickered again and then went off. Allan shuffled on the bench beside her.

"What are you doing?" she asked, her nerves making her tetchy.

"Nothing. I just..."

The lights came back on again. When she looked at Allan, he was holding something in his hands. A small black box. It was open, with something sparkling inside.

A diamond ring.

Nina gasped, her mind twisting into a knot and leaving her confused. "Allan, what are you...?"

"Nina Jones, will you—"

Going dooooown!

Nina let out a scream as the lights went off again and gravity disappeared. Her stomach leapt up into her mouth as she fell, fell, fell. The rapid descent seemed to go on forever, and her legs tensed to the point of cramping. She held her breath, closed her eyes, prayed for it to be over.

Gravity returned. The drop halted.

"Oh my God! I'm going to have a heart att—"

Welcome to the bottom!

The lights came on, the doors opened. A giant scowling devil's face—bathed in crimson light—let out an ear-piercing shriek.

Laughter and yelping filled the cabin as the lift launched upwards.

Nina screamed again, but Allan was cackling hysterically. He still held out the ring and was looking at her expectantly.

The lift leapt up through a muddy shaft, its doors still wide open. It felt like they were moving through the earth itself.

"What are you doing, Allan?" she asked breathlessly.

"A-asking you to m-marry me."

"Seriously. Right now!"

"Yes! I love you, Nina. Will you be my—" He let out a scream as the lift plummeted again.

Nina's breath caught in her throat as they plunged back down to face the devil again. This time, its giant, tooth-filled mouth was wide open. Its eyes swirled with actual flames and a hot gust of air rushed across the benches. Everyone screamed in glee. The teenager beside her gripped the metal railing for dear life.

Welcome to Hell, said a booming voice.

"I can't believe you're asking me to marry you now," she said, not sure if she was angry or elated.

"I wanted it on the ride photo. What's your answer?"

She shook her head, resting on anger. "Of course I'll marry you, you absolute moron—I love you—but this is going to cost you."

"You're worth any cost," he said.

The lift was still halted in front of the devil face. Everything was bathed in flickering crimson light. Nina knew the ride wasn't over yet. At some point they would shoot back up again, but that was okay. The ascent was much better than the fall.

She began to relax. Nothing had broken—no bolts had pinged free. In fact...

This is pretty damn cool.

The lift began to rotate. The devil's face disappeared to the left as the ride vehicle turned to the right. Muddy walls met the riders, with thick tree roots snaking back and forth. It was wonderfully immersive. It even *smelled* like they were deep underground.

"This is amazing," someone said.

"I didn't hear about this part," said someone else.

Nina noticed Allan was frowning. He was still holding the ring, but he was no longer looking at her.

"What is it?" she asked him.

"I watched like five on ride POV videos of this ride. I've never seen this."

"Seen what?"

The lift rotated more until the devil's face was completely gone. A dark tunnel lay ahead of them.

Allan shook his head. "I don't understand."

"It's part of the ride," Nina said, but couldn't help but notice several other riders also looking uncertain.

The lift lurched forwards into the tunnel. Crimson light gave way to darkness. The cold air turned stale. Everyone fell silent.

This was a ride unlike any Nina had ever experienced. The cost of building a shaft into the earth like this, and then a second, horizontal one, must have cost a fortune.

This is all just part of the fun, right?

So why is Allan so freaked out?

Welcome to hell, said the booming voice again, but it came from behind them now, from the other shaft. They were several feet inside the horizontal tunnel, now entrenched in complete darkness. The air grew colder and colder.

One of the riders began to freak out. Whoever was sitting beside them did their best to calm them down, but they sounded close to panic themselves.

"Allan?" Nina paused a moment, took a breath. "This is okay, right? Why are you being so quiet?"

"I just... never expected this."

"Okay, fine. That's the point, though, right? It's an unexpected twist to freak us out."

"Yeah..." He cleared his throat. "Except in this day and age, there *are* no unexpected twists. You can watch a complete video of any ride before it even opens to the public. There are entire channels on *YouTube* dedicated to ride POVs. None of them have shown this part."

Nina had a sinking feeling, her stomach draining through her legs and into her shoes. She shivered against the cold.

The darkness broke ahead—a tiny sliver of yellow light growing larger. Nina let out a sigh of relief, knowing they were about to come out onto the secret exit platform, laughing and trembling. Allan was having her on, or just trying to scare her, but...

Why would he want to scare me half to death right after proposing? He's not a complete idiot.

"I want to get off," someone yelled. "This isn't right. This bit isn't supposed to happen."

And then the panic began.

"Stop the ride."

"I don't like this."

"This is fucked up. I can't see a thing."

"Calm down," Nina shouted, flabbergasted to be the voice of reason in a group of strangers. "It's okay. The end is right up ahead."

"We're still underground!" someone yelled. "We're supposed to go back up to the top."

Nina didn't want to argue, so she hugged herself in the dark and kept quiet, even as others grew louder. She was comforted when Allan's hand found her leg.

At least, it better be his hand.

The lift trundled forwards, no longer enclosed by walls and a ceiling—the metal shell must have gone back up the shaft leaving only a platform with the benches. They finally entered the light ahead, moving along a steel track into an open area with concrete walkways on both sides. As expected, the riders had entered some kind of exit station. Except it was barely lit and there were no ride operators in sight.

A second section of track joined the first, and the other ride vehicle appeared and trundled in front of them, taking the lead. Its riders were just as freaked out as the ones on Nina's platform.

God, I get it now. It all makes sense. Allan has arranged this entire thing. He's set it up as part of his proposal. He probably got in touch with the park months ago. I'm going to kill him.

He wouldn't usually be this cruel.

The two ride vehicles came to a simultaneous stop between the two concrete walkways. It was time to get off. Nina thanked God. The relief was the only thing keeping her anger at bay.

Clunk!

The metal railings in front of the benches suddenly leapt forwards into their laps, clamping down and pinning everyone to their seats. Nina yelped in surprise, but Allan, beside her, groaned in pain as his thicker legs were painfully squeezed. "What the fuck? Help!"

If he was acting, Allan was far more talented than she'd realised.

The other riders cried out in shock and pain, too.

"Let me off," someone bellowed. "I'm gonna go ape shit if you don't let me off right now."

But no one came. No staff appeared. No messages drifted from hidden speakers, bidding them to disembark. The two platforms were empty islands surrounded by cold earth and featureless cement.

Then Nina spotted movement.

Something edged along the wall, slinking and curling. In fact, whatever it was seemed to come from a smaller tunnel in the earthen walls up ahead. It looked like... like some kind of *lizard*–a salamander or one of those cute crested things you saw in fish shops sometimes. Nobody else seemed to notice. They were too busy trying to extricate themselves from the steel railings that were pinning them against the bench.

Allan was still holding the ring box out in front of him, like he'd been frozen the whole time, and when she nudged him, he blinked and seemed to exit a daze. "Wh-What?"

"Look over there. That thing on the wall."

Allan turned his head, but the slinking creature had gone. The platforms were lit by a smattering of weak ceiling lights, but most of the space was gloomy and unlit. Nina sensed movement ahead, but couldn't quite locate it.

Then movement suddenly seemed to come from everywhere.

More creatures poured out of the smaller tunnel, and then from other tunnels Nina hadn't spotted. Dozens of them appeared. They made strange chittering sounds, almost cat-like.

The other riders noticed the lizards and screamed a shrieking chorus. Nina joined in for a moment, but then stopped herself. It wasn't going to help anything.

"This isn't right," she said. "Allan, what is this?"

The box with the engagement ring fell from his hand and tumbled to the floor, forgotten now as he clawed at the railing across his lap, fighting desperately to get free. "W-we need to get the fuck out of here."

"Allan, what is happening?"

"I don't know. I don't fucking know."

One of the creatures leapt from the concrete platform onto the other ride vehicle. A woman wailed in horror, then gargled in pain. Something awful was happening to her.

And then happened to everyone else aboard the vehicle as more and more lizards leapt from the concrete. All Nina could see were people thrashing about in the gloom, battling with the creatures and unable to escape.

Everyone was screaming. Then, one by one, the screams stopped, until there was only silence coming from the other vehicle.

Those riders sitting on the benches along with Nina and Allan fell silent, too, staring in horror at something none of them understood. On the concrete walkways, several more of the lizards appeared, coiled up and ready to pounce. Their pink eyes barely seemed functional, and their forked tongues appeared to be edged with tiny hooks as darted in and out of their hungry mouths.

There was a loud *clonk*.

Nina realised the metal restraints in the other car had released, rising back into an upright position. The riders were finally free to move—and they did.

What? Are they okay?

The first person to stand up was an overweight man. His silhouette was a large blob, yet he leapt onto the platform with surprising grace. He landed sure-footed on the concrete and turned around. As the light caught his eyes, Nina saw something familiar.

The man was expressionless. Glum and vacant, like the ushers upstairs had been.

More and more riders exited the vehicle, all of them with the same vacant stares.

Now that the other ride vehicle was nearly empty, it provided a clearer view of the remaining passengers. Nina watched as a lizard leaped into a woman's mouth and forced itself down her throat. Her neck bulged as her trachea snapped like a wet twig. She convulsed and thrashed, before finally becoming still. A moment later, she rose up like a zombie.

"No..." Nina shook her head and yanked at the metal across her legs. "No, no, no." The teenager beside her started begging for his mother. She wanted to help him, but she had to help herself. "They're taking people over," she cried out.

"It's okay," said Allan, and he wrapped his arm around her and pulled her closer. But it wasn't okay, so she pushed him away.

More creatures leapt from the platform, now landing on the riders in *her* vehicle. A woman in front of Nina choked and gagged as a lizard forced itself inside of her.

Tears streamed down Nina's cheeks.

The world lit up ahead, a bright orange shining light.

The muddy walls parted ahead of the tracks, revealing yet another shaft, this one climbing sharply upwards. There was a pair of new ride vehicles inside of it, side by side and identical to the one Nina sat in. Their benches were empty, but the zombies on the walkway shuffled over to them and sat down. Then the vehicle on the left rose upwards into the shaft.

Nina put the pieces together in her almost-shattered mind.

They're heading up to the exit. They're going to get off the ride like normal, and nobody will know what's happened to us. They're... they're imposters.

Allan seized up beside her.

Nina turned her head and screamed as she found herself face to face with a lizard. It seemed to enjoy her fear, staring at her through pink, puffy eyes. Then it buried its entire head inside Allan's mouth. She was powerless to look away as her fiancee struggled and gagged as the thing invaded his throat, tearing him apart from the inside. Allan's brown eyes stared at her, wide with terror. Then the light disappeared from them.

"Allan...?"

Another lizard leaped from the platform and landed on Nina's chest. She grabbed it with both hands, trying to fight it off, but it was slippery and strong. Before she knew it, it was inside her mouth and clawing its way towards her throat, tearing apart the soft flesh of her palate. It felt like a thousand fishhooks inside of her, dragging downwards into her belly and carving a bloody furrow through her tender flesh.

The pain suddenly stopped, but Nina didn't feel anything else change. In fact, she felt exactly like herself, but when the restraint lifted, she rose with no input from her own mind. She still saw through her eyes, but she did not control what they looked at. Every movement came as a surprise, and when she tried to feel her body, she felt nothing.

A few seconds later she was sitting on the other ride vehicle and rising upwards. Rising back to the earth, where more innocent people were queuing in their hundreds to get on this ungodly ride. Inside her mind, Nina shrieked, but nothing came out of her mouth. It no longer belonged to her.

A Discount for you

GET 15% off your next Iain Rob Wright book with voucher code:
NEXTREAD15

Just visit: **iainrobwrightstore.com**

One of Horror's most respected authors, Iain Rob Wright is the writer of nearly 50 books, many of them bestsellers. A mainstay in the horror charts, Iain is a prolific producer of unique and original stories. From his apocalyptic saga The Gates to his claustrophobic revenge thriller ASBO, Iain writes across a broad spectrum of sub genres, creating both beloved series and standalone titles.

For more information
www.iainrobwright.com
author@iainrobwright.com

Printed in Dunstable, United Kingdom

66236440R00231